TO SEE
THE DAWN
BREAKING

W.R. CHORLEY

76 SQUADRON OPERATIONS

FOREWORD

Between August 1914 and November 1918, the English and German Empires engaged in a war of quite titanic proportions. It was said to have been a war to end all wars, but a politically impotent Europe in the middle '30s helped to produce a climate ripe for a resumption of hostilities, which eventually broke out in September 1939.

This book is chiefly concerned with the second conflict and in particular the bombing campaign as remembered by the men and women of one unit, namely 76 Squadron of the Royal Air Force. Because of the sheer scale of this savage campaign, I have attempted to link the many individual contributions to the general run of events as the war progressed, though towards the end in 1945 with Bomber Command at its zenith the story becomes, perhaps, less personal.

It has not been possible for me to mention every squadron character by name and for this omission I apologise. Many of those stalwarts who formed the backbone of the squadron are no longer alive: to mention just two, 'The Colonel' and 'Pop' Bligh whose names must bring memories flooding back. Both were men of mature standing and I often wonder what their private thoughts were as they watched the young aircrews going willingly out to battle, often never to return. Therefore, I will try to set the tone of this book by quoting from a letter sent to me by Squadron Leader John Crampton who commanded B Flight at Holme-on-Spalding Moor from mid-1944, through to the end of the main bombing campaign in April 1945 and who writes in appreciation of just one of whom I have mentioned:

'We were blessed with a wonderful Adjutant, 'Pop'Bligh. He had served in the First World War and so must have been at least fifty. However, he kept us on our toes and frequently disapproved of our youthful behaviour. And yet, no matter what time of day or night we took-off on operations, dear old 'Pop' Bligh was always at the start of the runway, standing beside his bicycle, to wave us goodbye.'

Certainly not forgotten are the Commonwealth aircrews who came to serve with 76 Squadron, neither are the Norwegians who brought with them a special brand of enthusiasm to sustain them through their years in exile. I am proud to be able to recount so many of their stories.

For the younger generation who read this book, I sincerely trust the experiences relived in the following pages by so many of the participants, now nearly 40 years on, will never be repeated. I am sure this must have been the earnest hope of men like 'Pop' Bligh who, in May 1945, realised that no more would they need to go out onto a windswept Yorkshire airfield and wave farewell to the men in the bombers.

Bill Chorley
Sixpenny Handley, Salisbury
March 1981

To
Andrew

First published 1981, Midland Counties
Copyright ©W.R. Chorley, 1981
Reprinted 1996

ISBN 1 900604 02 7

By the same author:
In Brave Company:The History of 158 Squadron
with Capt. R.N. Benwell

Cover Design: Keith Woodcock
Production: Compaid Graphics
Cover Photograph: Gilbert Duthie

Printed and bound in the United Kingdom

Published by Compaid Graphics
Little Ash, Street Lane,
Lower Whitley, Warrington. Cheshire, WA4 4EN

CONTENTS

Chapter One

SEPTEMBER 1916 to JUNE 1941

The awful conflict of the First World War had been in progress for two years and forty three days when on Friday 15 September 1916, number 76 Squadron Royal Flying Corps was formed as a home defence unit at Ripon in Yorkshire.

For the background of events to this historic occasion it is necessary to look back in time to the autumn of 1915 and the Zeppelin airship attacks on London and the home counties. These attacks revealed a woefully inadequate defence system, which until this time had rested mainly with the hard worked RNAS squadrons. Lord Kitchener, it is said, inquired of Sir David Henderson, then Director General of Military Aeronautics 'What are you going to do about these airship raids.' Pressed for an immediate answer, Sir David replied it was the responsibility of the RNAS, to which Kitchener is alleged to have retorted 'I do not care who has responsibility, if there are any more Zeppelin raids and the Royal Flying Corps do not interfere with them, I shall hold you responsible.'

Words are often easier than actions. in the short term it was decided to form ten home defence squadrons, these to be based at suitable locations between Dover on the south coast and Edinburgh in the north. But before this decision could be implemented, events on the Continent dictated a different policy and by the summer of 1916 England's defences had been reduced to just six squadrons.

Early on a hot, cloudless summer day on 1 July 1916 the Allied armies opened the Somme offensive. From the musty trenches, where in some discomfort they had waited for days as the artillery pounded unceasingly at the German forward areas, thousands of men laden with equipment scrambled from their positions and walked out into the open and on towards the enemy trenches. In seconds the first casualties occurred as enemy machine-gun fire swept the close packed lines of advancing infantry. By the end of the day the exhausted survivors crouched in captured trenches and listened numbly to the pitiful cries of their wounded comrades. The dreadful slaughter of the Somme had begun. Overhead the Royal Flying Corps patrolled, dodged *Archie* and frequently engaged in wheeling encounters with the pugnacious opponents.

At home the toll of the war was borne in every town and village. Few were the families who escaped the briefly worded telegram from the War Office notifying the loss of a loved one. Each day the obituary notices swelled the nations newspapers. On the day of the squadron's formation, the official casualty list reproduced in *The Times* listed 146 Officers and 5,628 other ranks killed, wounded or missing in action. Amongst the twenty-three Officers remembered individually by family request were two from the Royal Flying Corps, whilst the supplement to the *London Gazette* bore names of 1,330 servicemen honoured by the award of the Military Medal for their bravery.

Somewhat appropriately *The Times* carried a report on the presentation to Lieutenant W. Leefe Robinson V C of a cheque for £500 in recognition of his destruction of a Zeppelin on 3 September at Cuffley, Hertfordshire. For once this illustrious paper had erred, for Leefe Robinson had in fact brought down a Schütte-Lanz, a mainly wood constructed airship which some experts of the day considered was ahead of the Zeppelin in several respects. But to the lay public all such devices were

'Zeppelins' and the shooting down of one was still a heady occasion. Such news must have given Major Murray food for thought as he prepared to take over command of 76 Home Defence Squadron. The possibility that his squadron may soon be 'interfering with the enemy' must have seemed a reasonable prospect.

Equipment, mainly a mixture of B.E.2c and B.E.2e types, however, was slow in reaching his squadron. An establishment of eighteen machines had been set, but it is highly unlikely that half of this number had arrived by the turn of the year. Cumbersome in appearance, the B.E.2's with their twin-exhaust stacks sticking up at right angles forward of the top wing's leading edge proved reasonably effective, though climbing was a laborious business for the 90 hp RAF.1A engine. Issued alongside were B.E.12's and 12a's, both versions powered by the 150 hp RAF.4A engine, the 12a being distinguished by its unequal-span wings. The armament deemed suitable for engaging the Hun intruders was the stalwart .303 Lewis gun mounted over the top wing on the B.E.2c. The B.E.12 and 12a had a similar calibre Vickers gun synchronised to fire through the propeller arc and, perhaps with future intent in mind, many were fitted with an additional Lewis gun mounted to fire over the top wing. From his headquarters at Ripon racecourse, Major Murray had control of three satellite stations, each accommodating a single flight. At Copmanthorpe, a few miles southwest of York, A Flight set up home, whilst B Flight settled at Helperby east of Ripon leaving C Flight to take up residence at Catterick, no doubt to act as guard for the Teeside towns. Conditions at these stations were to say the least primitive, and confidence amongst the pilots was not helped by the uneven airfield surfaces. in order to provide some assistance towards making a night interception possible, a searchlight unit was installed.

For close on a year the squadron operated without seeing anything resembling an intruder, but during the night of 21/22 August 1917, a Zeppelin was tracked over northern England and the squadron was alerted to investigate. Two B.E.2e's took off from Copmanthorpe and two similar machines, plus a B.E.12 operated from Helperby. Neither flight saw anything of the enemy and on return one of the Copmanthorpe aircraft and a Helperby B.E.2e crashed on landing. Just over a month later, in the early hours of 25 September, 2nd Lieutenant William Wallace Cook, a New Zealander, flying from Helperby sighted three different Zeppelins, all part of a ten-strong force attacking coastal shipping and targets in Yorkshire and Lincolnshire. His B.E.2e had neither the speed, nor the ceiling to permit an effective attack, but as events will show this did not deter the tenacious Cook. He caught sight of his first Zeppelin, the L55, at a quarter to two, held at 16,000 feet in the Skinningrove searchlight, but she pulled away rapidly as he climbed to follow her out to sea. Roughly an hour later he spotted the L41, briefly caught in one of the Humber searchlights, and again the Zeppelin easily made off before he could approach to within range. Deciding that his best hope of catching a raider was to wait for them returning over the coast, Cook flew out to sea. His intelligent anticipation paid off and at three in the morning, east of Hornsea, he sighted his third Zeppelin of the night. Cook could not coax his sluggish machine closer than 800 yards, but nevertheless he fired off four drums from his Lewis, but with no visible effect.

Cook now estimated he was sixty miles out to sea and after battling his way home against a strong westerly wind, he landed with only a few pints of petrol remaining. A crew from another squadron was not so lucky, they disappeared without trace. This was the squadron's only contact with the enemy in the First World War and Cook was later awarded the Military Cross. Furthermore, it has since been assessed Cook's long range fire did hit the Zeppelin, for the L42 is reported to have landed with two bullet holes in a gas cell. This particular Zeppelin had bombed shipping in the Humber and its course and time over the area coincides with Cook's patrol and subsequent combat.

8

In March 191 8, the squadron put up aircraft on two consecutive nights and though no airships were sighted, one of A Flight's B.E.12b's attracted the displeasure of an anti-aircraft battery at Howden. The 12b's had only recently reached the squadron. These were standard B.E.12 airframes adapted to take the 200 hp Hispano-Suiza engine in the hope of producing sufficient performance to cope with the latest Zeppelins operating at heights ranging between 18,000 and 20,000 feet. The B.E.12b had no Vickers gun, relying on a single, or a pair of Lewis weapons for the business of nightfighting.

Command, in the meantime, of this rather scattered squadron passed in February 1918 to Major Wilson and it was under his direction that the squadron saw out the remainder of the war. By the end of hostilities in November 1918, the B.E.s had given way to Avro 504K's and Bristol F.2b's and it was thus equipped when the squadron disbanded at Tadcaster on 13 June 1919.

Some evidence of the squadron's existence at Helperby survived until at least the late 1960s. Here one of the brick and wood-built hangars still stood, and inside, painted on a board fixed to one of the trellis roof supports, could be seen a fading letter 'B' which suggests a link with B Flight that operated from this airfield in 1917.

In the mid-1930s amidst gathering war clouds casting dark shadows across a weakened and politically divided Europe, the Royal Air Force embarked on the formidable task of expansion. Preparations for any future conflict went ahead apace. Squadrons that had been disbanded in the years following the Armistice were reformed, usually by splitting up existing units to provide a nucleus of experienced personnel so vital for the emerging squadrons. Thus on Monday 12 April 193 7, B Flight of number 7 (Bomber) Squadron based at Finningley in Yorkshire was re-numbered 76 Squadron. The initial strength of the new squadron consisted of five officers, six airmen pilots, thirty-six airmen and four Vickers Wellesley single-engine medium bombers. Wing Commander Graham was appointed to command, but before the month was out Squadron Leader George, a tall thick-set man with a dark moustache, neatly clipped, had assumed control.

It is worth recording at this stage that B Flight of 7 Squadron had only recently received the Wellesley and until issue of the twin-engined Whitley heavy bomber in March 1938, the remainder of the squadron was obliged to continue with the ungainly and now obsolete Heyford. Losing B Flight and its newly acquired aircraft could not have been too well received, for despite appearances the Wellesley was a considerably advanced design. A useful top speed in excess of 200 mph was available, if required, whilst a maximum load range was in the region of 1,000 miles.

Finningley in 1937 was a somewhat spartan place. The airfield was grassed surfaced and the men lived in butted accommodation. However, before the end of the year work had started on the construction of permanent living quarters around the drill square, and this led to much higher standards of personal comfort. One of the favoured meeting places off camp was Georges Cafe at the bus terminal in Doncaster and here the airmen of 7 and 76 Squadrons swopped many a tale and expounded on the latest rumours buzzing around this fast expanding station.

The squadron quickly settled to the task of working-up to operational readiness, though new pilots were rather irked by the order requiring them to fly for a minimum of five hours with the retractable undercarriage system locked in the down position. Although it was usually operated as a single pilot aircraft, the front cockpit taking up the whole of the space from side to side, provision was made for the carriage of a second-pilot. In order for the second-pilot to change places with the man at the controls, a rather complicated procedure was evolved as Major F.A. de V. Robertson was to write in an issue of *Flight* -

'It is rather amusing to watch this operation. The relief comes up behind and releases a catch, which allows the pilot's seat to tilt backwards until his torso is horizontal and his thighs perpendicular. Even though, for our benefit, the operation was carried out inside a hangar, and the first pilot knew what was going to happen, the expression on his face as he felt himself beginning to go over backwards raised an unsuppressible smile from the spectator.'

Little imagination is necessary to visualise what the outcome would be under the stress of operational flying, perhaps with the pilot at the controls wounded, or severely impaired.

For the 1937 Royal Air Force display at Hendon a flight of five squadron aircraft, closely followed by a formation of Whitley's drawn from 10 Squadron, thrilled the gathered crowd with a simulated bombing attack. Throughout the summer months the strength of the squadron gradually increased and a dozen Wellesleys were on charge as autumn approached. The daily routine of flying training was well established and although news from Germany was not encouraging, the immediate threat of war had receded.

By this time America had won the Ryder Cup for the first time on British soil, the course at Southport proving our golfers downfall, and at Wimbledon, too, America triumphed when J.D. Budge disposed of Germany's von Cramm to take the Singles Championship. The long hot summer days produced some splendid rowing at Henley, and on county grounds up and down the country Yorkshire plundered runs aplenty as they made sure of heading Middlesex in the County Championship. J. B. Priestley's new play *Time and The Conways* opened at the Duchess theatre; it was, indeed, an idyllic summer. The horrors of the Spanish civil war did not make pleasant reading at the breakfast table, but it all seemed so far away in the world of 1937.

During the autumn a German Military Mission led by General der Flieger Staatssekretär Milch arrived in England. *The Times* on 19 October quoted the General as saying 'this was an opportunity to destroy mischievous rumours and to create an atmosphere of comradeship and friendliness.' The mission was duly dined in the presence of Viscount Swinton, Secretary of State for Air and senior Royal Air Force officers who included Bomber Command's new Air Officer Commanding-in-Chief, Air Chief Marshal Sir Edgar Ludlow-Hewitt.

The squadron's chance to show off its paces before the mission at Mildenhall in Suffolk was dashed by inclement weather over the East Anglian countryside, and four days later the Wellesleys were flown to the armament practice camp at North Coates Fitties. Here the poor weather of the past few weeks persisted and in consequence the planned bombing training programme was frequently disrupted. A slightly disheartened squadron returned to Finningley in mid-November to continue the winter training schedules.

With the first signs of spring the squadron headed north, this time to Evanton in Scotland, where for a month the air-gunners were given intensive air gunnery practice on the nearby ranges. One incident, believed to have taken place during the camp, greatly embarrassed one young air-gunner. Returning in a 'Vic' formation of three aircraft from a drogue firing detail, he forgot to cock and clear his gun and as a result accidentally sent half-a-dozen bullets through the tail of the Wellesley flying on his port side. Despite this alarming moment, the camp was judged to have been hugely successful and everyone was in high spirits on return to their Yorkshire home.

In July 1938 Squadron Leader Pearce took command of a now thriving squadron.

The outlook from the continent of Europe was again forbidding and by late September the situation was giving cause for some alarm. As the news worsened Pearce informed his squadron that in the event of war the Wellesley force would be expected to operate at night, each crew to consist of two pilot/navigators and a wireless operator/air gunner. Cecil Smith, a young wireless operator, posted into the squadron at the height of the crisis recalls with some misgiving the prospect of becoming operational:

'Had the war started then I'm afraid the Wellesleys and their inexperienced crews would have been rather inadequate. Although the aircraft was very reliable and able to climb to colossal heights, the bomb load was very limited and the armament comprised one old Lewis gun firing .303 bullets which were a constant pain in the neck because of frequent faults that were sometimes difficult to clear. Both the guns and the radio equipment were a continual source of trouble. The radio was a 1082 receiver and 1083 transmitter, and these had to be nursed very gently to achieve any worthwhile results.'

Throughout the early part of October tension remained high, and during this time the Wellesleys lost their familiar squadron identity, the number '76' on the fuselage being replaced by the more anonymous letter combination of 'NM'. The chill of war was felt throughout the squadron. Cecil Smith continues:

'Whenever possible the bombing and air firing range off Catfoss, about ten miles north of the Humber was used. Air firing was carried out on a drogue target towed by another aircraft, and one had to be very careful to avoid firing towards the land when the aircraft was turning. it was very easy to get carried away, especially if the Lewis gun happened to be functioning well and I was admonished by irate pilots once or twice for sending a few stray shots towards the cliff tops. Needless to say our results were not very spectacular, although it was very exhilarating.'

Gradually the Munich crisis as this period is more familiarly known, receded and the modernisation of the Allied forces moved steadily forward. There could be no doubts whatsoever as to where Germany's expansionist programme under the guidance of Herr Hitler was leading. War clouds were inexorably gathering on the horizon.

By the end of the year 22 Wellesleys were held on charge, but a replacement was waiting in the wings. For just on a year 7 Squadron had used the Whitley, but for both Finningley based squadrons a much lighter bomber was in the offing. Sadly, Squadron Leader Pearce who died at Marlborough on New Year's Day never saw this change, and it was left to Squadron Leader Whitehead to see out the squadron's last days with the Wellesleys. On 10 March 1939 six Anson trainers came across from 7 Squadron to assist pilots in their conversion to the twin-engined Hampden bomber. Sleek, almost fighter-like in appearance, the new Hampdens were eagerly awaited.

A month later on 13 April, the same day that Wing Commander Allan took over from Squadron Leader Whitehead, two squadron pilots were detached to Waddington in Lincolnshire to convert onto the Hampden, although on paper the first allocations of the new bomber had been made to 76 Squadron on the last day of March. As a measure of the rapid expansion of the time no less than sixteen Hampdens were held on squadron strength by the end of April and a full training programme had been set in motion. A similar picture was unfolding on 7 Squadron and for the first time since the rebirth of 76 Squadron, both squadrons were using similar aircraft.

Conversion to the new bomber went smoothly and on 20 May the huge crowd enjoying the Empire Air Display at Doncaster airport were treated to a display of formation flying by squadron aircraft. Gazing down at the sea of upturned faces as Flight Sergeant Couch crossed in front of the airport buildings was Aircraftsman Cecil Smith. Although still having to contend with the vagaries of the infamous 1082/1083 wireless set, young Smith was full of confidence for whatever the future might hold in store.

On 1 June came a change in direction. The need for increasing aircrew training, especially amongst pilots and observers, resulted in certain squadrons being required to adopt a training role. Subsequently, both 7 and 76 Squadrons reverted to the role of a Group Pool squadron, though both units maintained their separate identities. The emphasis now lay in training Royal Air Force Volunteer Reserve pilots and observers up to operational standards. For this youthful band of fliers the Hampden was a far cry from the once leisurely weekend flying in Harts and Hinds.

The first batch of eight pilots earmarked for conversion training arrived at Finningley on 1 June, and in general their standard of flying ability was judged to be high, Unfortunately, the same cannot be said of the early intake of observers, some of whom seemed to be lacking even the basic skills of air navigation. in addition to the aforementioned categories of aircrew trades, wireless operators and air gunners arrived to swell the number of trainees, thus imposing a considerable strain on the resources of both station and squadron.

During the early part of August a major Home Defence exercise occupied the squadron. For a period of six days between the 5th and the 11th, daily formations of between two and three aircraft were maintained, sortie times being in the region of five hours. In Nazi dominated Germany the clarion call for war was strident. Following the invasion of the Sudetanland and Czechoslovakia, only one final act of treachery by Herr Hitler's henchmen remained. Under the pretext of alleged Polish atrocities. German ground forces with full air support marched into Poland on 1 September. France and Great Britain could stand idly by no longer.

Three days later at 11 o'clock on Sunday 3 September 1939, the British ultimatum calling for the complete withdrawal of German troops from Poland expired, In the absence of any response from Germany, the sombre-toned voice of the Prime Minister, Neville Chamberlain, broadcast to the free-world that Great Britain, Australia, New Zealand and France had declared a state of war with the German nation.

Amongst the many who heard this news was Aircraftsman 'Nobby' Hall, on duty in the squadron's Signal Section:

'It was more or less what we had been expecting, and our daily routine altered little as a result. We had received an influx of Class E reservists at the end of July, mainly those in the trades of carpenter, blacksmith, airframe mechanics who were popularly known as fabric bashers, wireless operators and armourers. Gun pits had been constructed around the perimeter from sandbags, and Lewis guns installed. At the beginning these were manned by airmen from all sections of the camp and instructions in their use was enthusiastically given by personnel from the armoury section.'

The next day Bomber Command dispatched its first operational sorties against German shipping lying in Schillig Roads near Wilhelmshaven. Twin-engined Blenheims drawn from 107 and 110 Squadrons based at Wattisham in Suffolk spearheaded this opening attack[1] from which five of the ten crews sent failed to return. The relentless struggle that was to last for over five years had started.

76 Squadron, probably to their chagrin, were not involved in these early forays. The daily grind of training continued, air firing at Squires Gate, low-level bombing practice on the Misson ranges, these were the tasks of immediate concern. A move, too, was in the offing. On 23 September the squadron took leave of its Yorkshire home and flew south to Upper Heyford in Oxfordshire. Here, still in

---

1   German warships at Brunsbüttel were also attacked by Wellington bombers of 9 and 149 Squadrons, but few, if any, results were observed. 9 Squadron lost two crews when one of its two sections were intercepted by enemy fighters.

company with their colleagues from 7 Squadron, the Hampdens came under the control of Headquarters 6 Group, forming Group Pool Training Squadrons for 5 Group. The embryo of what would later be known as an Operational Training Unit was in the being.

For a few weeks the strength of the squadron fluctuated as various demands were made upon its capacity. Order and counter-order followed each other in quick succession as the Royal Air Force took up the gauntlet of air warfare. Squadron Leader Oldfield who had commanded B Flight before the war was appointed Chief Flying Instructor, Flight Lieutenant Sheehan took over the duties of navigation officer, and Flying Officer Jones became Chief Ground Instructor. Overall command still lay in the capable hands of Wing Commander Allan.

Since its formation in 1937 the squadron had built up an enviable accident free record, but with the urgency of wartime training it could only be a matter of time before this fine record was broken. The inevitable happened on 24 November when Pilot Officer Hynes flew into a tree whilst practicing night-flying. Hynes, by good fortune, escaped unharmed, but his Hampden was damaged beyond repair. Less than three weeks later the first Hampden fatality occurred when on 11 December in conditions of failing visibility Pilot Officer Stevens flew into some trees just beyond the airfield.

The first Christmas of the war passed. Poland had long since fallen, but apart from minor ground patrol skirmishes and air reconnaissance, activity on the western front remained quiet. On the Continent the weather was foul, and over the United Kingdom conditions were not much better. At Upper Heyford the biting cold days gave way to heavy snow in late January and the airfield was closed to flying until 7 February. A partial thaw was followed by further heavy snow, and in general throughout the month of February little productive flying was accomplished.

Within a few days of the March flying programme beginning, the squadron experienced a further serious accident. Pilot Officer Edmonds stalled shortly after taking off for a night-flying exercise on the 4th, and though he managed to flatten out before striking the ground, his Hampden crashed heavily and burst into flames. Rescuers pulled young Edmonds from the cockpit, but he was grievously burnt.

Two days later Sergeant Loadsman had a miraculous escape from death. During the course of a low-flying detail Loadsman flew into a line of 11000-volt electricity cables near Eynsham on the Oxford to Witney bypass. The force of the collision ripped open the wing leading edge and wing-tip on the starboard side, swinging the bomber into a flat turn. With a horrendous screech of tearing metal the cable bit deep into the aileron before sliding across the undersurfaces of the wings to the bomb-doors and free of the Hampden. A very shaken pilot regained control and flew home without further incident.

Hopes of becoming operational rose momentarily when on 4 April a signal was received from Bomber Command headquarters ordering the squadron to standby for a move to West Raynham in Norfolk and prepare for operations. This order, however, was never implemented, but the second part of the signal instructing the training elements of 7 and 76 Squadrons to merge and form number 16 Operational Training Unit was actioned, the official date of disbandment being entered in the Squadron Operational Record Book as 22 April 1940.

After eight months of war and without dropping a bomb, or firing a gun in anger, the squadron was for the time being placed in limbo. For the groundcrews, at least, little changed. Life continued very much in the pattern of previous months:

'The old rivalry between the two squadrons still existed. The squadron numbers were still painted on all the equipment, and the squadron offices in the hangars maintained their separate identities. All we seemed to do was training exercises with the night-flying taking place from our satellite field at Brackley. The work was very demanding and although Banbury and Oxford were within easy reach we seldom got out of camp. Usually by the time we returned from our sections the bus would be already full with Station Headquarters types, all decked out in their best blue.' *(Sergeant Leslie Collett — Fitter II E).*

A year went by, a year during which the fortunes of war went much against the Allies. Within a few weeks of the squadron's demise the 'phoney war', as the period up to May 1940 is popularly known, exploded in a holocaust. Early in April, Denmark and Norway fell, then on 10 May a terrible blow struck the low-countries. Neutrality of states meant little to a regime flushed with the heady taste of total power. Holland and Belgium, even tiny Luxembourg, felt the full weight of the enemy forces, the proud city of Rotterdam being particularly heavily blitzed and many of her citizens killed,

In the confusion of armoured spearhead attacks the British Expeditionary Force fell back on Dunkirk where glorious history was duly made in the closing days of May 1940. No doubt encouraged by events in Northern Europe, Italy's Fascist dictator Mussolini decided to throw in his lot on the side of Hitler. Mussolini was no stranger to such conquests having savaged Abyssinia as far back as October 1935. Now his ambitions lay towards Egypt and the rich spoils of the canal zone. Soon the North African continent would boil over into fierce desert warfare.

On 21 June, France accepted the terms of an Armistice offered by the German High Command and capitulated. Great Britain and the Commonwealth countries stood alone to face the triumphant German forces.

Fortunately for us, more than tacit support was forthcoming from North America, while from the oppressed lands of Europe thousands fled to the Free World to continue the fight to liberate their beloved homelands.

Nonetheless, despite the triumph of Fighter Command in the 'Battle of Britain' in the late summer of 1940, it seemed inevitable that a German victory would soon follow as a relentless stranglehold encircled our island home. in the Atlantic marauding packs of enemy U-Boats were daily sending thousands of tons of essential supplies plunging to the ocean depths. All that remained was a grim determination never to yield to the Nazi yoke,

It was against this dark backcloth of events that 76 Squadron was reborn, this time as a heavy bomber squadron from C Flight of 35 Squadron. A founder member of the re-formed squadron, Sergeant Leonard Smith recalls his feelings at the time:

'I had completed over half a tour of operations on Whitleys with 10 Squadron at Leeming when I was told to report to Linton-on-Ouse for conversion on to four engined Halifaxes. One of the aircraft on the Conversion Flight was the Halifax prototype and this, being considerably lighter than the operational version, would fairly scream off the ground. This gave everyone considerable confidence as the Halifax did not have too good a reputation at the time, being very prone to drift on take-off and ground-loop if not corrected in time.'

Leonard Smith was slightly older than most of his squadron companions, a factor that probably led to his commissioning soon after the squadron was declared operational. it is also interesting to note that his personal Flying-Log records the date of re-formation at Linton-on-Ouse as 12 April 1941 under Wing Commander Bufton, whereas the squadron records indicate 1 May 1941, with Wing Commander Jarman taking command on the 28th.

One of the squadron's first flight engineers was Sergeant Leslie Collett, recently re-mustered from his ground trade of fitter 11 E, but already experienced in Halifax operating techniques with 35

Squadron:

'At Linton we had a local course on the Halifax, instruction being given by a very senior flight engineer who spurted an Air Force Medal and who was affectionately known as 'Pop'. We then had a course at the manufacturers works, first at Cricklewood and then at Radlett. On return to Linton we crewed up and commenced operations without any operational training whatsoever. As our numbers increased and more aircraft became available, about half of us went to 76 Squadron.'

Training continued apace with much of the initial pilot instruction being given by Squadron Leader Tait and Flight Lieutenant Lane. Squadron Leader 'Tom' Sawyer joined from 10 Squadron in the middle of April to assist with the conversion programme and the first crew!; were deemed proficient by the middle of May. Leonard Smith, who had viewed the prototype Halifax with such admiration, went solo on 11 May and two days later was himself assisting Sergeant Sturmey to reach 'First Pilot' standards. A handful of experienced Halifax crews arrived from 35 Squadron, theirs being the first squadron to receive this type in the winter of 1940, and over the weeks 76 Squadron became the second Halifax squadron to be declared operational.

Incidents during the training phase were relatively few, though shortly after moving to Middleton St. George, Sergeant MacDonald's Halifax swung on landing in a slight cross-wind and while turning sharply to avoid an obstruction, the undercarriage collapsed. This mishap effectively closed the main runway and Pilot Officer Lewin who was in the circuit was committed to landing on the secondary runway. His approach was good, but after touching down his aircraft veered to the right and seconds later the undercarriage gave way under the severe stress. Damage to both machines was quite substantial and whilst MacDonald's aircraft was eventually repaired and returned to service, Lewin's was struck off ' to become a ground instruction airframe.

Before these events, Linton-on-Ouse was bombed and strafed during the night of 11/12 May by a trio of Ju 88s, the presence of two heavy bomber squadrons being their prime incentive. Fires broke out in and around a number of installations and every available airman was called out to fight the flames. Sergeant Saunders and Aircraftsman Maleod were particularly to the fore in these efforts, both being mentioned in the squadron records for their exceptional courage and initiative while under fire. Tragically, Linton's Station Commander, Group Captain Garraway OBE[2] was struck and killed by fragments from an anti-personnel bomb whilst leading a team to extinguish a serious incendiary blaze. Thirteen members of the station were killed and a similar number were wounded, but the Halifaxes, well dispersed, escaped damage.

On 4 June, the squadron vacated Linton-on-Ouse, heading north to Middleton St. George, a bomber station in the county of Durham. From here 76 Squadron went to war for the first time on the night of 12/13 June 1941.

---

[2]   Group Captain Garraway had only taken up his appointment as Station Commander the day before the raid. His successor, Group Captain John Whitley DFC, arrived on 23 May.

Chapter Two

JUNE 1941 to NOVEMBER 1941

During the night of 12/13 June 1941, Bomber Command dispatched a total of 339 aircraft to attack the key railway marshalling yards at Hamm, Soest, Osnabrück and Schwerte, plus the important chemical works situated at Huls. A very high percentage of the command's available strength was being committed.

Included in the 'Battle Order' for the first time were three 76 Squadron crews captained by Flight Lieutenant Hillary, Pilot Officer Lewin and Pilot Officer Richards. In view of the occasion it is worth recording in some detail the outcome of this operation.

The principal objectives were the four marshalling yards and ninety-one aircraft were assigned to Soest, eighty-eight to Hamm, eighty-four on Schwerte and sixty five f or Osnabriück. Over Germany a thick blanket of ground haze persisted, a problem not uncommon to the Ruhr Valley[3] which supported a vast complex of coalmines, steel plants, power stations, oil refineries and factories, all geared towards maximum war production. This hazard, coupled with the formidable flak and searchlight batteries afforded good protection to the German war-machine for despite ever improving operating techniques in Bomber Command, it would be many months before attacks on the Ruhr towns could be carried out with any guaranteed degree of accuracy in marginal weather conditions such as prevailed this night.

Nonetheless, it is true to say the command was proving a tenacious adversary to the Nazi ambitions and 12/13 June was no exception.

Over Soest, reserved exclusively on this occasion for 5 Group, the Hampden crews encountered extensive medium cloud and this, coupled with the ground haze, made their task extremely difficult. Less than fifty per cent of the force claimed to have attacked the primary target, but those that were successful reported explosions and fires in the vicinity of the yards. One crew, who bombed from 2,000 feet, claimed to have seen a warehouse completely gutted by fire, whilst another sighted what was thought from their description to be an ammunition train on fire.

At Hamm where sixty-four Wellington crews from 3 Group bombed, results were a little more encouraging. Aircraft early over this target managed to start some good fires and these helped to guide their less able colleagues. Eventually, fifteen Hampden crews weary from a fruitless search for Soest, spotted these same fires, and so bombed Hamm as an alternative. Their journey had not been entirely in vain.

The yards at Osnabrück and Schwerte escaped serious damage, although a total of fifty-three Wellington crews from 1 Group claim to have recognised Osnabrück. At the last major objective, the chemical plant at Huls, very little success seems to have been achieved. From the nineteen aircraft dispatched, only three Stirling and two Halifax crews attacked, these claiming to have left some fires burning in the target area.

The squadron's fortunes were low. Pilot Officer Lewin who had been the last to take-off at 23.34 hrs. returned within the hour with failing engines. A similar fate befell Flight Lieutenant Hillary who was

---

3   See Chapter Five for a detailed description of this area.

airborne for just over five hours and must, therefore, have spent some time over enemy occupied territory before returning to base with his bomb-load intact. Pilot Officer Richards faired a little better. Unable to locate Huls he jettisoned his bombs over Essen. Results, he confessed, were difficult to gauge, but some incendiary fires were glimpsed as he set course towards the North Sea.

Despite this rather gloomy appraisal it must be borne in mind that at this stage of the war Bomber Command was the only force available to the Allies capable of carrying the war to the enemy, a task that its crews continued to discharge to the utmost of their ability until the invasion of 'Fortress Europe' in the summer of 1944, and beyond. The cost in aircrew lives during this period is almost too terrible to contemplate. And let no one be under the illusion that these young men were unaware of the dangers facing them. All recognised the fact that their chance of survival was at the best slender, yet only a handful failed to measure up to the final call. A quite senior pilot at the time, Wing Commander David Young, who before the year was out would take command of the squadron, wrote:

'I remember one young pilot, a charming and gallant lad of twenty or so. He was my second pilot on a trip to Düsseldorf and on his first trip. Things got a bit sticky and I was concentrating on the bombing-run and then getting clear of the target area. I looked round to see how he was reacting; absolutely deadpan, so I thought he'll do and got on with the job in hand.

Poor fellow, he died as so many others before he lost his illusions.' Its operational debut accomplished, the squadron joined in a further five mainforce attacks before the month was out. Sergeants MacDonald and McHale succeeded in locating the Rhineland city of Cologne on the 16th, but indifferent weather prevented an accurate assessment of their bombing. The remaining operations were directed against the German ports of Hamburg and Kiel, where the Germania Shipyards came in for attention from five crews led by Squadron Leader Sawyer on the 20th. This was 'Tom' Sawyer's final operation with the squadron as he was being promoted to the rank of Wing Commander and given command of 78 Squadron at Croft. His Flight in 76 Squadron went to Squadron Leader Walter Williams, destined to fly just one heroic sortie as will soon be recounted.

During the dual attack against Kiel and Wilhelmshaven on the 23rd, the squadron suffered its first losses on operations when Pilot Officer Stobbs and his all NCO crew were shot down by a Messerschmitt Bf110 flown by Oberleutnant Eckart of II/NJG1. Eckart made his interception southwest of Hamburg and following a brief engagement sent his victim down at Eilendorf, a small village near Buxtehude. In the last dying moments as the stricken Halifax hurtled earthwards, Sergeant Lipton managed to extract himself and parachute to safety. He was the sole survivor. The victorious Eckart had but just over a year to live. During an interception on 30 July 1942 his aircraft was hit by return fire from the bomber he was attacking. Eckart baled out, but died when he struck the tailplane of his Messerschmitt. At the time of his death he was serving with 7/NJG3 at St. Kap and had run-up a tally of twenty-two nightfighter victories. Today Eckart rests alongside some of his victims in the Lommel Cemetery, Belgium. On the day prior to the loss of Pilot Officer Stobbs, Hitler ordered 'Operation Barbarossa' - the invasion of Soviet Russia was under way and the uneasy alliance between the Fascist Party of Nazi Germany and the Communist leaders of the USSR was over. The German forces now found themselves committed to war on two major fronts, as well as supporting activities in the Mediterranean theatre of operations. Only two powerful notions remained outside the net of war; the United States of America and in the Far East the much underestimated people of Japan.

Early in July the squadron received instructions to commence daylight close formation flying over the sea. No indication was given at this stage as to the possible outcome of this training, but on most days small formations of bombers were dispatched to fly in close company with each other over Bridlington Bay.

In the meantime the pattern of night attacks continued. Wing Commander Jarman led his squadron for the first time on 2 July when Bremen was attacked in overcast weather. Variations in bombing heights ranged between 8,000 and 1 5,000 feet, but few results were seen through the clouds. Three nights later Flight Lieutenant Hillary made three runs over Magdeburg. Fires from his incendiaries broke out near the main railway station on the north bank of the Elbe, and later he put down a stick of high explosives across the railway lines to the northeast near the Wallstrasse. it is highly likely Hillary was trying to hit the military installations lying to the east of the station. On this same operation Sergeant Dunlop was taken ill at the controls of his aircraft, but an attack was still pressed home after his observer, Pilot Officer Jones occupied the Pilot's seat.

Further drama came on the 8th over Merseburg, home of the I G Farben Leuna synthetic oil plant. Squadron Leader Bob Bickford's Halifax was trapped in a cone of searchlights. Within seconds the crew felt their aircraft falter as the first pattern of shells exploded around them. This was no place to linger, Kicking hard on the rudder pedals and at the same time pushing forward on the control column, Bickford sent his damaged bomber into a series of stomach turning gyrations. Such was the violence of his flying, the instruments on his flying panel ceased to function correctly. The artificial horizon toppled as speed built up and height was quickly lost, the gyro compasses swung in wild confusion. Oxygen masks were practically pulled from the faces of some of the crew, limbs felt heavy as the gravity force increased and at more than one position nausea overtook the crew before the lights and flak faded into the distance.

Course for home had been barely established when a cannon-shell from an unseen night-fighter burst inside the nose. Sergeant Kenworthy, the flight engineer was wounded, as was Bob Bickford, but their attacker failed to press home his advantage, and Linton was eventually reached where the wounded received prompt medical attention.

Gradually the squadron was settling into an operational routine. Some problems still existed with unserviceable equipment, but the squadron strength was increasing steadily.

Seven crews set off in the late evening of the 14th to bomb the main railway station at Hannover in favourable weather conditions. All reached the target area, which was easily identified despite the glare from numerous searchlights. Heavy flak could be seen bursting over the town and Leonard Smith, who was stealthily trying to avoid the probing beams, caught sight of an unfortunate Whitley crew well and truly trapped in a cone of lights. The enemy searchlight operators were following every move of the luckless bomber and when last seen it was still being pursued by a relentless barrage of shells. Meanwhile, the raid was progressing steadily and fires could be seen breaking out in several areas of the city, hopefully some of these coming from the Gummiwerke chemical factory that had been assigned to the Group's Wellington crews.

On return Sergeant Harry Drummond landed his flak scarred Halifax at Linton-on-Ouse. Visibility was bad at the time and a long float after crossing the runway threshold had left Drummond with little room in which to bring his bomber to a halt. Still travelling at speed he could see the perimeter hedge rushing into view through the early morning mist. Pumping desperately on the brakes Harry Drummond attempted to turn off the runway, but his speed was too high and the huge bomber lurched into a screeching skid. At this point, not surprisingly, the undercarriage collapsed under the strain and the Halifax came to rest on its belly, flaps and undersurfaces buckled and torn from passage across the uneven ground. Minutes later Pilot Officer Ireton arrived over the fog-shrouded airfield. Unable to select full-flap due to battle damage, Ireton's bomber careered into the overshoot area where the undercarriage duly gave way. Linton's crash and recovery teams had plenty to occupy them in the chill of a mid-July morning.

By day the formation training exercises continued, the ground crews often working around the clock to keep as many aircraft as possible fully serviceable and ready for operations.

Then, on the 22nd during a training sortie, tragedy struck, Pilot Officer Blackwell was returning to Base after an uneventful day cross-country exercise. Everything aboard was quite normal as he began his landing approach, wheels and flaps down, the engines giving off a throaty roar as coarse pitch was selected, when without warning a Hurricane fighter flew across his path. Probably Blackwell's immediate reaction was to pull back on the controls to avoid a certain collision, but in doing so he stalled and went into a spin. in the height available to him recovery was impossible and with a sickening crash the Halifax struck the ground killing all five crew members, Young Blackwell had not been long with the squadron, having recently transferred with several of his crew from 78 Squadron.

Two days after this tragic accident Wing Commander Jarman, accompanied by five crews flew south to Stanton Harcourt, a satellite airfield for Abingdon in Oxfordshire. The recent formation flying practice was about to be put to the acid test.

For months past the Royal Navy and the Royal Air Force had been keeping a close watch on three German battlecruisers, the *Scharnhorst, Prinz Eugen and Gneisenau.* Following several successful actions against Allied shipping in the Atlantic, the *Scharnhorst and Gneisenau,* with their attendant support ships, had retired to the French port of Brest. Within the last few days, however, *Scharnhorst* had slipped her moorings and moved southeast down the Bay of Biscay to a new berth at La Pallice. Her departure had not passed unnoticed.

Intelligence reports on these menacing vessels were being continually sifted by the Admiralty and Air Ministry, while the War Cabinet, under the direction of the Prime Minister, Winston Churchill, was not blind to the stimulus to national morale which would result if one or more of these surface raiders could be sunk, or disabled.

Such a possibility was not lost on the German High Command, who had long since taken the necessary measures to protect these highly-prized capital ships. The coastal ports were ringed by experienced flak and searchlight personnel, while battle-seasoned fighter units were on immediate call from the surrounding airfields. Each harbour was a veritable fortress, and when not exercising at sea the three vessels lay anchored behind a protective screen of anti-submarine nets. To date all attempts by Bomber and Coastal Command[4] to breach these formidable defences had failed.

During the evening of 23 July, Bomber Command dispatched a force of heavy and medium bombers against the *Scharnhorst* at La Pallice. Weather conditions were good, though with no moon some crews had difficulty in plotting an accurate landfall on the French coast. Nonetheless, a high proportion claimed to have identified La Pallice, which from all accounts was well illuminated. Only spasmodic flak was encountered and the command was much encouraged by the news from 3 Group that one of

---

4   'On 6 April 1942, Flying Officer Kenneth Campbell flying a Beaufort torpedo-bomber from 22 Squadron died in a gallant attempt to sink the Gneisenau then lying in the inner-harbour, Rade Abri at Brest. For his heroic actions Kenneth Campbell was posthumously awarded the Victoria Cross.

their Stirling crews had succeeded in hitting the *Scharnhorst* damaging her superstructure.

The next morning a follow-up attack in daylight was launched involving a total of 149 bombers. Of this total, ninety-nine aircraft supported by a strong escort of Spitfires were directed against the *Gneisenau* and *Prinz Eugen* at Brest, whilst a diversionary force of thirty-five Blenheims from 2 Group, also with fighter escort, made for the well defended harbour at Cherbourg. The remaining fifteen bombers, all Halifaxes drawn from 3 5 and 76 Squadrons, were ordered to fly unescorted to La Pallice and bomb the *Scharnhorst*. The key to the success of the Halifax force lay in the simultaneous timing of the Brest and Cherbourg raids, which it was hoped would result in the *Luftwaffe* concentrating its fighters on these ports, thus leaving La Pallice relatively unprotected.

It was a beautiful summer morning when the Halifax crews went out to their aircraft drawn up around the perimeter of Stanton Harcourt airfield. All were bombed-up and fuelled, the air-gunners noting, possibly with feelings of apprehension, the plentiful supply of machine-gun ammunition ready belted and gleaming in the feedtrays. Last minute exchanges between ground and aircrew took place before the calm of the surrounding countryside was broken by the sound of sixty Rolls-Royce Merlin engines bursting into life. From across the airfield small groups of station personnel gathered at the end of the duty runway, their voices drowned by the sound from the lumbering bombers taxying into orderly position.

First away at 10. 35 hrs. to the unheard shouts of encouragement was Wing Commander Jarman, followed a minute later by Flight Lieutenant Lewin. During the next nine minutes ten Halifaxes were airborne comprising of Harry Drummond and the entire force of 35 Squadron led by Squadron Leader Bradley.

Then came a delay involving 76 Squadron's second flight led by Squadron Leader Waiter Williams. This interruption in the carefully prepared timetable would, before the day was out, prove disastrous for the majority of those concerned. Their leader, Walter Williams explains what happened:

'Engines were started just after ten o'clock, but unfortunately one of my formation had engine trouble on the run-up and there was a delay of some twelve minutes while the crew changed to the reserve aircraft.

'Over the radio I agreed with Wing Commander Jarman that we would rendezvous over Swindon. in the event we never met up and I therefore set course for the target alone with my formation.'

We will leave Squadron Leader Williams and his flight and return to the mainforce, now well ahead and on course for the first turning point over the Lizard. Flying at a thousand feet in brilliant sunshine the force had no difficulty in completing the first leg. Shortly before midday the rocky outcrops marking the Cornish coastline slid away beneath to give way to a shimmering sea, blue and tantalising.

The second leg extended across the Western Approaches to a position over the Bay of Biscay southwest of Brest. During this leg over the open sea the bombers remained at a thousand feet, in order to delay until the last possible moment detection by the enemy radar stations. Already, signals from the radio beacons at Barfleur on the Cherbourg peninsular and St. Brienc located near Etables were being intercepted. Later transmissions from the beacon at Quimper southeast of Brest would provide a useful reference for the navigators busy checking and re-checking their positions.

So far, apart from the delay of Squadron Leader Williams flight, nothing untoward had occurred, but shortly before the end of the second leg Sergeant Hutchin, the second pilot in Harry Drummond's crew, sighted what he thought was a submarine. His observation, viewed in the light of events to come, may have been significant. Most certainly an alert message could have been signalled, though no documentary evidence has been unearthed to support this supposition. Perhaps we shall never know.

Six minutes after this incident and just short of the hour from leaving the English coast, the mainforce turned onto the final leg. A lengthy run of over 250 miles lay ahead - La Pallice was still over an hour's flying time away - during the course of which the Halifaxes climbed to their operational height of around 14,000 feet.

Visibility remained perfect, dancing flashes of sunlight sprang fleetingly from places where the drab camouflage had been scratched from the upper surfaces of the wings. In the slipstreams of the leading aircraft their followers gently bobbed and weaved, All eyes strained for a view of La Pallice.

Reward came a few minutes after two o'clock in the afternoon, and within seconds the first enemy fighters were reported. As the bombers crossed the coast there could be no doubt whatsoever in the minds of all that a stiff fight awaited them.

High above the unescorted Halifaxes the German fighter pilots peeled off and dived at the tightly bunched formations. For the next fifteen minutes the bombers were continually attacked by both fighter and murderously heavy ground fire. Casualties were soon inflicted. From the squadron Flight Lieutenant Lewin was first to fall, his Halifax coming down near Aiguillon on the approach to La Pallice. Next to go was a 35 Squadron machine captained by Flight Sergeant Godwin, his aircraft being last seen spinning seawards with smoke pouring from its shattered engines.

Stunned by the sudden loss of two of their number, the survivors manoeuvred as close together as possible to afford each other maximum protection. All held a steady course for the *Scharnhorst,* now clearly visible through the countless flashes of gunfire. Heavy flak was bursting, raining shrapnel in all directions and still the enemy fighters pursued the bombers, exchanging a deadly hail of fire with the sweltering airgunners now fighting for their very lives.

Harry Drummond's aircraft shuddered from a succession of strikes. From the rearturret Flight Sergeant Begbie called to say he had hit one of the fighters. His excited cry was followed almost immediately by a muffled explosion and a piercing yell of pain from Begbie. Calmly, Drummond ordered two of his crew to the rear to render what assistance they could to their stricken colleague. Maintaining station Harry Drummond kept going, the sight of his leader's aircraft ahead a reassuring sight. Suddenly his eye caught sight of a fighter closing for a head-on attack:

'There was a blinding flash in the cockpit, followed by an acrid smell and a howling gale. He had shot through my windscreen missing me by a hair's breadth.

'When the smoke cleared, I turned to speak to my second-pilot only to see his head lying on the floor beside the edge of the armour plated bulkhead. Then his eyes and lips smiled and he picked himself up and resumed his position in the astrodome.' Sergeant Hutchin had been fortunate indeed to escape injury, but there was no time for further enquiry. The bomb-doors on Wing Commander Jarman's Halifax had swung open, this was it. Drummond hung on grimly to his controls, the backs of his hands bleeding from where splinters of perspex had punctured the taut skin. He felt a slight judder as his own bomb-doors opened, and then a perceptible lift as, relieved of its load, the Halifax rose upwards. Later it was assessed that their bombs had undershot the *Scharnhorst* by the narrow margin of 300 yards.

Close in Drummond's tracks, 35 Squadron were now running through the inferno of enemy fire. Bombs from Flight Sergeant Greaves aircraft were seen to explode across the ship, but in the confusion of battle his bomber was never seen again. The sky above La Pallice was now a boiling mass of bursting shells through which the Halifaxes continued to fly.

Squadron Leader Bradley's aircraft was continuously buffetted by a succession of well aimed salvos which momentarily jammed shut his bomb-doors. Inside the fuselage it was an awful shambles, his wireless operator Sergeant Bolton lay dead near his radio set, blood pulsating from a gaping wound in his chest. Alongside Bradley in the cockpit his co-pilot sat ashen faced, his left thigh and shoulder burning from the pain of shrapnel splinters embedded deep in his flesh. Despite these dreadful conditions someone managed to free the bomb-doors in time to alleviate the need for a second bombing-run.

Also in dire trouble was Warrant Officer Holden of 35 Squadron. Until now his aircraft had escaped serious damage, but with the ship almost in the bomb-sight, a burst of *flak* exploded beneath the forward fuselage. Shards of flying metal were sent coursing through the nose wrecking the bomb-release mechanism. The same burst seriously damaged the mainplanes, and the port main tyre was punctured. Before anyone could take stock of the situation, machine-gun bullets raked the Halifax. In the close confines of the rear-turret Pilot Officer Stone caught the full weight of fire and was left dying. At the twin-beam positions, both gunners staggered back from their guns severely wounded, but displaying fortitude of the highest order, Sergeants Perriement and Smith resumed their positions and continued to fire at their attacker. Later, poor Smith fell into a coma, so dreadful were his injuries.

It was probably at this time in the attack with the survivors of the mainforce clearing the target area that Squadron Leader Williams led his lone flight on to the scene. His small force was already reduced from three to two aircraft, himself and Flying Officer McKenna, Flight Lieutenant Hillary having being forced to turn back with persistent engine trouble. Coming up to La Pallice Walter Williams writes:

'We could see no fighters, nor could we see any other Halifaxes. We continued our bombing-run, but my bomb-aimer did not release our bombs because he was not satisfied that he had the ship in his sights. So, we continued through the area of the target and made a return run.'

This calm, matter of fact statement from Walter Williams makes no mention of the fact that he was flying through a curtain of heavy *flak*. In his mind he must have surely realised his chances of surviving the second run were minimal. it is highly probable that similar thoughts were going through the mind of young McKenna as he gamely followed his leader over La Pallice. The accurate ground fire continually harassed his aircraft, and while banking over La Rochelle to make the return run his Halifax took a direct hit. out of control the bomber plunged into the sea taking its entire crew to their deaths. Walter Williams was now alone:

'Just after releasing our bombs the aircraft suffered what appeared to me to be flak damage to the starboard side. Glycol streamed from one engine, which eventually lost power and finally stopped. I headed out to sea and was then attacked by a single fighter which had appeared on the scene. The second engine on the starboard side failed, and I was unable to maintain height.

'Eventually we ditched some seven or eight miles off the French coast.'

Considering the circumstances it was a text-book ditching. Norman Kershaw, Walter Williams wireless operator takes up the story:

'I had got out an S 0 S indicating we had been hit by flak and fighters, also a message in plain language that the *Scharnhorst* had been hit [5] . The next thing I remember is lying in the fuselage with water

---

5   It can only be assumed Norman Kershaw had been given some evidence to suggest the Scharnhorst had been damaged. Squadron records make no mention of damage being inflicted, but 35 Squadron in their assessment clearly credit Flight Sereant Greaves with hitting the vessel with his bombs. It is quite possible bombs from other aircraft struck, or fell near the ship, but in the turmoil of the action these went unreported.

lapping around me.

'I can vividly recall lifting my nose back into place, but no pain. I struggled down the fuselage thinking I must get out of my harness. Up on the wings I could see some of the crew and a dinghy bobbing on the water. The next moment I was in the sea struggling to get my flying-boots off, and then I passed out.'

Willing hands quickly dragged the unconscious wireless operator into the dinghy. Overhead the enemy fighter made several low passes above the forlorn crew pitching in their frail rubber craft, but mercifully no further shots were fired.

After about thirty minutes a French fishing boat chugged alongside and took all seven shocked survivors aboard. Heading for La Rochelle the little craft, with its pitiful human cargo, was intercepted by a *Kriegsmarine* vessel. For Squadron Leader Williams and his crew the remainder of the war would be spent in various prisoner of-war camps.

And so the battered survivors fought their way clear of the enemy defences. In ones and twos the Messerschmitts turned away, the flak guns fell silent. Smoke drifted lazily into the summer air as an uneasy calm settled over the harbour at La Pallice. Soon the curious would venture out to view the remains of three shattered Halifaxes, and it would not be long before Sergeants Phillips, Finlayson and MeLeod, the three survivors from Lewin's crew would join Walter Williams and his men on their way into captivity.

With one engine stopped Harry Drummond found himself gradually falling behind what remained of his formation. Dried blood caked the backs of his hands, his chest still ached from the blast effect of the cannon-shell exploding. Fatigue lay heavily upon his entire body. in the rest-position Flight Sergeant Begbie lay sedated from the morphine injection gently given by the navigator, Monty Dawson. Unknown at the time to the rest of the crew, Dawson himself nearly collapsed through lack of oxygen, but now he was busy at his charts plotting their homeward course.

Shortly after pinpointing their landfall over the Cornish fishing port of Fowey, a second engine failed. Drummond, however, was determined to reach Stanton Harcourt. Sergeant Fraser, the wireless operator, was ordered to alert the station of their plight, and to the immense relief of all on board an ambulance could be seen awaiting their arrival.

The time was a quarter to six in the evening. Five minutes later Wing Commander Jarman, who had delayed his approach in order that Harry Drummond might land first, brought his battle-scarred aircraft to rest. The day's work was over.

From St. Eval in Cornwall and Weston Zoyland in Somerset, news came that their surviving colleagues from 35 Squadron were safely down. This had been a brave, but costly operation, highlighting the tremendous risks involved in sending unescorted bombers in daylight against a well-defended target. The courage of the crews is beyond question, and their bravery was rewarded by at least five hits on *the Scharnhorst* which necessitated her immediate recall to Brest. Furthermore, claims for seven enemy fighters destroyed were submitted, though this figure was later reduced to four. The fierce air battle had not been entirely a one-sided affair.

With the chastening experiences of La Pallice fresh in mind the squadron probably welcomed a return to the slightly less hazardous task of night bombing. It should be borne in mind that the full might of the *Luftwaffe's* night-fighter force had yet to be felt. The sophisticated control systems responsible for inflicting heavy losses on Bomber Command in 1943 and the first quarter of 1944 were still in the embryo stages. For the present the defence of the 'Third Reich' lay primarily in the skilled hands of the flak and searchlight crews.

Operations in August commenced on the 2nd with four crews led by Squadron Leader Bob Bickford, now recovered from his wounds received over Merseburg, joining in a small attack by thirty-two aircraft on Berlin. Principal amongst the targets assigned were the Air Ministry buildings and the Friedrich-strasse railway station. This was the squadron's first visit to the German capital and, in the event, few of those taking part saw anything of note. The night was extremely dark, thus making route pinpointing very difficult, whilst in the vicinity of Berlin a thick ground haze blotted out most of the ground features. The majority of crews released their bomb-loads on an estimated time of arrival over the city, certainly not the most effective means of attack, but in the circumstances no other alternative was possible.

A few fires and explosions were reported, and later it was suggested that some damage may have been caused in the Steglitz area. Some bombs fell in parts of the city between Pankow to the northwest and the Friedrichstrasse station, but damage in these areas was minimal.

Ten nights later Berlin was attacked again. This time the raiding force was increased to seventy, including seven crews from the squadron. An injudicious route was ordered, landfall coming between the notorious hot spots of Amsterdam and Rotterdam. Understandably, many crews were unhappy about this, and it is likely the more experienced made their own plans for reaching Berlin. in the event the weather conditions again proved difficult, resulting in many crews bombing secondary targets well away from the capital. Sergeant Hutchin, now a captain in his own right, bombed the inland port of Bremen, but at least two, Pilot Officer Peter Dobson and Harry Drummond reached the general area of Berlin. By the light of searchlight beams Drummond witnessed the end of one of the attacking force:

'I was fairly certain at the time that I was watching the end of Christopher Cheshire's aircraft. We were right over the target and I sat there, powerless to help, as the bomber dropped from sight in a cone of lights.

'On return the next morning I flew down to see his brother who had telephoned the squadron for news. It was a sad occasion.'

By chance, Flight Lieutenant Leonard Cheshire had operated to Berlin this same might with 35 Squadron. He also had seen a bomber going down in circumstances similar to those described by Harry Drummond, and later he was to write in his classic book *Bomber Pilot*[6] , 'I hope to God it's not Christopher.' A member of his crew who had followed the grim course of events taking place not half-a-mile away from their aircraft, quickly chimed in 'No, sir, it looks more like a Wellington than a Halifax.' No one, I am sure, could be certain, and research undertaken during the preparation of this book suggests Christopher Cheshire's aircraft fell near Parnewinkel, a small town lying well inland roughly on a line midway between the ports of Bremen and Hamburg. From his crew five, including Cheshire, survived to become prisoners- of -war.

In clarifying this, no criticism of Harry Drummond is intended. Bomber Command lost ten crews that night and in the circumstances it was quite understandable to believe the aircraft seen going down was that of a highly respected squadron colleague.

In the pale light of an early dawn two squadron Halifaxes remained unaccounted for. Shortly after five o'clock Sergeant McHale's aircraft was reported in the circuit, but while turning at low altitude the bomber stalled. With an awful crash the Halifax struck the ground and burst into flames. Crash-crews

6   First published in 1943 by Hutchinson & Co.

reached the blazing wreckage within minutes, but there was little anyone could do for the seven crew. The unhappy task of informing the next-of-kin fell to the acting adjutant, Leonard Smith, now a Pilot Officer, who himself felt a great personal loss in that his regular navigator, Sergeant Stan Mayes was amongst those killed. By the late morning it was quite obvious that Sergeant Whitfield and crew would not be returning. A further seven letters required the immediate attention of the acting adjutant.

Whitfield, it turned out, had suffered the cruellest stroke of misfortune. Proceeding SSE of Bremerhaven his aircraft came under sustained attack from a night-fighter flown by Lieutenant Autenrieth of 6/NJG 1. Set on fire Sergeant Whitfleld ordered his crew to bale out, and evidence clearly shows all were successful in obeying his instruction. Tragically five, including Sergeant Whitfield, fell into a marsh near Wittstadt and all were drowned. The two survivors, Sergeant Kenworthy who in the July had been wounded on operations to Merseburg and Flight Sergeant Bone were soon picked up by the authorities. Bone never saw England again. Less than a month before the war in Europe ended he died, possibly as the result of an erroneous strafing attack by Allied fighters on a column of prisoners being force-marched by the retreating German forces.

The inclement weather continued. Seven operations were mounted before August gave way to September and none were particularly successful. During the penultimate attack, mounted against Frankfurt, Squadron Leader Bob Bickford was killed when his aircraft crashed near Pocklington, From the survivors it was learnt that one of the starboard engines failed, and shortly afterwards a second motor began to misfire. The order to bale out was given, but although Bickford succeeded in getting out of his cockpit the canopy of his parachute fouled the tailplane and he was dragged down to his death. The following day the body of the rear-gunner Sergeant Duckmanton was found, his parachute had failed to deploy.

This spate of losses were hard to bear for in the late summer of 1941 trained aircrews were at a premium. Indeed, this desperate shortage within the squadron is reflected in minimal participation in the two mainforce attacks sent to Berlin during early September. On the 11th four Halifaxes were ordered to proceed to Stradishall in Suffolk. Armed and refuelled all four took-off in the late evening and set course for the Royal Arsenal at Turin in northern Italy. Harry Drummond, one of the four pilots involved, recalls brief memories of the outward leg:

'Heavy rain was falling as we flew towards Chartres, but over France the weather cleared and we were flying in brilliant moonlight. it was a wonderful experience to see the Alps so clearly and one of my crew remarked *'Thomas Cook* would have charged a mint of money for this before the war, and here we are actually getting paid for the privilege.'

A few crews strayed from their tracks and encountered a salvo or two of Swiss anti-aircraft fire, but in the opinion of most this was aimed to explode well out of harm's way. Eventually all reached Turin where the defences were slight by comparison to recent experiences over the German mainland. Everyone was able to concentrate on making a good bombing-run and as the mainforce turned for home parts of Turin were well alight. Operations against the Italian targets were considered by the majority to be a 'piece of cake', the worst hazard being fatigue from the long hours spent at the controls. On this occasion, however, Flight Lieutenant Leonard Smith was in for a rather unpleasant surprise:

'We arrived over Turin at 14.000 feet in clear weather. The *flak* was ineffective and I was in two minds whether or not to carry out a low-level attack, or to remain at my present altitude. Fortunately, I decided on the latter for no sooner had my observer called out 'bombs gone' than there was a rush of air and for a few seconds the Halifax seemed out of control.

'It transpired that out bombs had released in a single salvo, leaving the bomb-doors jammed in the open position. This caused considerable drag and reduced our airspeed accordingly.

'To add to our problems the weather turned sour on the way home. Crossing the French coast we attracted some flak, but eventually we arrived over North Forehand short of petrol and in very murky weather. After making a number of 'Darkie' calls some searchlights were switched on as a guide and a few minutes later I saw a flarepath ahead of us. just as we were about to land a Wellington cut in from the side, its pilot obviously intent on getting down come what may. I shouted to my flight engineer 'have we got enough petrol to go around again'. His reply was not encouraging 'don't climb too much skipper, or we will never make it'.

'Somehow I eased my way around the circuit and landed off the second attempt. Within fifty yards of turning off the runway all four motors cut for lack of fuel.' This proved to be Leonard Smith's last operational sortie. His primary task for the remaining years of the war was instructing pilots in the art of Beam Approach flying. The majority of his pupils went into Bomber Command, more than a few eventually serving with 76 Squadron.

Three nights later Harry Drummond completed his tour of operations when the harbour at Brest was the primary target. obtaining a good pinpoint on Point de Diable, Harry commenced his bombing-run. The *flak*, as expected, was fierce and of the harbour little could be seen through the defensive smokescreen set off at the first sound of the approaching bombers. Bombs were released and once clear of the target area course for Base was set. For Harry Drummond the wheel had turned a full circle. At the start of his tour six months previously he had set out in company with Sergeant Cope in a Whitley bomber of 78 Squadron, their target - Brest.

Homecoming on that occasion was no doubt exhilarating. Now, half a year later, and fully aware of the perils that faced him each time his name appeared on the 'Battle Order' Sergeant Drummond[7] looked forward to some respite.

On return to Base he was greatly saddened to learn that Pilot Officer Hutchin who had flown with him to La Pallice in July was dead. Details are scant, but it is affirmed that Hutchin, while on the outward leg to Brest, got into difficulties near Bedford. His crew escaped by parachute, but Hutchin was found still at the controls of his wrecked bomber.

Brest was again visited on 2 October. The customary hot reception duly awaited and Flight Lieutenant Wright struggled back to land at Boscombe Down, the metal fuselage of his aircraft ripped and torn by numerous shrapnel splinters.

Apart from a long night haul to Nuremburg on the 12th, coastal targets occupied the squadron for the remainder of the month. November was quiet until the 7th when Berlin was attempted on a night best remembered for its numbing cold. Pilot Officer 'Jock' Calder and Sergeant Herbert attacked in what both considered to be the general area of the city, whilst Squadron Leader John Bouwens, recently arrived from 51 Squadron to take over B Flight, went for the docks at Flensburg as a last resort.

---

7   Commissioned soon after leaving the squadron, Harry Drummond later flew in the 1,000 bomber raids launched in
     1942 and ended the war as a Wing Commander flying instructor.

This was the last raid on the German capital by Bomber Command in 1941. In retrospect it proved to be the last major operation mounted against this target for over a year.

Although improved equipment was reaching the command in the shape of the Halifax, Stirling and Lancaster bombers, with the versatile Mosquito soon to appear, the bombing campaign was proving to be an uphill struggle. Losses were mounting steadily, especially amongst the new crews arriving as replacements on the squadrons. Fresh from training, few had yet fully mastered the skills required to handle a heavily laden bomber engaged in the rigours of operational flying. Time was not on their side, nor on that of their leaders. The day to day requirements frequently required Squadron Commanders to send raw crews on major operations without the prior benefit of less demanding sorties. A policy of seconding newly arrived pilots to a seasoned crew was maintained whenever possible, though with hindsight it is doubtful whether this practice helped to reduce casualties. An examination of squadron losses clearly indicates those at most risk to be the 'freshers', as the new arrivals were popularly known. As one young pilot of the day put it:

'You shut your mind to what lay ahead. Each day was lived to the full in the expectation it could be your last.'

With the turn of the year fast approaching the emphasis still lay in attacks aimed at the German battlecruisers. Soon, added to the now familiar names of *Scharnhorst, Gneisenau* and Prinz *Eugen,* the name Tirpitz would feature in the operational briefings.

Between the end of November 1941 and the closing days of April 1942, the squadron was involved in nine attacks against these targets. Four were directed on Brest and four were delivered against the Tirpitz, the other operation being an abortive attempt to locate units of the German battlefleet in the North Sea on 12 February, The events of these operations will now be considered in some detail, along with the actions by the other bomber squadrons similarly engaged.

Chapter Three

NOVEMBER 1941 to JUNE 1942

During the afternoon of 25 November 1941, a strong force of bombers took off from bases in northeast England for an early evening raid on Brest. Four squadron crews were engaged, and all arrived in the vicinity of the target at around quarter to seven. Searchlight beams were already busy probing the evening sky, accompanied by the now familiar flash given off by countless guns firing from in and around the harbour entrance. Sergeant Herbert's bomber shook violently as a salvo went off directly ahead of its flight path. Red hot shrapnel sliced through the perspex of the nose turret, fragments of the spent charge ricocheting dangerously inside the confines of the forward compartment. No one was injured and Herbert maintained his course.

As with previous operations the German defenders flooded the basins with smoke, through which sticks of bombs tumbled setting off explosions on jetties and starting some fires amongst the paraphernalia littered around the docks. The prime objective of their attention escaped. it was without doubt a most frustrating encounter. A little over three weeks later Wing Commander Jarman handed over the reins to Wing Commander David Young, and within a day of his arrival the new CO ordered his squadron to commence intensive daylight formation flying practice. it is unlikely that many crews had time to brush up on this procedure for after tea on that same day, 17 December, the reason behind the order was unveiled. A daylight assault on Brest was in the offing. Immediately six of the most experienced crews were ordered to attend briefing. Security was tight, movement of all personnel being confined to the Base area. The next morning all six, Wing Commander Young at their head, took-off and made for the first rendezvous point over Linton-on-Ouse. Excellent work by the groundcrews ensured 'Jock' Calder's departure after his Halifax developed brake trouble whilst taxiing, thus necessitating a prompt transfer to one of the reserve aircraft.

Linton was duly reached, by which time the squadron had linked up with 10 Squadron operating from Leeming and flying their recently acquired Halifaxes for the first time on operations. From Linton 35 Squadron were already airborne, bringing the Halifax force up to seventeen aircraft, the single casualty being Wing Commander Marks, leader of 10 Squadron. He had been forced to jettison his bomb-load into Filey Bay and put back to Leeming with a jammed starboard undercarriage.

In misty weather course was set for Lundy island in the Bristol Channel, where it was planned to meet two squadrons of Stirlings from 3 Group. En route Squadron Leader Packe's Halifax began to misfire and he was obliged to break formation and head for Boscombe Down with his engine instruments fluctuating wildly. The 4 Group contingent was now reduced to sixteen Halifaxes. Through the mid-December murk, the shape of Lundy island came into view and all were relieved to find the Stirlings ready on station.

Over the Channel, the rocky outcrops of the Lizard peninsula fast disappearing from view, the weather improved. On schedule and with nine twin-engined Manchesters from 97 Squadron making up the rear formation, the mainforce neared the French coast. Here, lazily wheeling in the pale blue December air was the welcome sight of a strong fighter escort. Fighter Command had already carried out part of its task. Squadrons of Spitfires and Hurricanes had swept the surrounding areas inducing the Messerschmitts to rise like a school of fish to the bait. A general melee had resulted and now only a handful of enemy fighters remained in the air. The time was coming up to half past twelve. At Base lunch would just about be ready to serve as Wing Commander David Young takes up the story.

'The *flak* was very heavy and concentrated over the target, so I led my chaps out about 400 yards to the right and swung in from a slightly different angle to that originally intended. This was an instant decision and was criticised afterwards, but it was right. We did a very steady bombing-run and had excellent photographs to show as proof, right over the ships.'

Flying in the same formation as Wing Commander Young was Flying Officer 'Hank' Iveson, who now continues:

'I could see the Stirlings going in first, and we were due next followed by the Manchesters. A few 109s were still causing trouble as the Stirlings made their attack, but all had disappeared by the time we arrived. The flak, however, was most intense as we ran in, still in Vic formation from the west and it was very accurate owing to our straight and level approach. One burst went off just above us and a piece of shell came through the astro hatch narrowly missing my second pilot, Pilot Officer Perry.' in the face of this accurate fire the mainforce held good order, 10 and 35 Squadrons attacking in line astern. No one was bombing short this time as stick after stick straddled the two docks containing the enemy vessels. Several direct hits were scored and photographs taken from Iveson's aircraft show his two sticks bursting on the dockyard walls.

While this furious activity was in progress, a high percentage of the enemy fighters that had scrapped with the Hurricanes and Spitfires earlier in the day, had landed and were now being frantically rearmed and fuelled. With the bombers fast clearing the target area, the German fighter pilots rose once more to do battle. From above the remaining Spitfires slanted downwards to meet this renewed threat. Whirling dogfights broke out, but some of the Messerschmitts were getting through to the bombers as witnessed by 'Hank' Iveson:

'East of Brest the enemy fighters were still scrapping away. One latched itself onto a Stirling and gave it a terrific pasting. A fire broke out and the Stirling went down, but not before the gunners were rewarded by seeing their attacker go down in flames.' It is most likely young Iveson was watching the end of a 15 Squadron machine piloted by Flying Officer Bunce. Several of his squadron companions reported Bunce going down in the manner described above, one adding that the rear gunner was still bravely defying the enemy fighter as the Stirling went into a near vertical dive. It must have been a gallant sight to behold.

Several of the bombers had been hit by *flak*, or damaged by the fighters. Wing Commander Vernon Robinson of 35 Squadron was in very serious difficulties with two engines out of action and a third damaged. Displaying superb airmanship Robinson successfully nursed his crippled Halifax away from the target area, setting course for the southwest coast of England. Gradually he lost height and at a quarter past one in the afternoon he was forced to alight in the sea. His was a textbook ditching and the entire crew were able to scramble into the aircraft's dinghy before the battle damaged Halifax slipped beneath the foam capped waves of the English Channel. A few hours later all were rescued by an RAF high-speed launch sent out from Penzance.

Before this drama was enacted, 97 Squadron with their Manchesters had braved the enemy fire. A Bf 109 pounced on Pilot Officer Stoke's aircraft, quickly sending it down out of control. Flak harried the remainder, one shell in particular inflicting severe damage to the rear fuselage and elevators of Wing Commander Balsdon's machine. His rear gunner Flight Lieutenant Wright was wounded, and nearing their Base at Coningsby a radio call was sent asking for an ambulance to be standing by. Shortly before four o'clock, and in fast fading light, the crippled Manchester was sighted nearing the airfield. it can only be assumed Wing Commander Balsdon was unhappy with his approach, or perhaps the Manchester was not responding to the controls. Whatever the reason, those watching on the ground saw the nose, of his aircraft slowly rise as power was increased, as if the pilot was attempting to go around the circuit again. Then with an awful suddenness the inevitable happened, the Manchester stalled and crashed onto the airfield. There were no survivors from the crew of eight.

Just before darkness fell David Young brought his squadron into Boscombe Down. Fog had crept in over the northern bases and it would be four days before the Halifaxes could return to Middleton St. George.

From this gallant operation five bomber crews and one fighter pilot failed to return, while a total of eight enemy aircraft were claimed destroyed. Material damage to the German ships was not as severe as hoped and before the end of the month another attempt would be sought.

This came on the 30th, with the attack timed to commence in the middle of the afternoon. At the squadron commanders conference held before the operation, disagreement arose over the methods to be employed, 'When it was suggested that we should attack in line astern I held three pencils in my hand and then pointed them about five degrees apart, but one person still could not see that if we went in my way we would each get a third of the flak until the bombs were released. However, it was two to one at the end of the meeting and I was overruled.'

This rejection of Wing Commander Young's reasoning will later be seen to have had an unhappy outcome. But this was some hours away. The squadron's departure was not without hindrance. Sergeant Morin, a Canadian, was obliged to make a last minute change of aircraft following the discovery by his rear gunner of a faulty turret.

The route was similar to that flown on the 18th and everyone was much relieved on nearing Brest to see the escorting Spitfires tucked in at 20,000 feet, some 4,000 feet higher than their charges. As decided at briefing the three Halifax squadrons went into line astern, Vernon Robinson at their head. Next came 76 Squadron, followed by three 10 Squadron machines headed by Squadron Leader Webster.

The doubts expressed earlier by David Young became abundantly clear to all as the enemy gunners quickly gauged the height and course of the leading bombers. One or two sighting shells exploded, and then Squadron Leader Middleton of 3 5 Squadron, flying immediately ahead of David Young took a direct hit. Shell splinters from this same burst struck the 76 Squadron leader's Halifax causing it to swerve violently to the left, and into the path of 'Hank' Iveson. For a second or two a mid-air collision seemed unavoidable and it was a much relieved Iveson who found himself in clear skies flying next to Sergeant Herbert.

His respite was brief. A tremendous flash, followed by a bang, clearly audible above the roar of his engines, sent hard splinters of shrapnel thudding into his aircraft. Most of the perspex from the front turret disappeared, and an icy blast of air roared into the cockpit. Later it was discovered that the undersurfaces of the forward fuselage were pitted in more than a dozen places,

The three 10 Squadron machines were next to feel the full weight of the ground fire. Flight Sergeant Whyte's Halifax was riddled from stem to stern, but his crew were left unharmed. Squadron Leader Webster's bomber was damaged in the area of the rear turret and to a lesser degree in the port wing-flap mechanism, while Pilot Officer Hacking emerged from the smoke relatively unscathed.

Over the harbour a few enemy fighters darted in and out of the smoke puffs marking the shell bursts, pressing home their attacks with tenacity. in the confusion 'Hank' Iveson's rear gunner, Sergeant Holmes, fixed his sights on a Bf 109 and gave it two short bursts of accurate fire. To his delight the enemy fighter spun away, out of control and with flames streaming from its engine cowling. The majority of fighter attacks, however, were being driven off by the escorting Spitfires. David Young again takes up the story:

'My tail gunner called out 'fighters coming up - swarms of them' I replied, 'OK, keep me informed of any attack.' About ten seconds later he let out a yell 'It's alright, the cavalry have arrived. Spitfires are tearing into them'. And so they were, long range Spitfires had been sent to meet us over the target, including a Polish [8] squadron, and the impression of those of us who saw the battle was that the Poles did not open fire until they were reading the instruments in the 109s cockpits.'

Still the unremitting flak continued. Squadron Leader Packe's aircraft was hit in the starboard outer engine knocking away an exhaust pipe. A shower of sparks leapt like angry fireflies over the upper surface of the wing. On Packe's starboard beam a bright red flash marked an explosion directly beneath Pilot Officer King's machine enveloping it in smoke and flame. When next sighted King's Halifax was gliding down, the outer motor on his starboard wing stopped. In a cloud of spray the Halifax struck the water. Two Spitfires lingered above watching for any signs of life, but no one from this young Canadian pilot's crew survived. Today their names may be found in The Books of Remembrance at the Royal Air Force Memorial, at Runnymede.

As the survivors headed north of Brest the enemy fighters swooped in for a final attack. In Flight Sergeant Whyte's Halifax his rear gunner, Flight Lieutenant Roach, made his last call 'fighters, I am firing'. The rest of his words, if any, were blotted out by the roar and fury of machine-gun and cannon shells, their lethal charge rendering awful damage to the tail and port wing. The attack left Whyte with only one operative engine, but gamely he drew away maintaining airspeed by holding the Halifax in a slightly nose down attitude. His crew were ordered to take up ditching positions, and this was successfully accomplished some eighty miles south of the Lizard Point. For seven vital minutes the bomber remained afloat, long enough for it to be established that Flight Lieutenant Roach had died at his post. Exhausted, the numbed survivors huddled in their dinghy to spend an uncomfortable five hours before being rescued by an RAF Air Sea Rescue launch.

Very few results from this second strike at Brest were observed. The intense ground fire had called for continual evasive tactics which had split the bombers on their bomb runs, and had not the Spitfires been on hand the *Luftwaffe* would have surely enjoyed a field day. In the event losses were restricted to three bombers and three fighters. As for the earlier raid on the 18th claims against the enemy amounted to eight Messerschmitts destroyed. The ships, by now quaintly christened Salmon *and Gluckstein by* those charged with their destruction, remained intact.

'In spite of the fact that our photographs showed bomb-bursts around and alongside the ships, little damage had been done. The reason these raids did not sink either of the ships is obvious now, but was not at the time, even to the higher command. We were using two thousand pound armour piercing bombs of doubtful vintage and they were certainly not good enough for these ships which were not as old as our bombs.' This wry observation by Wing Commander Young illustrates well the problems facing the command at the end of 1941. Even more alarming, perhaps, to the senior officers in Bomber Command

8   This was 306 Squadron, then based at Church Stanton in the Blackdown Hills, south of Taunton, Somerset

was the knowledge that in the short term little in the way of improvement could be expected.

This should not be interpreted as criticism of the aircrews. Almost without exception everyone concerned with the bombing offensive was giving of his all. The sad fact facing the planning staff at High Wycombe, nerve centre of Bomber Command headquarters, was that men and equipment were not reaching the squadrons in sufficient quantity for the command to be effective. However, the end of year figures for the squadron were quite encouraging. A total of 162 Halifax sorties had been dispatched, from which 127 had been claimed as successful. Although these figures pale when compared to, say the summer of 1944, it was for the time an excellent achievement.

The first attack on the Tirpitz involving 76 Squadron took place on 30 January 1942. Her position at the time in Aasen Fjord near Trondheim required the squadron to move a detachment up to Lossiemouth in Scotland. From here, in weather that can only be described as 'disappointing', five crews headed out towards the forbidding coastline of Norway, The events of the next ten hours are now told by Flight Lieutenant 'Hank' Iveson:

'The weather forecast was for cloud from 2,000 to 8,000 feet, with heavy icing. Immediately after take-off we commenced climbing to get above the cloud, but to my concern we were still flying 'blind' at 15,000 feet, though thankfully the icing had by this time ceased. This high cloud broke up as we neared the Norwegian coast, but a layer of strato cumulus remained at 7000 feet, persisting all the way to the target area.

'Without sighting anything we flew north where gradually the cloud could be seen to be breaking up. I estimate that within two hours the area around Trondheim would have been clear, for there was a strong northerly wind blowing.

'Feeling extremely disappointed we flew home via the Shetlands, remaining above the worst of the weather. With a full moon setting in the west and dawn breaking in the east, it was a truly amazing picture.'

This long slog home in indifferent weather presented the crews with as much danger as the flak and searchlights. Even the slightest track error at these latitudes could lead to fatal consequences, thus Sergeant Harwood's ditching, and subsequent survival, was little short of a miracle. Soon after turning for home the wireless equipment failed and in the wan light of dawn all that could be seen was the empty stretch of sea. By this time Harwood was well overdue, but at least someone had the good sense to alert the aerodrome at Dyce. From here 416 and 60 3 Squadrons were scrambled in the slender hope they might find the lone bomber and guide it to safety.

Out into the half light flew the Spitfires, anxious eyes hoping for a quick sighting of Harwood whose fuel reserve was now critical. Aboard the Halifax equally anxious eyes, eyes raw from the fatigue of long cold hours in the air, strained for a glimpse of land beneath the grey mist of cloud.- Then, just when hope seemed all but gone the thin blur of a distant coastline loomed into view.

Elation, however, quickly changed to abject despair for almost in the same moment came the unmistakable splutter of engines misfiring through lack of fuel. Their course was run and Harwood had no choice but to commit his aircraft to a ditching. Summoning all his reserves of energy and skill Sergeant Harwood set his bomber down in the icy sea four miles out from the fishing port of Aberdeen. Two of his crew were slightly injured as the Halifax slewed drunkenly through a sheet of water, but moments later all were able to scramble clear and reach the dinghy bobbing gently in the swell. Rescue was not long in coming. Soon all were recuperating from their ordeal of the hours past, while at Dyce the Spitfires were recovered without incident.

A week later the detachment returned to Base without mounting any further operations.

On 11 February six crews bombed the huge inland docks complex at Mannheim, deep beyond the Ruhr. The sky was clear and aided by flares dropped from selected aircraft some good results were achieved. Meanwhile, as the Mannheim force headed for home, hundreds of miles away to the west, events in the English Channel were beginning to build towards an action that subsequently would come close to toppling Winston Churchill and his War Cabinet. The German Battlecruisers *Scharnhorst, Gneisenau* and Prinz *Eugen,* escorted by a cavalcade of destroyers and E-boats had broken out of Brest and were in the Channel. Steaming at speed this formidable array of warships held course for the Strait of Dover. The weather was awful. High winds lashed at the fleet, rolling seas broke across the open decks sending sheets of freezing spume dashing along gangways and slapping into the upper works. Lookouts, their faces and hands tinged white and blue with the cold ducked involuntarily as the wind whipped the spray around their exposed positions. Overhead the enemy fighter pilots no doubt cursed their superiors as they strove to maintain visual contact with the fleet.

For several vital hours the ships remained undetected and when at last alerted to what was happening the attempts to sink, or at least cripple part of this armada failed, By noon on the 12th the main elements of the enemy fleet were racing through the narrows towards the North Sea. With each passing minute safety was coming that much closer.

But something desperate was being attempted. From Manston in Kent Lieutenant Commander Eugene Esmonde and his crews ran across the rain soaked tarmac towards their waiting Swordfish. Minutes later Esmonde, followed by five more torpedo laden biplanes, were lost from view as they headed through the lowering cloud and rain towards the Channel. A promise of fighter escort perhaps gave faint hope to those young Fleet Air Arm crews of 825 Squadron as they neared the Kentish coastline, but, not surprisingly in the dreadful conditions the waiting escort could not be seen.

Undeterred Esmonde led his crews out over the sea, the rain and wind buffeting at their frail craft.

Through the gloom the enemy vessels came into view and immediately Esmonde's force were engaged by all manner of defensive fire. it must have been an awesome sight, the flash of gunfire, the streaming trails left by tracer mixed with the red burst of exploding shell. Hit after hit was registering on this gallant band, but none turned away. When last seen all were holding unswerving course towards the dark outlines of the German battlecruisers.

Later, a handful of shocked survivors were plucked from the sea, but Esmonde [9] was not amongst them.

The cruisers were unscathed and during the afternoon 76 Squadron was caught up in the general confusion of action over the North Sea as aircraft of Bomber and Coastal Command searched in vain for these elusive targets. By the early hours of the 13th it was grudgingly acknowledged that the enemy vessels were safe in the sanctuary of their home waters.

Two days later on the 15th, the British and Commonwealth forces fighting in Singapore surrendered to the Japanese. The news was about as bad as at anytime in the war to date.

It was against this sombre panorama that the squadron faced up to the last months of winter. Although unrealised at the time a new appointment was made on 22 February that for Bomber Command would

---

9   To mark his actions that day the country bestowed on Lieutenant Commander Eugene Esmonde it's highest accolade for bravery, a posthumous Victoria Cross.

have a far reaching effect on the remaining course of the war. On that day Air Marshal Sir Richard Pierce officially handed over the office of Air Officer Commander-in-Chief, Bomber Command, to Air Chief Marshal Sir Arthur Harris. Within a few weeks of his appointment it became crystal clear to all that the total destruction of the German war-machine by bombing was the new commander's sole aim. With singleness of purpose Harris pursued his plan with an almost cold fanaticism until the end of hostilities. The rights and wrongs of the decisions he took on the way to his ultimate goal have been fiercely argued over by historians, and will no doubt continue to be the subject of discussion for many years to come. But this is all done in hindsight. At the time few opposed his plans, or questioned the wisdom of his decisions. There can, however, be no doubt whatsoever that under his direction Bomber Command meted out terrible retribution on the civilian population of Germany for the folly of their leaders in believing they were the natural masters of western democracy.

For the present, however, the squadron was still much occupied with the Tirpitz. On 27 March David Young took a dozen crews and aircraft north to Tain. Here a strike for the 29th was planned, but at the last minute the operation was postponed for twenty-four hours. The route still lay towards Aasen Fjord, now well fortified with flak and searchlight batteries, and it was the destruction of these defences, plus the anti-aircraft guns aboard Tirpitz that required the special attention of 76 Squadron. To achieve this aim a mixed load of 4,000-lb blast-bombs and 500-lb high explosive charges were winched by sweating armourers into the bomb-bays. At other dispersal points similar teams of men hoisted 1,500-lb depth charges into the waiting 10 and 35 Squadron Halifaxes.

The weather outlook was favourable as the mainforce flew out below 1,000 feet, the sky above overcast and uninviting. The dark shadow of Sumburgh enabled navigators to make one last positive fix before laying off their courses for the as yet unseen shores of Norway. Cold, cramped hours later the hard snow packed hills of this still ice-cold land slipped away beneath as the bombers clawed for height through clear skies. But as the force penetrated deeper inland the first ominous wisps of a milky-fog could be seen swirling through the valleys below.

By the time Aasen Fjord was reached conditions had deteriorated to such an extent that it was impossible to see the Tirpitz, Nonetheless, five crews pressed home their attacks, Flight Lieutenants 'Hank' Iveson, Peter Warner, Flight Sergeant Lambeth, and Sergeants Borsberry and Harwood all claiming hits on flak and searchlight positions.

Their companions faired no better. Once more a long and difficult journey had been accomplished with little reward for the tenacity of the crews involved. The weather, that until now had been found reasonable, changed for the worse. 'Hank' Iveson describes his flight home with all its inherent dangers:

'After flying at 13,000 feet we descended into thick clouds, encountering severe icing at 8,000 feet. Full power was needed to get away from these conditions and in doing so it was obvious that our margin of petrol was going to be critical.

'We managed to obtain a fix on Sumburgh, so we came out of the clouds, dropping down to 1 000 feet, only to discover that most of Sumburgh was fog-bound. My fuel state was such I knew we would not reach Tain and with my wireless operator (Pilot Officer Craine) transmitting distress calls we set course for Wick.

'I had just told my crew to prepare for ditching when I saw the Wick beacon signalling. Landing lights on, we went straight in, cutting the inboard motors as we crossed the boundary hedge. Three-quarters of the way down the flare-path I realised the brakes were not working, so not wishing to go through the fence and perhaps end up in the local churchyard, I swung the aircraft off to the right. The undercarriage held and after bouncing around the perimeter track we came to a halt.'

'Hank' Iveson's fear of finishing up in the churchyard was a distinct possibility as the church was below the level of the airfield,

One squadron crew was missing from this operation. Squadron Leader Burdett had been heard calling for assistance shortly before midnight and later a message was received from 14 Group headquarters indicating his aircraft had passed over Sumburgh at around 01.20 hours. This was about the time that 'Hank' Iveson was 'bouncing around the perimeter' at Wick, but for Squadron Leader Burdett and crew there would be no safe homecoming. Their demise is calculated at approximately sixteen miles south of Sumburgh in the Shetland Islands. An intensive sea search was mounted around the islands, but no one from this Halifax was ever found.

From 10 Squadron came word that Squadron Leader Webster and Pilot Officer Blunden, a New Zealander, were missing. Worse news was soon to come from 3 5 Squadron. Here three crews had failed to return, Bushby, Archibald and the Canadian Steinhauser, all Flight Sergeants. Forty-two airmen had been swallowed up without trace, a tragic loss that was felt deeply throughout all three squadrons.

For another five days the squadrons were held in readiness. Each day the crews reported to the briefing rooms, but on 5 April all were told to proceed to their respective bases. In the prevailing weather conditions, this was no easy matter and at the first attempt only two squadron crews succeeded in reaching Middleton St. George. The next day saw an improvement and seven crews flew south, leaving two unserviceable Halifaxes at Tain for repair.

The respite from Tirpitz operations was short-lived. On the 21st an advance party of groundcrews set out on the uncomfortable journey by rail to Tain. Aircrews flew in on the 23rd and the familiar 'on', 'off' situation occupied everyone for the next three days. Then, on the 27th a strong force of heavy bombers, including for the first time a dozen Lancasters from 44 and 97 Squadrons, took-off and made for Trondheim. Latest intelligence reports suggested the Tirpitz would be found near Aavikaunet on the northern bank of the Fetfjorden, northeast of Trondheim.

This time the weather remained clear and on nearing the Tirpitz the night sky was transformed into a kaleidoscope of frightening colours. From the shores of the fjord a barrage of heavy flak, accompanied by tracer fire, came hurtling upwards. Thousands of brightly shining balls cut through the chill night air, the evil red tinged smoke from exploding shells clearly visible as the bombers swept across the still water. Ahead, staining the surface of the fjord, a creeping smudge of black oily smoke surrounded the ship, through which a deluge of bombs and depth charges plummeted, sending pillars of spray cascading amongst the low flying aircraft. The *flak* was terrible. Wing Commander Don Bennett [10] leading 10 Squadron was hit and was last seen slipping away northeastwards towards the snow encrusted hills. Flight Lieutenant Pooles and Pilot Officer McIntyre, both of 35 Squadron, were brought down, but miraculously all eleven squadron crews emerged relatively unscathed.

Gradually, the smoke drifted away, the roar of aero engines receded into the distance as the last nervous sweep of a searchlight beam lit the surrounding hills and died. The Tirpitz remained defiantly afloat.

Hit by *flak* when making his second run over the target, the return leg for Flight Sergeant Kenny Clack was a somewhat eventful affair as his flight engineer, Sergeant Bill Lawes explains:

---

10   Later Air Vice-Marshal Bennett, wartime leader of 8(PFF) Group.

'I checked the instruments and discovered one engine temperature winding itself off the clock. We hung on to all four motors until we were well clear of the gunfire, and then I feathered the overheating engine and took stock.

'A petrol tank was holed and its fuel gauge was rapidly lowering. The bomb-doors were open, creating an unwanted drag. I fed the remaining motors off the holed tank for as long as possible, after which we had a council of war. The alternatives were to make for Sweden, or try for Scotland. We opted for the latter as there were supposed to be many ships along our return flight path, just in case anyone had to ditch.

'At around dawn we were flying at 9,000 feet in light cloud, and with no sign of land a sea landing seemed inevitable. But, as we were mulling this possibility over, I spotted a flashing beacon which was identified as an airfield just to the north of Tain. Not long afterwards we were down after nine hours and fifteen minutes in the air. it was not a moment too soon, for within a few seconds of touching down all three engines stopped through lack of petrol.'

A follow-up attack 24 hours later was equally frustrated by the defensive smokescreen. And now, with the first gentle touch of early spring lifting the shield of darkness, there seemed little profit in maintaining such a force of heavy bombers at these far flung Scottish bases. Thus, on the 30th Wing Commander David Young led his squadron home to Middleton St. George. Targets in Germany once more beckoned.

One final word on the Tirpitz is, however, worth recording, For nearly three years this formidable vessel would survive all manner of attack. Throughout this time she proved a dangerous adversary facing the Allied convoys plying through the guarded waters around the North Cape. For the merchant seamen and their naval escorts, the supply runs to Soviet Russia were always fraught with danger.

Significantly, it was from the air that death eventually reached out to around 900 of her crew. On 12 November 1944, a combined force of Lancaster crews picked from 9 and 617 Squadrons and led by Wing Commander Tait succeeded once and for all in capsizing this proud ship in Tromso Fjord.

Long before this however, recognition of what had been so valiantly attempted by the three Halifax squadrons manifested itself in the summer of 1942 with the detachments of 10 and 76 Squadrons to the Middle East. The intention at the time was for this combined force to strike at units of the Italian Fleet in the Mediterranean. This, as it will be explained, did not materialise, but the expertise gained in the first four months of 1942 would be put to good use against the Axis defenders of Tobruk.

From his headquarters at High Wycombe, Air Chief Marshal Sir Arthur Harris was actively preparing plans for his part in the destruction of Germany. Already he had shown his hand to deadly effect on the Baltic seaport of Rostock where in four nights between 23 and 27 April, considerable fire damage had been inflicted. Earlier, on 3 March he had sent his bombers, 235 in all, to bomb the Renault works at Billancourt in the western suburbs of Paris. From the outset the emphasis of this raid lay in a heavy concentration of aircraft over the target, and the outcome was hugely successful. However, Harris knew that the prime targets lay in the Ruhr, where war production continued to increase despite all his close attention.

During the night of 10/11 April, Pilot Officer Mike Renaut and Sergeant Harwood wrote their names and that of the squadron into the history books when they successfully delivered the first 8,000-lb bombs on Germany. Appropriately for the occasion the Krupps works at Essen was the target for this latest addition to Bomber Command's increasing arsenal of weapons.

Sergeant Harwood was first to attack, his run from 17,000 feet above the Ruhr being timed eight minutes before the midnight hour, A satisfying glow of fire marked its point of impact.

For the next thirty minutes bombers arrived over Essen, and amongst those in the closing stages of the attack was Mike Renaut. The defences had by this time warmed to their task and Renaut's Halifax was shaken repeatedly. This was the most dangerous time as the bomb-aimer guided his pilot towards the aiming point. Far below the spurt of fire could be seen chasing through several areas of the darkened city, while all around the air vibrated from bursting shells.

Inside the unlit fuselage Renaut's crew busied themselves with the task at hand. To be occupied helped close the mind to the inherent dangers from without. Near the end of his run the half expected blow fell, and it came just as the nose, relieved of the weight of 8,000-lbs of explosives, rose momentarily from its course. A particularly close burst of *flak* had sent red-hot splinters of steel through the forward fuselage. The carnage could have been dreadful, but in the event only his wireless operator needed medical attention and Renaut limped across the North Sea to land at the coastal aerodrome of Docking near Hunstanton in Norfolk.

May opened with a raid on Hamburg on the 3rd. Towering walls of cloud hid the sprawling dockland, but if any of the attackers had doubts as to their position, these were quickly dispelled by a curtain of flak marking their approach across the Elbe. it should also be mentioned that more and more crews were becoming skilled in the use of 'GEE' and against coastal targets, such as Hamburg, this aid was proving most useful in target identification. Scientific involvement on both sides in the campaign was increasing daily. Far removed from the brisk business of battle, men and women worked unceasingly in the laboratories to provide the night-bomber forces with the best in equipment. The Germans, it should be realised, were certainly no laggards in the field. Allied bomber crews already had a most healthy respect for the heavily armed Junkers and Messerschmitts and the men that flew them. interceptions by nightfighters were on the increase and as the enemy's airborne radar and ground control systems improved, no lessening from this quarter could be expected.

Let us, therefore, pause for a moment to examine the table of losses inflicted so far upon the squadron during night operations.

Date	Target	Aircraft Captain	Loss to:
23 Jun 41	Kiel	Pilot Officer W K Stobbs	night-fighter
5 Aug 41		Karlsruhe Sergeant T A Byrne	unknown
13 Aug 41	Berlin	Flight Lieutenant C C Cheshire	*flak*
13 Aug 41	Berlin	Sergeant C E Whitfield	night-fighter
12 Oct 41	Bremen	Sergeant E B Muttart RCAF	night-fighter
31 Oct 41	Dunkirk	Sergeant C S O'Brien RCAF	night-fighter ?
10 Apr 42	Essen	Flight Sergeant J H Lambeth *flak*	
12 Apr 42	Essen	Sergeant K F Lloyd-Jones RAAF	*flak*
27 Apr 42	Dunkirk	Sergeant P C Morris	lost control
3 May 42		Hamburg Sergeant J B Williams	night-fighter

On the 8th Harris again focussed his attention on a Baltic coastal target, no doubt hoping to repeat the successes gained at Lubeck in late March and the April raids on Rostock. On this occasion he chose the town of Warnemunde, a target that amongst its industries included a Heinkel aircraft production plant.

Planning for the attack was quite complex, and with hindsight it was far too ambitious for the quality of the forces available to him. In effect the raid was split into three phases, which will now be explained. The initial attack was to be confined to eighteen aircraft carrying high explosives, bombing by this force to be completed within five minutes of Zero Hour. Immediately following this phase, 104 aircraft - the mainforce - would bomb during a forty-five minute period using General Purpose bombs, and lastly, sixteen bombers would come in at low-level to complete the destruction of the works. This third phase, it was estimated would take ten minutes.

On paper a clearly defined set of objectives had been set out. to which it was added 'between Z plus 20 and Z plus 60, sixty-two aircraft will attack using incendiaries and from Z plus 5 to Z plus 50, twelve aircraft will make low-level attacks on searchlights.' From this review of the planners intent, it can be readily understood that timing of the three waves was the key factor. in the event this close attention to time went sadly astray. From the outset the Warnemunde defences were alert and well co-ordinated. Hundreds of searchlight beams swept back and forth, dazzling those crews in the leading waves, and it is very doubtful if the dozen crews briefed to nullify these positions met with any tangible success.

Valuable time was lost as the first arrivals searched vainly for some discernible landmark, and it was this hesitant start that gave encouragement to the flak gunners who quickly added to the general discomfort of the raiding force. Soon, any cohesion that may have existed was lost as the high flying bombers delivered their attacks in a piecemeal fashion.

The remainder faired no better. Pilots, blinded by the searchlight glare, blundered across the town at dangerously low altitude, light flak and tracer following their path. Not surprisingly losses were severe. From 193 crews dispatched, nineteen failed to return, including Pilot Officer Moorhouse whose wrecked bomber was found in the light of morning on the outskirts of Rostock.

This overall loss bordering on ten per cent was a savage blow.

Despite this reverse of fortune Harris struck back at the end of May in most spectacular style, when he launched the heaviest air attack of the war to date. His target was the Rhineland city of Cologne and by using nearly every available bomber at his disposal, including machines drawn from other commands and training units, he mustered a force totalling just over 1,000 aircraft. The squadron was well represented, twenty-one crews in all with Squadron Leader 'Jock' Calder, head of the Conversion Flight, flying an aged Halifax B 1 for the occasion.

The 'heavies', in the main, made up the final waves, and on their arrival Cologne was seen to be well alight with much smoke drifting across the Rhine. For nearly three hours the city was pounded by high explosives and incendiaries. Fires raged unchecked in several areas and by morning much of Cologne was without water, gas or electricity. Reports telling of fractured mains and other damage had often to be relayed to the hard pressed authorities by hand as broken telephone lines severely disrupted this common form of communications. Tram services in certain parts of the city were non-existent, while above, an ominous pall of smoke hung in the early summer skies. Early attempts by a Mosquito crew to photograph the destruction was partially thwarted by the smoke column, and it was several days before Allied intelligence could gauge the full extent of damage. For Flight Sergeant Alun Lloyd, one of the navigators operating that night, Cologne holds other memories:

'I was only recently married and my wife, Hilda, came up to Darlington during the day of the raid. Naturally, I could not leave the station to meet her, or explain my absence, and when I eventually reached the house where she was staying, in the early hours of the next morning, I had to throw stones up to the window to attract her attention.'

Two nights later on 1/2 June, a second 'thousand-plan' raid was attempted, this time on the Ruhr industrial city of Essen. It is no secret that many senior officers wished Harris had chosen an easier target, for the industrial haze of the Ruhr valley made Essen a notoriously difficult place to find.

Twenty-one crews were briefed and, perhaps to his vexation 'Jock' Calder found himself once more allocated the veteran B.1 from the Conversion Flight, For seven of the twenty-one crews, a new role was asked of them. No doubt recognising the problems associated with Essen the plan called for a special marker force of twenty Wellingtons to head the main attack. This force was tasked to release flares over the target area, and the seven carefully chosen squadron crews headed by Squadron Leader 'Hank' Iveson were ordered to provide a back-up by laying down a mixture of incendiaries and high explosives. if successful, the mainforce should have a good guide on which to deliver the meat of the attack. Shades of a Pathfinder Force were in the making.

As on so many past occasions success, or failure, depended much on the outcome of the weather. The forecast was not too encouraging and over the North Sea the mainforce found itself trapped between two thickish layers of cloud. Nearing the Dutch coast the lower band of cloud broke up slightly, but in general conditions over the Ruhr were poor. This resulted in the majority of crews either wandering off track or falling well behind schedule. Even the marker force, in the opinion of 'Hank' Iveson had strayed to the west of Essen, and though he was satisfied with his own attack it is unlikely that the primary objective, the Krupps works, was damaged to any degree.

Over a wide area of Germany bombers were flying about in some confusion searching for any landmarks that would enable them to establish their position. Sergeant West on this his seventh operational sortie as captain must have held a good course throughout and as 2 a m approached his Halifax was flying westward over Belgium and nearing the town of GrezDoiceau. Unseen, but already trailing the speeding bomber, was a night-fighter flown by Oberleutnant Prinz zu Sayn-Wittgenstein of III/NJG 2 Stealthily Sayn-Wittgenstein edged his fighter into an attacking position and moments later West's aircraft staggered from the blows of exploding cannon shells. in the seconds that followed four of his crew leapt free of the stricken Halifax. West and one of his gunners, Sergeant Thompson, were not amongst them.

Of the four survivors, two were made prisoners, but Sergeants Wright and Norfolk evaded the search parties and in the weeks that followed made their way to freedom. Norfolk is known to have received help initially from the village of Gottechain, and by the July he was in Brussels. From here, under the protective shield of the famous 'Comet' escape-line, he was brought down to the Pyrenees and before the month was out Sergeant Norfolk was safe in Gibraltar. The Essen raid had marked the squadron's first 'home-runs' of the war.

Two nights later, from an attack on Bremen, two experienced crews failed to return. It can only be assumed that the North Sea claimed Pilot Officer Philp and crew, four bodies from his aircraft being washed up later on the beaches of the Frisian Islands. Of Flight Sergeant Stell, already an 'old-hand' with eight operations - including one on the *Tirpitz* - to his credit, a little more is known for the remains of his bomber were found roughly fifteen kilometres north of Alkmaar near the little Dutch village of St. Maartenvlotbrug. The wreckage bore the unmistakable signs of air combat and Stell's Halifax was later claimed by Hauptmann Heimut Lent.

On 8/9 June Squadron Leader Peter Warner's crew had a most fortuitous escape from death. High over Essen their aeroplane received a direct hit from flak which shattered the port-outer engine and sent the bomber into a spin. For several terrifying minutes, during which time the Halifax lost 1 5 000 feet, Warner wrestled desperately with the controls, eventually regaining level flight at 2,000 feet. Three petrol tanks had been holed by the blast and for a while it seemed unlikely that Base would be reached. That it was is a measure of Peter Warner's skill as a pilot and the determination of his crew working under the most trying conditions.

The port of Emden was raided on two consecutive nights in late June. From the eleven sorties sent to this target, Pilot Officer Norfolk was the only casualty. Hit by flak over Emden, Norfolk was gamely making his way towards the North Sea when his Halifax was intercepted in the early hours of 21 June by Oberleutnant Prinz zur Lippe. A sharp exchange of fire followed Lippe's opening burst, but to no avail. Norfolk called to his crew to bale out, holding the crippled bomber as level as possible to aid their chances of survival, Initially five, at least, made good this chance, Flight Sergeant Salway the rear gunner who was unable to reach his parachute making his jump clinging to his friend Sergeant Smith. This was a brave decision for both airmen to take, and sadly for Salway the jerk of Smith's deploying canopy tore free his tenuous grip and he fell to his death near the little hamlet of Houwerzijl. Smith and three others survived; at Vierhuizen the bodies of Pilot Officer Norfolk and Sergeant Charlesworthy were removed from the remains of their aircraft.

The climax of this busy month came on the 25/26 when Harris sent nearly a 1,000 aircraft winging towards Bremen for the third and final 1,000 plan raid. Lying abroad the river Weser southwest of Hamburg, Bremen's docks were amongst the busiest in Europe. To destroy these installations would give Bomber Command much satisfaction. But, as with the strike aimed at Essen earlier in the month, Harris would be denied success.

The weather was unfavourable throughout northwest Germany with much of the land hidden beneath rolling walls of cloud. Occasionally crews would catch sight of the area surrounding the docks, and then the clouds would close in, forever teasing those trying to select their aiming points. In sheer desperation Flight Lieutenant Mike Renaut dived his bomber through one of the tantalising gaps, levelling out at 2,500 feet above the town. This sudden appearance of a low-flying bomber galvanised the defences into action. Searchlight beams quickly illuminated Renaut's aircraft, the rapid crack from light flak guns was quick to follow. From the nose compartment came a despairing cry from his bomb-aimer to say he was completely blinded by the glare, but Renaut had spotted his target. Shouting to his incapacitated bomb-aimer to release on his command, Renaut held his line.

By now the flak gunners were finding their range. Burst after burst sent shrapnel thudding into the Halifax, but nothing vital was hit. Then, to the immense relief of all on board, the nose of the bomber lifted, the roar from the four Merlin engines increased and with the light flak and tracer still hosing towards them, Renaut regained the sanctuary of the clouds. As he climbed at full power his rear gunner called up to say their bombs were bursting amongst the packed warehouses bordering the docks.

'Jock' Calder, to his dismay, was fired upon by a Wellington. Before he could take avoiding action bullets hit his outer starboard engine puncturing its glycol tank. A thin stream of coolant could be clearly seen fanning away into the slipstream, leaving Calder little choice other than to jettison his bombs and turn for home.

Shortly after this incident 'Jock' Calder came under attack from an unidentified night-fighter, but several well aimed bursts of return fire discouraged the enemy pilot from pressing home his attack. Several hours later Coltishall in East Anglia received one sorely damaged Halifax.

For the vast majority of those serving on the squadron, this operation was their last over Europe for many months to come. The infamous "sixteen day" detachment to the Middle East was about to be announced.

Chapter Four

A MIDDLE EAST ADVENTURE

The Western Desert of North Africa in the summer of 1942 saw two battle-hardened armies locked in hard combat. Driving from the west across the sands of Libya was the all powerful German Afrika Corps, supported by their Italian allies and led by one of Germany's most brilliant field commanders, General Erwin Rommel. His immediate objective was the port of Tobruk, but this master tactician had his eyes set on the canal zone of Egypt wherein lay Alexandria and the Nile Delta. Beyond were the rich oil-fields of the Caucasus and the Persian Gulf. Rich, satisfying pickings all.

Opposing this resolute Axis commander was the Allied commander-in-chief General Auchinleck with his principal force, the men of the 8th Army commanded by General Richie.

For two years past the fortunes of both sides had alternated between rapid advances, followed by equally swift retreats with neither side in the ascendency for any length of time, The very geography of North Africa determined that the bitter desert fighting be confined to the relatively narrow coastal belt sandwiched between the sands of the Sahara Desert and the shimmering waters of the Mediterranean sea.

By the July of 1942, the length and breadth of this extended battleground was strewn with the debris of war, grim memorials to the many hard fought campaigns of the recent past.

On 15 June, Rommel opened a new offensive, sending his dusty armour spearhead columns rolling due east towards Sidi Rezegh and Belhamed. In support of this advance the *Luftwaffe* moved quickly to protect the panzers. Air superiority was of prime importance to the generals on both sides, and though beyond the scope of this book it should be remembered that some of the most savage air fighting of the war took place over the barren soil of the Western Desert.

Rommel's move brought rapid success. Within six days General Auchinleck, with heavy heart, signalled the surrender of the beleaguered garrison of Tobruk. His anguished decision was greeted with much concern in Allied circles, while in the enemy camp Rommel jubilantly amended his plan to halt his forces on the Egyptian frontier. Orders were flashed to his field commanders - cross at your will. His instructions were enthusiastically carried out and by nightfall of 24 June advanced formations of the Afrika Corps were on Egyptian soil.

Fighting a dogged rearguard action the Allied ground forces fell back to establish a line of defence at Alamein. On 1 July, Rommel threw in a strong armoured attack on the Alamein line, while at the same time Axis airforces based in Sicily struck hard at Malta.

For the first four days of July 1942, the situation around Alamein remained critical, but determined Allied counter attacks prevented Rommel's forces from making the crucial breakthrough. Over Malta the airfighting was by no means over and would continue at a violent pace for the first half of the month.

This was the background to the situation when the squadron was ordered to send sixteen aircraft and crews, plus groundcrews, to Palestine. At Leeming 10 Squadron received similar orders and preparations were immediately put in hand. A sixteen-day detachment was envisaged, during which time the squadrons experience gained in attacking German shipping would be further tested in operations against the Italian Fleet.

During the last few hectic days spent at Middleton St. George, accidents robbed the squadron of three experienced crews.

The first tragedy was witnessed by Corporal Ray Hancock of 78 Squadron, who later wrote in his diary: 'A horrible prang today involving a 76 Squadron aircraft that hit an Oxford head-on. The Oxford came down in little bits, the halifax in a tight spiral dive to hit the ground just the other side of the hedge from where one aircraft was being worked on.' So died Pilot Officer Bingham and crew, also the pilot of the 15 16 Beam Approach Training Flight Oxford.

Shortly after 15. 30 hours the next day, Sergeant Ashton was just about to climb away from the airfield when both port engines 'cut'. This sudden loss of power occurred with the Halifax barely fifty feet above the ground. Slowly, at first, the bomber drifted to the left and then with swing increasing it climbed a further one-hundred feet, before banking over and diving into the ground. Ashton and four of his crew died instantly, his rear-gunner Pilot Officer Higgins DFM, sorely injured, died three days later in Darlington hospital.

On the day that Pilot Officer Higgins lost his battle for life, Flight Sergeant Tackley experienced an engine failure during a routine cross country exercise. Lightly loaded, the situation did not seem too serious and Base was eventually reached on the three remaining motors. His landing approach was perfect, when without warning a second engine 'cut' and his Halifax crashed just short of the runway. From the ten persons on board, Tackley was the most seriously hurt and he succumbed to his injuries the following day.

Despite these tragic events work on preparing for the squadron's departure continued apace. Long range fuel tanks were installed and as June gave way to July aircrews were kept busy carrying out fuel consumption tests.

At last everyone was ready to go, and at 03.52 hours on 10 July Flying Officer Bill Kofoed sped down the dark Middleton St. George runway and climbed slowly away towards the south. Seven minutes later Flight Sergeant Granger opened up his four Rolls-Roycd Merlin engines to full power and in a gathering crescendo of noise moved off down the duty runway. 'Hank' Iveson was next to go at 04.00 hours, followed in the next thirteen minutes by Flight Sergeant Thomas, Flying Officer Bickerdike, Pilot Officer Wickham, Pilot Officer Geoff Raymond and Flight Lieutenant Bryan.

Course was established for Gibraltar. The first part of the Middle East detachment were safely underway.

Four days later Wing Commander Dav;d Young, Squadron Leader Peter Warner, Flying Officer Knox, Pilot Officer Kenny Clack, Flight Sergeant Brown, Flight Lieutenant Mike Renaut, Flight Sergeant Harry Alcock and Pilot Officer McIntosh RAAF followed in that order.

Surprisingly, considering the hazardous nature of the flight, all went reasonably well. 'Hank' Iveson, leader of the advance flight penned in his notebook:

'Passed down the west coast of Wales and Spain, came in close to the shore-line. of Portugal and through the Strait (of Gibraltar). A pipeline broke on the pressure side of the hydraulic pump, depositing a considerable amount of hydraulic fluid. To save the pump I feathered the port inner propeller and as we neared Gibraltar I ordered the undercarriage locks to be unfastened. With a satisfying thump the wheels fell down and we went straight in.'

The eight and a half hour flight was over. Crammed with equipment and carrying three passengers in addition to a full crew, passage over the Bay of Biscay must have been quite nerve wracking. But with the arrival of Geoff Raymond at 13.40 hours all were safely accounted for and no enemy fighters had been sighted.

The next day seven aircraft were ready to leave, the eighth, captained by Flight Lieutenant Bryan, being delayed with a defective tyre. No one was blind to what lay ahead. Palestine beckoned from the eastern end of the Mediterranean. For much of the time the flight would be at risk from attack by Axis aircraft patrolling out of Sicily to port and Libya to starboard.

Fuel tanks were filled to capacity as crews viewed with some misgivings the prospects of getting into the air off Gibraltar's 1,300 yards runway. Their chances were not improved by only the- lightest of winds. Slowly the Halifaxes crept forward to gather in a queue at the entry point to the runway. The sea looked dangerously near at hand. With straining eyes, breath held, the departure of the first aircraft was viewed with more than passing interest. Slowly to start with, but quickening perceptibly as the airscrews bit at the late afternoon air, the first Halifax rolled towards the glassy waters of the outer harbour.

With much relief the onlookers saw the wheels lift clear, but the next few minutes were just as anxious as the bomber continued to fly just clear of the sea before climbing laboriously away into the distance.

The remainder followed without incident, and the formation droned eastwards towards Malta. No landing here on this bomb-bruised rocky island; Malta was purely a marker before setting course towards the void of the Nile Delta. In the event Flying Officer Bickerdike was forced to interrupt his journey here with defective engines, but the remainder, thanks to excellent navigation, reached their objective safely.

Bickerdike made his first attempt to rejoin his colleagues on 12 July, but was soon back at Luqa with one engine badly misfiring. It is said that his jettisoning of fuel prior to landing was not well received by the authorities.

For several days he remained firmly grounded whole groundcrews changed the unserviceable engine for one taken from a grounded Hurricane. Unorthodox though this may have been, it worked and Bickerdike arrived at Aqir on 20 July.

By this date David Young's party had arrived, their sole absentee being Flight Sergeant Brown delayed at Gibraltar. He, too, joined on the 20th.

At Aqir the myth of the "sixteen day" detachment was soon laid to rest once and for all. It was made emphatically clear that 10 Squadron, now under the command of Wing Commander Seymour-Price and 76 Squadron were firmly under the control of Middle East Command. Thoughts of bombing the Italian Fleet were quickly dispelled. Tobruk was to be the maximum effort objective for the newly arrived Halifax force. Rommel desperately needed supplies in order to continue his push towards the Canal Zone and the Mediterranean was his principal supply route with Tobruk his key harbour. All available Allied resources were being concentrated to deny Rommel his equipment. The seas of the Mediterranean would in the weeks ahead become a horrific killing ground.

With barely a pause to gather breath, 76 Squadron was ordered to commence bombing operations on 15/16 July. Led by 'Hank' Iveson, Geoff Raymond and Wickham, plus Flight Sergeants Granger and Thomas flew down to the advance base at Shallufa, from where a successful raid on jetties and harbour installations was mounted.

To everyone's delight the Tobruk defences were slight, comprising nine searchlights and a few bursts of inaccurate flak. One pilot later wrote:

43

'What a piece of cake. The Wellington pilots consider Tobruk to be a 'hot' target. They should try the Ruhr, that would shake them.'

With commendable ease both squadrons slipped into the groove of Middle East operations. Flying on alternate nights and pooling their resources to keep their aircraft serviceable against the ravages of the frequent desert sand-storms, the task of reducing Tobruk to an untenable harbour got under way. On some nights only one aircraft was available as on 19 July when Flight Sergeant Granger took a 10 Squadron crew to 'see the sights'.

David Young flew his first sortie on 23 July, running into some quite hostile ground fire. At Aqir the following morning crews gathered around Flying Officer Knox's Halifax which had gained the dubious distinction of being the first from the squadron to be hit by *flak* in the Middle East. It was not badly damaged, but it did provide a good talking point for a couple of hours amongst the curious.

Two nights later a burst exploded in the path of Mike Renaut's aircraft, and his observer Pilot Officer Frank Collins was badly wounded by perspex splinters entering his eyes. Huge fires were started in the area of the docks and these were further stoked up by a brisk attack on the 27th.

Shipping and petrol installations were hit on the 29th, sending columns of smoke billowing into the clear desert sky. The flash of guns firing could be seen quite clearly from the surrounding sand dunes, while from the harbour the dull red glow of fire reflected upon the oily water.

On the last night of the month, five crews delivered another strong attack. Flying low across the harbour Geoff Raymond's gunners opened fire at the shipping gathered alongside the wharves and later, clear of the town, strafed enemy motor transport moving down the road towards Bardia. One crew, however, was in trouble; their Halifax had been caught in the fierce flak barrage and now Pilot Officer Wickham was limping for Base with his port inner engine smashed.

His problems further intensified when the outer starboard motor failed with Alexandria some 160 miles distant. All moveable equipment was thrown out and distress calls were transmitted. Shortly before six o'clock in the morning, and still between five and ten miles southeast of Alexandria his two air gunners, Sergeant Maltwood and Flight Sergeant Gillies were baled out. A last frantic search for Heliopolis was unsuccessful and Wickham crash-landed on the gritty desert strip at Landing Ground 90. No one was hurt and it was not long before the crew were reunited with each other.

Since the arrival of 'Hank' Iveson's flight, the squadron had operated on eleven nights, dispatching a total of fifty-one sorties; a most creditable effort from air and groundcrews alike. At 205 Group headquarters the staff could afford a few grim smiles now that the Wellington force was backed by this small, but seasoned band of Halifax crews. The enemy were being hit around the clock. Air power would be the key factor in the outcome of the land-battlest to follow and slowly the ascendancy in this direction was being gained by the Allies.

Auchinleck, meanwhile, had attempted to break out from Alamein. For eight days between 19 and 27 July, a fierce armoured battle swayed back and forth. The natural desert heat was intensified by burning tanks and half-tracks, gutted lorries and shattered guns lay in confusion across the sand. Here and there hastily erected crosses marked temporary burial grounds. By night the sky was tinged with an awesome light, tracer patterns danced in deadly earnest across the forward lines. At the end of the month Auchinleck's men were still rooted at Alamein.

August, by comparison, was quiet, but certain events occurred which in due course would leave an indelible mark on the history of the war.

The first was tragic. Auchinleck was due to receive a new commander for his 8th Army, having himself commanded this formation since the fall of Tobruk in June. The new commander was to be Lieutenant General Gott. On 7 August, Gott boarded a 216 Squadron Bombay transport aircraft to fly to his new appointment, but his aircraft was intercepted by a flight of Bf109s and the general was killed. His place at the head of the 8th Army was taken by Lieutenant General Bernard Law Montgomery, while General Auchinleck found himself relieved by General Sir Harold Alexander.

Little of this affected the day-to-day existence of the squadron. In truth August was little different from July. Tobruk was still the priority target and as such it received considerable attention. Maximum effort was still the order of the day and during the first ten days of the month thirty sorties were flown. The attack on 4 August was easily the best, explosions ripped through the rubble-strewn streets and a broad column of smoke was left drifting across the harbour.

On 10 August an advance party flew from Aqir in Palestine to Fayid in the Canal Zone. This was a welcome move as it dispensed with the chore of operating from a forward base, and both squadrons were settled in their new home by the 14th. Servicing standards improved and on most nights, when required, the squadron could muster eight or more aircraft.

Gradually the garrison town of Tobruk was being reduced to little more than a smouldering pile of rubble, while the harbour was a desolate scene of rusting hulks and bomb-blasted jetties.

On most visits the return flights were carried out at low-level in the hope of catching enemy road transport. Such targets were gleefully dealt with by the air-gunners, thus robbing Rommel's forces of some of the supplies still evading the nightly deluge of bombs. A further diversion following a raid on the 25 August gave David Young's crew the opportunity to shoot-up a landing ground, possibly at Sidi bu Amud. With their pilot yelling encouragement the gunners needed no second bidding as the Halifax roared over the barren strip at 200 feet.

From this same mission Flight Lieutenant Bryan landed his fire-blackened bomber at Fayid with his wireless operator Sergeant Lythgoe badly burnt about the face, arms and legs. It transpired that Lythgoe was attempting to dislodge the photo-flash flare stuck in the flare-chute when, with a near blinding flash, the pyrotechnic exploded. For several minutes the ensuing blaze raged unchecked, and from the ground it must have appeared that the entire bomber was alight. Searchlight beams quickly settled on the Halifax, but Bryan soon lost this unwelcome complication. Gradually the flare, still jammed firmly in the chute, burned itself out and succour was given to the unfortunate wireless operator.

Another successful raid was made on 28 August. Flight Sergeant Granger scored a near bulls-eye on the number 3 jetty, the explosions that followed sending debris cart wheeling into the sky. The next night crews from IO Squadron concentrated their efforts on the harbour, followed on the 30th by yet another heavy attack involving five squadron crews. For Geoff Raymond, the return journey was not without incident:

'While still about two hours flying time from Base we were in some difficulty. The port outer had been feathered after the oil pressure dropped to danger level and we had been unable to release, or jettison, the bombs in the wing-racks due to an electrical fault. With a full load of incendiaries in each wing cell we were slowly losing height as both inner engines were having to be nursed to avoid overheating.

'About ninety minutes later we were over the Delta approaching Bdbeis and although down to just under 3,000 feet, we were maintaining height and I had high hopes of reaching Base.

'Without warning the port inner engine failed completely and all attempts to feather the propeller were unsuccessful. It was just about possible to hold the aircraft on course, so I tried to restart the port outer, hoping this engine would last long enough for us to reach Bilbeis. This action of mine proved quite useless. The propeller ran wild and while trying to get it to feather, the starboard inner caught fire.

'My situation was now desperate with both port engines failed@ their propellers windmilling, the starboard inner on fire, the bomb-load still in the wings and very little height remaining, I was left with no alternative but to attempt a night crash-landing in the Delta.

'I gave the crash-positions order and my wireless operator and navigator went immediately to their stations. My flight engineer stayed a few seconds longer, firing off a couple of Very cartridges to give me some light for the crashlanding. In the light provided we just managed to clear a clump of palm trees, touching down just beyond them.

'When the aircraft finally came to a rest, I was a little dazed and was sitting, apparently quite unconcerned, watching the wings burning fiercely. I was brought back to my senses by the frantic shouting of Sergeant Coates urging me in no uncertain terms to get out.

'Scrambling through the pilot's escape hatch and running down the top of the fuselage, I saw my wireless operator caught up in the second escape hatch. I disentangled his harness, pulled him out of the fuselage and dropped him to the ground, jumping after him without further delay.

'As the remaining members of the crew could not be seen, I went back into the aircraft and found the navigator lying unconscious on the floor. There was no sign anywhere of the gunners, so with the help of Sergeant Coates, I dragged my navigator out of the wreckage and beat a hasty retreat.'

The next few minutes were rather confusing. A dazed, and still badly shocked crew gathered to watch the flames consume what remained of their aircraft. Of the two gunners, there was still no sign until, in the dying light of the fire, the rear-gunner Sergeant Paine was spotted making his way towards the small group of survivors.

Geoff Raymond again takes up the story:

'Apparently my tail gunners intercom had packed up completely and he did not hear the crash-position order, so was still in his turret when we crashed. On impact the turret broke completely away, finally coming to rest in some mud, a considerable distance from the main wreckage.

'Incredibly he clambered out, shaken but otherwise unhurt. Sometime later we were picked up and taken to an army hospital. Here, the following morning, my mid upper gunner Sergeant Hill turned up looking dishevelled, but in one piece. He told me that when the port inner packed up the intercom became very distorted, and my call to the flight engineer to get the port outer going sounded to him like 'get out'. While wondering if it was a bale out order, he saw flames from the starboard inner and being unable to raise anyone on the intercom he decided it was, and promptly baled out.

He hit the ground seconds after his parachute opened, but landed in the mud of the Delta and was unharmed.'

The sequel to Sergeant Hill's narrow escape was somewhat amusing. By the time he arrived at the hospital his mud-caked flying clothes were giving off a smell which, to put it mildly, was quite repugnant. Fearful that he may have swallowed some of the evil smelling mixture, the doctors were loath to allow him much freedom, much to Hill's disgust.

But for Flying Officer Peter Earle, the navigator, this close reprieve from death was tragically short. Discharged from hospital he was immediately screened from further operations, and because of his experience in the workings of 'GEE' he was posted home to England. Within a few hours of leaving the squadron he was dead, killed when the aircraft he was travelling in crashed in Malta.

September opened with heavy raids on Tobruk's still functioning harbour. Heavy, accurate flak was encountered and two Halifaxes were damaged. In the desert fighting, Montgomery had already scored his first success by repulsing a sharp Panzer thrust at Alam el Halfa at the southern end of the defence line. On the 3rd he counter-attacked with armoured columns forcing his opponent to break off the engagement and withdraw, bloodied.

This change in fortune for the Allied ground forces brought a change in targets for the two Halifax squadrons. The island of Crete was the new focal point and a hurriedly arranged daylight raid on the aerodrome at Heraklion was ordered for 5 September. Five squadron crews were quickly assembled and briefed, plus a handful from 10 Squadron, including Wing Commander Seymour-Price.

Shortly before four o'clock in the afternoon the force was airborne flying northwest above the warm waters of the Mediterranean. Within minutes of taking-off Pilot Officer Kenny Clack was seen to break formation and turn for home, a thin stream of smoke issuing from a broken outer starboard engine. This must have been a galling. moment for young Clack, not yet twenty-one years of age, but whose determination and drive had been an inspiration to all those who were fortunate enough to know him.

in the clear evening light the Halifaxes, still keeping close formation, crossed the craggy island coast. Maintaining height at 8,000 feet the force ran through a hail of *flak* which, though heavy, was not particularly effective. Good order remained and 'Hank' Iveson's flight held course towards the aerodrome, now in view and tightly packed with aircraft, especially on the northern side of the runways.

Bomb-doors swung open and in unison Iveson's group bombed, obtaining an excellent concentration. The events of the next few minutes proved rather lively and are best left to his description:

'Our bombs gone we put our noses down and made for the north coast of the island. We turned just in the nick of time as the gunners had by this time gauged our height and the first really accurate salvos arrived as we were banking.'

This shell pattern inflicted slight damage to the Halifaxes flown by Mike Renaut and Flying Officer Bickerdike. Iveson continues:

'I then saw the other formation coming in from the west and run into some pretty intense *flak*. One Halifax was hit and caught fire and I last saw it flying south with some parachutes deploying. I recognised Sevmour-Price's machine close in towards the mountains, his gunners exchanging fire with a twin-engined aircraft. Of the third aircraft (Flight Lieutenant Hacking of 1 0 Squadron) there was no sign. Away to starboard I could see a fighter, so I led my chaps down into the valley and flew towards the sea at maximum speed. it was, on reflection, rather a bumpy ride.'

The Halifax seen by 'Hank' Iveson burning and flying south was that of Flight Lieutenant Bryan. In his account, Iveson attributes his colleague's demise to the vociferous ground-fire, but it is possible that Bryan and his crew fell victim to an attack from a Bf 109 piloted by Feldwebel Liebhold, a young fighter pilot serving with Ill/JG27. From his crew Sergeants Robinson, Jones, Young and Blatch escaped by parachute, but Flight Lieutenant Bryan along with his wireless operator Sergeant Potts were killed. Their deaths were the only fatal casualties suffered by the squadron in the Middle East. The loss of this crew holds particular memories for Sergeant Bill Lawes who with Sergeant Young from Bryan's crew had started to construct a sailing dinghy.

'We had commandeered an empty hut and 'liberated' timber, aircraft dope, old engine covers and sundry bits and pieces for the construction. The sails were made from sheets 'borrowed' from the Americans. The craft was still unfinished when Young went missing and the next thing that happened was that the Station Commander sniffed out the project. I found myself on a charge of stealing air force property, but the Squadron CO got to hear of it and he managed to get the charge squashed. I finished off the boat and we all used it on the Bitter Lakes.'

Two days after the Heraklion adventure and without operating further, 205 Group headquarters ordered the amalgamation of the surviving aircraft and crews to form 462 Squadron, a Royal Australian Air Force Squadron. On the face of it a most curious move as at the time there were relatively few Australian personnel serving with either 10 or 76 Squadrons. Wing Commander David Young was appointed to command this new squadron [11] and life continued very much as before. Valiant work by the groundcrews ensured that the tired Halifaxes would continue to meet the tasks needed of them, until such times as replacements arrived from England.

Within weeks of the recent round-the-clock operations, Montgomery opened his Alamein offensive. A fortnight later, hundreds of miles away to the west an American, Lieutenant General Dwight Eisenhower, was in command of the Allied troops pouring ashore in French North Africa. Rommel was effectively caught between two very determined armies. The desert campaign was moving swiftly towards a triumphant conclusion in favour of the Allies.

In no small way 76 Squadron, aided by 10 Squadron, had helped pave the way towards this victory. 76 Squadron alone had taken part in thirty-two attacks dispatching a total of 183 sorties, a most creditable achievement and one that reflects well on all those concerned.

In 1943 the survivors of the Middle East detachment returned to England. By this time Peter Warner had been promoted to Wing Commander and taken over 462 Squadron, only to be killed on operations over the Mediterranean.

After leave, the majority of this happy band of flyers were posted to Conversion Units as instructors. At Rufforth David Young, now a Group Captain, managed to gather under his wing many of his old squadron - Renaut, Iveson and Clack to name but a few. As the war followed its course, so the ties that held them together for close on three years were loosened. Many were reposted for a further tour of operations and Kenny Clack and 'Hank' Iveson we will meet again. Mike Renaut was duly promoted to Wing Commander and was given command of 171 Squadron flying Halifaxes on radio counter measures from North Creake in Norfolk.

Some were killed whilst instructing. Flight Sergeant Thomas was one; he died when a wing came off the Halifax he was flying. Happily, though, the majority survived and no story of 76 Squadron can be complete without mention of these Middle East adventurers.

---

11   Following a varied existence in the Middle East, 462 (RAAF) Squadron was renumbered 614 Squadron in March 1944. Reformed in the August at Driffield, Yorkshire, 462 Squadron was for a few months loosely associated with 76 Squadron in that both served in Number 4 Group.

Chapter Five

JULY 1942 to APRIL 1943

When Pilot Officer McIntosh RAAF took-off from Middleton St. George on the morning of 14 July 1942, he left behind him a small home echelon of the squadron in the capable hands of Squadron Leader 'Jock' Calder. Since the turn of the year this officer had been charged with the important task of organising the squadron's Halifax Conversion Flight.

Now, with the departure of the Middle East detachment, 'Jock' Calder found himself with very few trained crews at his disposal. Circumstances would decree that the squadron's contribution to the European theatre of bombing operations would be severely limited. Nonetheless, for operations against the shipbuilding yards at Vegesack on 19 July, one Halifax and crew were loaned out to 78 Squadron. Sadly, this venture ended in disaster when within a short time of take-off Flight Sergeant Belous, the captain, radioed to say he was returning to Base with engine trouble.

Nothing further was heard, until it was reported that a Halifax had crashed near Yarm. Inside the wreckage were discovered the bodies of Belous and that of his flight engineer Sergeant Hebron. Thankfully, the remainder of the crew were safe after bailing out on their pilot's command.

A week later on the 26th, three crews took off for Hamburg. Sergeant Nicholson was successful in his attack, but a badly misfiring port inner engine forced Pilot Officer Ronnie Waite to return a shade earlier than expected. It was for this recently qualified pilot his first experience of three-engined flying. The third crew captained by Sergeant Butt failed to return, his Halifax crash-landing an hour before midnight at Buxtehude, near Hamburg, with the loss of three young lives.

Both Sergeant Nicholson and Ronnie Waite reached Saarbrucken on the 29th and the same pair were employed two nights later when Dusseldorf was the primary target. Nicholson's sortie was relatively trouble free, as was Ronnie Waite's until he passed over Oudorp, Holland in the early hours of 1 August, heading towards the North Sea and home.

The first warning of danger came from his rear-gunner Pilot Officer Glasgow, who caught sight of a Ju 88 flying on their port quarter. He judged the enemy fighter to be about 1,000 yards distant and closing. Almost immediately from the mid-upper position Sergeant McAuley shouted to say he could see a fighter away to starboard, but it was from the port side that the first wicked streaks of gunfire [12] came.

'We were hit several times. One shell exploded somewhere near the navigator's compartment. It made a terrific crash and filled the cockpit with smoke. I looked at my instruments and found several of them unserviceable. Then I tried to speak to my crew, but the intercom was 'dead'. This was a hard blow as I did not know if any of them were hurt.'

---

[12] Close research into this combat leads me to believe only one fighter was involved, and in the heat of the moment Sergeant McAuley misreported their assailant.

Indeed, a dreadful dilemma for Waite. Casualties had been inflicted. McAuley was dead, Sergeant Poole RCAF his navigator was in pain from grazes where a cannon shell had passed across both his wrists, angry red weals already forming, and Sergeant Miller, also of the RCAF, was wounded slightly in one leg.

The crew of the Ju 88, Hauptmann Herbert Bonsch, Feldwebel Otto Botcher and August Willie were already dead, or about to die. Possibly blinded by the flash given off from his own gunfire, Herbert Bonsch had continued to close until a collision seemed almost certain. At the last moment he pulled up sharply, presenting Glasgow with a perfect target. For at least ten seconds Glasgow sent a stream of machine-gun bullets into the underbelly of the Junkers, and now it was falling, almost vertically.

Inside the nose of the Halifax Sergeant Geddie, the wireless operator, applied bandages to the badly burnt arms of Sergeant Poole who, despite his injuries, continued to give course instructions to his pilot. The flight engineer, Sergeant Greenwood, meanwhile had forced open the bulkhead door jammed by the exploding cannon-shell and was now tending to the fuel-cocks. Amidships, Sergeant Miller was gently removing the dead body of McAuley from the shattered remains of the mid-upper turret.

Nearly two hours later the Halifax crossed the southeast coast, but their plight had worsened considerably:

'With our rudder controls and ailerons not working, the chances of making a safe landing were remote, so I decided we must bale out. I sent my flight engineer off with the necessary instructions, and then sat, waiting. As the navigator lifted the escape hatch the slip-stream blew papers and dust all over the place.

'I could not see whether the crew were going out alright, but in a few moments my engineer came forward to say that all had left and he was now going himself. I straightened up the controls as best as I could and followed him out.'

Shortly afterwards Ronnie Waite landed in a field cropped with mustard plants. Ridding himself of his parachute he managed to waken the occupants of Newlands Hall at Roxwell, Essex. It was not long before a welcome cup of tea was being pressed into his hands, and within the hour he was relieved to hear that the rest of his crew were safe.

Later, the six survivors travelled first to Chelmsford before starting on the long journey northwards. A few miles away in a mangle field at Fristling Hall Farm the burnt remains of their bomber were already under guard of the local air-raid wardens from nearby Stock, The body of Sergeant McAuley had been removed from the wreckage and in the morning a still inflated undercarriage tyre was discovered lying over two fields away from the main crash area.

On 5 August, Squadron Leader Leonard Cheshire arrived to take over command of the home echelon. From the outset of the bombing offensive in the summer of 1940, this young ex-Oxford University undergraduate had made a distinct mark in the hurly-burly of night bombing. His enthusiasm had not passed unnoticed and now he was tasked to rebuild the squadron into an effective fighting unit.

His first operation with 76 Squadron came on 11 August when he joined in a mainforce attack by 152 aircraft on the industrial town of Mainz. The aiming point was the chemical works and after depositing his bombs into the growing sea of fire, Cheshire continued to orbit the target area while his crew took photographs of Mainz burning below. One particularly fine shot revealed the flash from high explosive bombs ripping through the centre of the town.

One week later the Pathfinder Force commenced operations. Ever since the operational debut of 'GEE' as a navigational aid for bombing in August 1941, certain high ranking officers had been advocating the setting up of a target finding force to spearhead the night attacks. Amongst the campaigners for this elite force was Group Captain Bufton who, as a Wing Commander, had commanded the squadron for a few weeks on its reformation just over a year ago.

Harris, supported wholly in this instance by his Group commanders, was totally opposed to the establishment of a specialist group, though he freely acknowledged the benefits to be gained from such a force. His own thinking was on the lines of each group providing one squadron to lead the mainforce, the premise being that the resulting competition from other squadrons within the groups would increase the efficiency of that particular group, and in turn the effectiveness of the entire command.

After months of argument and discussion between the interested parties, little had been achieved, and the situation seemed deadlocked. At this juncture the Air Staff came down firmly on the side of Bufton, and Harris received orders to implement the setting up of this new force without further delay.

Although understandably annoyed at the Air Staff's decision, Harris sent for the man he considered most suitable to head this new force, Wing Commander Donald Bennett whom, it will be recalled, was last mentioned 'slipping away towards the snow encrusted hills' surrounding Trondheim. His successful escape will be seen to have a far reaching effect on the ensuing bombing offensive.

Operations for the new group got off to an inconclusive start on 18 August when the U-boat installations at Flensburg, some sixty miles north of Kiel, were the target. No squadron crew took part in this attack which was marred by high winds and poor ground visibility, and it was 1 September before three crews, led by Flight Lieutenant George Dixon, at last witnessed a Pathfinder Force (PFF) led attack. The two crews that returned were not over impressed. Saarlouis to the northwest of Saarbrucken had been marked by mistake, but at least some material damage had been inflicted on the industrial area. Of Pilot Officer Sherwood there was no immediate news. Next of kin of the missing crew would, in due course, endure the private agony of learning that loved ones had failed to return from operations.

Fortunes improved the next night when the docks at Karlsruhe came in for close attention by a strong force of bombers, including three from the squadron. The forecast winds proved inaccurate, but this error was realised by the mainforce and Karlsruhe was left with a column of smoke drifting upwards to 6,000 feet.

The improving techniques of the command, however, were still being firmly challenged by the German defences, and against Duisburg on 6 September Sergeant Bill Richardson, making his operational debut as captain, had a close encounter with the defenders of the Third Reich. Approaching the Ruhr his aircraft was intercepted by a prowling fighter and some damage was sustained before evasive tactics lost their attacker. Course was resumed, and a short while later Richardson was coned by searchlights. His first attempts to lose the clinging beams of light were unsuccessful and several well aimed salvos caused further damage to the Halifax. Eventually he was free, bombs were dropped and a safe return made. Throughout the ordeal his crew had responded magnificently shouting words of encouragement to each other as each threat to their survival was met and dealt with.

Sergeant Al Moir experienced some difficulty in closing his bomb-doors and the trip home was made with the port wing wanting to drop, unless held with some force by young Moir. No doubt his inspired flying on this occasion impressed his distinguished second pilot, Group Captain McKechnie, Station Commander of Middleton St. George.

Frankfurt was chosen for 8 September, but as on the 1st, PFF laid their markers well away from the primary target, resulting in the Opel and Michelin factories at Russelsheim being bombed. This error of around fourteen miles caused a few blushes amongst Bennett's staff.

Two nights later five squadron crews flew to Dusseldorf. On return the debriefing intelligence officers learnt that the streets of Dusseldorf were lit by vivid pink flashes, quite unlike anything witnessed before. There is little doubt the crews were seeing the command's latest innovation, the 'Pink Pansy'. This superb 4,000lb incendiary bomb emitting a distinctive pink red glow on impact. As a Target Marker weapon, the 'Pink Pansy' would find good employment in the mounting campaign ahead.

Bremen and its docks were well hit on 13 September, two square miles of the port area being left ablaze. Pilot Officer Campbell's gunners fought a long engagement with a night-fighter whose persistent sniping badly damaged the bomber's starboard mainplane. From his rear-turret Sergeant Burman harried the enemy pilot with a steady stream of accurate return fire, which eventually convinced the enemy plot to break away and seek a less tenacious target.

Three nights later Pilot Officer Lex Campbell RAAF failed to return from Essen, though on this occasion his rear-gunner was Sergeant Moffatt. Whilst over the Pas de Calais their Halifax was set upon by a night-fighter and sent down out of control. Seven bodies were taken from the wreck lying at Rubrouck Nord and amongst this sad tally was the body of Flight Sergeant Geddie who less than two months previous jumped for his life over the countryside of Essex.

A near mid-air collision came close to robbing the squadron of Flying Officer 'Judge' Hardy. Weaving gently to port he was suddenly aware of another Halifax banking to starboard and coming straight at him. Hardy immediately pushed with all his might on the controls and as his aircraft responded the other Halifax crossed directly overhead. The sudden force of his actions tore the bomber's Eisan from it's position in the rear fuselage, depositing the contents over the roof of the centre fuselage. A few minutes later a rather worried wireless operator reported 'a most serious oil leak'.

This operation to Essen was the last attempted by the squadron from Middleton St. George. During the morning of 17 September, the squadron flew down to Lintonon-Ouse from where Sergeant Richardson carried out a solo attack on Saarbrucken on the 19th.

A heavy assault on the U-boat base of Flensburg was launched on the 23rd. It will be recalled that high winds and bad visibility spoilt the last attack made on this key target. This time the mainforce encountered a thick belt of low cloud extending seawards over Kiel Bay which effectively shielded the port. Descending through the overcast many individual attempts were made to get at the submarine pens, but the light flak defences were co-ordinated and extremely hostile.

On 1 October, following an abortive effort on 26 September, Harris again sent his crews to Flensburg. The *flak* was terrible and Harris was denied revenge. One crew who undoubtedly got through the defences, albeit at the cost of their lives, was that captained by Pilot Officer Atkinson RCAF. Flying on this his fourth operational sortie, Atkinson's aircraft crashed in the St. Pauli district of the town, wiping Number 11 Backensmuhle off the town's map.

During the evening of 8 October five crews led by 'Judge' Hardy dropped mines in the Terschelling area without meeting any opposition. Not all such sorties were so uneventful as Sergeant George Griffiths remembers:

'The drill was to navigate to the centre of the selected island (in the Frisian Island chain) at about 500 feet, then fly to one end and leave on the given heading for so many minutes at an agreed airspeed and drop your mines from a given height. As I turned along the coast, we were caught by a searchlight and completely blinded in the middle of a steep turn. I shouted to my gunners who opened up simultaneously and put the searchlight out, just in the nick of time. As I regained my vision the altimeter was reading zero.'

Shortly before the middle of the month, Kiel with its harbour and associated submarine works was given a good pounding that lasted for over half-an-hour. Six squadron crews assisted in this, though it was only through the sterling services of the groundcrews that George Griffiths was able to participate. His first Halifax developed an engine fault, but the 'spare' aircraft was made ready in record time, enabling him to make his contribution towards the night's work.

Cologne was visited on the 15th, this being the command's first major raid on this target since the massive assault at the end of May. Stronger than forecast winds upset a number of crews and photo-plots afterwards revealed that Bonn, well to the south along the Rhine, had attracted some of the bombing. Sergeant Sawatzky RCAF jettisoned his bombs on to an unidentified airfield in Holland after his starboard inner engine failed. This proved to be his penultimate operation for after leaving for a mining detail on 8 November his aircraft was not heard from again.

During the night of 22/23 October, Bomber Command commenced a series of major raids aimed at the industrial cities and ports lying in the north of Italy. These attacks were specifically launched in support of the pending Allied landings in North Africa, code named 'Torch'. The squadron's first involvement came the following night with Wing Commander Cheshire taking six crews to Genoa, under attack from a force of 122 aircraft. Flying with the squadron as second pilots were three Norwegians, Lieutenants Gunnar Halle, Bjorn Naess and Erik Sandberg. In the weeks ahead all three would command their own crews and become the fore-runners of a long association between the Royal Norwegian Air Force and 76 Squadron.

Clear skies over the Alps afforded crews a magnificent view of the towering snow capped peaks, but the first ominous signs of cloud were beginning to slip beneath the approaching bombers, shielding the land from view. By the time Genoa was reached the cloud-base was reaching downwards towards 6,000 feet, thus making identification of the docks no easy task. Most certainly, on this occasion, Savona on the opposite side of the bay to the west attracted far more than the nine aircraft detailed for this target.

Nonetheless, some damage was inflicted. George Dixon, now a Squadron Leader, broke through the cloud-cover and witnessed several good areas of fire to the east and west of the harbour confines. Turning away from the target area, Leonard Cheshire's Halifax was picked up by an Italian biplane, probably a CR 42. His rear-gunner on this occasion was Flight Lieutenant Gilbert who later wrote in his report:

'The fighter made a diving attack from the starboard quarter firing short bursts which included cannon and tracer. The tracer was seen to pass in front of and to starboard of our aircraft. Return fire was given and the skipper easily evaded the enemy fighter by going into a diving turn to starboard.'

Course was resumed and soon afterwards the Italian pilot made a second half hearted firing pass. A repeat performance by Cheshire quickly lost the fighter, whose pilot did not seem particularly aggressive and the long return flight to Base passed without further incident.

Aboard Sergeant Richardson's aircraft all was far from well. Shortly after crossing the south coast his rear-gunner Sergeant Sutcliffe called to say he had trapped a leg in the turret mechanism and was, as a result, in some distress. Richardson decided to land as quickly as possible and was soon approaching Benson in Oxfordshire. One can imagine his desire to get down quickly for the sake of his unfortunate gunner, but as the airfield he was approaching was in darkness, it may have been more prudent of him to seek a more welcome haven. However, he committed himself to this unfamiliar aerodrome, overshot the runway and crashed. A fire broke out, but at last good fortune prevailed and the entire crew scrambled from the wreckage with little more than minor cuts and abrasions, though it is said Sutcliffe's leg was rather sore for several days thereafter.

Genoa was revisited on 7 November, a Saturday, and to the delight of everyone the weather was fine.

Marker bombs from the PFF fell squarely across the docks and the mainforce quickly converted a large area along the waterfront into a blazing inferno. The weather worsened during the return flight across occupied France and running short of fuel Flying Officer Anderson and Flight Sergeant Richardson, none the worse for his crash a fortnight earlier, landed at Manston whilst Pilot Officer Elliott put down at Upper Heyford.

Missing from this operation was Flight Sergeant 'Slim' Thom RCAF. Crossing the French coast his Halifax had flown through several bursts of light *flak* and unbeknown to him at the time pieces of shrapnel had found their way either into the engine coolant system, or into some oil tanks. it was not long before his flight engineer, Sergeant 'Red' Owen noticed a slight rise in the engine temperatures, though the increase was very gradual and Thom flew on, deep into France.

Gradually, the blackened-out city of Reims slipped away beneath. Ahead lay the Marne, always a useful guide, but before the river was reached events took a turn for the worse. From the isolation of his mid-upper turret Sergeant Larry Horne takes up the story:

'We were flying straight and level, when without warning an outer motor burst into flames. The fire was quickly extinguished and while we were discussing our chances of crossing the Alps on three engines, one of the inner motors caught fire.

'That decided it. The pilot immediately ordered the bomb-load to be dropped 'safe', and turned for home, trying to restart the first engine that had caught alight. It was soon obvious he was having no success and when flames started to come from one of the remaining two engines, the order to bale out was given.'

Larry Home was last to leave, and his late departure may have been the root cause for his eventual escape to Switzerland, where he remained until October 1944. But what of his companions? Two, Sergeant Norman Gorfunkle the navigator and Sergeant Derek Reed the rear-gunner, landed close to each other in a wood near Chaumont St. Aignan. Reed was shaken, but otherwise unhurt, but poor Gorfunkle had suffered a very severe throat injury and he now lay where he had landed, barely able to move. Rather than leave his injured friend, Derek Reed remained with him and both were captured shortly after daybreak. By this time Gorfunkle was in very poor shape and he died a few days after being admitted to a Reims hospital.

'Red' Owen remembers very little of his capture. He landed heavily across a pile of logs and for the next seven days floated in and out of consciousness. A distinct feeling of being bitterly cold and a hazy recollection of riding down a country lane in a truck filled with soldiers remains in his memory. Owen finally came to his senses in the same hospital room at Reims where Norman Corfunkle had died earlier in the week.

Now, apart from Sergeant Horne, only the pilot remained at large. Thom was to give his captors a good run for their money, but eventually luck deserted him and whilst attempting to cross the Pyrenees into Spain he was taken prisoner.

Two nights later the emphasis of attack was switched to Hamburg. Six crews under George Dixon were detailed, but a change in wind direction sent the majority of the mainforce well to the south of track. Flying above the cloud-cover and operating just beyond the limits of 'GEE' aids, the attack[13] failed.

---

13   Since the late summer enemy countermeasures were effectively jamming the "GEE" transmissions, reducing its
        working range from well over 300 miles to around 200 miles.

Flying Officer Anderson strayed into the Bremen area where his aircraft was heavily engaged by flak. Control was lost for a moment or two and as the Halifax lost height Anderson shouted to his crew to leave the aircraft. Sergeants Killnee' Peace claimed his bombs struck a warehouse containing bales of cotton, the fire, he said, burning most satisfactorily.

Turin was visited on the 18th where Flight Sergeant Richardson counted nineteen good areas of fire, all burning within the target area. The onslaught continued on the 20th with nine crews joining in a raid by 233 bombers on this industrial target. Eight returned to report on excellent fires and much destruction, their verbal claims being well supported by good aiming point photographs. Similar to Flight Lieutenant Smith's eventful return from Turin of over a year ago, 'Judge' Hardy was to experience some problems within minutes of clearing the target area:

'The bomb-doors would not close and after climbing over the Alps we lost an engine with about four hours flying still ahead of us.

'When we crossed the English coast, I decided to make for Linton where to my dismay visibility was very bad. We were given a priority landing, but on finals with flaps down, the undercarriage failed to operate. I was left with no choice but to overshoot. in attempting this I could not get the aircraft to climb above 500 feet, and what with juggling with throttles and looking at my instrument panel, I lost sight of the flarepath. I continued to fly in a wide circle, and just when all seemed lost the runway appeared straight ahead.

'With my flight engineer pumping down the undercarriage a good landing was accomplished. Later he told me his efforts were aided by the knowledge that the fuel gauges were showing empty.'

Of Sergeant Wisely RNZAF there was no immediate news and it has since been established his entire crew perished when their Halifax crashed at Bardonecchia, Italy. There was no evidence of a bomb-load in the wreckage and it may be safely assumed that the Halifax was homeward bound when the tragedy occurred.

By this time the allied landings inNorthAfricaweregoingextremelywel4theenemy's grip in this part of the world was, with each passing day, weakening perceptibly.

On 22 November six crews, including Gunnar Halle and Bjorn Naess RNAF operating for the first time as captains, attempted to strike at Stuttgart. A thick ground haze made their task extremely difficult and it is unlikely that any major damage was caused to Stuttgart's industries.

The general pattern of successes against the Italian targets counterbalanced by the relative failure to interfere with the workings of towns on the German homeland continued into December. This should not be interpreted as an adverse comment on the skill of those conducting these attacks. The plain truth is the weather over northern Europe for the last two months of 1942 was exceedingly bad, Time after time crews returned frustrated by sudden changes in the forecast wind direction, while near unbroken cloud seemed to be a nightly feature over Germany at this time.

A fine example illustrating these frustrations occurred on 2 December when a mainforce attack on Frankfurt was ordered by High Wycombe. Of the nine squadron crews involved, Flying Officer Anderson returned with his bomb-load intact and his Halifax showing signs of flak damage. His crew had been unable to locate anything through the cloud cover. The remainder claimed to have reached the general area of the target where, in their unanimous opinion, the PFF marking had been weak and totally ineffective. There was no improvement when Mannheim was raided on the 6th, indeed Flight Sergeant Al Moir filed his report with the words:

'I am not certain where my bombs fell, but estimate somewhere in an area fifteen to twenty-five miles southwest of the target.'

This honest appraisal was probably echoed by more than one crew at debriefing, though young Hillier's would not be returning to this ritual. Sergeant John Theckston, the mid-upper gunner and one of the five survivors, tells what happened:

'I was in the turret when the flashing and banging commenced and I heard the skipper give the order for everyone to bale out. Somehow, my Mae West had inflated and I found myself held tight, dangling half in and half out of the turret. I still had my helmet on and I could hear the pilot asking if anyone remained, so I quickly let him know I was stuck. My senses told me he was still at the controls, keeping the aircraft flying as I fought to free myself. The flames had nearly reached me by the time I clipped my parachute on, so calling out I was ready to jump, I went out through the side door, not a moment too soon.'

For two days John Theckston enjoyed a strange freedom, but he was then betrayed and taken prisoner. Before being taken to Dulag Luft at Frankfurt, he was placed in the guardhouse at Bar le Duc airfield. Here he was spoken to by a young *Luftwaffe* pilot who claimed he was responsible for shooting Hillier's Halifax down. The German's command of English was excellent and he described in some detail his visit to the wreckage, and the discovery of two bodies. One, he said, was wearing good quality gauntlets, and from other points made during his conversation, John Theckston was left in no doubt that his pilot had been killed.

Three strong attacks on Turin were delivered between 8 and 11 December, the first two being most successful. George Dixon, to the amusement of his crew, completed the second of the three raids in his stockinged feet. He had forgotten to don his flying-boots and the crew had not been airborne long before it was realised that the nails in his service shoes were having an adverse effect on the aircraft's compass. It is not recorded the amount of feeling left in his toes on return, but his feet were safely clad in more suitable footwear for a visit to Duisburg later in the month.

The third attack on Turin was an abysmal failure. Severe icing, coupled with violent electrical storms forced the majority to turn back and from the ten squadron crews operating, only two reached Northern Italy. Pilot Officer Norman Black RNZAF was one, the other was Cunnar Halle who was confident he reached the primary target area after flying for over 300 miles without navigational aids, a most commendable achievement. But it is from the navigator in Norrnan Black's crew, Sergeant Ted Strange, that an account is given of problems met and overcome, nearly forty years ago:

'Conditions were extremely bad and soon after take-off we were flying in cumulus cloud. Navigation was entirely by 'Dead Reckoning' and as we couldn't break cloud, even at about 21,500 feet, the situation was less than satisfactory.

'Towards the target a minimal break in the cloud enabled the bomb-aimer to provide me with a pinpoint, stated to be on the River Po. From this pinpoint we agreed on a 'Dead Reckoning' timed run into the target and as, on approach, considerable searchlight activity appeared through the thinning clouds below we felt we may have made Turin[14] after all. We bombed and turned for home.

'Shortly after, heading north there were small breaks in the clouds above, so I went back to the astro-dome with an oxygen bottle and sextant to take some star shots. This proved difficult owing to the

---

14   Later, when the navigational log was re-plotted, it was realised Milan and not Turin, had been bombed. Nonetheless, it was still a highly creditable performance and one which gave the entire crew much satisfaction.

cloud interference and only one shot was secured before I found myself succumbing from lack of oxygen. I must have called out for the bomb-aimer came back to see what was wrong, but I collapsed on him, which could have been more embarrassing but for the prompt action of the flight engineer who witnessed the incident.'

Still flying in cloud Norman Black recrossed the channel, but with little sign of improvement in the weather, and with the crew in some doubt as to their exact position it was decided to break radio silence and ask for assistance. Ted Strange continues:

'Help was obtained from a station on the east coast, which quickly confirmed my previously discarded plot as being correct. At once I gave an alteration of course for Base, but then we were instructed to divert to Acklington as Linton was closed due to bad weather. This airfield was along the track we were following, so we called up and landed, even before the runway lights were fully switched on.'

it was three days before the crew returned to Linton, where forty-eight hour leave passes awaited them. In general, however, the Italian campaign had gone well. Here are some impressions from those that took part:

"So contemptuous were we that in place of the usual bomb-symbol painted on the nose of the aircraft to denote successful completion of a German sortie, the Italian targets rated only an ice-cream cone." *Sergeant 'Lucky'Clarke - Pilot.*

"My memory of these Italian trips is of long flights, lots of cloud, little or no opposition south of the Alps." *Lieutenant Gunnar Halle RNAF -Pilot,*

"Few of us took a trip to Italy very seriously, for we did not look upon the Italians either as natural fighters, or as being very committed to the war. It was noticeable that although there was a great deal of *flak* on going into the target, as soon as the bombs started bursting the flak virtually died out. In other words, the gunners decided that their priority lay in getting underground." *Wing Command Leonard Cheshire Commanding Officer.*

The final observation is made by a member of the stalwart groundcrews Sergeant Syd Garratt, an engine fitter by trade:

'We used to sit in Nissen huts out on the aerodrome in the most uncomfortable wicker-basket armchairs, trying to get some sleep. The designer of those chairs must have been an expert in keeping people awake; the back wasn't high enough to rest the head, and the sides were too high to rest the arms. They really were an instrument of torture.'

This last letter of comment only lightly hints at the loyalty fostered between the aircrew and their ground counterparts. After a long day spent in preparing the aircraft for the night's business, many of the groundcrew, like Sid Carratt, chose not the relative comfort of their bed, but quite voluntarily remained out on the airfield in makeshift shelters waiting for the bombers return. As one of his contemporaries put it to me 'To see your crew home safely from the target was reward in itself'.

For the squadron the year ended on a high note. The target was Duisburg in the Ruhr and after the disappointments of early December, the PFF were in good form. Markers clearly defined the northern and southern edge of the aiming point, between which the mainforce bombed with some vigour. The steel plants at Hamborn and Hochfeld, both part of the Thyssen organisation, were hit, while in the Beeck district and in the Old Town bordering the docks, good fires were started.

A fierce *flak* barrage harried the bombers, now streaming towards the Dutch coast. Receding from view Duisburg was burning, the glow from fires still being quite distinct as the last of the attackers headed across the North Sea. Two squadron crews were not amongst them. At Weeze/Norh Geldern the winter earth claimed 'Charlie' Peace, while Flying Officer Anderson had been picked off over Liedern Bockolt by Oberleutnant Bauer of Ill/NJG 1. Each Halifax had been carrying a full complement of eight men, and the names of the sixteen aircrew are now recorded on the memorial stones at the Reichswald Forest Military Cemetery.

Taking stock at the end of the first full year of operations it will be seen that the squadron had sent a total of 446 sorties against European targets, including minelaying operations. The Middle East detachment had flown a further IS 3, taking the overall figure to beyond 600 sorties. Casualties had been severe; twenty-six crews had failed to return from operations and a further nine had been involved in operational, or training accidents. Morale was high in the squadron and throughout the command for, during the last few weeks of 1942, a steady increase in trained aircrews had reached the squadrons. Equipment, too, was improving, though problems with engine failures would persist throughout the life of the Halifax, despite the skilled attention of those that attended them. Therefore, let the last words of 1942 belong to Sergeant Bill Tidy, a fitter IIA, who served with the squadron from August 1942 until April 1943.

'The perimeter tracks were constantly busy with the coming and going of petrol bowsers, tractors pulling long loads of bomb-trolleys, crew-buses and a host of other miscellaneous vehicles hurrying from one dispersal point to another like bees visiting flowers. Dropping some glycol off there, some urgently required spare part labelled 'AOG' (Aircraft on Ground), or perhaps a special tool drawn from stores needed for the removal, or fitting of a part.

'The constant hustle and bustle of each day kept everyone on their toes, though accidents did occur from time to time, one of which I clearly recall resulted in the death of an armourer. Pneumatic bags were being experimented with, these being placed under the wing tips and then inflated, thus enabling an aircraft to be lifted off the ground without the use of the normal hydraulic jacks. This allowed jacking of aircraft on occasions when crashes occurred, or when undercarriage failures took place on the soft grass covered surfaces. On this occasion the bags were being used with the fuselage bomb-doors open, while the armourer worked on the bomb-racks. The wind was fairly strong at the time, and a sudden gust caused the Halifax to slide sideways, trapping the poor man half in and half out of the bomb-bay.

'This was a silly accident, but such mishaps happened due to the anxious times and the urgency at which we were trying to get things done.

'One irksome event, I remember, was marching out to the dispersals after early morning muster, a time wasting factor to say the least when there were numerous bicycles that could be made use of. We regulars had had our share of 'bull' and parades before the war and we were only interested in doing the job we had been trained to do. But, nonetheless, we all felt part of a team, closely connected with our flying crews, doing the occasional test-flight with them and, of course, sharing many a drink at the local when operations had been scrubbed.'

The inclement weather of the past month spilled over into 1943. Rain and poor visibility severely hampered operations, though Wing Commander Cheshire and his crew succeeded in operating on consecutive nights in the middle of the month. His first operation was to Lorient where, despite the attendant difficulties presented by drifting clouds, some success was achieved. A large oil-fire was started on the east bank of the Scorff river and further damage was caused in and around the submarine pens.

Late the following afternoon he was airborne, heading for Berlin. This target had been ignored by Bomber Command throughout 1942, but with the PFF getting into its stride Air Chief Marshal Harris decided the time was ripe to revisit Germany's capital city. Just over 200 bombers set out and within hours of take-off the mainforce were ploughing through 10/10 cloud covering the Baltic and the whole of northern Germany. A key turning point at Neuwarf went unmarked, hidden beneath thick drifting clouds, and though conditions improved slightly as Berlin was approached, the snow covered landscape prevented accurate pinpointing by the PFF. Little wonder, then, that few crews witnessed the 250-lb Target Indicator bombs dropped by the PFF for the first time.

By the 17th an improvement in the weather over northern Europe gave Harris the opportunity for a second crack at Berlin. A force totalling 187 aircraft, including PFF, mustered and Berlin was reached at around eight o'clock in the evening. The *flak* was quite heavy and increased in strength as the mainforce, which had become somewhat scattered on the long outward leg, arrived in isolated groups over the capital. This loss of concentration led to the main weight of bombs falling to the south and Southwest of the aiming point.

Captain Gunnar Halle RNAF timed his attack at 20.17 hours, while the last squadron crew reported over Berlin was captained by Flying Officer Lambert who released his bomb-load at 21.19, a good hour after Halle. The subsequent night bombing photoplot reveals Lambert's bombs exploding in the Schoneberg area of the city. Cunnar Halle's attack gave rise to a few smiles afterwards .

'Just as we dropped the bombs, we were engaged by heavy flak, concentrated and well aimed, In the Halifax the navigator's position is on top of the escape hatch, and it so happened that the hatch cover was not properly fastened. Every time we had a close burst, the cover would lift a little from the air pressure of the explosion, with the result my navigator Vikholt was bouncing up and down like a jockey. Since then we all noticed that he carefully checked the hatch cover before each flight.'

The majority of the squadron bombed in the twenty minutes between 20.30 and 20.50 hours, including George Griffiths who arrived on the scene with one engine out of action. After bombing his flight engineer reported the bomb-doors were still open and height was lost to about 11,000 feet as feverish efforts were made to retract the doors by means of the hydraulic pump. This loss of altitude was instantly detected by some flak batteries and for a novice crew this realisation by the enemy may well have signalled their doom. To the experienced the problem, although unpleasant, was not insurmountable as George Griffiths explains:

'We were being well and truly sorted out as I altered course into each salvo, the next one bursting each time on the opposite wing tip. Gradually I worked my way out of range of the guns, by which time another engine was giving trouble.

'Our homeward route lay northwest into the southern Baltic and then across Denmark in a straight line to Flamborough Head. I decided, and the crew agreed, that if the second engine packed up before we left the Danish coast, we would turn back and bail out over Sweden, rather than attempt the North Sea crossing on two over-heating engines in mid-winter. The chances of surviving a ditching in such circumstances, I considered, were somewhat minimal.'

Fortunately their fears went unfounded and after a long strength sapping flight, Base was reached in the early hours of the 18th. Here it was discovered a piece of shrapnel had pierced the fuselage adjacent to the containers holding the carrier pigeons, neatly amputating the beak from one. Sam, as the bird was so named, made a good recovery and was later awarded the Dickin medal as well as making the headlines in the 'Daily Mirror'.

At around the same time that George Griffiths was skilfully avoiding the attentions of the German flak gunners, Flight Lieutenant Hull was completing his bombing-run in relative peace. Satisfied bombs were gone and doors closed, Hull steered towards the northwest, warning his crew to keep a sharp look-out for fighters. His warning was indeed timely, for within ten minutes of leaving the target area his aircraft was approached by a Ju88. Coming in from the port quarter the night-fighter closed to within 200 yards, but prompt evasive tactics, coupled with accurate return fire from Sergeant Matthews in the rear-turret prevented the enemy pilot from making good his attack.

Two crews, captained by Captain Bjorn Naess RNAF and Sergeant Gold, failed to return and with the loss of Bjorn Naess the squadron suffered its first Norwegian casualties - his navigator was a fellow Norwegian, Lieutenant Bjarne Indseth. His Halifax was never found. Sergeant Gold's aircraft was discovered, wrecked, a kilometre southeast of Glashutte near Hamburg, the entire crew killed.

Thick fog hung dank over the Yorkshire wolds preventing further operations until the 21st when four crews left for a mining sortie off the Frisians. En route to the dropping zone the force passed over an enemy convoy which promptly opened fire. The naval gunfire was accurate and may well have accounted for Sergeant Holmes, for no trace was ever found of his aircraft.

Two nights later Lorient and its strategic submarine installations came under heavy assault from 109 bombers. Situated on the west coast of France, this key target would continue to attract concentrated attacks until the middle of February. One of the most devastating raids took place on 7 February, when against weak opposition over 300 aircraft, including six from the squadron, pounded the town with high explosives and incendiaries. Marking by the PFF was extremely accurate and this opening phase was well backed up by the first wave which left a lake of incendiary fires as a bright visual guide for the second wave. Into the gathering inferno high explosives tumbled, creating numerous explosions and causing terrible destruction. Afterwards, it is reported, the entire civilian population of Lorient was evacuated.

On the 13th an even stronger force than that despatched six nights previous made towards Lorient. In the clear moonlight Ile de Groix was clearly seen and over the harbour the visibility was perfect. The main objectives in what was to be a two pronged attack, were the cast and west docks. Incendiary fires were soon started and it was not long before the entire area shook beneath the weight of exploding 4,000 pounders. The Keroman area, in particular, suffered badly and vast areas on either side of the Port Militaire were gutted by fire. inland, to the west, the airfield at Kerlin/Bastard attracted a fair share of the bombing and it is in this vicinity that the night photoplots for Gunnar Halle RNAF and Sergeants Cursley and Perks have been identified.

For several hours after the departure of the mainforce fires raged unchecked. Evil smelling black smoke rose high from the direction of the oil storage tanks to hang like a ragged funeral robe over the desolate town.

The final attack, the ninth in the series, was pressed home with much vigour on the 16th. On this occasion 360 aircraft passed over Lorient in less than half-an-hour, leaving the already ravaged Keroman area further devastated. A number of crews witnessed a most vivid eruption coming from the docks, suggesting a direct hit had been scored on an ammunition store.

This spate of heavy raids, which probably had a greater effect on morale than any benefit derived from material damage caused to the well defended submarine pens, provided a pointer to operations over the Ruhr still to come. Out of the nine attacks, the squadron had been involved in seven. Fifty-five sorties had been despatched without loss, though on the 16th this fine achievement came within an ace of being spoilt. Sergeant Cresswell was fast approaching the end of his take-off run when an engine on the starboard side 'cut'. The sudden loss of power caused the Halifax to veer violently, but Cresswell corrected the swing and struggled into the air on three engines.

Airborne, he ordered his flight engineer to feather the still windmilling propeller, and then with a near full load of fuel and bombs still on board he landed without further incident at Marston Moor. Without doubt this was a most commendable performance from a crew that had only started their operational tour just three nights previous.

Soon after leaving for Wilhelmshaven on the 19th, Norman Black's navigator received a most painful injury. The unfortunate victim, Pilot Officer Ted Strange, tells what happened:

'On take-off, as always, I was back in my crash position and as we became airborne I obtained permission to go forward. While climbing over a spar, the aircraft lurched and my left knee hit one of the protruding studs, doing damage which was not apparent at the time. Fortunately, for once, I was wearing long underpants and their material stopped excessive bleeding. It was not until our return that I became aware of the pain and after debriefing was sent to Sick Quarters for attention. Over the years since I have, at times, suffered much discomfort and received hospital treatment for bone chippings in the left knee.'

Although no one could have known at the time, this injury to Ted Strange saved his life, as we shall discover during the next few pages.

Meanwhile, over the target area Sergeant Cresswell's crew experienced further anxious moments, this time when a photo-flash flare exploded prematurely in the chute. The flash-back injured the mid-upper gunner, who was later treated for facial burns during the return flight. A more distressing start to their tour is hard to imagine.

The cause of this accident was probably due to the flare jamming in the base of the flare-chute, a not uncommon happening as Gunnar Halle RNAF remembers from first hand experience:

'The difficulty was that the flare-chute was so long you could not reach the flare from above if it became stuck, so following a sortie when our flare lodged for a few seconds, my mid-upper gunner said he was taking a broom handle along to give the thing a wallop. And that was exactly what happened; the flare again stuck in the bottom of the chute, but with his broom handle ready my gunner managed to push the flash out. just as it left the aircraft, it exploded under the tail, temporarily blinding my rear-gunner.'

On the 25th it was the turn of Sergeant Sanderson to make the news. Like the unfortunate Cresswell, Sanderson lost engine power at the critical point in the takeoff run. On this occasion the loss was so severe that the Halifax refused to climb and Sanderson was left with no choice, other than to crash-land. Ahead lay a small wood and in making a desperate attempt to clear the trees, the bomber stalled. Why this crew did not die within the next few seconds is little short of a miracle. Somehow, Sanderson managed to force the nose down and with a tearing of tortured metal the aircraft skidded wildly across a field. Moments later a shocked crew scrambled from the exit hatches with only superficial bruises to show for their ordeal.

After these alarms, it is pleasing to record that both Cresswell and Sanderson would eventually complete their operational tours, but I doubt if either will ever forget those terrifying experiences of February 1943.

Gradually, the bone chilling days of winter were giving way to the promise of spring. On the last day of February fourteen crews flew as part of a force of 436 aircraft attacking the French port of St. Nazaire. Excellent marking of the docks was followed by a heavy concentration of bombing which left an estimated 140:acres of the town destroyed, or badly damaged. Worst hit was the area lying to the west of the Bassin de St. Nazaire. Here, power-houses, a cold storage plant, electrical sub-stations and sundry warehouses caught the full weight of the raid. The submarine pens sheltering units of Grossadmiral Donitz 6th and 7th Submarine Flottillen escaped, though minor damage was inflicted on the thick concrete roofing structures.

This had been an extremely busy month for the squadron. Crews had been involved with twelve major operations, as well as giving support on two minor details, Turin by Erik Sandberg RNAF and Pilot Officer Al Moir on the 4th and a mining sortie flown by Sergeants Cresswell, Hoover, Nevines and Perks on the 18th. All had been accomplished without loss.

For the people living in the occupied countries and to the German population at large, the growing power of Bomber Command was slowly being realised. Harris, aided by his staff, had succeeded in arresting the gradual declining strength of the command, evident in the closing months of 1941 and the first half of 1942. Now came the task of building from sound foundations a force that in the months to come would be capable of unleashing upon the cities of the Third Reich a terrible destruction. Uppermost in his planning during the late winter of 1942/43, was a concentrated assault on the industrial centres of the Ruhr. Here, he knew, he could hurt Germany most.

On the map, following the Rhine river back towards the Swiss frontier from the North Sea at Rotterdam, the area of what we know as the Ruhr Valley is soon reached. Tracing our path from the river's eastbankwe discover a multitude of towns and cities linked by good road and rail communications, plus a network of canal systems, the most important of these being the Dortmund-Ems canal curling northwards into Germany, Many names, as familiar to those that flew against them as their own, catch the eye; Bochum, Bottrop, Duisburg with its vital docks, Dusseldorf, Essen - dreaded Essen and its Krupps armament factories - Gelsenkirchen and Sterkrade, areas noted for their synthetic oil-refining plants, Hagen, the Hamm marshalling yards on the north-eastern edge, Krefeld and the like, all are there.

From the earliest days of the bombing campaign, these towns had featured often at the target briefings, and hundreds of sorties had been dispatched to the 'Happy Valley', to give the Ruhr Valley its name in contemporary aircrew parlance.

So far, very little damage in real terms had been inflicted, though it was not for the want of trying. One reason was that despite its size, towns in the Ruhr Valley were notoriously difficult to locate. Haze, nearly always thick, was a very common feature, while spewing forth continuously from the hundreds of smoke stacks were the waste products from hundreds of factories, now gearing towards all out war production. At Essen, and no doubt the same can be said of the other major manufacturing towns, the production lines at Krupps were manned around the clock, the workforce only retiring to the air-raid shelters at the last possible moment. Indeed, it was not unknown for production to continue throughout an alert.

As could be expected the Ruhr was also well defended by man. Flak and searchlight batteries guarded all approaches, while the numerous airfields of the occupied low-countries provided the *Luftwaffe* with ideal bases for its fast expanding nightfighter forces.

On 5 March the first hammer blow aimed at the Ruhr fell on Essen, but before describing this event, we will return to the beginning of the month and tell of a quite stunning attack on Berlin. On the day of the attack, a tension that one airman said 'was quite electrifying' gripped the entire station. Flight Sergeant 'Lucky' Clarke, a pilot who had been flying with the squadron since the previous autumn, was one of the fourteen captains listed on the squadron 'Battle Order'..

'The 'signs and portents' around lunchtime were that it was to be a longish trip, eight or nine hours, and was to be a 'blaster' with an 'urban' mix of 1,000 and 500 pounders, plus incendiaries. The consensus was somewhere like Munich, which was incomprehensible and inexplicable as very, very few would be privy to the secret at that stage of the day. Someone had told the groundcrew NCOs that it was to be 'a big one' and, presumably, to give everything that bit of extra care. That is surmise only, but the men at dispersal certainly knew something special was on.

'When, later that afternoon, we assembled for briefing, there was already a charged atmosphere - excitement, anticipation, 'sweat and butterflies'. I recall, to this day, the gasp when the route-map was unveiled. That red line stretching eastwards to the 'Big City' itself. For most of us, probably all, this was our first Berlin trip.'

Phil Clarke's last assumption was not quite accurate since Squadron Leader Fletcher and Flight Lieutenant Hull had taken part in the January operations on this target.

The PFF opening was both accurate and well concentrated, the skill of those concerned being rewarded by some good follow-up bombing from the mainforce in the face of a stiff *flak* barrage.

Sergeant Sanderson is believed to have been the first squadron pilot to arrive over the capital. He timed his attack four minutes after ten o'clock, and was soon followed by Phil Clarke, Cresswell and Cursley. Fires were already observed to be taking a hold and later these reached such an intensity that the city's own fire-fighting teams were overwhelmed and brigades from Leipzig were sent racing into Berlin to render assistance.

Severe damage was caused to a number of important buildings, including the offices of the Air Ministry.

The next day many Berliners walked to work, not by choice but by circumstance, picking their way through the rubble-strewn streets, their boots grinding to a fine powder the millions of fragments of glass scattered in confusion like particles of crushed ice. Around them lay clear evidence of the severity of the raid. Trarn lines were broken, escaping gas left a pungent smell and water was forcing its way through the dozens of fissures in the road surfaces. It would be several days before these services were restored. Here and there groups of smoke-grimed anxious people heaved at the rubble of a crumpled building, perhaps a life was trapped beneath the debris.

The command had not escaped lightly. Seventeen crews were missing, including two from the squadron. Half-an-hour before the attack opened Norman Black RNZAF had sent a message indicating his Halifax had been attacked by a fighter and his reargunner Sergeant jack Ryder had been badly wounded. Nothing further was ever heard from his crew, but available evidence suggests they may have fallen to the guns of Leutnant Denzel, some forty kilometres west of Texel. Norman Black's loss was particularly hard felt by his navigator Ted Strange, still recovering from his knee injury but looking forward to resuming operations with his skipper.

The second crew, captained by Squadron Leader Fletcher, came down in Belgium, victim of a night-fighter. His bomber crashed four kilometres north of Casterle. From the crew of eight (Fletcher had with him a second pilot gaining experience), three survived, two as prisoners, the third man, Flying Officer Souter-Smith successfully making contact with a resistance group known as 'Portemine'. He was smuggled into Brussels on 20 March and, it is reported, was still in the city until at least 16 May.

As already mentioned briefly, the opening assault on the Ruhr took place on 5 March, with the initial blow centred on Essen. Racing ahead of the mainforce were eight OBOE equipped Mosquito light bombers; their mission, to put down the first markers. Five were successful, their red target indicators straddling the aiming point and these were quickly supplemented by the backers-up dropping a succession of green markers. For the mainforce of over 400 bombers, a good start had been achieved. On arrival of the twelve squadron crews, all operating in the first wave, Essen was well alight. Columns of -black smoke could be seen drifting across the markers lying amongst the production sheds of Krupps. To his disgust Flight Sergeant Tom Gallantry's bomb-doors jammed and his load was later dumped into the North Sea.

By the end of the attack it was estimated that nearly three square miles of Essen were engulfed by fire, in the centre of which lay the Krupps armament works; a most encouraging start to the 'Battle', and 'OBOE', used here for the first time on a large scale as a target marking device.

Losses were fewer than might have been expected. Fourteen crews failed to return, this total including Flight Sergeant Milan, a Canadian, whose aircraft disappeared without trace.

The deep penetration raid to the marshalling yards at Nuremburg on 8/9 March was, by comparison, disappointing. The first markers were scattered far and wide of the aiming point. George Dixon reported several areas of woodland burning on the outskirts of the town, though later on in the attack some substantial damage was inflicted on the town's industrial areas. Fires were started at the rolling stock works of Reichsbahn Ausbesserungswerk, while the Suddeutsche Apparatefabrik plant producing radio equipment and the M.A.N. diesel engine works were hit during the course of the attack. Flying as a second pilot to Flight Lieutenant Wetherley was the Commanding Officer designate,. Wing Commander Don Smith whose previous operational experience had been in the Abyssinian campaign of 1940-41.

Three nights later he led the squadron on a strike directed at Stuttgart. The defences were very active; as Tom Gallantry was soon to find out:

'Most of the *flak* was bursting at around our height, or above it, the rest seemed to be exploding at about 10,000 feet. I decided we would stand a better chance of an accurate run-in if we bombed from 12,000 feet, so I descended to that height and my bomb-aimer fixed the aiming point and commenced directing me on to it. Everything was proceeding smoothly, we were lined up nicely on the target, and whilst I could hear the clump of exploding shells and shrapnel hitting the aircraft, we didn't seem to be in any great danger. Then, just as the bombs were released and the aircraft rose in the air, there was the most terrific bang, a brilliant flash of light and we were tossed about like a cork. The instruments were spinning wildly and I had no idea of the attitude of the aircraft. My immediate reaction was to ask to see the fires in order that I could bring the plane back on an even keel. Eventually I straightened out and asked everyone to check for damage.'

The Halifax had been badly knocked about. At first Tom Gallantry considered their chances of clearing the target area as somewhat minimal.

'The starboard outer propeller was windmilling and we were getting no power from the engine. I tried to feather the airscrew, but was unable to do so due to damage in the mechanism. The elevators were not responding to the controls and soon it was found that the cables between them and the control column had been severed. Fortunately, the trimming tabs were still in operation and I was able to keep the Halifax level by using these. The rear turret was stuck and a check in this direction found the hydraulic pipes to it were broken.

'I managed to turn the aircraft on a course for home. We could have headed for Switzerland which was nearer, but I felt confident that if we were able to continue as we were, we should at least get back to an airfield near the south coast. We had on board a second pilot, an Australian, who was experiencing his first trip, and whilst I would not say he was actually enjoying the situation, he did not seem over perturbed and he only broke the silence to ask if every trip was like this one.

'The three remaining engines were still running smoothly, but the unfeathered motor was causing a fair amount of shaking. That, plus the lack of elevator control, was making it hard work to keep the aircraft reasonably steady and on an accurate course. Altitude was being gradually lost, but I calculated we should make the south coast with enough leeway to effect a landing. However, when some thirty to forty miles from the French coast the port outer started to overheat. We tried everything to keep it going, but eventually I had to feather the propeller and trust that we would be able to continue on the two inner engines. The extra power these were being asked to give caused their temperatures to rise, but I still felt we could make it to England with just a little luck. By this time we were down to about 5,000 feet and as we crossed the French coast this loss of height became more marked.

'Eventually the English coast passed beneath us and we sent out a distress signal asking the nearest airfield to give us assistance to land. The two inner engines were showing signs of throwing in the sponge, so I decided it would be impossible to land in these circumstances, and we would have to abandon the aircraft. I commenced turning until the Halifax was heading back towards the channel, ordering the crew to bale out through the front hatch. As each man passed me, he gave a 'thumbs up' sign. My relief at getting back this far was tinged with apprehension at the thought of having soon to make that leap into the dark. By now the plane was on a southerly heading, so I unfastened my harness, adjusted the trim as best as I could, and made my way down into the nose compartment. For a few seconds I sat on the edge of the escape hatch, my feet dangling in the slipstream, before pushing myself out. The tailplane of the Halifax disappeared over my head. I grabbed the ripcord, pulled it and found myself floating quite gently through the air.'

Less than an hour later Tom Gallantry walked up to a searchlight battery post. Transport to the nearest aerodrome was quickly arranged and here the entire crew were reunited. Sergeant Len Exton, the navigator, who played a crucial part in their ultimate survival plotted their near demise in the area of Brighton.

Essen was revisited during the evening of the 12th. Good fires were left burning, though not on the same scale as the first attack. All the same, the distinctive flash given off from high explosive bombs could be seen from as far away as the Zuider Zee. Wing Commander Don Smith's return was rather eventful:

'We came into land on three engines, the port outer having given up over the Dutch coast. With full flap on and an unserviceable undercarriage, we overshot the runway and crashed. Everyone was out in record time, my navigator getting his intercom lead tied up with the fixed aerial and trying for a few seconds to untangle the mess before ripping his helmet off. The fire tender was quickly on the scene, covering everything and everybody with foam, almost before we were out of the aircraft. By a stroke of good fortune nothing caught fire.

'In the morning we inspected the damage. To the groundcrews' evident satisfaction the remains of J Jinks were strewn over an area of some 200 yards and her back was irremediably broken. We were not entirely sorry either.'

Let us pause for a moment and consider some of the problems of three engine flying. Such procedures were certainly practised during conversion training, and in normal circumstances a competent pilot should experience little difficulty in coping with such a situation. However, at night, with the bomber fully laden with fuel and bombs, perhaps flying in marginal weather, the difference between stalling and maximum speed was quite small, and it is not difficult to imagine the consequences following an engine failure. It is now generally acknowledged that not all Halifax losses were attributable directly to enemy action. Loss of control, either through an engine failure, or stalling, was now a factor being considered. This having been said, it is perhaps typical of Leonard Cheshire that he should try to do something practical about this worrying problem.

'I therefore took a Halifax up to 12,000 feet and put it into a tail stall. The result was I simply could not get her out of the resultant spin, finally having to cut back both of the motors on the outside of the spin, open the other two to maximum throttle and with both feet on the rudder bars force the controls forward with all my strength. I just about managed to right her in time. I might add to the great indignation of my wireless operator who wanted to know what the idea was.'

Wing Commander Cheshire repeated this test with various Halifaxes, always with he same hair raising results. The poor streamlining of the aircraft also concerned him:

'My way of overcoming this problem was to remove the mid-under gun turret and replace it with a clear vision panel. The effect of this was to give us an extra nine miles an hour, which I considered more valuable than the extra gun. I doubt if we got official permission, but when one's life is at stake these little things do not seem to matter too much.'

But to overcome the first problem, something more than the removal of a gun turret was going to be necessary. Cheshire pleaded, unsuccessfully, for design changes to be made to the Halifax tail section. No one, it seems, was willingly to interfere with the smooth running of the production lines. Undeterred, he flew down to Boscombe Down and persuaded the Research Institute here to take the matter up. This they did with tragic results for one test-crew and its Polish Test Pilot. The fault, as he suspected, lay in the shape of the tail fin and in time the original triangular shaped unit was changed for a more square and angular design.

For the next week inclement weather prevented the command from operating in force, though a good attack on the U-boat base at St. Nazaire was made on the 22nd. This was followed by a rather confusing affair over Duisburg, when some of the mainforce bombed ahead of the PFF markers, and the month ended with two heavy raids directed at Berlin. By far the most successful of these two attacks was the raid on the 27th when a force of nearly 400 bombers flew through a heavy flak barrage to inflict quite serious damage to property on either side of the River Spree. Good fires were seen spreading east of the Alexander Platz and as one squadron pilot remarked:

'Quite a pretty sight and one which most of us would have paid 10/6d to watch on a peacetime 5th of November.'

His comments would prove quite prophetic, for in the winter of 1943 Sir Arthur Harris would launch an all out assault on Germany's capital city.

The second visit was marred by dreadful icing and a higher than normal percentage of the attacking force turned for home well short of Berlin. Those that did fight their way through returned with stories of near intolerable conditions in their aircraft, the isolated gunners suffering particularly badly in their cramped draughty turrets. it had been an awful night, the day that followed was little better as the personal effects of Flight Lieutenant Wetherley's and Sergeant Cursley's crews were collected, parcelled up and sent to Uxbridge.

April started with a visit to Essen. The enemy defences were well co-ordinated and hundreds of powerful probing searchlights swept the skies between the Dutch coast and the Ruhr. intermittent heavy flak harried the mainforce and there is evidence of bombs being scattered haphazardly over wide areas of the Ruhr.

Flight Lieutenant Hartnefl-Beavis was coned for eight minutes, and he was fortunate to escape relatively unscathed from the radar predicted *flak* that burst alarmingly close to his Halifax.

At Essen the locomotive shops attached to the Krupps complex were badly damaged, this being a good blow against the German war effort, for the Essen works were the second largest in Germany after Henschel of Kassel.

Gradually, the effectiveness of Bomber Command was being felt by the German civilian population and intelligence reports for the time suggest that several members of the Nazi hierarchy were sent to the worst devastated areas to deliver morale boosting speeches to the suffering populace.

On 7 April Wing Commander Leonard Cheshire formally handed over the squadron to Wing Commander Don Smith. As the squadron diarist wrote:

'What the squadron has lost, Marston Moor will gain. it was under the character and personal supervision of Group Captain Cheshire that the squadron became what it is today - one of the best in Bomber Command.'

Don Smith was now destined to lead the squadron through what would prove to be one of the most hazardous periods in the entire history of Bomber Command.

The night following the Group Captain's departure, Duisburg was attacked. Thick cloud hid the target from view, but a satisfying glow from many fires reflected through the overcast as the last of the bombers turned for home. Sergeant Cresswell's aircraft was attacked by a pair of single-engined fighters, tracer from one narrowly missing his wing tips as he twisted and dived to evade their attention. in the morning everyone was saddened to learn that Flying Officer Elliott was missing from this his 22nd operational sortie. Accompanying Elliott as a second pilot was Flying Officer Rogers DFM, but, sadly, no one from this crew has ever been found.

Night-fighters were again well in evidence on the 14th when Sergeant Carrie's Halifax came under fire as he flew home from Stuttgart. A few seconds before the attack two Ju 88s had been sighted in the clear moonlight running in from dead astern. One was displaying a light in the nose, but it was his companion that opened fire first.

Evasive action was immediately taken as the second fighter commenced firing. By this time Carrie's rear-gunner Sergeant Wanless was in action. For several seconds the deadly flash of tracer fire swept around the weaving Halifax, and then with a resounding explosion a cannon shell burst in the bomber's nose compartment mortally wounding the bomb-aimer Sergeant Weir. In sheer desperation Carrie threw his aircraft into a stomach wrenching corkscrew. As the Halifax responded, so Wanless at last got the measure of the second fighter, sending bursts of machine-gun bullets thudding into its undersurfaces. For a split second the Ju 88 hung in the air, before flicking over into a spin and falling away burning furiously. His companion, probably unnerved by what he had witnessed, was last seen well astern and out of range of the triumphant Wanless. It was a very shaken bomber crew that returned to Base.

The Skoda works at Pilsen in Czechoslovakia was the intended target for 3 27 aircraft on the 16th, while a slightly less powerful force set course for a raid on Mannheim. First reports suggested the Pilsen attack had been a success, despite heavy losses totalling thirty-seven crews. But, as more and more photo-plots were examined it became painfully obvious that the majority of bombs had fallen well away from Pilsen - a wretched disappointment. The Mannheim raid, however, had faired much better. Sergeant Bill Elder RNZAF reported three good areas of fire and from the night photoplots it was assessed that some five-and-a-half acres of the Joseph Vogels tank and motor vehicle components factory had been damaged by fire. Some bombs had fallen on the Kaiser Wilhelm barracks, others on the Carl Phillip palace causing some fire damage to this historic building. From this target eighteen crews failed to return, taking the command's loss to well over fifty crews.

All in all it had been a costly night, especially for the squadron with three crews missing from Pilsen. From the twenty-one aircrew only two escaped with their lives. Sergeant Wombwell, the mid-upper gunner in Sergeant Wright's Halifax down at Mundelsheim was safe, as was his counterpart Sergeant Mitchell from Sergeant Webb's crew. By sheer chance this crew came down southwest of Mannheim at Lachen-Speyerdorf. The third bomber, captained by Sergeant Wedderburn was discovered near Liesse, northeast of Laon in France. There were a number of tragic coincidences, with six of those killed sharing surnames in common.

This was the highest casualty rate suffered by the squadron since the daylight raid on the *'Scharnhorst'* in July 1941.

By contrast the raid on the Baltic Sea port of Stettin four nights later was most rewarding. Headed by Don Smith, fourteen crews joined a mainforce of over 300 aircraft, the majority of which reached and bombed Stettin. Visibility was excellent throughout and all considered the enemy target defences to be ineffective. Not so the crews manning the *flak-ships* moored off the Danish coast and it is likely that the majority of the twenty-two aircraft lost on this operation fell to these formidable gunners.

Flight Sergeant Bawden received a drubbing from such a vessel three miles west of Naestved. His hydraulic system was shot through, while less serious damage was caused to the tailplane and port wing. Before he had time to recover from this battering, a nervous Lancaster gunner opened up, but fortunately his aim was poor and Bawden limped for home.

Stettin had been quite badly blitzed. Installations in the Didiewerke complex responsible for producing much needed material support for Germany's iron and steel industries were :set on fire. 'The dockland did not escape either. Here several acres containing wharves, warehouses and shipbuilding yards were left cratered with sundry fires burning merrily. The raid also turned out to be a tremendous morale booster for the inhabitants of occupied Denmark. Many, it is said, ran from their homes and completely disregarded the 'black-out' regulations to wave and cheer the low-flying bombers roaring over their rooftops.

With the success of Stettin, and the ever lengthening hours of daylight reducing the opportunity for long-range attacks, Harris concentrated his forces on the relatively close Ruhr towns. The onslaught on targets in the occupied countries and the German mainland was rapidly becoming a twenty-four hour operation. Under cover of darkness, often in appalling weather, the crews of Bomber Command set forth, while by day the American Fortresses and Liberators of the Eighth Air Force were gradually getting into their stride, penetrating deeper and deeper into enemy territory. Round the clock bombing, a dream a year ago, was fast becoming a reality.

To achieve this aim the skill and resources of thousands of people were needed. In the Dominion and Commonwealth air training schools aircrews of all trades were being instructed in the various skills of flying, while at home in the aircraft and armament factories throughout the land production was maintained around the clock to keep pace with the insatiable demands of war. Production was reaching high enough levels to allow Bomber Command's losses in equipment to be made good almost overnight. The equipping of the remaining Wellington squadrons with four-engined types continued and new squadrons were forming as more and more fresh faced airmen emerged from the training system.

In the closing weeks of April 1943, the squadron exchanged its Halifax BIIs for the marginally better Mk Vs, and so equipped it continued 'The Battle of the Ruhr' with a vengeance.

Chapter Six

MAY 1943 to NOVEMBER 1943

As the last hours of April 1943 faded into the dawn of May, eight crews joined the mainforce steering a course for Essen. Severe icing was encountered and over Essen thick cloud prevented all but scant visual reference to what was happening below. Flares were going down in abundance and later some crews claimed to have seen a mixture of red and green Target Indicators burning inside the target area.

Dortmund was singled out for attention on 4 May, substantial damage being inflicted on the town centre and around the docks. To the east of the Kanal Hafen some forty-five acres of industrial works received heavy fire damage.

On the 12th it was the turn of Duisburg with a total force of 572 aircraft employed. Accurately placed red Target Indicators went down from the OBOE Mosquitoes, quickly followed by a deluge of greens. Through the *flak* came the mainforce, Wing Commander Don Smith amongst the squadron contingent of twelve crews:

'On this trip we backed-up the PFF and obtained a good photograph of the Aiming Point. We had little trouble from icing, though a good many fighters were in evidence. Our load consisted of seven 1,000 pounders and the furthest of these landed 750 yards from the Aiming Point'.

Undoubtedly, this was the heaviest attack of the war to date on Duisburg. Around the main station at Meiderich the destruction was of a scale that prevented trains from entering this normally busy station for nearly a week. Perhaps of more importance the steel producing plants of Von Thyssen were hit, also the reheating furnaces of the Vereingte Stahlwerke at Hamborn. Large quantities of rolling stock were totally destroyed and some damage was caused to the local coal mines and coke ovens of Celsenkirchener Bergwerke.

A similar picture of destruction unfolded in the wake of the Bochum raid on the 13th. On this occasion the town's two most important steel works operated by Bochumer Verein were severely damaged. At the height of the bombing the outside scene left two squadron aircrew flying in separate aircraft with indelible impressions:

'Heavy flak was exploding all around, just barrage at the time, nothing predicted. Everyone was keyed up as the skipper put the aircraft into a shallow dive to cross the target. Over the intercom I could hear the bomb-aimer calmly asking for minute changes of course as the markers came into his sights. A slight jar, bombs gone and that's it. Already the navigator is giving a course that will take us away from the target area. Soon there is general easing of tension as Bochum recedes further and further into the distance.'

The other remembered:

'Searchlights were everywhere, unbroken walls of them. It was as light as day and the whole of the Ruhr valley seemed to be lit up by the moon and lights. Near the target there must have been fifteen large cones with between thirty and forty beams in each. The lights would wave about until they found somebody, then all the beams in the area would fasten on to that aircraft and shells would be pumped up the cone just like water spurting from a park fountain.'

Ten nights later Harris switched his bombers back to Dortmund. Well over 800 aircraft were ordered and the results by this strong force well surpassed the destruction achieved here on the 4th.

It is not surprising, therefore, to learn that the enemy defences were responding to the full as the command maintained its direct threat on the industrial heart of Germany. Searchlights swung back and forth in an unceasing hunt for the invading bombers, but by far the most feared menace facing those venturing forth over the Rhineland in the summer of 1943 was the night-fighter. The risk of interception was growing nightly and for the most part the odds lay in favour of the defending fighter crew. Vigilance by all was the key to survival.

Over Dortmund the *flak* barrage was both vicious and accurate, the night sky being alive with bursting shells:

'We had been coned and held by the searchlights for a time, when there was a tremendous bang beneath the rear of our aircraft. For several minutes we fell out of control before recovering and resuming our course. I then discovered that brute force on the control column was needed to prevent the bomber from stalling and I had to be assisted by my flight engineer in keeping the nose down.

'We struggled along producing little in the way of airspeed, even at full boost. Later my rear-gunner informed me that amongst all our troubles, we had lost an elevator. Soon afterwards, I believe in the region of Zwolle, we were hit by a fighter and what little control I had vanished. The aircraft nosed up and stalled. I had no option but to tell everyone to get out.' *Sergeant Clifford Cousins - Pilot.*

This brief account illustrates well the dangers facing a partially crippled bomber. By the time Sergeant Cousins crossed the borders of Holland, his aircraft was well isolated from the returning stream of bombers. Little wonder then that Lieutenant Augenstein of 7/NJG 1 was able to increase his tally of night-fighter victories.

From Cousins aircraft five survived, both gunners either dying in the sharp encounter, or failing to leave the falling bomber. Flight Sergeant Bawden, who had so narrowly avoided being shot down on the Stettin raid in April, had earlier fallen victim to Lieutenant Rapp, a colleague of Augenstein's. His Halifax crashed three kilometres northwest of Greven whilst still outbound for Dortmund.

This attack, then, had cost the squadron two crews. Sergeant Cousins was a relative 'fresher', but Bawden's loss represented a very experienced crew that had been operating since late February. However, a near third disaster was only averted through a measure of luck and good teamwork.

During the home-leg flight, Sergeant Ward and his mid-upper gunner, Pilot Officer Hyett, spotted a Ju 88 away to port on a course parallel to their own. For several minutes the two aircraft held their course, until suddenly the enemy pilot banked sharply towards the Halifax, opening fire at 200 yards range. On seeing the first spurt of tracer, Ward turned towards his assailant, at the same time shouting to Hyett to commence firing. His gunner's response was immediate and effective and moments later the Ju 88 swooped beneath the Halifax. Ward resumed his original heading, but still visible and now flying ahead of the bomber, the Junkers could be clearly seen turning steeply, the enemy pilot setting himself up for a renewed assault, this time from the port quarter.

Once again Ward turned to meet his attacker. From his cramped position in the rear turret Sergeant Cameron RCAF caught sight of a dark blur racing past, tracer from Hyett's guns hosing in hot pursuit. Quickly adjusting his sights Cameron opened fire. For the next few seconds the night-fighter could be seen jinking madly to avoid their combined fire, before at last it vanished from view.

Two nights later during a raid on Dusseldorf, Pilot Officer Ross RCAF reported an inconclusive combat near Cologne. in the event neither aircraft opened fire, possibly because his rear-gunner Flying Officer Campbell was convinced the other aircraft was a Wellington. This mystery, however, was never resolved. On the 27th Ross was one of fourteen squadron crews ordered to attack Essen. Slightly less than three hours after leaving Linton, his Halifax was intercepted by Lieutenant Augenstein and sent down at Leer, some five kilometres southwest of Burgsteinfurt. Ross, along with four others from his crew, survived but Campbell who was certain he had seen a Wellington in his sights two nights previously, died along with the navigator, Sergeant Anderson.

The last major attack in the May was launched on the last Saturday in the month, the 29th, with Wuppertal-Barmen the target. Clear skies and good visibility enabled the PFF, their Lancaster element using H2S for the first time on operations, to identify this relatively small target. For the inhabitants of Wuppertal it was their misfortune that the markers were tightly bunched and accurately placed. Hard on the heels of the PFF came the mainforce. Huge fires sprang up, leapfrogging from street to street consuming everything in their path. High explosives sent shock-waves coursing through the battered structures, further hampering the desperate attempts of the defenders to bring the raging inferno under control. Throughout the night and well into the Sunday the fires burned and appliances from neighbouring towns were called upon to help stem the uncontrolled blaze. Before the summer battle was over, the Wuppertal brigades would respond to similar calls from these same neighbours as Harris sent his men time and time again to the Ruhr.

To add to the misery of those being bombed, it should be remembered that further widespread destruction had been caused by a very special raid carried out in the middle of the month. This was the Dams raid by sixteen Lancasters of 617 Squadron, led by Wing Commander Guy Gibson. The dams at Moehne and Eder were successfully breached, releasing millions of gallons of precious water and flooding the Ruhr and Eder valleys.

For those people bowed beneath the Nazi yoke, the news bore a note of encouragement. Their awful plight was not forgotten. Before continuing with the events of June, we will look briefly at what it was like for the aircrews operating in this violent summer of 1943. Unlike the soldier in the front-line who is constantly facing the enemy, the men of Bomber Command lived an existence of opposites. On the bomber bases life, in general, was good. When not operating there was little demanding work to be done:

'Living relatively in the comforts of home created a rather unreal situation and feeling. An incredible contrast between war and peace. I remember so often when waking up from a few hours sleep after returning from a trip, I felt that the night's action might just as well have taken place in a dream.'

So wrote Lieutenant John Stene RNAF. A young flight engineer, Ferris Newton posted in with his crew early in May 1943, was already acutely aware of the sharp divide separating the aircrews in their enclosed world of operations from the reality of life going on around them. These notes, recorded in his diary, no doubt reflect the feelings of dozens of his contemporaries:

'Went back to the Mess to try and eat the special meal put on. I had had a very funny feeling in the pit of my stomach ever since being told I was on operations that night. I was both curious and anxious at the same time, wanting to know how I would react in the face of danger, and to know what it was really like on 'the other side'.

The ritual of briefing is neatly outlined.

'We moved in small silent groups down to the intelligence section. First we entered a room cluttered up with photographs, maps, chairs, technical papers and confidential Air Ministry publications. In the far wall another door giving access to the briefing room. The atmosphere caught you by the throat the moment you put your foot inside that door.

The first thing you saw when entering was the big map nearly covering the whole of the wall behind the platform. When the covers were pulled back the big splashes of red indicating defended areas were plain to see the 'Wingco' said "We have routed you through a gap in the Ruhr", we used to give a nervous laugh.'

Next, the feelings of a bomb-aimer, Gilbert Duthie, recently arrived and quickly caught up in the whirl of operations:

'I had lost half of my crew in a fighter affiliation exercise at Rufforth, and arrived on the squadron as a 'spare bod'. My first operation was with a New Zealander doing the last sortie of his tour, but thereafter I was attached to a regular crew. To start with every trip seemed to be to the 'Happy Valley', flak, violent manoeuvres to get out of the searchlights, the Stirlings seemingly far below and silhouetted against the burning incendiaries which outlined the pattern of the streets. The odd parachute in the midst of all the confusion, a twin-engined aeroplane on a diametrically opposite course passing too quickly to recognise and as near to a collision as we ever came. The shallow dive to the coast, which we usually crossed amidst displays of light flak and tracer.' Fleeting impressions, locked in his mind forever.

Sergeant Ken Parry, a navigator destined to be severely wounded on operations to Peenemunde later in the summer, writes:

'Our first trip to Stettin in the Baltic was uneventful and seemed a 'piece of cake'. But we were faced with stark reality on our next few trips which were all to the Ruhr. The aircraft received flak damage on a number of occasions, particularly on raids over Gelsenkirchen and Bochum.'

Ken Parry was crewed with a quite remarkable pilot, Ken Hewson, an American by birth. Between 4 May and 24 June, Ken Hewson took his crew on thirteen consecutive operations, a record unsurpassed in the history of the squadron.

The groundcrews, as ever, were fully involved in the battle. Syd Carratt the engine fitter, whom it will be remembered spent many a night in the ill-comfort of a wicker armchair, recalls:

'The engine damage at this time was often extensive. It was common for an aircraft to come back on three engines, occasionally two. Sometimes we would get away with just a cylinder block change, but more often than not it would be a complete engine change. We would remove the cowlings and see con-rods sticking through the crankcase, everything smashed to pieces. A team of four men could change an engine in just over four hours, start after breakfast and have the engine running before we went to lunch.'

Also very much to the fore in all these events were the civilian inhabitants of the Ruhr towns. As our own people had suffered in the enemy raids of 1940/41, and on a reducing scale since, the pendulum was fast swinging in the reverse direction. In the summer of 1943 the German at home proved he could take it 'on the chin' as well as anyone, the difference being that 'his chin' was to be the focal point of attention for the next two years to come. From this unidentified German housewife and mother, some very different sentiments to those expressed earlier in this chapter:

'It was an inferno. Bomb followed bomb, streams of phosphorous flowed from a above and incendiary bombs fell without interruption. It is a miracle we are still alive.

'Our district is completely in ruins and only western parts of Essen remain standing. it is difficult to visualise what everything looks like now. Thousands of people have been left without a home. We are all completely worn out. Only ruins are to be seen which ever way one looks. If everything is going to be destroyed, including our house, it would be better for you not to come here. I shall not be able to stick it. Approach of darkness always makes us shiver in anticipation of air raids.'

Written in the spring of 1943, this letter was found a few weeks later on the body of her husband, killed on the Eastern front. Whoever this unknown German soldier was, he met his death many miles from his homeland, sad in the belief that his home and family were unlikely to survive his homecoming.

I have mentioned several times the capability of the *Luftwaffe's* night-fighter force, and I do not intend to dwell at any great length on the composition, or control of the German defensive system. Several excellent books have been written explaining the workings of this force, and I can thoroughly recommend Alfred Price's fine study of the subject published under the title 'Battle over the Reich'[15] . It is suffice to say that many of the innovations employed by the spring of 1943 stemmed from one man, Generalmajor Josef Kammhuber, and it is appropriate now to include one account written by an airman charged with the task of trying to carry out Kammhuber's instructions. As it will be seen, such instructions were not always easily complied with. Uffz. Heinrich Scholl was a young radio operator flying in a Ju 88 during the early summer of 1943, and here he describes his crew's unsuccessful attempt to engage a Stirling somewhere over the Ruhr. The flight engineer, Karl Chus, had been the first to sight the bomber flying some distance ahead of their fighter. Heinrich turned around from his seat positioned behind the pilot, Leutnant Bruno Heilig:

'All I could see was a dark shadow, and immediately I had to return to my instruments and the radio conversation, so I had little time to observe what was happening. During my now increasing occupation with the radio conversation, I waited anxiously for the sound of shots from our cannons, which I wanted so much to hear. However, everything in the cockpit was quiet. During my conversation with the ground controller, which was following a normal course, I looked over the sides of the cockpit and through the canopy. The dark night sky seemed to grow slightly darker and with a reflex action I glanced upwards. I thought a shot had hit me, for scarcely thirty metres away and to one side, was a Short Stirling. It was flying exactly on our course and was slightly slower than ourselves. I snatched at the double MG machine guns, but dared not shoot since I had no order to do so from my pilot. I quickly grabbed the radio microphone and in my highly agitated state called the pilot and told him that scarcely thirty metres above me was a Stirling. I posed the question, should I shoot, but he did not answer and without his permission I could not fire. Slowly the enemy bomber wandered off behind us and it was then he must have seen our outline for it dipped its left wing down, made a powerful swoop and vanished into the darkness of night below us, also without having fired a shot.'

This account illustrates well the discipline of the night-fighter crews and though perhaps a freeness of hand may have brought them victory, it was this same discipline that was achieving considerable results in their favour as the bombing of the Ruhr towns gathered pace. The increasing percentage of Allied bomber losses can be directly attributed to the skill of the *Luftwaffe* night-fighter crews and the table published at the end of June 1943 makes sombre reading.

Finally, before threading our way through the month of June, a letter from a Dutchman, patiently waiting for his country to be liberated:

'In the past winter months British bombers would begin flying over between seven and eight o'clock in the evening. But in the spring the raids started later. Suddenly, all the dogs would start to bark and howl. When this happened, then we knew that after five or ten minutes, first in the long distance, the sound of *flak* explosions creeping nearer and nearer. Next, some few minutes later, more searchlights begin to light

---

15   Published by Ian Allan in 1973, though no longer in print at the time of going to press.

the night sky and then the drone of many engines fill the air with noise. Although afraid, one had to look outside. Between the hectic sound of explosions from *flak* shells, the metallic clatter of falling shell splinters on the streets and roofs. Sometimes, a more high engine noise could be heard and we knew that this was mostly night-fighters. Our hearts then go out to the men in the bombers.'

These are the memories of Leo Zwaaf who, as a schoolboy of sixteen, was arrested in Rotterdam by the Gestapo.

Yes, May 1943 was a month never to be forgotten by the inhabitants of the Ruhr, or by those who flew against them. Equally heavy raids were planned for several weeks to come, but this dreadful unleashing of power by Bomber Command had arrived on an unprecedented scale. The steel industry, in particular, had sustained very severe damage and some disruption in supply would be felt throughout the remaining summer months.

Rain fee on most days at the start of June, and the squadron did not operate until the 11th when eighteen crews visited Dusseldorf. Cloud obscured the Aiming Point from time to time, but some good fires were left burning. Two crews, those captained by Sergeant Phillips and Wilson, failed to return. Sergeant Wilson, flying for the first time on operations, was shot down by a Bf 11OG-4 four kilometres south of Bladel, a small Dutch town southwest of Eindhoven, by Oberleutnant Barte. In his combat report Barte states he fired 332 rounds from his twin MG 151 cannons, and 1,616 rounds from the four nose-mounted MG 17 machine-guns. Only Sergeant John Lobban, the navigator, survived this devastating encounter. In the brief time remaining between living and certain death, Lobban frantically strove to open the escape hatch beneath his plotting table. His entire body felt heavy as the bomber spun with ever increasing velocity. For several minutes his frenzied struggle went unrewarded, until a crack and an inward blast of icy summer air signalled he might yet survive. Casting aside his flying-helmet, John Lobban jumped into the void below:

'I drifted down peacefully. Far below a blinding flash indicated petrol tanks exploding. By manipulating my parachute cords I avoided landing in the inferno, and I offered up a prayer of thanks when I realised I was not seriously injured.'

For nearly three months John Lobban, aided by the resistance avoided capture, but the end came in a seedy hotel on the outskirts of Bordeaux. The Gestapo had, through the connivance of a traitor, successfully infiltrated his particular evasion line.

Bochum was next in line, particularly widespread damage being inflicted in the area around the town's north station and at the Eisen and Huttenwerke steel plants. The night is remembered as being extremely bright, giving the defending night-fighter crews the chance to make visual sightings almost at will. Nearing Texel on the homeward leg Sergeant Ken Hewson's Halifax was approached by a Ju 88. The events that followed are clearly described by his rear-gunner, Sergeant 'Dave' Davis:

'I spotted him flying about 800 to 1,000 yards dead astern and slightly above us. His shape was clearly silhouetted in the first early light of the day. He did not look too dangerous and I think he was being radar predicted onto us.

'I called to AI in the mid-upper turret to verify my recognition, but before he could reply I saw his tail tip up and I shouted to the skipper to corkscrew, the direction not mattering as our attacker was approaching from astern.

'My pilot's response threw me backwards against the bulkhead doors, causing me to lose sight of the fighter as it dived into the dark part of the sky. A long burst of tracer came snaking below our starboard wing, so I touched my firing button and gave a short reply into that part of the sky from where I imagined his fire lay. He replied, and again missed.

'Then I saw him, his wing span wider than my Graticule Ring, about 150 to 200 yards away. He was breaking away in a climbing turn to port, so I opened fire into his belly. To my satisfaction I saw him catch fire and break up into flaming pieces as he disappeared into the North Sea.'

For several minutes the blazing remains of the night-fighter continued to burn on the surface of the water, as jubilant bomber crew continued their journey westwards the dawn breaking behind them.

On 16 June the squadron left Linton-on-Ouse and by the evening of the same day were settling into their new home at Holme-on-SpaldingMoor, a new aerodrome north of the Humber and close to the towns of Beverley and Hull. This move from the comforts of a permanent pre-war station with all the trappings of solid comfort, even in war, to a typical war-built airfield, sparse and cold, was not entirely welcomed. Sergeant Lauric Brown, the flight engineer in Sergeant Ken Myers crew recalls:

'Linton had been shared by 76 and 78 Squadrons [16] and this had generated a friendly rivalry in all respects, even to seeing which squadron could be the smartest when led by their COs on marches around the airfield. Whether this friendly rivalry really helped, I do not know, but things never seemed quite the same after we left Linton for Holme.'

Soon the comforts of Beningborough Hafi, home of Lady Chesterfield at Newton on Ouse, of 'Old Nick's' ferry behind the hall, twopence to go across, sixpence return after 9 pm - and it invariably was after an evening spent in the Alice Hawthorn at Nun Monkton - would just be memories.

The first operation from this new base come three nights later when nine crews, headed by Flight Lieutenant Sanderson, joined in a most successful attack by 290 aircraft on the Schneider Amiament works at Le Creusot in central France. This was a relatively small target, calling for particular care in bombing.

Ken Hewson and Hickman opened the squadron's accountant 01.53 hours, Sergeant Hickman reporting his bombs straddling a row of machine erecting shops. Five minutes later Flight Lieutenant Sanderson released his bomb-load on to a rolling mill at the Breuil steelworks just to the north of the Aiming Point, his navigator, Squadron Leader Nigel Bennet being most strangely employed.

'I spent most of my time over the target area hanging out of the forward escape hatch, holding a cine camera. As might be expected, the results were not very good. I think it was the first time that anybody in 4 Group had used a camera on operations. Later on, with a fixture of my own invention, I was able to lean further out of the escape hatch and maintain a much steadier grip.'

One of the last crews to attack was captained by Pilot Officer Carrie. By the time Carrie found himself over the target, many fires were raging giving off quite largo volumes of smoke. His bomb-aimer had great difficulty in sighting the markers, but eventually he was confident of his position and Carrie's bombs arched into the blaze below. Only two aircraft, Halifaxes from 10 and 408(RCAF) Squadrons, were lost and all agreed this raid had been a welcome diversion from the ceaseless journeys to the Ruhr.

However, it was a return to the familiar stamping grounds on 21 June when the town of Krefeld felt the full weight of a strong attack which lasted for nearly an hour. Red and green Target indicators lay in profusion, covering the centre of the town and it was not long before the first fires took a hold. From one street to the next it was a similar horrifying scene as the rain of incendiaries, mixed with the lethal high

---

16   78 Squadron moved to Breighton, another wartime constructed airfield with similar comforts those afforded by Holme.

explosives, blasted over 9,000 acres of Krefeld into a smouldering ruin.

These relentless attacks were bringing out the very best from the crews. Flight Sergeant Bill Elder RNZAF was plagued by engine trouble almost from the start of the Krefeld operation and he would have been quite justified in turning back. He refused to do so, reaching the target area to make his contribution towards the destruction of this industrial centre.

Mulheim and the Elberfeld district of Wuppertal came next on the agenda, though Elberfeld escaped the horrors of its neighbour, Bannen. Mulheim was not so fortunate, substantial damage being caused to the town's centre, despite the degree of protection offered by the clouds on that balmy summer night. From Mulheim Pilot Officer Carric failed to return. Flying with Carrie as second pilot was Holme's newly appointed Station Commander, Group Captain Wilson - an Australian. By awful chance he was the second Station Commander lost on operations with the squadron in 1943. On 10 April, Group Captain John Whitley, then commanding Linton-on-Ouse, was posted missing after taking off for Frankfurt with Flight Lieutenant Hull. Intercepted by a night-fighter over Belgium, Hull's aircraft fell near Hirson. Four, including Hull were killed, but the remainder, Group Captain Whitley, Pilot Officer David and Sergeants Davies and Strange evaded capture. In the case of Pilot Officer Carrie, shot down by Oberleutnant Baake northwest of Utrecht, near Zuilen, seven, including the Group Captain survived to become prisoners, the sole casualty being Sergeant Huke the flight engineer, whose parachute failed to deploy.

Towards the end of June, Harris turned his attention towards Cologne. Badly damaged in May 1942 by the first of his '1,000 plan' attacks, Cologne had made a good recovery in the ensuing twelve months. Between 28 June and the second week of July, three punishing assaults laid waste these repairs and created much new damage to boot. The squadron was involved in two of the three raids. On the first attack crews bombed through cloud, releasing their loads on an estimated time over target, which was not very satisfactory, or on the Parramatta flares put down by the PFF. Pilot Officer John Maze attacked by the latter method and was rewarded by the sight of a vivid blue explosion which seemed to reverberate for about a minute. Squadron Leader Vivian Bamber also remembers this attack, but for slightly different reasons:

'Before briefing we had been given a lecture by a Royal Artillery Officer on German *flak*, one of the points being the number of seconds taken by a shell to arrive at the aircraft's altitude, plus additional time for the gunners to set the fuses. On our bombing run with the doors open, we were coned, but believing in that earnest RA officer, I pressed the stop watch, allowing myself another twenty seconds on my present heading. Almost immediately, long before the twenty seconds were up, we heard four shells burst. To hear them they must have been pretty close and the right hand side of my cockpit canopy disappeared. The RA chap had forgotten to mention predicted *flak*.'

This incident came close to killing Bamber's navigator who happened to be standing beside his skipper, target map in hand. A red-hot shell-splinter ripped through the map to leave an angry weal across the backs of his fingers on both hands.

Squadron Leader Bamber's crew were not the only ones to be shaken by the *flak* barrage. Heading away from the Rhine, Sergeant George Dunn's aircraft was engaged by the ground fire as his flight engineer, Ferris Newton remembers:

'There were a few searchlights wandering about and as we approached them they all went out. The skipper seemed to sense a trap and he had just warned us to be on the alert when a 'master' searchlight snapped on to us. These 'master' lights were controlled by radar and seconds later three or four other beams came up, coning us well and truly. George kept his head well down, concentrating on his flying instruments and taking violent evasive action. Having got us coned, up came the *flak*. The first burst seemed to be dead in front of the nose, the next was just off the port wing and the third was just a hell of a clatter and bang. The kite shook, making my hair stand on end. It seemed like hours before we got out of those beams, but George was tops. Eventually, the 'master' light went out and we were in the clear.'

Ferris Newton was now busy checking for any possible damage and it was several minutes before he reported all systems were still functioning. From the pounding, he had quite expected to find major structural damage, but to his amazement only a dozen or so smallish holes could be found in the central fuselage skin and nothing vital to their safety had been hit.

Night-fighters were also active. Nearing Cologne one opened fire on Sergeant Ward's aircraft. Machine gun and cannon fire hit the nose of the bomber, wounding the navigator Sergeant McDougall in the chest. As his colleagues rallied to his aid, Sergeant Cameron RCAF drove off their attacker with a series of well aimed bursts, while Ward turned towards the North Sea. With a wrecked intercom and a badly injured airman, it would have been foolhardy to continue. Twice in the last six weeks death had courted this crew.

But if fortune had been kind to Sergeant Ward, such blessings had avoided his companions Sergeants Coles and Parritt. Neither returned and Parritt's Halifax was found at Vottem, eighteen kilometres north of Liege in Belgium, while the bodies of Coles crew were discovered between Duisburg and Dusseldorf at Angersund.

These losses brought the total to seven for the month. Compared with some squadrons in the Group, a quite low total. Much has been written about the chances of survival in Bomber Command, and there can be no argument that the command sustained very severe losses in 1943, and in the first half of 1944. Selecting as an example June 1943 and taking the raids involving the squadron, the published casualty returns show:

Date		Target	Sorties Despatched	Failed to Return
11 June	1943	Dusseldorf	783	38
12 June	1943	Bochum	505	24
19 June	1943	Le Creusot	290	2
21 June	1943	Krefeld	705	43
22 June	1943	Mulheim	557	35
24 June	1943	Wuppertal	630	33
25 June	1943	Gelsenkirchen	473	30
28 June	1943	Cologne	608	25
Totals			4,551	230[17]

Despite these awful figures, crews were getting through their tours. From the squadron in this same month of June Pilot Officer Cresswell who, it will be remembered, had such an eventful start to his tour, was posted to 24 Operational Training Unit at Honeybourne, and Pilot Officer Hoover went to 1664

---

17   These figures have been taken from AIR241256 and do not take account of casualties sustained in accidents during the course of these operations.

Conversion Unit at Croft. Flying Officer Jagger after only three trips was given up to the PFF and 35 Squadron at Gravely, this practice being quite common and not universally liked by either Group, or the PFF. Others who had survived from the early spring raids included Phil Clarke, Tom Gallantry and George Griffiths, all completing full tours. Al Moir and Bill Richardson had been screened slightly ahead of their contemporaries, but Moir had been tragically killed soon afterwards in a flying accident at Marston Moor. Two of the Norwegians were safely through, Erik Sandberg and Cunnar Halle, but many of their fellow countrymen would not be so fortunate as we shall in time discover.

July 1943 commenced with a heavy raid on the east side of Cologne. in clear weather everyone saw the well placed markers and much destruction to the industrial areas on this side of the Rhine was achieved. The flak barrage was strong. Sergeant Gordon Greenacre's aircraft was hit in several places and his rear-gunner Sergeant Brawn received a painful wound.

Disorientated Greenacre wandered from his intended course and their return to an emergency landing at Flartford Bridge near Basingstoke was only accomplished with much difficulty. This must have been an unnerving experience for this young crew operating for only the second time, but Gordon Greenacre would prove to be a pilot of quite exceptional courage in the coming months of the campaign.

A more seasoned crew captained by Ken Hewson turned in an equally spirited performance on Gelsenkirchen on 9 July:

'Persistent engine trouble prevented our aircraft from getting above 8,000 feet and on arrival over the target I estimated our position from the Wanganui flares drifting down above us. No sooner had I called 'bombs gone' then we were coned, and in getting clear of the lights we lost the use of the port outer engine. More seriously, we strayed off track and arrived over Bonn where we were chased by more searchlights.

'For sometime after leaving the Ruhr we flew along in cloud and when eventually this thinned we discovered we were over Paris. The shortest possible route to the coast was taken, by which time dawn was breaking. After what seemed an age we arrived at Base and after one overshoot we touched down on the grass. The brakes failed and we crashed through a boundary fence, crossed a field, and came to a stop with the aircraft wrecked. ' *Sergeant 'Taff' Isaacs - Bomb Aimer.*

For slightly differing reasons Sergeant George Taylor, the wireless operator, also remembers the occasion well:

'I had always fancied recording Gelsenkirchen in my log-book ever since the summer of 1941 when I was at Feltwell. it was a crew member from one of the resident squadrons who, on his return, told me he had been to Gelsenkirchen the night before and as the name appealed to me at the time, it bad always stayed in my memory. When I was afforded the opportunity of visiting the place myself, I was more than enthusiastic and tried to convince the others it would be 'a piece of cake'. However, after our belly-landing they seemed to lose faith in my forecasts of operational conditions.'

Ken Hewson had got his crew home under the most difficult circumstances. It would have made a happy ending to say all were unharmed, but 'Taff' Isaacs was taken off to hospital with a painful spinal injury which prevented him from operating for over a month. The rest, however, were declared fit in time for the next operation, Aachen on the 13th.

Altogether twenty-four squadron aircraft were prepared fort his attack on Aachen, a manufacturing town on the western edge of the Ruhr, not far from the border with occupied Holland.

From the outlying dispersal points the twenty-four Halifaxes headed towards the duty runway. Soon the familiar sounds of heavily laden bombers gathering speed and clawing for height in the late evening air echoed across the airfield, drowning the cheers of those gathered to watch their departure. Thirteen, including Ken Hewson, had taken off without difficulty. Now it was the turn of Leif Hulthin RNAF. From the caravan a steady green light signalled that he was clear to go. Slowly at first, but quickening with each passing second, his Halifax rolled forward. In the rear turret Sergeant Bill Freeman was aware of the tail rising into the air, the dark surface of the runway receding into a diminishing blur. The events of the next half-hour are best left to his description:

'A swing developed which the skipper over-corrected for we started fishtailing violently until eventually the undercarriage collapsed and we swung off the runway on the port side, breaking the port wing. A fire broke out immediately and I heard someone call 'get out quick, we are on fire.' I swung my turret to beam, opened the door and ripping off my oxygen mask, dropped out backwards. It seemed ages before I hit the ground and I can only assume that the kite must have finished up nose down with the tail high in the air. The rest of the crew got out through the forward escape hatch and despite being encumbered with my bulky flying-suit, I quickly caught them up.

'On reaching the perimeter of the aerodrome we jumped into a ditch, where a rollcall revealed Leif to be missing. He was soon spotted, however, standing on top of the aircraft directing the hoses of the crash-tender personnel. Every so often he would jump down and look under the aircraft, ' judging the state of the bombs which must have been 'cooking' merrily by this time Despite the frantic attempts by the crashcrew, who I give full credit to for reaching us so quickly, it was plain to see the blaze was out of control. Eventually Leif decided to leave the aircraft, but when the crashtender driver tried to start the appliance, it refused to start. Everyone finished up running over to the comparative safety of our ditch, where we watched our aircraft burn. Tracer bullets, Very lights of all colours were flying through the air, until at last with a tremendous roar the bombs exploded leaving a great hole in the runway and debris scattered all around.'

This horrific accident effectively stopped all further take-offs, probably to the chagrin of those waiting behind the unfortunate Hulthin.

Their colleagues, meanwhile, flew through cloudy skies lit by a bright moon. Over Aachen the clouds persisted, but through the occasional gaps fires could be seen taking a grip. Damage was caused to the electrical engineering works of Garbe Lahmeyer, the armaments components factory of Maschinenfabrik Krantz and the Phillips works. The Aachen-Sud goods yards received a plentiful supply of bombs and if in the morning the bemused population wondered why the trams were taking longer than usual to arrive, the reason was simple; two depots containing a large number of cars had been destroyed.

The 'Battle of the Ruhr' was over, the 'Battle of Hamburg' was about to begin. Before this next ferocious onslaught commenced, twenty-three crews joined in an exclusive 4 Group attack on the Peugeot Motor Works two miles to the north of Montbeliard, a thriving town west of Basel on the Swiss frontier. Currently engaged in the production of tanks and lorries for the Wehrmacht, the Montbeliard works had so far escaped the attentions of Bomber Command.

In perfect visibility the Halifaxes arrived over the town in the early hours of 16 July and from an average height of 7,500 feet made their bombing-runs. To his extreme annoyance an electrical fault prevented Sergeant Les Falgate from releasing his bombs, but his twenty-two companions had no such problems. Sergeant Little was first in at 01.49 hours, while last to bomb were Sergeants Griffiths and Troake who bombed in unison at 02.05 hours. In the space of just over fifteen minutes parts of the works had taken a tremendous battering. The mangled remains of vehicles lay in confusion on the wrecked assembly lines, a further telling blow had been dealt to the enemy's armaments capability.

For the majority the long return flight across France passed without incident. Gradually crews relaxed their vigilance as the first pale shafts of light flooded the countryside below.

Approaching the town of Goole, south of the Humber, Wing Commander Don Smith snapped out of his feeling of contentment when both starboard engines cut. On his command, three crew members hurriedly departed through the forward escape hatch, while his rear-gunner eventually made good his exit minus his flying-boots which he left jammed fast in the mechanism of his turret. For the remainder there was no time to jump and seconds later the bomber skidded to a halt in a potato field. Apart from a liberal supply of potatoes and bent propellers, the Halifax was little damaged, It had been a copy-book forced-landing.

On 24 July the first of four major night raids on the port of Hamburg was launched. Air Chief Marshal Sir Arthur Harris and his staff had given careful thought to this operation, code-named 'Operation Gomorrah'. By night, it was planned, Bomber Command aircraft would pound the target with high explosives and incendiaries, while by day it was hoped the American Eighth Air Force would maintain the impetus. For the citizens of Hamburg there was to be no respite. To help counteract the increasing threat from the German night-fighters, the mainforce would use Window operationally for the first time. It is not within the scope of this account to enter into the technical details of this device; suffice to say it consisted of strips of paper coated in a metallic substance and cut to a predetermined length, before being packed into bundles - each weighing about one pound. Released into the air the bundles, their protective wrapping removed, would break open allowing thousands of strips to drift, setting up a confused clutter of images on the enemy radar screens. Window was an immediate success and the lives of many aircrew were saved, only twelve aircraft failing to return from a force of well over 700 bombers.

The opening attack was a success. The mainforce, approaching the city from the north, tight on the heels of the PFF markers, put down a mixture of high explosives and incendiaries which started off fires that burned unchecked long after the last of the bombers had departed. The majority of the bomb-loads fell, as intended, north of the Elbe and west of the Alster, the expected 'creep-back' extending back for a distance of seven miles from the Aiming Point.

On 2 5 July, and the following day, the Americans sent in two daylight raids, which although not on the scale of Bomber Command's night effort were, in their own right, quite damaging. Bomber Command in turn split their effort with a decisive attack on Essen, This was an attack full of incident for the squadron and for two crews in particular. First, Sergeant S H Bates, rear-gunner to a Norwegian pilot, Sergeant Bjercke:

'I heard the bomb-aimer call "the doors won't open" and our pilot, being the dedicated man he was, decided to do another orbit and make a re-run over the target. You can imagine how I felt, and the rest of the crew. Here we were over one of the most heavily protected targets in Germany and we were going to do it all again. The flak was pretty strong and searchlights were pointing everywhere, but on the second run everything went perfectly and we flew home without further incident.'

The same cannot be said about Flight Lieutenant Shannon RAAF. Over Essen his Halifax (actually it was George Dunn's favourite aeroplane) shed a propeller and with a resounding crash the still spinning blades hurtled into the bomber's forward fuselage, gouging a sizeable hole. In the understandable confusion that followed as Shannon fought f or control of the plunging bomber, his mid-upper gunner, Sergeant Waterman, baled out. Waterman's colleagues were about to follow suit, when Shannon got the Halifax back on to an even keel. With the three remaining motors running smoothly,

Shannon headed for Holme. Hours later he successfully crashed-landed his severely crippled aircraft, which in the circumstances held together remarkably well.

The second visit to Hamburg far exceeded the successes of the first attack, This time the mainforce crossed the German coast and held an easterly course to a point northwest of Lubeck, then it turned southeast crossing over Lubeck, before wheeling to come at Hamburg from the direction of Ratzeburg. Five minutes before 1 am on Wednesday, 28 July the first of the PFF yellow Target Indicator bombs crashed into the streets below, roughly two miles east of the city centre. Less than an hour later the last of the mainforce cleared the area - all twenty-four squadron crews were through, but not without incident. Pilot Officer Bill Elder RNZAF had just completed his bombing-run and his mid-upper gunner, Sergeant Smith, was still busy feeding Window down the flare-chute when a night-fighter attacked their aircraft from below. Immediately Elder started to corkscrew, but it was not long before the Halifax was hit by several bursts of fire. One of the port engines was knocked out and his reargunner, Sergeant Heggarty called to say he had been wounded. Almost at the same moment a cannon shell exploded against the starboard side and Sergeant Smith fell dying, shot through the neck. Splinters from the explosion hit the mid-upper, slightly wounding the flight engineer, Sergeant Berry, who had relieved Smith just a few minutes earlier. Their plight was indeed desperate and to everyone it must have seemed just a matter of time before their attacker delivered a coup de grace. But the tenacious Elder was far from being finished. Continuing to twist and weave, despite being hampered in his efforts by a 'dead' engine, Elder gradually drew away from his assailant. With heartfelt relief the survivors realised the fighter was gone, the long flight home lay before them.

Eventually the cast coast was reached and Sergeant Clarke contacted Holme by wireless. Instructions were passed ordering them to proceed to an aerodrome at Shipdham. Bill Elder, fully aware of their still precarious position, wisely decided to bale out his crew. Four, including the second pilot, a Canadian, left without delay, but poor Heggarty was too incapacitated to operate his parachute and he was helped to the rest position by Sergeant Berry. Satisfied Heggarty was as secure as possible, Berry made his way back into the cockpit and announced he was going to stay and help with the landing. Summoning up all his last reserves of strength, Elder commenced his approach, the undercarriage left retracted on purpose:

'I did a right hand circuit and was committed to my landing, when the watch office gave permission for another aircraft to take-off for night circuits and bumps. However, the pilot saw us and did not take-off. We landed with a screech on our belly, overshot the runway and bashed the starboard engines out on some tree stumps. The three of us climbed out and soon a fire tender was on the scene and put out a fire which was beginning to burn. Poor Smithy was removed and the wounded were taken off to hospital, while I went to the watch office, remaining there until they had news of the four who had baled out.'

Bill Elder had not long to wait. All were safely down with only a few bumps and bruises to show for their terrifying experiences,

Two nights later twenty-three crews set out across the North Sea for yet another strike at Hamburg. Twenty-two returned; Sergeant Bjercke RNAF, who had made two runs over Essen on the 25th, was missing. Crippled by *flak*, Bjercke's Halifax was finished off by a night-fighter. From his crew five survived; none had been with the squadron for more than three weeks.

The final blow was launched on 2 August and for the first time the mainforce were routed in from the south. The weather could not have been worse. Violent electrical storms raged, rain, hail and strong winds buffeted the bombers as their crews gamely tried to hold their courses. Severe icing prevailed and this hazard alone caused many crews to abandon their task and turn for home. For those who did struggle through the dreadful weather conditions, pinpointing the Aiming Point proved near impossible. From the squadron seven crews claimed success. Captained by Lieutenant Gunner Hoverstad RNAF, and

Sergeants Row, Ward, Alf Kirkham, Ken Hewson, Troake and another Norwegian, Fridtjof Giortz, these seven were confident they reached the environs of Hamburg. For Hewson's rear gunner, Sergeant A! Atkinson, it had been the most agonising experience of his young life. The continuous flash of lightning had completely destroyed his night vision and now he sat petrified as sparks arced violently across his four Browning guns:

'Nothing on Cod's earth would have got me to touch those guns. All the time we were in the storm I was trying to screw myself into a ball so that no part of me touched the metal parts of the turret. Somehow I managed to get my feet underneath me and I just crouched on the little rubber pad that served as a cushion until we flew out of the storm. It was years later that I learnt about the bonding of aircraft in order to earth them.'

As well as having to cope with the weather, more than a few crews came up against night-fighters. Battling his way towards the burning city, Sergeant Troake was alerted to the presence of three Ju 88s on his port beam and flying parallel with the Halifax. Two of the trio turned towards his bomber, but as they drew near a flash of lightning lit the heavens with a blinding light destroying completely the night vision of both invader and defender alike. When at last the effects of the flash wore off the nightfighters had vanished.

Somewhere in the general area of Hamburg, Flight Lieutenant John Maze fought off two separate attacks. The first came from a Ju 88 that was spotted against the backcloth of a towering bank of cloud. The enemy fighter opened fire as Maze corkscrewed to port and its tracer passed harmlessly to starboard. Twenty minutes later a Fw190 was seen approaching from the port quarter, but clever evasive tactics by Maze and a discouraging burst of well aimed fire from Sergeant 'Rammy' Ramsden in the rearturret frustrated the enemy pilot's intentions.

Despite the shortcomings of the last operation, Harris had scored a resounding victory. Damage on an unprecedented scale had been achieved and much of Hamburg had been reduced to little more than smoke blackened ruins. Between the early hours of 25 July and the debacle of 2 August, over 40,000 men, women and children had been killed, the great majority of these dying in the firestorm that engulfed the densely populated Borgfelde and Hamm districts following the second Bomber Command attack. The stunned survivors had plenty to tell the teams of examiners sent to report on what remained of the port and shipbuilding facilities. Their findings could not have made light reading for the German hierarchy, still shaken from the recent devastating attacks on the Ruhr towns, At least Milch, then head of the *Luftwaffe,* was alarmed for he wrote:

'These attacks on Hamburg strike deep at our nation's morale. it we do not succeed in smashing these terror attacks by day[18] and by night very soon, then we must expect a very difficult situation to arise for Germany.'

Prophetic words in part for which, in Germany's case, there would be no solution. For Sir Arthur Harris the dream of forcing the enemy to surrender unconditionally through the sheer weight of bombardment from the air looked for awhile like being realised. in the remaining weeks of August and throughout the autumn, he maintained a broad spectrum of attacks, aimed specifically at the industrial heart of Germany.

---

18 Here Milch was referring to the American day-bombing offensive. On 18 August 1943, in the aftermath of Peenemunde, Milch committed suicide.

Italy was not entirely shelved from his plans, and shortly we will read of a successful raid delivered on Milan. But triumphant though Hamburg may have been, the Axis response was positive. Even as the last of the mainforce turned for home in the storm lashed hours of 3 August, the *Luftwaffe* had come part way towards counteracting the effectiveness of Window. A long and very bitter winter campaign in the skies over Northern Europe lay before the men of Bomber Command. Victory, scented at last, was still well into the future and for many quite beyond their wildest hopes:

'Somehow we managed to adjust to the situation and carry on in spite of the strain of seeing our friends and colleagues disappear, one after the other. We knew we had a job to do and we accepted the fact that we were 'playing for keeps' every time. We also knew the statistics and the odds for - or against - survival. I often think back and remember all those friends whose luck ran out too soon.'

Major John Stene RNAF - Pilot and Flight Commander A Flight.

'There were some very fine men in 76 Squadron and many of them died. it was rough in 1943 and one has to remember that the chances of finishing a tour were very remote, and what is more we did not really expect to. My flight engineer even carried his shaving kit and spare clothes, just in case we were unavoidably detained on the other side.' *Sergeant Alf Kirkbam - Pilot.*

'Most of us were very young and perhaps we were just not imaginative enough, or maybe one has a defensive mechanism which 'puts up the shutters' when one is in danger. Whatever the reason, I don't think that we as a crew ever consciously considered that 'we' would not return; others yes, but not us.'

Sergeant Laurie Brown - Flight Engineer.

Another flight engineer, Sergeant Maurice Manser who crewed with Alf Kirkham and who flew with his change of clothing, recalls:

'Throughout all our training no one ever explained what it was like on operations. We just did not know what to expect and after our first few trips I was both surprised and pleased to find how steady my nerves had become.'

The pairing of Maurice Manser with Alf Kirkham had a rather odd beginning. During training Maurice had 'lost' three pilots on familiarisation sorties as second pilots, and he was now resigned to a short life on operations. He admits he was most surprised to wake one morning and find Alf Kirkham had returned from his 'shake-down' trip, so deciding it was a good omen he announced he was going to stay with him.

But now, one final account in this section and again it is a flight engineer, Flight Sergeant Phil Tweedy DFM who flew his tour of operations with Erik Sandberg:

'It seemed that I went from the 'new boy' to the 'old sweat' in a very short time. I cannot say I was not afraid, for every operation could be the last, and somehow I never enjoyed the traditional operational meal which was usually bacon, egg and chips. Courage, I think, is the ability to suppress fear; some have it, others don't, and some are not afraid to say they are not courageous.'

Some were surviving by the narrowest of margins. Sergeant Troake and John Maze both had recent memories of close encounters on the Hamburg raids, but on Nuremburg and Milan respectively, each came within an ace of destruction. Sergeant Troake was nearing Saarbrucken on the outward leg to Nuremberg on 10 August, when cannon-fire raked across his Halifax. Rapid, and effective, evasive flying by Troake prevented the enemy pilot from capitalising on this surprise attack, but not before the life ebbed from his second pilot, Sergeant Whittlesea. Displaying commendable fortitude Troake regained his heading and continued on to Nuremburg. Wisely, he had decided that their survival lay in remaining with the mainstream of attack, rather than face the inherent dangers of an isolated return.

Tracer coming up from below his port quarter was John Maze's first indication of attack. in the next second a cannon-shell blew a hole in the rear fuselage, wrecking the hydraulic lines to the rear turret and wounding its occupant 'Rammy' Ramsden in the legs. The force of the explosion blew the tail trimmers away, destroyed the intercom and the emergency call lights, leaving maze' deaf' to any evasive instructions. His only course of action was to corkscrew and trust his attacker would not be skilled enough to follow him through these manoeuvres. For several anxious minutes John Maze continued to throw his bomber through the sky, until he was satisfied the fighter was no longer with them. Without the aid of the trimmers, the return flight to an emergency landing at Thorney Island was most difficult. Here, his second pilot Sergeant Waitt received treatment for a painful eye injury, while to his surprise John Maze was torn off a dreadful strip by the local Air Traffic Control officer who was upset that his Halifax had arrived in the middle of local night-flying practice. Maze, had in fact, landed here in error for nearby Ford, but in the circumstances he was just thankful to be down in one piece.

This last action gives rise to an interesting observation. From the wording of the intelligence report, it seems just possible that John Maze had been attacked by a fighter fitted with upward firing cannons, set in the fuselage aft of the pilot's cockpit. If this was the fact, and indeed it is now common knowledge that such devices were used to good effect in 1944, then it is little wonder that the loss rate in Bomber Command crept steadily upwards throughout the winter of 1943/44, for this weapon was near impossible for the bomber crew to combat effectively.

The raid on Milan had been a huge success. Not only were rail communications badly disrupted, but the Breda steel and locomotive plants were badly damaged. Two crews, however, were missing. Pilot Officer McCann, a most experienced captain flying his twentieth sortie, was shot down near Bemay in northern France, and there was no news either of Leif Hulthin. The sad procedure of informing next-of-kin was carded out, and two days later the father of one of Hulthin's crew arrived at Holme to pick up his son's personal belongings. The occasion was difficult for all concerned, but for once anguish gave way to joy when it was announced Leif Hulthin's aircraft was in the circuit. For the father it must have been like waking from a terrible dream.

It transpired that within minutes of bombing Milan the aircraft's oxygen supply failed, rendering a return over the Alps quite impossible. Undeterred, Hulthin turned about and flew south, his navigator Sergeant Murfitt working on a new course that eventually took them to Protville, an airfield in Algeria. Here the entire crew were decked out in tropical kit and dispatched for home via Gibraltar laden with oranges and other tropical fruits not seen for many a year in war-gripped England.

Five nights after Milan, Harris dispatched a force of 597 heavy bombers to bomb rocket installations at Peenemunde, Hitler's secret weapons establishment on the island of Usedom in the Baltic. Activities on the remote barren island sixty miles northwest of Stettin had first attracted the attention of Allied intelligence in December 1942. By the following April this interest had intensified to the point where it was felt that the Prime Minister, Winston Churchill and his War Cabinet should be alerted. Further evidence provided by two photographic reconnaissance sorties flown in June 1943 clearly revealed the advanced stage of testing reached by the enemy scientists and technicians. it was assessed that if counter measures were not taken, and quickly, the enemy would soon be in a position to unleash destruction on a scale of unprecedented fury upon the towns and cities of Great Britain. Even more alarming, our defensive system as it stood would not be able to stop such an attack, for Hitler would not be sending conventional manned bombers, but rockets packed '.with high-explosives and travelling faster than sound. To illustrate the magnitude of what was facing the populace of our island home, a conclusion reached by our intelligence was that just one of these devices failing on a built-up area could cause up to 4,000 casualties. Bearing in mind that the Hamburg operation had involved the command in the sending of over 3,000 sorties, and the dropping of over 8,300 tons of bombs, then it is little wonder Allied intelligence was extremely worried by events taking place on Peenemunde. The pendulum of war, swinging favourably for the Allies in the late summer of 1943, now looked like being dramatically reversed. The importance of this target was, in due course, forcibly brought home to the twenty squadron crews gathered at the briefing given on the 17 August.

'We were advised that if the target, which none of us had heard of before, was not destroyed we would 'go back again and again, regardless of losses'. That is a verbatim quote indelibly imprinted in my memory. '*Flying Officer Reg McCadden - Navigator.*

Such words could have left little doubt in the minds of those present, Peenemunde was going to be no easy task. Much of the route lay over the open sea and for several dangerous hours the mainforce would be operating well within the range of the German night-fighter units guarding the Baltic approaches.

Mindful of such a situation the planners included in the overall structure of the attack a diversionary raid by eight Mosquito light bombers on Berlin.

This, in the event, proved highly successful, for the German commander of the 1st Fighter Division incorrectly assessed that this was where the command's main objective lay and he marshalled his forces accordingly. it has been reported that a quite farcical situation developed over Berlin. The flak gunners, hearing the concentrated sound of many engines converging over the capital, opened fire and continued to do so with some accuracy, despite their night-fighter colleagues loosing off the colours of the day, Eventually after milling around, dodging the *flak* and no doubt cursing the ineptness of their ground controllers, the night-fighter crews realised that the main attack was going in far to the north. By this time the majority were low on fuel, but it was still a considerable number that sped towards the coast where they engaged the last waves of bombers.

In view of this Ken Hewson, now commissioned, was singularly unlucky to be attacked from the air. Even more unfortunate is that it seems very likely that his adversary was another bomber. Substantial damage was inflicted on the nose of his aircraft and Ken Parry, his navigator, received upper arm and shoulder wounds of such severity that he never flew operationally again.

But in general the squadron had an easy passage. Sergeant Griffiths, Alf Kirkham and Ken Hewson - bloodied - all bombed at seventeen minutes past midnight, Sergeant Eric Wright, Warrant Officer Ken Myers and Flight Lieutenants Sanderson and Hodson followed a minute later and the rest were well clear by the time Flight Sergeant Holmes bombed at exactly half-past the hour. Alf Kirkham writes:

'Our trip was fairly uneventful, the usual searchlights and flak, but little fighter activity. Things changed, however, once we reached the target. I had never seen so many aircraft over a target at one time and we had great difficulty dropping our bombload. The *flak* was accurate, but it was nothing compared to targets like Essen.' Although Alf Kirkham experienced some problems on his bombing-run, the squadron records clearly show that everyone was through the target area inside of fourteen minutes. Markers were plentiful, and the PFF had put down spot fires on the tiny island of Roden, a few miles to the north of Peenemunde, as an aid for the timing of bombing-runs. Flight Lieutenant Ted Strange was flying with Eric Wright:

'Just as the markers went down I came up from my plotting table to stand by Eric as we bombed. In the moonlight I could quite clearly see people on the ground running for the shelters.'

In the clear moonlight conditions, the various Aiming Points were soon identified and well saturated with high explosive bombs. Numerous buildings received direct hits and debris from these flew high into the air. Towards the end of the attack smoke and dust practically obscured the Target Indicators and the official intelligence report[19] suggests that the defenders set off a smoke-screen in order to protect Peenemunde's secret installations. By this time the last of the squadron aircraft had departed and our final account comes from Flight Lieutenant 'Tam' Readhead, the squadron's Flight engineering leader:

'The target area was a mass of flames as we set course for our return trip. There was a brilliant glow in the sky which we could see for a long, long time. Our collective opinion was, it must have been a 'wizard prang'.

For 'Tam' Readhead, it was the last operation of his first tour. He had been with the squadron for a year, flying the majority of his sorties with Al Moir. Now, with a well deserved Distinguished Flying Cross to his credit, 'Tam' was rested. In due course he would fly a second tour of operations, this time with 462 Squadron, which, it will be remembered, was created partially from 76 Squadron aircrew in 1942.

It was estimated that the German rocketry programme at Peenemunde had been delayed by up to two months. This delay would prove just long enough for the Allies, though Bomber Command's battles against the 'V' weapons were not yet over as we shall discover in the summer of 1944.

An attempt on 22 August to hit the chemical works at Leverkusen on the north bank of the Rhine above Cologne did not meet with any tangible success. Thick banks of cloud hung near motionless over the target and crews report the PFF skymarkers as being 'barely discernible'. This was not the case the following night when over 700 heavy bombers pounded Berlin. Few crews experienced any problems on the outward leg. Turning points were well marked and the mainforce arrived over the capital in good order. 'This high concentration did give rise to one or two tense moments:

'During the bombing-run we nearly collided with another Halifax. I was listening to my bomb-aimer giving me 'steady, steady' when out of the corner of my eye I saw a large shadow closing in on us from the right. I pulled the stick back and saw the Halifax disappear underneath me. My bomb-aimer lost his voice for a few seconds and when he got it back it was at least one octave higher. He told me later 'Christ, I could have touched it'. *Second Lieutenant Fridtjof Giortz RNAF - Pilot.*

Moments later Fridtjof Giortz completed his attack. By this time fires over a large area of the capital were taking a hold and the defences were co-ordinating. The *flak* was extremely hostile, but by far the greatest fear was the possibility of encountering night-fighters. Giortz,himself, saw two in the light of searchlights, but was not attacked. Neither were the remainder of the squadron seriously troubled and for some crews their worst moments were yet to come. While the mainforce was recrossing the North Sea the weather was beginning to turn sour over the Yorkshire Wolds. Bill Elder RNZAF was amongst the first to reach Holme:

'On our arrival at Base the wind was blowing across the runway and I could not line the aircraft up for landing. I decided to overshoot, but left it too late and I felt something hit from underneath. Four propellers make a very good job of cutting a large hawthorn hedge, a better job than they would have made of a brick house which we just missed.'

For Pilot Officer Elder this was his second eventful landing in a month, and it provided a rather dramatic end to his first tour of operations.

Following the months second visit to Nuremburg, thirteen crews participated in an attack on Mönchengladbach, a town lying on the outskirts of the Ruhr west of the Rhine. There should have been

19   Public Record Office AIR 24/258.

fifteen squadron aircraft, but Flight Lieutenant Lemmon's Halifax was wrecked in a spectacular take-off accident. While travelling at high speed a tyre burst causing the bomber to veer sharply off the runway. The undercarriage promptly collapsed and soon flames were coming from the wings where ruptured petrol tanks had ignited. Scenes reminiscent of Leif Hulthin's crash a few weeks previously were re-enacted and eventually, with a tremendous roar, Lemmon's bomb-load exploded, a shaken crew viewing the proceedings from afar. Meanwhile, Flight Sergeant Holmes was anxiously waiting to land, his Halifax being damaged by the pilot's escape hatch blowing-out and striking a severe blow to one of the twin-rudders. Lemmon's accident put paid to his immediate plans and with some difficulty Holmes diverted to Riccall. The remainder continued completely unaware of the high drama affecting their squadron colleagues.

Bombing conditions were far from ideal. A persistent layer of thick cloud covered the Ruhr, and the mainforce was further hampered by the lack of skymarkers. A high percentage released their bomb-loads on an estimated time over Munchengladbach and it is very doubtful in the circumstances if any major damage was achieved. The *Luftwaffe,* however, were up in some numbers. Alf Kirkham's Halifax was intercepted:

'Without any warning we were attacked by two fighters and we were hit by cannon shells and tracer immediately. My navigator was badly wounded, a bullet struck me in the right leg, the starboard inner engine was knocked out, the intercom failed completely and to cap it all, we caught fire.'

This initial attack left a lasting impression on his flight engineer, Maurice Manser:

'There was a sound just like cardboard being ripped. I looked down and saw a line of holes crossing the fuselage floor. There was, at this stage, no sign of a fire, so I popped my head up into the astrodome to see if I could spot our attacker.'

It should be explained that a fire had in fact broken out in the area of the bomb-bay and Alf Kirkham was in very serious trouble. The events that will now be described Illustrate well the unstinting courage of a crew facing death, yet determined to survive.

Despite his wound Kirkham automatically went into the well practised corkscrew manoeuvre. Less than a minute later one of their attackers, a Ju 88, was spotted by the mid-upper gunner, Sergeant Whitter. The enemy fighter was climbing hard to port in readiness for a diving attack and as it banked so Whitter opened fire. For several seconds both fighter and bomber exchanged a fusillade of shots, Whitter's fellow gunner Sergeant John Dennis having brought his rear-turret guns into action. Bravely the enemy pilot continued to close through a hail of machine-gun fire, but at the last moment he was forced to break off in a steep turn to starboard. As he did so, John Dennis raked his undersurfaces with a sustained burst and the Junkers was last seen dropping away in a high speed spiral dive, trailing black smoke from both engines. But there was scant respite. Tracer coming from ahead warned Kirkham the second fighter was making its play, and a second later the unmistakable shape of a Bf 110 swept low over the bomber. From his mid-upper position Whitter had barely time to squeeze off one burst before the fighter came racing in off a tight turn. Dennis, too, was soon active and together the two gunners drove off this second attacker. The battle to survive had lasted for ten minutes; at last the crew could take stock of their situation.

Throughout the shambles of the fuselage the stink of cordite caught at heaving lungs. Flames were flickering through a sizeable hole in the floor of the centre section, while forward in the nose compartment a partially blinded Sergeant Harry Foster continued to work at his navigation charts, blood streaming from serious facial injuries. His awful plight was realised by Flight Sergeant Wicks who had left his radio in search of a fire extinguisher. Aided by the bomb-aimer, Sergeant Ward, Wicks got the wounded navigator into the rest position and then gingerly set off down the fuselage to check on the two gunners.

'Wires were hanging down all over the place. There was a jagged rent in the floor, almost large enough to fall through and where the main fuselage door should have been were three large holes. I reached the rear turret door and was relieved after much banging and shouting to find the gunner unhurt. On the way back I stopped by the mid-upper gunner. A bullet had torn a piece from one of his socks, but he seemed cheerful enough and gave me a thumbs up. After reporting to the skipper I returned to my set, wound out the spare aerial and spent the next hour sending out coded situation report4;.'

Several hours later Flight Sergeant Kirkham, weakened by loss of blood, crash-landed his Halifax on the small airfield of Bradwell Bay in Essex. Medical aid, thankfully, was soon forthcoming.

From this operation Squadron Leader Stuart failed to return. It is now known that within a few minutes of leaving the target area he was attacked by a pair of fighters and sent down out of control to crash on the main road between Roermond and Weert, just inside the border with Holland. From the falling bomber only Flying Officer William's, the bomb-aimer and Sergeant Doe, the wireless operator managed to escape.

Apart from Kirkham down at Bradwell Bay, the remainder were diverted to Riccall as the remains of Flight Lieutenant Lemmon's aircraft still lay scattered along Hohne's runways. This diversion, and subsequent late recovery to Base left very little time for servicing and preparation for the forthcoming raid that same evening. Consequently eight crews from the sixteen dispatched, turned back from Berlin. No one could be blamed, time was of the essence and on this occasion this vital factor ran out on the hard pressed groundcrews.

From those that did get through to the German capital, it was yet another night of hard fought running battles with the defending night-fighters, heightened by the successful introduction of a new defensive ploy. Satisfied that the mainforce were heading for Berlin, selected night-fighter crews, already positioned high above the city, were instructed to drop flare clusters marking the course of the approaching bomber stream. The execution of this plan was highly successful and as the Halifax and Lancaster crews turned onto their bombing-runs, the night sky was transformed into 'day' by hundreds of drifting flares.

Nearing the target Flying Officer Jimmy Steele spotted a single-engined fighter coming at his Halifax from the port beam. He shouted to his gunners that he was going to corkscrew, and the crew prepared to meet their attacker. Two more fighters, identified as Fw 190s, were seen by the rear gunner, Sergeant Harry Welch RCAF, climbing from the port and starboard quarters. Before either could open fire Welch gave the nearest fighter a good drubbing, but deftly the enemy pilot broke away, only to form up on his companion and continue to close from dead astern. Again the vibrating chatter of machine-gun fire was felt throughout the bomber, followed by a jubilant yell from Welch to say that he had hit the leading fighter. Although a victory could not be claimed, neither enemy pilot seemed inclined to continue.

Over the heart of Berlin squadron crews fought at least two sharp engagements. Flying Officer William's gunners drove off a Bf 110, while John Maze found himself the centre of attraction for the fifth time in less than a fortnight. His would-be assailant was a lone Bf 109 which attacked from the port quarter. Sergeant Bernard, firing from his rear turret, caused the fighter to break upwards and thus presented the squadron's gunnery leader, Flight Lieutenant Ashton with a near perfect target. Gratefully Ashton took his opportunity and sent the fighter plunging earthwards, seemingly out of control. For the second time in succession all squadron crews returned safely from Berlin, though overall the two attacks had cost the command 104 crews.

September opened quietly with a 'Gardening' operation on the 3rd, followed two nights later by a searing attack on the chemical and armament industries of Mannheim. Numerous fighter flares drifted into the bomber-stream as nearly 600 aircraft forged deep into Germany. Sergeant Thorp was attacked and later he made an emergency landing at Ford in Sussex where his rear-gunner Sergeant Marvin was taken to hospital with wounds to both legs and hands. Of Pilot Officer Schmidt RNZAF nothing further was heard and it has since been established that his Halifax fell victim to a night-fighter near Jagersburg, northeast of Saarbrucken. Despite losing thirty-four crews, Harris had given Mannheim a severe pounding. Well over 1,500 tons of high explosives had blasted parts of the city into rubble and the ensuing inferno sent up a pall of smoke that hung for almost two days, while the brigades worked to bring the fires under control.

On 6 September Leif Hulthin was attacked twice in quick succession as he ran towards Munich. His first assailant, who was showing a bright light, was clinically dispatched by some good shooting from his rear-gunner, Flight Sergeant Pringle, a sharp eyed Australian. The second fighter was sighted by Pringle's fellow gunner, Sergeant Brawn and his timely warning prevented the second attacker from avenging his colleague.

Sergeant Waitt's gunners also picked up a fighter displaying a light from its nose, but after one ineffective attempt to engage the speeding Halifax, the enemy pilot broke away and disappeared into the mantle of some nearby clouds.

In the middle of the month the squadron was involved in two attacks away from the German mainland. The first, on the 15th, was a successful strike against the Dunlop tyre works at Montlucon, some forty-five miles to the northwest of Vichy in France. This quite stunning blow followed hard on the heels of an American raid by Fortresses early that day in the Paris area, and was in the words of the official communiqué part of a new Anglo-American heavy bomber offensive'. The close concentration of the Montlucon bomber-stream and the consequences of the bombing was not lost on the late Sergeant Jeff Kirby, flight engineer to Jimmy Steele. On return he wrote in his diary:

'A Halifax almost crashed on top of us on the way out. Boy, what a shaky-do, but owing to the skipper's presence of mind we are alive to tell the tale. Over the target we saw huge columns of black smoke rising to 8,000 feet as we left.'

The second raid was aimed at further disrupting enemy communications with Italy through the Mount Cenis tunnel in southeastern France. in the event the weather en route was dreadful. Severe icing was encountered on the outward leg and neither this, nor the attack by 5 Group aimed at the Antlieor Viaduct carrying the coastal railway into northern Italy, between St. Raphael and Cannes, was successful. Nonetheless, some good fires were started at the Modane marshalling yards and for the Allied armies waging a relentless battle against stiffening enemy resistance in central Italy, this was welcome news.

Losses on these two French targets were light, though Jimmy Steele's crew witnessed the destruction of two Halifaxes as the mainforce neared the French coast on return from Modane. The first bomber was seen burning furiously on the port bow, while to starboard a second Halifax was locked in a fierce running battle with a single engined fighter. With a feeling of utter helplessness Steele's crew watched the fighter snapping away at the bomber, until at last a sheet of flame flared into the slipstream and with its gunners still firing the doomed Halifax dropped away out of control.

Fully awake to the dangers close at hand, Steele's gunners were ready when a fighter came in from astern. For a second or two Harry Welch RCAF was blinded by a light coming from near the fighter's spinner, but his fire was sufficiently accurate to prevent the enemy pilot from gaining any advantage. But now danger threatened from the port quarter, for a second fighter was closing unseen. it was to their good fortune that its fire was wildly inaccurate and as it crossed overhead, both turrets replied to deadly effect and the enemy aircraft was last seen on fire, spinning earthwards.

This same crew successfully beat off a menacing approach from a Ju 88 while visiting Hannover on 22 September. Here the bombing was well concentrated and fires were left burning over a wide area, However, reconnaissance would later prove these were mainly well to the southeast of the Aiming Point, though the Döhren and Wölfei districts had suffered very substantial damage. Two squadron crews, captained by Squadron Leader Turner and Sergeant Birger Fjaervoll RNAF were included in the twenty-five reported missing. Flying with Birger Fjaervoll was John Dennis who, it will be recalled, experienced a hazardous return from Munchengladbach with Alf Kirkham just a few weeks previously. In his wildest dreams John Dennis could not have foreseen the traumatic events that were destined to overtake him that night:

'We were attacked just after leaving the target. The starboard wing was set on fire and the intercom was put out of action. I had no idea what was happening up front, but as the flames got worse and I could make no contact with the others, I decided to bale out.

'I climbed down from my turret and made my way aft to the escape hatch and jettisoned this ready to jump. There was no sign of the rear-gunner, so I banged on the rear-turret doors and tried to open them, and as I was doing this the aircraft went into a dive, throwing me on to my back.'

For the next few terrible minutes John Dennis lay pinned to the fuselage floor, the gravitational forces preventing him from making any movement. Then, with a sickening crash, the Halifax struck the ground. Possibly in those last few seconds before the final impact the bomber either flattened out slightly, or struck some trees. The results were nonetheless devastating.

'I was thrown from near the rear-turret to the mid-upper position. My left knee hit the step near the turret and my parachute struck the main framework. Undoubtedly this helped cushion the blow. I was conscious of a fire burning ahead of me and I struggled madly to get out through a hole in the fuselage, but for the life of me I could not move. Then I passed out and when I regained consciousness I was lying half inside and half outside the fuselage. The fire had burnt itself out and all I wanted was a drink of water. There were some distinctly unfriendly looking chaps looking down at me wearing uniforms. I kept asking for water and one soldier replied 'Ja, Ja, wasser'. This was the extent of my first conversation with anyone from the Third Reich.' Scattered around were the burnt remains of the Halifax. Gently the soldiers lifted the grievously injured airman from the wreckage and John Dennis was soon on his way to a hospital at Vechta. Here the German surgeons fought for hours to save young Dennis's life. The crash had broken his back in four places and his left femur was badly fractured. For six months he lay encased in a plaster cast from his waist downwards to his left ankle. Throughout this time the nuns who nursed him attended to his every need, and by the time he was declared fit enough to be moved to Stalag Luft VI at Heyderkrug, John Dennis was able to converse quite fluently with them and his elderly guard, Joseph[20].

But what was the fate of his companions? Seconds before the Halifax went into its terminal dive, Sergeant George Old managed to jettison the escape hatch beneath his navigator's position and jump to safety. The remainder were either dead, or like Sergeant Dennis trapped by the gravitational force. Three

---

20   In 1955 John Dennis, accompanied by his parents, wife and youngest son returned to Vechta where over a bottle of Schnapps a quite moving reunion took place. The surgeon who saved his life in 1943 had since died, but his son now worked at the same hospital and he quickly arranged a tour of the wards, reintroducing John Dennis to Sisters Lutilla and Valginda, responsible for lavishing such care on one who was once their 'enemy'.

bodies were never found, such was the extent and savagery of the fire that followed the crash.

Further stiff opposition was met on the second attack against this medieval town. John Stene RNAF reported seeing an aircraft going down out of control near Hannover and eight minutes after bombing Flight Lieutenant Hodgson's crew were witnesses to a similar scene. The night sky in the immediate vicinity of the target presented an awesome sight. Fighter flares hung loosely in clusters throwing an eerie light across the heavens. The frequent splash of tracer marked the battles between attacker and defender as wave after wave of bombers tracked with determination over the multi-coloured markers.

At Holme the following morning the personal effects of two crews were collected. On the operations board showing the tally of completed sorties by each crew, the white chalked names of Pilot Officer Griffiths and Pilot Officer Hickman were removed in a few deft sweeps of a duster. Hickman had completed twenty-eight operations, his companion, Griffiths, twenty-one. Pilot Officer Hickman had been cut down within days of reaching the magical thirty trips and 'screening'; Griffiths would, had he lived, have been through in a little over a month.

On a happier note came the news that Flight Lieutenants John Maze and Sanderson were deemed to have completed their tours. For Maze a posting to headquarters at High Wycombe, while for Sanderson the prospect of instructing the command's young hopefuls at 18 Operational Training Unit.

The dominant feature of October 1943 centres around just four major attacks. Of these two were directed against the manufacturing town and key railway centre of Kassel, while Frankfurt on the 4th and a further visit to Hannover on the 8th completed the agenda. The raids on Kassel were particularly punishing. The vast Henschel works sited at Mittelfeld in the northwest outskirts, Rothenditmold on the western edge of the city and Werke Kassel in the town centre all received considerable fire damage. These plants were responsible for a wide range of war production, the principal being the construction of locomotives, Tiger tanks, anti-tank guns and spares for an assortment of truck designs. To maintain the necessary impetus demanded, thousands of forced-labour workers were billeted in Kassel and it was the mass destruction of their living quarters that caused the German authorities very severe post-raid production problems.

The opening raid was sent on the 3rd, Wing Commander Don Smith leading the squadron contingent of twenty crews. All ran the gauntlet of concentrated nightfighter activity. Over Kassel the weather was clear and Don Smith duly recorded bombing a cluster of green markers surrounded by a large area of fire. At this stage the worst fires were taking a hold in the outlying suburbs. The Fiesler Aircraft works at Bettenhausen was hit repeatedly and it was later estimated that some fifty-five Fw 190 fighters were lost on the production lines. In simple terms this represented about four weeks supply to the *Luftwaffe*.

The cost to the squadron was high. Four crews failed to return, the highest single operation loss since the reformation of the squadron in 1941, and the worst since last April when three crews were lost attacking Pilsen. In the confusion of battle it is difficult to assess accurately the order in which aircraft were lost, but it is believed Flying Officer Wilson, an Australian, was the first to fall, coming down over Vehne Moor eighteen kilometres southwest of Oldenburg. Two survived, including Wilson, but it is likely he was severely injured for he died in captivity some six weeks later.

Pilot Officer Thorp crashed at Lenstrup near Detmold, while at Moorhausen the grim discovery of six bodies marked the last landing for Flight Sergeant Waitt. The fourth bomber down was piloted by a Norwegian, Second Lieutenant Niels Eckhoff. Eckhoff had been forced to turn back when fifty miles short of Kassel. A blow of considerable force had torn a large hole in the metal cladding of the forward fuselage, through which had been sucked the bomb-aimer, Bob Coupe, and most of Sigmund Meieran's navigating equipment. Bombs were jettisoned and height lost in order to maintain flying speed. For the next forty-five minutes Eckhoff flew westward relatively untroubled, the North Star steady on his starboard wingtip. Sigmund Meieran takes up the story as the crippled Halifax approached Texel on the Dutch coast:

'The rear-gunner called 'fighter, fighter' and in that same second the flight engineer, who was standing next to me, yelled out in pain from being hit in his left leg. The entire rear section of the aircraft was ablaze. Hayes, despite the wound to his leg, and I grabbed some fire extinguishers and attempted to fight the fire, but it was to no avail. All extinguishing fluid gone, I turned around and saw the pilot directing me to get out. All the others had by then abandoned the aircraft and in the rush the flight engineer had taken my parachute. However, it did not take me long to find his and a few minutes later I landed in the sea.'

Fortunately for Meieran the wind was blowing off the sea and during the next half hour he was propelled like a small sailing dinghy across the water and up on to a sandy beach. The combat had driven their bomber northwards and now the shattered remains lay on a sandbank 400 yards east of Terschelling. Sigmund Meieran was captured twenty-four hours later trying to steal a rubber dinghy and soon he leant four others from the crew were alive.

Bob Coupe survived being catapulted out over the German mainland, ending up in hospital and sharing a room with an injured German night-fighter pilot who told him he had been in collision with a four engined bomber near Kassel. Coupe is convinced it was their Halifax that the German pilot had collided with.

Jens Skjelanger, the Norwegian wireless operator, was unhurt, as was Sergeant Coster the mid-upper gunner. Poor Hayes, who had tumbled from the blazing bomber wearing the wrong parachute, died from his injuries at Leeuwarden on the 6th, while Flying Officer Sherman never left the aircraft. Niels Eckhoff did, but his body was discovered dreadfully broken in a farm field, In Meieran's opinion, for he had the sorrowful task of helping to remove his skipper's remains, Eckhoff made his exit through the top escape hatch and in doing so struck either the mid-upper turret, or the tail assemble.

The second assault took place on the 22nd when despite very severe icing conditions, destruction was on even greater scale. The vast weight of explosives fell into an area covering seventeen square miles and encompassing the town centre. Fire damage was on a massive scale, especially at the Henschel works in the heart of the city. The marshalling yards did not escape. Administrative buildings, workshops and locomotive sheds were all hit and seriously damaged from the rain of incendiaries. Explosions from the 900 tons, or more, of high explosive bombs tore the close knit rail tracks asunder, cratering roads, smashing through gas and electricity mains and fracturing numerous water pipes, thus reducing the effectiveness of the town's fire-fighting force. The bewildered inhabitants could be in no doubt as to the purpose behind these crushing raids - total destruction.

Missing from this attack was Leif Hulthin. His loss was very hard felt throughout the squadron. Since his horrific take-off crash in July, he had flown on eighteen major attacks and was just past the half way point in his tour. Although no one survived the crash in a field near the village of Bahne northwest of Kassel, their deaths had a most profound effect on a young German schoolgirl who was one of the first to reach the burning bomber. Hearing the sound of the crash, she had rushed to the scene and was confronted by a most terrible sight. The Halifax had broken up on impact, throwing the bodies of the crew in all directions. Now they lay contorted on the broken and furrowed earth, three with their clothing still alight. One, the name is not known to her, was just barely alive, but he died in her presence. Little wonder such traumatic events are locked in her mind to this day. But it is the words of Sergeant Bill Freeman who flew with Leif Hulthin that close this account:

'I have nothing but admiration for all the members of my crew. The skipper always insisted on hitting the target and on one occasion he made three orbits of the target to make sure our bombs fell in the correct place. it was for me a very proud moment when in 1945 1 met his sister and father in Oslo.'

Winter was now fast approaching. Throughout the command morale was high for since the turn of the year the bombing campaign had increased tenfold. Across the breadth of Nazi Germany the lash from this mighty force was being keenly felt. No longer were the land battles going in favour of the Wehrmacht. On the bleak eastern front the prospect of a second Russian winter must have been a daunting thought for the German soldier. Along the spine of Italy fierce fighting still waged, but with each passing day the Allied armies were inching forward, ever forward. Increasing acts of sabotage from the resistance groups in the occupied countries continued to tie down large numbers of troops, so preventing their deployment to the battle fronts, and here it cannot be stated too strongly that Bomber Command's continual incursions over the major cities of the Third Reich was playing a major part in frustrating the German High Command's ambitions. The *Luftwaffe* was hard pressed to meet its commitments - for the German infantryman complaining bitterly of lack of air support, it was but cold comfort to be told his airforce comrades were locked in almost daily combat over the Fatherland. The halcyon days of 1939/40 had vanished for ever.

Dull, misty weather heralded the start of November 1943. At Holme there were no operations until the 3rd, when crews were briefed for an evening attack on Dusseldorf. For Sergeant Fred Hall, a navigator, the day had started quite normally:

'In the morning I met the rest of the crew at the Met lecture, after which I went out to our new aircraft and made my usual inspection. From there I went back to the Navigation Section to prepare maps and charts as we had been told we were on operations that night. The rest of the lads went about their business and after an early lunch, I returned to the billet to change into my flying clothes. There were no signs of the rest of the crew, so I presumed they had taken the aircraft up on a local air-test. It was a reasonably pleasant day, but from a flying aspect the weather was not so good. A thickish haze persisted, mixed with several areas of very low cloud and I was aware that all the aircraft seemed to be having difficulty in landing. However, I attended the navigators briefing and I can remember thinking Dusseldorf would be our first really short trip. Such thoughts were still running through my mind when I went to collect my parachute and was told my crew had crashed.'

It transpired that his pilot, Flight Lieutenant Jimmy Steele, had, as assumed by Fred Hall, taken off on a local flight. No doubt, bearing in mind he would not be flying far from the Base area, he decided to leave his navigator working on his charts, but he did take a young lady scientist, Miss Dorothy Robson B.Sc. Miss Robson was a familiar figure at Bomber Command stations, her work in the Instrument and Photographic Department at Farnborough necessitating her frequent trips to the bomber bases. By late 1943, Dorothy Robson was acknowledged to be a leading expert in the functions of the Mk XIV bomb-sight [21] and such was her enthusiasm and awareness in making certain the equipment was correctly installed, she often flew on air-tests checking the bomb-sight in operational aircraft. There can be no

<hr>

21   Designed by Professor P M S Blackett and Dr. Braddick.

doubt that she was so engaged during the late morning of the 3rd when in hazy weather Jimmy Steele took-off from Holme for a local air-test. No one will ever know for certain what went wrong during the flight, but around midday reports reached the airfield that a Halifax was down near Enthorpe, northeast of Market Weighton. Rescue services were soon at the crash-site, though there was little hope for any of the crew. Three had been killed outright, Flight Sergeant Roy Brawn RAAF the mid-upper gunner was pronounced dead within minutes of his admission to hospital, while Jimmy Steele and Flight Sergeant Harry Welch RCAF died the following day. Alive when lifted gently from the shattered remains, the vivacious Miss Robson, who was just twenty-three years of age, lived until the 5th. Her wish, expressed a few weeks before in a talk with her father, that her ashes should be scattered from the air was reverently complied with.

Against this background of sadness, twenty crews commenced taking-off in the early evening. Operations were under way. Two hours later Flight Lieutenant Dennis Hornsey was approaching Dusseldorf. Already he had taken evasive action crossing the Dutch coast near Texel.

'We were now in a quiet stretch, outwardly. To left and right cones of searchlights were up over two large towns where diversionary raids might be going on, or perhaps where a bomber had strayed off track. We were entering 'Bomb Alley'. Dark beneath us lay Belgium. This was a zone of great fighter activity.'

Indeed it was, for seconds later cannon-shells from Leutnant Otto Fries's nightfighter ripped into his port wing. The navigator, Sergeant Ron Glover explains what happened during the next thirty seconds or so:

'The first I knew of trouble was the feeling that the wing had run into something resembling a brick wall. I called up on the intercom for information, but was told to wait while contact was made with our two gunners.'

A pungent smell from cordite fumes was soon followed by the stench of smoke. Hornsey had by this time forced open the portside cockpit window and could clearly see the ominous flames taking a hold around the wing root. His attempt to blow the flames out by diving the Halifax met with no success and the order to bale out was quickly given. Ron Glover again:

'I set the Gravenor switch to blow up the 'GEE' set on impact and put the code books inside my battledress blouse. Before leaving I told the wireless operator what action he should take if the pilot rescinded the order after my departure, and promptly dropped through the escape hatch. My intention was to do a delayed fall as we had been flying at about 20,000 feet. Soon I was in cloud, where it was icy cold and I lost all sense of time. Pulling at the ripcord of my parachute I felt a tremendous tug as the canopy deployed. The rest of my descent was quite alarming. I felt a rush of air which I think was caused by bombs being jettisoned and then a flare illuminated quite near to me. Thinking I might be shot at, I started to climb up the cords towards the canopy. This caused the air to spill out and the flare soon disappeared. My parachute now started to oscillate through 180 degrees and I began to swing back and forth. I was very glad when this swaying reduced, but then I realised I was coming down right over a crashed aircraft which was in flames. By giving further tugs at the cords I drifted away from the fire and landed in a clearing of some woods.'

And here for the moment we will divert our attention to the second squadron crew destined not to return to Holme. Flight Lieutenant David Hicks RCAF had taken off without difficulty and was soon in the stream of bombers climbing sluggishly over the North Sea. Shortly after crossing the coast of Holland the freezing cold began to affect the intercom speech between Hicks and his rear-gunner Sergeant Davis. A lesser man than Hicks would have been tempted to turn for home, but instead he chose to send his flight engineer, Sergeant Ray Clough, aft with instructions to change helmets. Clutching two portable oxygen bottles to his chest, Clough groped his way to the rear, but the exchange of masks proved no easy task and while trying to regain his flight engineer's position, Ray Clough collapsed. His plight was quickly realised by the bombaimer, but he too passed out and only the prompt action by the wireless operator spared them both further discomfort. Clough and Sergeant Morrison recovered and David Hicks held his course for Dusseldorf, now coming into view. As he turned onto his bombing-run a four engined bomber was spotted on their port quarter going down, apparently out of control. in the next few seconds a loud explosion occurred in the area of the mid-upper turret of their own aircraft which, in all probability, killed its occupant Sergeant Elder and at the same time started a fire in the bomb-bay. The events of the next few minutes, as Hicks struggled to maintain control, are here best described by Ray Clough, who earlier had multiplied the sum of two sevens in order to satisfy his pilot he was fully recovered:

'I could see the glow beneath me and as the aircraft dived I took the opportunity to clip on my parachute. The pilot then levelled off and I stood on the astro-dome platform and looked out. I noticed the loop aerial had been shot away and was dangling loose on top of the fuselage. The bomb-aimer was asking for the bombs to be jettisoned and the rear-gunner was yelling that the fighter was coming in again. Sure enough he was clearly visible on our starboard quarter and as he fired I jumped down from my position. The next moment the engineer's panel fell in and a shower of perspex splinters spattered around me. I took off my oxygen mask and picked up a fire extinguisher, but there was no chance to use it because we were now spinning violently.'

This second firing pass by Leutnant Hensler had to all intents and purposes finished off David Hick's bomber. It is believed the shells that ripped through the astro-dome entered the cockpit killing, or incapacitating the Canadian plot. The centrifugal forces pinned young Clough to the floor, and then to his surprise the Halifax stopped spinning:.

'We seemed to halt in mid-air and a cone of searchlights lit up the cockpit. Through the shattered windscreen I could see the target area quite clearly and I gave up all hope of getting out alive. Then debris started to rush past me and a second later I was out of the aircraft and hanging beneath my parachute.'

The Halifax had literally broken into two pieces and Clough had been plucked off the floor of the fuselage by the air rushing through the open forward escape hatch. Two days later, on the Saturday, after gamely struggling through woods and marshes near Monchengladbach, Ray Clough was taken prisoner. Only one other crew member, Sergeant Bristow who had left his wireless set to aid the unconscious flight engineer, survived this brutal engagement. We will now rejoin Sergeant Glover.

Ron Glover was down near Lanaken in Belgium. Once over the initial shock of his landing, he began making plans to escape. To start with he was quite successful and many brave members of the Belgian resistance movement risked their all in getting the young airman into the evasion line. Unbeknown to Ron Glover, his pilot was receiving similar help, Dennis Hornsey had landed near the little hamlet of Uykhoven and in the weeks that followed he was smuggled southwards through France and into Spain. Sergeant Glover was not to be so fortunate. After being taken to Liege, where he lived for a few days with a greengrocer and his family, he was handed over to two men responsible for organising a local resistance cell. Now he was frequently on the move as it was suspected that the Germans had infiltrated the local escape lines. Four Americans and a Canadian joined his group and by degrees the little party worked their way southeastwards towards the Swiss frontier. But danger stalked their every move and in late December the four American airmen were arrested. Ron Glover and his Canadian companion split up for a few days, but both were together when the authorities picked them up in the town of Pontarlier on 23 December 1943. The Swiss border and safety was so tantalisingly near.

On 11 November the marshalling yards at Cannes in the south of France received a visit from a medium force of Halifaxes drawn from 4 Group squadrons. First reports indicated a degree of success, but later messages from the French underground told a different story, and for one crew this Armistice Day raid is best remembered not for the Haig Poppies dropped over Cannes, but for the mix-up at Holmsley South near Bournemouth. It was here that a number of the returning bombers were diverted, bad weather having closed the aerodromes to the north.

'On calling control we were given Number Two, but it was fifty minutes before we were able to land. The aerodrome was practically one large 'dead spot' for the radio. We were jumped up and down the queue and finally told to taxi to the end of the runway and turn right while we were still airborne! I tried cajolery and curses by turn, growing madder and madder from the endless delays.

'Afterwards I discovered there were three 'S' for Sugars' in the circuits, hence the confusion. We were not sorry, after a few hours sleep, to fly home to Base.'

One week after this incident, Wing Commander Don Smith led his squadron for the last time. During the past eight months his squadron had taken part in some of the most bitter night raids in the history of the war. His own personal tally stood at eighteen operations, fourteen of these being against major German industrial targets, including seven in the Ruhr Valley. His final objective was the Farbenindustric Chemical works at Mannheim. The night was dreadfully cold with temperatures falling to minus thirty degrees centigrade. Between Frankfurt and Mannheim the night sky was a near solid mass of probing searchlight beams.

Meanwhile, many miles away to the northeast a second force of heavy bombers were homing on Berlin. The 'Battle of Berlin' was about to start. For the next four months this target would occupy the priority spot in the operational planning at Bomber Command headquarters. Hundreds of airmen and hundreds of Berliners would not live to see the spring.

B.E.12 C3114, possibly not a 76 Squadron machine

Officer and NCO pilots, 76 Squadron, Finningley 1937

See Appendix Six (page 249) for more detailed photograph captions and credits.

Wellesleys stepped up in echelon, 1937

Wireless operators pose with a Hampden, Finningley 1939

Halifax B.I MP-D piloted by Pilot Officer Smith, August 1941

Halifax B.I L9530 MP·L with Flight Lieutenant Cheshire at the controls

Flying Officer Geoff Raymond, Middle East 1942

Ju88C6 of E/NJG 2, Gilez Rijen early 1943

10 and 76 Squadrons aircrew, Middle East 1942

Captain Gunnar Halle RNAF and crew, April 1943

Halifax B.V DK148 MP-G crash-landed 26 July 1943

Squadron aircrew prepare to leave for Hamburg 27 July 1943

Aircrew standing beside Halifax B.V DK204 MP-L, 27 July 1943

Captain Gunnar Halle RNAF and crew, April 1943

Halifax B.V DK148 MP-G crash-landed 26 July 1943

Squadron aircrew prepare to leave for Hamburg 27 July 1943

Aircrew standing beside Halifax B.V DK204 MP-L, 27 July 1943

Pilot Officer Bill Elder and crew, 27 July 1943

Aircrew and WAAF drivers, 1943

Drawing parachutes, 1943

Airborne for Milan, 12 August 1943

Sergeant Ken Hewson and crew, 1943

Pilot Officer Eric Wright and crew, 1943

Pilot Officer George Dunn and crew

Lieutenant Neils Eckoff RNAF and crew, 1943

Some remains of
Halifax B.V DK203 MP-A
recovered during 1980

Flight Lieutenant Jimmy Steele takes off for Kassel, 22 October 1943

Wing Commander Don Smith and crew, 1943

Waiting to board the transport, operations late 1943

111

Pilot Officer Jimmy Row and crew, 1943

Flying Officer Roy Bolt and crew, 1943

**Le Mans under attack
13-14 March 1944**

Flight Lieutenant Roy Bolt and crew being debriefed 21 April 1944

Warrant Officer Mickey Jenkins and crew, 27 April 1944

Lieutenant Carl Larson RNAF and crew spring 1944

Pilot Officer Valle RNAF receives the Distinguished Flying Cross

Flying Officer Neil Conway RAAF and crew, 1944

**St. Martin L'Hortier
under attack
5-6 July 1944**

Halifax B.III LK785 MP-T *Topsy*, **24 July 1944**

Halifax B.III LW648 MP-A *Achtung, The Black Prince*, **August 1944**

Halifax B.111 MZ516 MP-V *Vera the Virgin*, **September 1944**

A close up of the nose of *Vera the Virgin*

O-de-O with Flight Lieutenant Stu Orser and crew, 1944

Damage inflicted to Halifax B.III MZ528 MP-K

Pilot Officer George Rowley
and crew, 1944

Warrant Officer Espie RAAF and crew, 1944

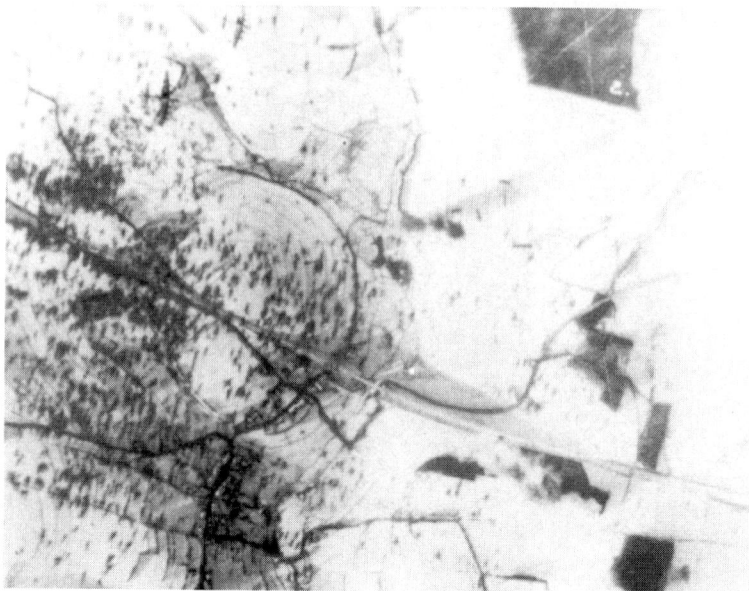

St. Vith under attack, 26 December 1944

Halifax B.III NA570 MP-P *Powerful Pete*, mid March 1945

Flying Officer Whittaker and crew, 1945

Halifax B.VI RG591 MP-A, April 1945

Halifaxes on operations to Bayreuth, 11 April 1945

Flight Lieutenant Peter Collins and crew, April 1945

Bomb-damaged Cologne, June 1945

Halifax B.VI RG553 MP-T falling out of control, 25 April 1945

B Flight and Dakota, June 1945

76 Squadron aircrew in Palistine 1945, staging to India

Canberra B.6 WH980 in flight

Canberra B.6 WH976, New Zealand 1959

Canberra B.6 WT206, Gibralter 1960

Canberra B.6 WJ757, Upwood 1960

Chapter Seven

A WINTER'S TALE

Before concerning ourselves with the events of the forthcoming battle, we will pause for a few moments and review the squadron's achievements in the two major offensives of the year, the Ruhr and Hamburg. Against the Ruhr targets the squadron had dispatched a total of 337 sorties for the loss of fifteen crews. In these figures I have included the attack on Essen on 25 July. I mention this as historians tend to include this raid on Essen in with the Hamburg offensive. Hamburg had produced ninety-one sorties, from which three crews had failed to return, while losses on other operations since the start of the year amounted to a further thirty-two crews missing. Nonetheless, throughout the summer the squadron's overall strength had grown and by the onset of winter it could, when required, operate at near maximum strength. This same period had witnessed the introduction of improved target marking techniques, especially the short ranged OBOE. As a counter measure to the increasing effectiveness of the German night-fighters, Window had been given its debut, and this had certainly forced radical changes upon the Luftwaffe. From the relative restrictions of flying in controlled boxes, the enemy night-fighter pilots were by the winter of 1943 operating more freely as his ground controllers became skilled in providing a running commentary on the raids coming time and time again on their towns and cities. Little damaged at the start of the year, the scale and frequency of Bomber Command attacks since the spring was ensuring their mass destruction and to use the analogy quoted so many times 'They that have sown the wind; they will reap the whirlwind'. As we shall now discover, those charged with bringing the 'whirlwind' were about to start the bloodiest battle yet in the night bombing campaign.

The squadron's first involvement in the 'Battle came on 22 November when in the late afternoon nineteen crews commenced taking-off from Holme to join forces with over 760 heavy bombers streaming towards the capital city of Berlin. Clouds covered the entire route, but the mainforce held station well and shortly after 8 pm a most concentrated attack commenced. Flying Officer Marin, a Canadian, was the first of the squadron crews to bomb and he was followed a few minutes later by Major John Stene, who had had his fair share of problems:

'We were well inside Germany and still had an hour to go to the target when the exhaust manifold on one engine blew open, producing an eight to ten feet long trailing flame, visible for miles. I feathered the propeller, but since we were in an early wave, it seemed wiser to continue and stay with the stream, rather than turn around and become a lonely straggler. With a full bomb-load and on three engines only, we kept losing altitude, but we still had 12,000 feet in hand when we reached the target. On the way home we restarted the flaming engine every time we ran into cloud-cover, feathering it again when we were out in the open. In this way we returned to Base without any further problems.'

Frankfurt was bombed with moderate success in the early hours of the 26th. Leading the squadron on this occasion was the Commanding Officer designate, Squadron Leader 'Hank' Iveson. 'Hank' Iveson was no stranger to '76' having first joined the squadron in late 1941 and continuing through to September 1942, by which time he was in the Middle East.

Two crews failed to return from this attack. Pilot Officer Troake, who had survived a number of very difficult operations, crashed between Wieslock and Malschenberg, small towns well to the south of

Frankfurt, past Heidelberg. Three members of his crew survived to become prisoners, including his American mid-upper gunner Staff Sergeant Flewell. The second crew was captained by Second Lieutenant Knut Lindaas RNAF and a description of their loss comes from his rear-gunner, Sergeant Fred Beadle:

'We overshot the target on our first run, but turned and bombed successfully on our second attempt. Flying away from Frankfurt we ran into extremely heavy icing. Within seconds the interior of the aircraft was glazed with ice and my turret was immobile because the electric connections were frozen solid. Eventually, when taking evasive action to avoid some searchlights we ran into a layer of clouds and iced up even more and the aircraft refused to answer to the controls. The intercom to my turret was frozen, but guessing that something was wrong I went forward to find the flight engineer trying to persuade the pilot to jump, which he refused to do. But he ordered us to leave, which we did from a very low altitude and landed safely in a snowstorm.' By remaining at the controls Lindaas must have realised his chances of survival were slender, but his proud Norwegian courage never deserted him and in giving his crew their best chance of living, Second Lieutenant Lindaas died. After the war Knut Lindaas was awarded the War Cross, Norway's equivalent to the Victoria Cross. it has further been established that Knut - and his brother - were on the Gestapo's wanted-list, and indeed his brother was arrested and murdered for his resistance activities. Possibly it was the knowledge of what fate had in store for him if taken prisoner that decided young Lindaas to stay with his aircraft. Today the brothers are united side-by-side in graves in Oslo.

The final attack in this grey month came on the 26th when Stuttgart absorbed more than 400 tons of high explosives and incendiaries. Considerable damage was inflicted on the giant Daimler-Benz engine works at Unterturkheim. At least a month's supply of aero engines were lost as explosions tore through the production lines. At the experimental sheds fires raged unchecked for several hours, but a photo reconnaissance sortie later revealed the engine test-bed buildings in the southwest corner of the plant had escaped virtually undamaged.

In the wake of a stunning raid on Leipzig on 3 December the weather closed in. For sixteen days the squadron remained firmly on the ground. During this period Pilot Officer Eric Wright, described by a member of his crew as being of 'frail build, but a most efficient pilot', was posted to fly Wellingtons with 20 Operational Training Unit. Lieutenant Fridtjof Giortz RNAF was dispatched to Kinloss, then home of 19 Operational Training Unit, a unit still equipped with the ubiquitous Whitley, while a third crew captained by Flight Sergeant Healey[22] were 'lost' to Pathfinders and 3 5 Squadron. Shortly before this trio departed, George Dunn and Ken Myers completed their tours and in the words of John Stene this pair 'represented the backbone' of A Flight - praise indeed.

A general improvement in the weather by the 20th resulted in a strong evening raid being sent to Frankfurt. 'Hank' Iveson lost the use of his 'GEE' equipment and this, coupled with a ten-degree variation between his compasses, all made for a rather difficult sortie, which he thinks culminated over Mannheim. Flying Officer Roy Bolt lost power from his port outer engine, so he elected to bomb Westhoofd as an alternative before turning for home. But for three crews their tours had ended abruptly - not for them the celebrations and fond farewells after thirty trips. Flight Sergeant Boddington was

22   Commissioned, Healey went on to serve with great distinction and was still operational in the late summer of 1944

down in the vicinity of Trais-Horloff, while an hour later, at eight o'clock in the evening, Flight Sergeant Lewellyn Cable came down at Dachsenhausen. From both crews men survived; four from Boddington's and a similar number from Cable's, including the squadron's Signals Leader, Flight Lieutenant Evans, who was sitting in for the crew's regular wireless operator Bryan Williams, in hospital with bronchitis. Of the third crew captained by Flight Sergeant Matthews little is known as all were killed. A wireless fix in the late evening placed their aircraft homeward bound over the North Sea and it is now thought Matthews met his end roughly to the west of Goeree island off the Dutch coast. The bodies of Matthews and that of his navigator Flight Sergeant Lamb, a New Zealander, were washed ashore and both are buried in Holland.

These recent losses brought the total to eleven since the beginning of November, but the squadron remained in good spirits and everyone responded well to the Christmas festivities. And, as though lifted by the two days of celebration, twenty-two crews took part in a very successful mid-evening strike against Berlin on the 29th. This attack was the eighth in the series and it marked the halfway point in the 'Battle'.

Operations in the New Year did not commence until 20 January. The first fourteen days of the month were devoted to intensive flying practice, while on the 15th the station awoke to find a thick dank fog hanging like a shroud over the airfield. All flying ceased for five days.

Earlier, on the 5th, Squadron Leader Kenny Clack DFM arrived to take command of C Flight, For this officer it was the start of his second tour of duty with the squadron. His first spell commenced in early 1942 and ended in the Middle East, after which he had returned to England and spent the best part of a year instructing at Rufforth. Kenny Clack was still not yet twenty-one years of age.

When operations were resumed the pattern was much as before; maximum effort against Berlin. On the 20th a total of twenty-three crews were involved, this figure including Wing Commander 'Hank' Iveson who had officially taken over from Don Smith on Boxing Day. Conditions at Holme were still far from ideal as Pilot Officer Les Falgate headed the queue of bombers rumbling towards the duty runway. Braving the bone chilling cold of a late January afternoon were the usual gathering of little groups of men and women waving and shouting God speed to their aircrew friends. The surrounding air throbbed as each aircraft awaited the signal to leave. At 16.14 hours Falgate was cleared by a steady green light shining from the airfield control caravan. Seconds later his fast accelerating Halifax vanished from view into the swirling mist.

It was quite dark by the time Flying Officer Burnand RCAF departed, leaving the little knots of groundstaff to stroll back to their sections with the sound of climbing aircraft gradually fading into the still night air. Now there was little to do but await the squadron's return.

For an hour or more the laborious task of forming up the mainforce was enacted. Gradually some 769 bombers passed through the main concentration point, from where the stream settled down on the first leg of the long haul to Berlin. Not all would reach their objective. Already technical malfunctions had overtaken three squadron crews. Aboard Burnand's aircraft the navigator reported a complete failure 6f his 'GEE' equipment, and similar problems were experienced by Flying Officer Bob Stewart RCAF. After some deliberations both captains decided to turn back. The third crew, captained by Flight Sergeant Jenkins, also encountered navigational difficulties, but installations on the Kiel canal received their bombload before course was set for Holme. The remaining twenty continued, their steady passage unhindered despite towering pillars of cumulus cloud that hid from view the frozen countryside beneath. individual tensions mounted as Berlin drew near and the stream prepared to run through the cauldron of flak blocking their approach. To some extent the cloud cover reduced the effectiveness of the searchlights, but there was no escape from the nerve tingling moments spent amongst the bursting shells. Flight Lieutenant Roy Bolt, a westcountryman, and Flight Sergeant Jimmy Cole probably spearheaded the squadron crews, each completing their bombing-run without undue difficulty. However, this was not the case for Pilot Officer George Whitehead, flying his fifth operational sortie as captain:

'I recall hearing my bomb-aimer[23] say "bombs gone, I can see them". These were the last words he spoke for at that moment we were hit in the nose by flak, and he was killed instantly. A large hole was torn on the front port side, causing severe wounds to my wireless operator's[24] head and neck. Our immediate problem was the complete loss of all navigational equipment; charts, protractors, log, flight plans, which all disappeared, sucked through the hole in the fuselage. All compasses were rendered unserviceable and an engine failed.'

Whitehead's was one of many bombers severely damaged by the flak barrage. Close at hand, but unseen, desperate battles for survival were commencing. Skilfully he turned away from Berlin, but it was not long before his difficulties were further increased by the flight engineer's inability to change fuel tanks due to damage to the fuel cock mechanism. Throughout this time an icy blast of air coursed through the broken nose section. Whitehead's navigator, Warrant Officer John McTrach RCAF takes up the story:

'We could keep nothing down unless it was tied, and it was terribly cold. The aircraft kept wallowing about making my attempts at astro-navigation near impossible, so I had to rely on Dead Reckoning. As we flew near to the Ruhr, I managed to get a fix on a diversionary raid, but we had to leave the mainforce while still over Germany as we were in no shape to ditch if forced down on the long North Sea crossing.'

McTrach's last sentence suggests the crew were resigned to coming down over occupied territory, though Whitehead was very determined to keep his aircraft flying for as long as possible. When at long last a break in the drifting cloud gave the crew their first sight of land since leaving Base, hopes rose momentarily, but nothing looked familiar, no landmark could be identified. By this stage their fuel situation was fast becoming critical and both port engines were overheating to a quite alarming extent. Wisely, Whitehead decided that there was little option left but to order the survivors to bale out. The final dreaded moments were upon them. Quickly the crew went about helping their sorely injured colleague:

'I was helped to the rear exit by the flight engineer and I still recall seeing his 'thumbs up' and gap-toothed grin as he assisted me on my way, but I could not hear a word he was saying. It was still dark and I seemed to be leisurely tumbling through space. I was really not experiencing any great pain at that time, just a numbness and an inability to rotate my head. The opening of my parachute remedied that to some degree with quite a severe jerk, for which I was not prepared. I had no idea of my height, or location and I was in a general state of dopeyness. There was a certain amount of swaying and I found it hard to raise my arms in order to grasp the lines and stabilize myself. Aware that the ground was not too far below I tried to assume a posture that would enable me to land without breaking any other piece

---

23   Flying Officer H D G Morris.

24   Sergeant Leonard Stokes. The flight engineer who helped him out of the Halifax was Sergeant Harry Fisher, one of two 'Fisher's' in Whitehead's crew. Both were destined to become prisoners in a very short while.

of my anatomy. Whilst musing on this I hit the earth rather forcibly. The area was a farmer's field, from sight unseen, but by touch a cow pasture.'

Leonard Stokes was down. For the moment we will leave him, in his wounded state, feebly tugging at his parachute cords. just a few thousand feet above George Whitehead was preparing to make his exit:

'I was not able to get out immediately because the aircraft could not be trimmed and wanted all the while to bank and turn steeply each time I let go of the controls. Eventually I got her facing some open countryside and flying level enough to allow me to step through the escape hatch.'

Shortly after Whitehead 'stepped through the escape hatch' the Halifax crashed near Lievin in the mining country southwest of Lens in northern France. Three of the crew, Whitehead, John McTrach and Sergeant 'Tich' Compton the rear-gunner managed to avoid the searching authorities and in due course all returned to England. Pilot Officer Whitehead tumbled into the back garden of a small terraced house occupied by a Polish couple and within forty-eight hours was in the care of a local resistance group. Taken south he crossed the Pyrenees into Spain and was soon in the safe haven of Gibraltar. From here he returned to England on 3 May 1944.

McTrach and 'Tich' Compton, although separated initially, later met up and both were hidden in the Pas de Calais area. From here they were liberated in the weeks following the invasion by units of the Canadian 2nd Army.

The body of Flying Officer Morris was found in the wreckage of the Halifax and the remaining survivors were taken prisoner, but before continuing let those last few hours of freedom spent by the badly wounded Sergeant Leonard Stokes be set down in his words:

'I got up after a while and lugging the parachute staggered into a wire fence. it was pitch black and I had no idea where I was. There was a depression, or a small ditch, at the fence so I dumped the parachute down and wrapping myself in its canopy, settled down to await the dawn. I was soaking wet, feeling lousy and shivering. The parachute afforded no warmth, so I huddled there and tried to rest. My head kept sticking to the silk and I spent a dreadful few hours unable to sleep. At first light I tramped the parachute down as best as I could and blundered under the fence and across the field. It seemed an endless trek, but was probably only a hundred yards or so until I came upon a farm. I made my way through the farmyard, encountering an elderly man leaving the building. Although only a few yards away he studiously avoided my presence. My calls to him only solicited a gesture which intimated I should go away. Murmuring a few pleasantries at his back I plodded on into the farmhouse, meeting a couple of men whose reception was most chilly. Either my pleas, or their language brought some women onto the scene. The first signs of compassion came from these ladies. I was taken into the house and laid gently on the floor. I was a bloody mess in every sense. A straw filled palliasse was brought in and I was deposited on it. The women kept flinching and grimacing about my wounds which gave me some misgivings, not knowing what medical shape I was really in. They did their best to wash my face and neck, making me as comfortable as possible. By this time the numbness was wearing off and a dull ache came over my head and neck. Reaction was, I presume, setting in. I felt nauseous and chilled to the bone. Possibly I passed out for suddenly, as if from nowhere, a couple of French Gendarmes were in the room looking down at me. 'Allo Tommy' were the first words from one; he then did a quick medical check on the back of my head. His English was limited, but he made it known that skilled medical attention was essential. This was inconceivable without German knowledge and he appraised me "the war is over for you". Whilst this was going on one of the women brought me a bible. She wanted to show me a page on which someone had written an RAF rank and name, her indication being they would

133

like to help me as they may have done others. After a period of time two men dressed in civilian clothes and obviously German, arrived. They were rather unpleasant in their questioning which, with their limited English and my deafness, proved a fruitless inquisition. Throughout the shouting the two Gendarmes watched over me, until at last I was lifted from the mattress and assisted outside into a vehicle. My last memories before lapsing into unconsciousness are the fond farewells of the women.'

Indeed, for Leonard Stokes the war was over. For several days he lay seriously ill in a French hospital and it was several weeks before he was fit enough to be released to an Allied prisoner-of-war camp.

In the hours while he lay semi-conscious in the folds of his parachute by the wire fence,, the returning bombers were being accepted at airfields stretching from East Anglia to near the Scottish borders. At Holme Pilot Officer Falgate, who had been first to leave, was recovered at 23.31 hours, his 24th operational sortie completed. Last to land over an hour later at 00.44 was Flight Sergeant Richards. At debriefing Richards indicated he had experienced difficulties in setting the aircraft's compasses and later his night photo plot revealed he had bombed a built up area in the southwestern suburbs of the city. in addition to the names of Pilot Officer Whitehead's crew entered on the missing aircrew sheet, details from Flight Sergeant Ive's and Flight Sergeant Parrott's crews were added to the list. No one, it was later learnt, survived from Flight Sergeant Parrott's Halifax, down fifteen kilometres northwest of Burgkem-nitz, and only two - both Australians - - Sergeant Buchan and Flight Sergeant Curry survived the ordeal that befell Flight Sergeant Ive RAAF. Both crews probably fell victim to night-fighters as enemy documents state twenty-two Halifaxes were claimed by their defences, twenty-one of these falling in air combat. Another hard fought round in the 'Battle' had been concluded.

The following night nineteen crews, including nine who had operated against Berlin twenty-four hours previously, took off for a late evening strike on Magdeburg. Within a few minutes of leaving Holme Flight Sergeant Firth was in very serious trouble. The Halifax commenced vibrating at a most alarming rate, so much so that Firth realised he would not be able to hold the bomber in the air long enough to make a forced landing. Frantically he shouted to his crew to bale out. In the next few seconds six anxious men leapt to safety, but for poor Firth there was no such opportunity and his young broken body was recovered from the remains of his aircraft. in the opinion of one very experienced pilot, Flight Sergeant Firth had unwittingly taken off with a liberal coating of frozen snow on his mainplanes.

For the remainder this tragedy probably passed unnoticed and as Magdeburg came slowly into view so a panoramic scene of fire mixed with the vivid flash of high explosives and marker bombs unfolded. into the frosty night air thousands of incendiaries tumbled from over 600 bomb-bays into the flames below. Millions of brightly glowing sparks rose into the air, scattering wildly in all directions. The stink of death lay heavy in the January air after the last of the bombers had departed. Losses were severe and the squadron suffered particularly badly. From three crews, Lieutenant Tor Anundskaas RNAF, Sergeant Bloomfield who this night was flying Roy Bolt's favourite Halifax and Sergeant Walker, there were no survivors, while from Flight Sergeant Boyes crew downed by a night-fighter over Helmstedt only three lived to relate their experiences, Boyes along with the remainder of his crew, was dead. Sergeant Walker is assumed to have come down in the North Sea. At 4.45 am a wireless message from his Halifax was received indicating he was preparing to ditch, but a minute later all contact was lost. in time the sea give up two bodies from this crew, the bomb-aimer Sergeant Abrahams being washed ashore at Texel, that of the flight engineer, Sergeant Hughes, being discovered on the bleak shore of North Beveland.

A further punishing blow at Berlin was delivered on the 28th. From over 200 miles distant on the return leg a distinctive angry red hue was clearly visible. Throughout the raid the mainforce had flown above a thick carpet of cloud, but the skills of the PFF allowed no respite for the war-weary inhabitants of Berlin. On this occasion all squadron crews returned safely, though it was only after some adventures that Sergeant Carl Larsen RNAF regained the safety of Holme, his Halifax badly damaged. Running in towards Berlin from over the Baltic sea, his aircraft was savaged by a Ju 88 which destroyed his port-inner engine. Bombs were jettisoned over Rostock and a course for the distant North Sea was established. At times the lone bomber was harried by flak, but the most anxious moments came with the approach of a second night-fighter. Sergeant Maurice Ransome, the mid-upper gunner, gives his impressions of this near encounter:

'Suddenly a twin-engined fighter appeared ahead of us and slightly above. Our navigator claims he could see the enemy observer's head looking around, everywhere but below him. He must have been guided onto us by radar and it seemed ages before the enemy crew must have told their control they had boobed and broke away from us.' February opened quietly. A change to the much improved radial-engined Halifax B.111 was in the offing. on the 15th, five of the squadron's faithful MkVs were ferried to Marston Moor, here to continue in service as training aircraft. Consequently, only nine aircraft could be made ready for the planned evening raid on Berlin. Of these seven are known to have got through to the capital city, which for once was bombed in conditions of near perfect visibility. Huge areas of fire engulfed large parts of this once proud city, now being gradually reduced to a bomb-blasted ruin. One squadron crew failed to return. High above Schwerin, approximately thirty minutes before the main bombing commenced, Hauptmann Werner Hoffman's night-fighter slid unseen behind Flight Sergeant Eaton's aircraft. Werner Hoffman signalled his presence with a sharp burst of cannon fire that alerted the bomber's wireless operator, Sergeant Bob Becker:

'I popped my head up into the astro-dome and saw the fighter immediately. He was sitting slightly above us firing through our mainplanes, left to right. The port-inner was on fire and our mid-upper gunner was in the next second blown from his turret on to the fuselage floor. He seemed not to be seriously hurt, but we were obviously a goner. The rear-gunner was returning the fighter's fire and I think may have hit him because as I went through the forward escape hatch. I nearly collided with a twin-engined aircraft that appeared to be burning.'

At this stage of the combat, no one aboard the mortally damaged Halifax were injured, but in the event only six lived. Sergeant Basil Upton, who had been blasted unhurt out of his mid-upper position, had the cruel misfortune to plunge through the surface of an ice-covered lake and drown. He had been filling in for Eaton's regular mid-upper gunner, Roy Wallis, injured in a flying accident a few days earlier. Hauptmann Werner Hoffman landed safely at Schwerin.

The next day Flight Lieutenant Bob West RCAF airtested the squadron's first MkIll Halifax. Disposal of the remaining B.Vs to various training establishments proceeded apace and three of the new bombers were prepared for operations on the 24th. At 18.27 hours Flight Lieutenant Lemmon climbed steadily away from Holme, followed in the next three minutes by Kenny Clack and 'Hank' Iveson. Eight hours later all three were safely home from Schweinfurt, the key ball-bearing producing plant in the very heart of Germany.

A raid on the Messerschmitt works at Augsburg followed. This time the command was following up a successful daylight attack on this target by elements of the American Eighth Air Force. To the grim satisfaction of the mainforce it was abundantly clear that the Augsburg fire services had been unable to quench the fires started by the Fortresses and thus aided by excellent route marking by the PFF, a further crushing blow was delivered.

Compared with the fortunes of a year ago, March 1944 was not a good month, although it did herald the commencement of the successful bombing campaign directed against the communications systems of the occupied low-countries and France. The first seeds for the long awaited invasion of 'Fortress Europe' were about to be sown. On the 6th Squadron Leader John Harwood headed fourteen crews sent to Trappes on the southwestern outskirts of Paris. The first bombs went down on these important marshalling yards shortlyafter nine o'clock in the evening and the outcome was received with some enthusiasm by the High Wycombe planners. Two visits were necessary in order to damage the yards at Le Mans in central France. A thick covering of cloud foiled the first attempt and only a handful of crews caught sight of the red Target Indicators put down by the Pathfinders. In the absence of any opposition parts of the mainforce made several attempts to relocate the target area, but the cloud cover persisted and the Master Bomber eventually called off the attack.

Raids on the beleaguered towns of our Allies had to be conducted with the utmost care in order to minimize the loss of civilian lives, but mistakes did occur. The raids on the yards at Ghent in Belgium resulted in the deaths of over 450 Belgian civilians, a tragic outcome and one that highlights the problems for a force schooled in Area Bombing now being ordered to achieve absolute pinpoint accuracy at night. But, to return to Le Mans. Conditions were much improved on the 13th. All markers were clearly visible and the mainforce had little trouble in giving the yards a thorough pasting:

'I recall seeing pictures taken shortly after the raid which indicated that the marshalling yards, as such, had been virtually destroyed. Also, and I am not sure if it was wishful thinking, an Intelligence Officer had ringed certain bomb craters and had appended the names of the crew that had dropped these particular bombs.' Flight Sergeant Guy Edwards - Mid-upper Gunner.

The raid on the industrial centre of Stuttgart two nights later was not nearly so successful. Drifting cloud obscured most of the markers and the few fleeting glimpses of the surrounding countryside were insufficient to establish the accuracy of the Target Indicators. it was several days before a photographic reconnaissance Mosquito swept high in the late winter air over Stuttgart, its cameras recording evidence of the recent attack. A few hours later the developed film clearly revealed the main weight of the bombing had fallen in two separate areas. The Oberturkheim district, roughly four miles east-southeast of the town's centre, was very badly damaged, as was the village of Musberg some seven miles to the southwest.

Fortunes improved on the 18th and 22nd when Frankfurt was subjected to two major attacks. Visibility was perfect on the first raid, which is noteworthy from a squadron viewpoint in that five crews flew in Halifaxes modified with a ventral gun position. The feelings of an occupant of this position are now given by Sergeant Nicholson who, along with ten other air-gunners, was posted to the squadron specifically to man these mid-under positions:

'Although not all that cramped, it was a cold and draughty place to operate from. Everytime Window was shoved out from the forward chute, it would blow back and rattle against the perspex. It was an easy position to vacate in a hurry, if necessary, as the point five inch gun was mounted with two release pedals, one on each side. You hit these hard with your feet and the gun fell away, leaving a fair size hole for one to get out of.'

From the five Halifaxes so equipped on this mission, only four returned. Flight Sergeant Joseph was sent down, probably by a night-fighter, at Preist. Seven from his crew survived, amongst them Sergeant Makens, the mid-under gunner, who may well have been the first to prove in action the designers intentions for a rapid escape. Flight Sergeant Noyes was also missing, his aircraft plunged onto 34

Ulmenstrasse. Four of his crew parachuted to safety, one of them landing on the roof of an apartment building in the Altkoenigstrasse. Lowering himself onto a balcony on the third floor, the dazed survivor made his way into the flat and down the stairs to the basement where he joined an equally dazed German family sheltering from the bombing. Together they sat until the attack was over. A most unusual incident.

Night-fighters were again active on the second attack, though Les Falgate's would be assailant was later identified as a 'friendly' Halifax. Frankfurt, however, was sorely hit. Huge bands of fire crept across the city causing some to seek refuge in the river Main, such was the ferocity of the raging fires.

Two nights later the 'Battle Order' was titled Berlin. Since the previous November this sprawling city had been the principal target in the bitter winter bombing campaign. Now for the sixteenth time the command was gearing itself for what would prove to be the final round. Spring was in the air, the available hours of darkness necessary for the Berlin visits were fast receding. From headquarters to Groups, from Groups to stations, the black metallic teleprinters sounded alarms, chattered and hummed, the paper rolls filling neatly with the mass of orders and instructions. The well practiced art of dispatching between 5,000 and 6,000 men deep into the Third Reich was swinging smoothly into operation. From the outlying dispersal points came the harsh roar of engines, announcing the start of the perfunctory air-test. Later these same dispersal pans would be alive with activity. Fitters and riggers, hands gnarled and stained, toiled over engines and airframes, crew chiefs cajoling, signing vouchers and casting experienced eyes over the work unfolding before them. From the fuel farms and bomb dumps, bowsers and squat powerful tractors emerged, each conveying its priority cargo to the waiting bombers. As the day wore on armourers sweated and cursed as bomb-loads were manhandled into position before being winched upwards into the cavernous fuselage bays. Others would be busy filling the ammunition trays with belted machine-gun bullets, the brass cases gleaming. on the wings refuellers tugged at unwieldy hose lines, a near maximum fuel load would flow into wing and overload tanks. Oil and coolant tanks, replenished as necessary, were not forgotten. inside the aircraft nimble-fingered electricians, instrument and radio fitters, all went about their respective tasks. Nothing could be left to chance.

Away from the hustle and bustle of the windswept airfield, Officers and Sergeants Messes were busy preparing flight rations; hot soup, coffee, sandwiches and chocolate, all would be welcome as the operation ran its course. in the briefing rooms an expectant band of men sat, their eyes taking in the large map of Europe festooned with thin spidery lines of tape snaking across the North Sea and by way of the Baltic sea continuing across Berlin, before stretching to the west, north of the feared Ruhr valley. Prominent red patches marked the well defended areas, and of these there were plenty. Such events as these took place at Holme throughout that blustery late March day. Now, with the light slowly dimming, a succession of intelligence officers mounted the rostrum to address the sixteen squadron crews gathered, for there were still not enough of the new Halifaxes on charge to involve all crews on the station. Even the occasional chuckles at a tired joke could not break the air of tension present in this awesome room.

As a measure of the movement that had taken place on the squadron during the four months past, only four crews listening to the pre-raid patter had been present in November. Perhaps a certain tiredness of eye singled them out from amongst their less experienced colleagues, but still attentive were Les Falgate, Roy Bolt, Lemmon and Bob West, their respective crews clustered around. Of their companions from the recent months the majority were dead, one-hundred to be precise. Some were languishing in prisoner-of-war camps, thankful to be alive even though not free. A handful, like George Whitehead, were on the run, but not all would make the safety of a neutral country. Flight Sergeant

Jackson, a navigator, from Davies' crew shot down at Cellessur-Plaine near Nancy on 1 March, had just about a month of dangerous freedom remaining. Two crews that had flown in November were still at Holme, but 'stood down' from this operation, five had been 'screened' and two, those of Flight Sergeant Healey and Warrant Officer Murray had moved on to Pathfinder squadrons.

The briefing over, there remained the task of collecting parachutes and flight rations and attention to the private tasks carried out by many prior to operations. This was the time when personal fears were surpressed in all manner of guises, and few would feel at ease until the crew buses arrived with their cheerful WAAF drivers to speed them out to the waiting aircraft. In the remaining minutes left before hatches were closed and engines started, the Halifaxes were formally handed over from ground to aircrews. Hopeful farewells and good wishes had been cheerfully exchanged. All was now ready.

First to leave was Pilot Officer Ross Forsyth RAAF, airborne at 18.45 hours. Less than half -an-hour later Flying Officer Gordon Greenacre's laden bomber staggered into the darkening sky. The operation was still in its early stages when aboard the leading aircraft the more experienced navigators realised, with some concern, that the forecast wind speeds were hopelessly at fault. This had a disastrous effect on the mainforce clawing for height on the outward leg. Long before the final turning point was reached the bombers were scattered and isolated. There would be no concentration over Berlin this night.

This unhappy state of affairs was already realised at Bomber Command headquarters as first a trickle and then a flood of reports came through from the wind-finders[25]. in order to fully appreciate the effect of the wrongly forecast wind on the 24th, it is necessary to look at some of the previous raid reports on this target. On 22 November, for example, seventeen squadron crews passed over the city within the space of fifteen minutes. In the two January attacks sixteen crews bombed inside of fourteen minutes on the 20th, while during the crushing assault of the 28th, only seven minutes spanned the ten crews involved. Now, with the mainstream in disarray, twenty-eight minutes would separate Flight Lieutenant Roger Coverley, first to bomb, and Flight Sergeant Innes, the last. Innes, in particular, went through a most gruelling experience. Flak continually bracketed his bomber tracking across the city at 19,000 feet. Inside the darkened fuselage his crew flinched, privately, as a hail of spent shrapnel rattled against the outside skin, the closer bursts sending splinters through the undersurfaces and mainplanes. With a feeling of great relief Innes completed his run and headed away from Berlin. Ross Forsyth was not finding it easy either, as his flight engineer Sergeant Owens remembers:

'We were slap bang in the middle of a load of searchlights and flak bursts. What appeared to be a dirty big blue light picked us out and this was followed by several others. I think it was our rear-gunner who shouted "for Christ's sake Ross, put your nose down" and put the nose down he certainly did, We levelled out at about 5,000 feet, low enough for the light flak, but we had lost those blinding beams and only suffered a little damage.'

Gordon Greenacre, whom we mentioned earlier as being last to leave had by this time flown into a middle order position in the stream. He, too, caught the full weight of the ground defences and was lucky to escape with only minor damage to his starboard fin. Greenacre's tour had been punctuated

---

25   Selected crews chosen to assess and broadcast the upper wind speeds to their respective Group radio stations. Here their reports were fed to command where the meteorological staff computed their findings into a mean windspeed. The 'new'wind was then relayed to the mainforce, the optimistic assumption being that the mainstream would be kept intact.'

with narrow escapes and he would return to Holme thankful that Berlin was behind him and the end of his long tour, for he had now been nearly a year on the squadron, was nearing completion. Alas, he was not destined to live to see the start of April.

Some crews were blown well past the Aiming Point by the strong tail-winds and then to their surprise found it impossible to turn about for a second attempt. Pilot Officer George jettisoned his load in the southeastern suburbs after being hit repeatedly in the starboard wing, while the Australian, Forsyth, mentioned earlier diving to escape the lights, secured a photograph of the Torgau area, again a positior-1 well to the south of the city. Later this crew, still drifting south of track in the gale force winds, would blunder over the Ruhr and here spend twenty agonising minutes being pursued from one cone of lights to another. it was certainly not Ross Forsyth's night and that he and his crew ultimately survived can only be attributed to his flying skill plus a liberal measure of luck, and to the remarkable strength of their Halifax which was hit time and time again by the ground fire.

In the aftermath of this difficult operation, command announced that seventy-two crews were missing, amongst them Flight Sergeant Marshall RCAF whose wrecked bomber was lying at Gatow, close to Berlin.

With barely time to draw breath, Arthur Harris sent his crews to Essen. Several thick layers of high cloud masked the approaches to the Ruhr, but the Pathfinders struck it rich and the mainforce responded well to their efforts. Much of the repair work carried out here in the autumn and winter was laid to waste, the relatively untouched areas to the south were badly blitzed and Krupps was further damaged.

One last major effort was called for to bring the winter's effort to a close, Nuremburg[26]. Two major raids launched the previous August had given the inhabitants of this distant city, lying some 230 miles south-southwest of Berlin, an insight of what lay in store. On 30 March 1944, a total of 779 aircraft took off to follow a flight plan that has, in recent years, been the subject of much controversy and argument. Over the continent the moon shone brightly, everyone could see for miles, the air was so crystal clear. No one, I suggest, as the mainforce crossed the coast above Knokke to fly above occupied Belgium could have imagined the scale of the carnage about to be inflicted Northeast of Charleroi the stream turned to run south of Liege before crossing the border and on deep into Nazi Germany. Long before this point in the raid was reached the enemy were well aware of the presence of a large force of Allied bombers. In fact, two distinct raid patterns had been charted and expertly studied One was plotted snaking across the North Sea in the direction of northwest Germany, thus posing a possible threat to Hamburg, or perhaps Berlin. The second raid, it was assessed, would come over the Belgian coast at least 300 miles south of the expected landfall of the force moving northeast. The fateful decision as to which raid posed the most danger was taken in the operations room of the 3rd Fighter Division at Deelen in Holland. it was from this control post that instructions were signalled to the Nachtjagdgeschwader ordering a concentration of their forces over the radio beacons, innocuously coded, Ida and Otto. Ida was sighted to the southwest of Cologne, Otto was located northwest of Frankfurt. The route would take Harris' bombers more or less directly between both beacons.

---

26   The full story of this operation has been set down by Martin Middlebrook in his now classic book 'The Nuremburg Raid'. His account is perhaps the most fitting tribute in recent years to the courage of the crews serving in Bomber Command. Another well told description of this infamous raid can be found in James Campbell's book 'The Bombing of Nuremburg'.

For the staff at Deelen their choice proved perfect. From night-fighter bases as far afield as Westerland on the island of Sylt to Coulommiers near Paris, an assortment of fighters, fuelled and armed sped towards these beacons. Later, night-fighters normally held for the defence of Berlin would be sent winging towards the Ruhr valley.

Light from the moon bathed the bombers in an eerie sheen. Amongst the veteran crews there was probably a dreadful awareness that the run to Nuremburg was going to be no easy passage. Their worst fears were soon realised as first one and then another aerial combat was sighted and reported, usually by the vigilant air-gunners. The turning point forty miles north-northeast of Schweinfurt would prove one reference point too far for many young crews, their funeral pyres were already marking the way to Nuremburg.

'How we managed to avoid combat before we got to the target, I shall never know. From the time we crossed the Rhine until we turned at the end of the long leg we were surrounded by running battles to such an extent that my navigator[27] gave up logging the number of aircraft shot down.'

This good fortune, here remembered by Flight Lieutenant Roy Bolt, was not in his case to hold, but for the moment we will leave Bolt and his crew and examine the fates of his less fortunate colleagues.

Roger Coverley had taken off for Nuremburg happy in the knowledge that the target was not Berlin. He had already completed one tour of operations with 78 Squadron, and was at the time of Nuremburg well into his second. All went well until he was attacked by a Ju 88. A fire broke out amidships, but this was quickly dealt with, and although some damage was caused to one of the starboard engines Coverley was able to continue. The next assault was far more lethal. Unseen Feldwebel Otto Kutzner, who had flown from Vetcha to join the fray opened up the bomber's starboard wing, rupturing fuel lines and starting a furious blaze. Horrified by the suddenness of this unreported attack, which was not surprising as Feldwebel Kutzner was flying below the Halifax and was thus effectively shielded, Coverley tried desperately to get away from the fusillade of cannon fire. But to no avail, rudder and elevator controls were already shot away and he could sense the nose of his aircraft wanting to pitch upwards despite his efforts to maintain level flight. He knew that if the crew did not escape within the next few precious seconds all would likely be lost. Calling to everyone to jump, Roger Coverley remained in his seat. Only when he felt all must have left the crippled Halifax did he concern himself with his own survival.

'The flight engineer had passed me my chest pack parachute just in case before going back after the first attack to see what he could do about the fire aft. Now something hit me in the face, knocking my oxygen mask off and temporarily blinding me. I got out of my seat, fell backwards down the steps leading to the nose and found myself outside the aircraft. I cannot recall clipping on my parachute, but it was there when I reached for and pulled the handle.'

Coverley's grim resolve to stay at the controls was justly rewarded, and the sole casualty, sadly, proved to be Sergeant Motts, his flight engineer. The body of this young airman from Lincoln was found three days later suspended in a tree, the burnt remains of his parachute canopy draped around him. Scattered over a wide area of the wooded hillside, less than a mile northeast of the village of Hamm an der Sieg, lay the burnt and buckled remains of what had once been their aircraft. In cold statistics it had been the 22nd to fall.

---

27   Flying Officer Fred Hall.

Further to the northeast, thirty miles it is judged, Squadron Leader Kenny Clack along with six of his crew died when their Halifax exploded in a pulsating ball of fire. Clack, not yet twenty-one years of age, had barely time to shout 'prepare to bale out' when the end came. As the Halifax tore itself apart Flight Sergeant Guy Edwards, the mid-upper gunner, realised he was being propelled through a gap opening before him in the fuselage side. For some inexplicable reason he survived.

Far below Oberieutnant Martin Becker resumed his hunt for further targets. From a study of the chart showing where each bomber fell, it is probable that Becker was patrolling near beacon Otto, and it is likely Oberleutnant Gustav Tham was similarly engaged when he picked up Flying Officer Gordon Greenacre's aircraft. With practiced precision Tham eased the controls of his fighter gently until he was satisfied that he was holding station with the onward speeding bomber. Only then did he press the firing button. High above the small town of Nieder-Moos a sudden curve of spreading fire marked Greenacre's end. Invisible from the ground the form of Sergeant Henthorn, his wireless operator, tumbled through the forward escape hatch. For a second or two, it could not have been longer, the Halifax continued in its gentle bank and then with an horrendous roar, it blew up. Molten chunks of metal mixed with stinking pieces of smouldering rubber rained earthwards, some of it narrowly missing the flight engineer Pilot Officer Monk who had survived the explosion and was now floating beneath a white parachute, badly shocked, but otherwise relatively unharmed,

Greenacre, like his two fellow pilots before him, had fallen to night-fighter fitted with upward firing guns. Surprisingly, Allied intelligence - normally well informed knew little about this device, which comprised of cannons mounted at an angle in the upper fuselages of some night-fighters. In the Bf 110 the modified gun mountings were in the roof of the cockpit and adjusted so their fire went almost vertically upwards. It is very likely that during the recent winter raids the Luftwaffe had scored successes with machines so fitted, but it was for the cold clinical dispatch of so many bombers on Nuremburg that the expression 'Schrige Musik' will be best remembered.

Now we will rejoin Roy Bolt and crew, surprised at having reached their objective without being involved in combat. His bombing-run, also, had been trouble free and now in Bolt's own words:

'We were heading south and feeling a lot happier.'

His euphoric frame of mind was soon rudely shattered:

'Without the slightest warning we were hit in the centre fuselage and in the starboard inner engine. At first I thought it was the sound of flak bursting below us and I shouted to the wireless operator to push out some Window. Then I smelt cordite and my rear-gunner called "flames are coming from the fuselage." I could not see any fire from the cockpit and concluded that the nearly empty overload fuel tank in the bombbay must be burning. My flight engineer was certainly aware of the blaze for he had opened an inspection hatch in the floor and was trying to douse the flames with a portable extinguisher. His task was hopeless, so I decided to try and blow the fire out by diving the aircraft. With the bomb-doors open I made two dives, losing several thousand feet in the process, and with relief the flames went out during the second attempt.'

Course had been barely resumed before Sergeant Harry van der Bos in his rear turret sighted a fighter 600 yards away on their port quarter and closing fast upon them. In the face of this renewed threat Bolt reacted calmly, his mind well drilled for his required actions:

'My rear-gunner called off the fighter's range and at 400 yards he shouted 'dive port'. With ten degrees of flap, climbing rpm set and a 60-degree diving turn, we could turn inside a Spitfire and I now proved we could also out-turn a Bf 210 by the same manoeuvre. The enemy pilot and my own gunner opened fire simultaneously as I dived to port and both continued to exchange, fire until the fighter broke off at fifty yards, flicked onto his back and went straight down. All the time I could see his tracer curling past to starboard, not one of his rounds making contact. We later claimed him as a probable, but if he survived he had certainly had enough.'

Roy Bolt had been extraordinarily lucky. That he and his crew had survived can only be attributed to their training and operational experience. There had been no panic, no unnecessary shouting over the intercom and now each member of his crew turned to his allotted task and quietly went about the business of getting their damaged bomber home. From his navigator, Fred Hall, came instructions to re-establish their course, while Sergeant Jack Bates the flight engineer set to work to assess the extent and severity of the damage. During the first attack the petrol feed to the inner starboard engine had been damaged and fuel was flowing from the hole at an alarming rate. To reduce the critical petrol loss, the damaged engine was stopped and the throttles of the three remaining motors were set at minimum power settings. Both pilot and flight engineer watched the fuel gauges with anxious eyes. It was going to be a close run thing. To ease their passage towards the still distant English coastline, Bolt trimmed the Halifax slightly nose down. Height was being slowly sacrificed for speed, but gradually the coast of France drew nearer and after what seemed an eternity the channel was crossed. By this time their fuel situation was critical and survival lay in getting down at the first available airfield. For sometime past QDMs had been received from the coastal aerodrome of Ford near Bognor Regis, but at the last moment Roy Bolt was unable to raise the Ford aerodrome controller. By a stroke of good fortune the flare path at nearby Tangmere was lit and with only an estimated five minutes flying time left available to him, Bolt steered towards this new haven of hope. That he could not make contact with flying-control was the least of his problems, for he was already in the circuit, the damaged engine restarted, when a new crisis struck:

'As I turned downwind Jack reported that the starboard undercarriage uplock release handle had been shot away and only the port main wheel had lowered. To give him time to try and sort the problem out, I made another quick circuit. Using the aeroplane's axe he quickly hacked a hole large enough in the uplock cable housing to enable him to get a hold on the wire cable and manually release the jammed undercarriage leg. There was no chance of a further circuit as my tanks were virtually empty. The landing that followed was not one of my best as the starboard tyre had been punctured. By maintaining power on the starboard outer, I prevented the wing from striking the ground until we lurched rather unsteadily to a standstill on the grass beside the runway.'

In the light of day one of Holme's engineering staff flew down to Tangmere to inspect the damage inflicted on Roy Bolt's Halifax. To his concern he discovered a cannon-shell had pierced the main spar on the starboard side and, in his opinion, the bomber was beyond economical repair. indeed, he added, why the wing had not folded under the kinetic energy spent by the cannon-shell was little short of a miracle.

In closing the account of this operation, we will report briefly on the fate of the survivors from the three aircraft shot down.

While the engineering officer from- Holme was deliberating on Roy Bolt's aircraft at Tangmere, Roger Coverley was making his way, generally westward:

'I had a bar of chocolate and Horlicks tablets and although I was cold, I was not frozen. At one stage I dug up some leeks from a vegetable garden and ate them raw which put me off of that vegetable for a very long time. The woods were a festive sight, decked in a mass of Window and strewn with Allied propaganda leaflets.'

Four days later his bid for freedom ended as he attempted to cross the Rhine, possibly near Bonn. The remainder of his crew, apart from the unfortunate flight engineer, were already captured. Guy Edwards was also in custody. On being taken to a cell, Edwards was surprised to find Sergeant Henthorn from Gordon Greenacre's crew sitting forlornly on a bunk:

'On the day of the raid I had met Sergeant Henthorn standing by a bus stop near the camp dressed in his best uniform, and here he was, still in that same attire in a Luftwaffe cell. He told me the crew had been promised three extra days leave after the Nurernburg operation.'

Altogether twenty-two men from the squadron had failed to return. Squadron Leader Kenny Clack had with him a second pilot by the name of Flight Sergeant Mogalki, a Canadian, who had only been on the squadron a matter of days. Nine from the twenty-two were now alive but this figure would eventually shrink to eight on 19 April 1945. On this day, with the Wehrmacht retreating in confusion on all fronts, Allied prisoners from camps in the east were being force-.marched westwards away from the advancing Soviet armies. One such column, containing Flight Sergeant Bauldie, Roger Coverley's rear-gunner, was attacked by an Allied fighter. After it had flown away Bauldie was one of several left lifeless in the ditches and paths raked and churned by Allied cannon-shells. it is most likely that Flight Sergeant Bone, whom it will be recalled was shot down on operations to Berlin in August 1941, died during this same attack; also a third squadron airman, Flight Sergeant Lawton, a flight engineer, shot down in March 1944 while operating to Berlin with Flight Sergeant Marshall RCAF.

Numbed, the command absorbed the terrible news of ninety-eight aircraft and crews missing, plus a further ten aircraft written off in crashes in the United Kingdom. Deelen's commander Generalmaj or Walter Grabmann had, through his decision, scored a notable success. Nine days elapsed before the squadron answered again the call to battle. Fourteen crews trooped into the briefing room, only two it should be noted, Pilot Officer George and Flight Sergeant Ian Weir, a New Zealander from Tauniaruniu, had been employed on Nuremburg. The majority of the remainder were fresh-faced youngsters eager to get going on operations. Their enthusiasm would not be denied them in the weeks and months to come.

Their target for this early April night was the rail marshalling yards at Lille in northern France. On return crews reported the yards effectively bombed in bright moon light conditions; Flying Officer Jimmy Watt RCAF returned on three engines after a)flak shell passed through one of his motors without exploding. This, the BBC visiting Holme at the time decided, was worth a picture or two, the groundcrew were - I suggest - less enthused, though later the incident was commemorated by an all white bomb-symbol, the fifth to be painted on the nose of this particular Halifax and in lieu of the usual white outlined bomb. Apart from jimmy Watt's narrow squeak, the raid had passed without incident and the command diary records only the loss of a single 35 Squadron Lancaster. The relentless battle was continuing unabated.

Chapter Eight

APRIL 1944 to SEPTEMBER 1944

With the arrival of the spring in 1944 came a general awareness that the war was swinging firmly in favour of the Allies, From the distant Pacific theatre the cinema newsreels were showing the Americans fighting a bloody island-hopping campaign against the Japanese. Territory lost in the first furious months of 1942 was now being reclaimed, but at a high cost in human lives. From the Middle East the news was most encouraging. Here the Allies were in control, though northwards across the Mediterranean a tough land battle was still being fought along the rocky spine of Italy. Although the Italians had capitulated the previous September, the German forces under Kesselring were denying the Allied armies an easy passage as they inched towards the Po river valley. On the eastern front the rapid German advances of 1942 and 1943 had faded and now, with supplies dwindling, the Wehrmacht were being forced to give ground before the powerful Russian divisions. The shell of Nazi domination was splitting apart.

Here in England preparations for the invasion of the western wall of Europe were gathering momentum. The Supreme Allied Commander, General Dwight Eisenhower had triumphed in his skirmishes with the politicians and was firmly at the helm of operational policy and planning, At his direction Air Chief Marshal Harris had been ordered to gear his bombing offensive towards the destruction of communications in the occupied countries. The men of Bomber Command who had carried the war to the German homeland for four long, costly years stood poised to strike at the very vitals of the enemy supply lines. in this key pre-invasion role they would not be found wanting.

As recorded, Lille was bombed with some success on 9 April and before the month was out the rail centres at Tergnier, Ottignies, Villeneuve St. Georges, Montzen and Acheres had all received close attention from Bomber Command. of these targets the yards at Tergnier were subjected to two attacks, the first on the 10th, the second on the 18th. Tergnier was of some importance to the railway system. Traffic passing north from Paris into Belgium was routed through these yards, as was the east-west flow between Laon and Amiens. It was the Halifax crews from 4 Group that dominated these attacks and on both occasions the mainforce met fierce night-fighter opposition. Sergeant Peter Chipping threw off a fighter's challenge on the 10th, while on the 18th Flight Sergeant Smith's gunners fought a sharp battle over the target area with a freelancing Fw 190. For several seconds the enemy fighter absorbed the punishing fire from Smith's rear-turret and then, with flames streaming past its tail, it dived into the ground. Warrant Officer Johnston's crew claim to have damaged a Ju 88, but although the squadron suffered no losses from the thirty-one sorties sent, the command lost sixteen Halifax crews from the two raids, probably all to night-fighters. The Tergnier yards were well punished. Near cloudless skies allowed everyone a clear view of the target on the 10th, but indifferent bombing spoilt what should have been a devastating attack, Fortunes improved considerably on the 18th, though, initially, confusion reigned after the PFF put down two widely separated sets of markers. Fortunately for the inhabitants of the town the Master Bomber was able to correct this error and an excellent bombing pattern followed, which more than atoned for the niggardly efforts of the 10th.

Ottignies, fifteen miles southeast of Brussels, received a good pounding on the 20th, Flying in cloudless skies all but four of the 175 Halifaxes bombed in the wake of the PFF opening. Flying Officer Morton diverted to Woodbridge in Suffolk after losing the use of his starboard outer engine, and to his annoyance Lieutenant Carl Larsen RNAF was obliged to return early with unserviceable hydraulics.

For the raid on Villeneuve St Georges in the southeastern suburbs of Paris the raiding force split into two groups, each group heading for a separate Aiming Point within the sprawling conglomeration of lines and switching points. An interval of half-an-hour elapsed between the dual strikes, which were carried out in marginal weather conditions. The final assault in April was aimed at the yards at Achères on the opposite side of Paris to Villeneuve. It was planned that OBOE Mosquito bombers would mark this target, but in the event the Target Indicators were put down by the Master Bomber, Squadron Leader Cresswell. The mainforce, including twenty squadron crews, followed up his target marking with an excellent display of controlled bombing which tore the heart out of the Achères yards. Sandwiched between the raids on Ottignies and Villeneuve were two heavy attacks on industrial targets in Germany, namely Dusseldorf and Karlsruhe. Nearly 600 heavy bombers went to Dusseldorf on the 22nd and crews returned to speak of extremely heavy night-fighter activity. Squadron Leader Somerscales, recently arrived to take charge of B Flight, was shot down by a night-fighter as he approached the Ruhr from the direction of Holland. Burning furiously, his bomber crashed at Gulpen, just a few kilometres east of Maastricht. Somerscales and his midupper gunner, Flight Sergeant Poole, were killed, but the remainder parachuted to safety. Three were rounded up and taken prisoner, but the bomb-aimer, Flying Officer Wingham, along with the navigator, Flying Officer Lewis, successfully evaded capture and eventually returned to England.

Flight Lieutenant Lemmon was equally unfortunate. Shortly after completing his bombing-run a savage night-fighter attack left his Halifax blazing like a torch, Four from his crew jumped in time, Lemmon and two others died in the burning remains of their aircraft down near Osterath. The demise of this crew was a particularly hard blow for the squadron for the majority were well within sight of finishing their tours, having been with the squadron since the mid-summer of 1943.

Two nights later an even stronger force visited Karisruhe. This, in the opinion of most who took part, was an ineffective attack spoilt by the large clouds of smoke drifting across the target area. For Warrant Officer Fuery RAAF Karlsruhe holds memories of jammed bomb-doors on the run-in and after these had been forced down in time to avoid going around again, the discovery they were stuck in the open position, so imposing a considerable drag on the return journey.

Later, as the mainforce recrossed the English coast, enemy intruder aircraft intercepted the bomber-stream. Carl Larsen saw the end of one bomber:

'We had our navigation lights on and had just broken open the coffee flasks for some welcome refreshment when tracer fire passed in front of my aircraft and entered the bomber flying on my left side. I immediately shouted to my gunners to be on their guard and switched my lights off pretty quickly. The bomber that had been hit was on fire and I watched it go all the way down in a curve to crash near Peterborough.' Carl Larsen had undoubtedly witnessed the end of a squadron colleague, Pilot Officer Dibbins. Only the rear-gunner, Flight Sergeant Anderson, survived and he was found in a badly wounded state.

On return to Holme several crews were understandably very upset at being given no warning that intruders were operating. Blandly, one senior officer present at the debriefing told Carl Larsen there had been no enemy aircraft over the British isles:

'This made me very angry. in that case, I told him, we are shooting our own aircraft down and if that is so I will not fly for you anymore. Later that day I was called in to see this same officer, who by then had learnt the true facts. At least he was decent enough to apologise for his stupidity.'

April had been busy for the squadron as the table below will show:

Date	Target	Sorties Dispatched	Primary Attacked	DNCO	FTR	Remarks
9 Apr	Lille	14	14			Marshalling Yards
10 Apr	Tergnier	10	10			Marshalling Yards
18 Apr	Tergnier	21	21			Marshalling Yards
20 Apr	Ottignies	23	21	2		Railway Centre
22 Apr	Dusseldorf	22	19	1	2	Industrial Target
24 Apr	Karisruhe	20	20			Industrial Target
26 Apr	Villeneuve St Georges	22	22			Marshalling Yards
27 Apr	Montzen	21	21			Railway Centre
30 Apr	Achères	20	19	1		Marshalling Yards
	Totals	**173**	**167**	**4**	**2**	

May 1944 would turn out to be busier still as the pre-invasion raiding rate was stepped up. For everyone, ground and aircrews alike, the summer of 1944 would see the level of operational activity rise to outstanding proportions.

The opening attack in May came on the 1st with seventeen crews employed against the railway centre of Malines situated a few miles north of Brussels. Broken cloud over the Belgian countryside afforded some protection to this target and four crews refrained from bombing as they were uncertain of their position. Sergeant Clithero drove off an enemy aircraft that closed in on Flight Sergeant Innes' Halifax, but in general the Malines raid was a quiet affair.

Late in the evening of the 6th a dozen crews assembled in the main briefing room at Holme, where they were informed that the yards at Montgassicourt northwest of Paris would be their target. One crew was left behind with an engine fault, but the remaining eleven, headed by Squadron Leader John Harwood, carried out a stunning attack. A further piece in the intricate jigsaw slotted neatly into place with the bombing of gun emplacements at Berneval on the 9th. These particular batteries were sited on the French coast southwest of Dieppe and as such were well away from the actual invasion beaches of Normandy, This mattered not for unfolding was a gigantic plan of deception aimed at keeping the German High Command guessing as to where the blow would eventually fall.

Following the Berneval raid, seventeen crews flew to Lens on the 10th and here, from an average height of 7 000 feet and in clear weather, plastered the marshalling yards with high explosives.

Coastal batteries at Trouville, opposite Le Harve and much closer to the planned invasion site, took a pounding on the 11th. At least sixteen crews should have joined the force earmarked for this attack, but Flight Sergeant Strattford crashed on take-off. Unhurt, Strattford and his crew scrambled clear from the ruined bomber, retiring to a safe distance as the flames took an unquenchable hold on the wreckage.

The following night the marshalling yards at Hasselt, midway between Louvain and the Belgian/German frontier, came in for attention in weather that turned out to be disappointing. One Halifax, piloted by

Warrant Officer Jenkins, lost the dinghy hatch cover on take-off. Within a short while Jenkins returned, his bomber vibrating badly and suffering from stability problems. Hours later sixteen crews were safely back at Holme, but of Flying Officer Jack Newcombe there was no immediate news, and it is believed that his Halifax fell to the guns of Oberleutnant Herman Greiner. Jack Newcombe's crew was amongst the most experienced on the squadron. All were on their second tour, Newcombe having completed his first tour with 78 Squadron, and flying as his navigator was Squadron Leader Shove DFC, then commander of C Flight. The majority died in the crash at Hadschot, but it is known that Flying Officer Harold Reeder and Flight Sergeant Reading survived, Harold Reeder, safely hidden by the resistance, Reading less fortunate a prisoner-of-war. The news of Jack Newcombe's death, he was just twenty-two years of age, was received with much sadness by his family in the little community of Torrington in North Devon and amongst his many friends in the Southern Railway Division at Exeter where he had been articled to the Divisional Engineer.

With the completion of the Hasselt operation, the squadron paused to draw breath. Six operations had been mounted in the first twelve nights of the month, now a welcome break for a week lay ahead.

The return to the fray was marked by twenty-four crews, under Squadron Leader Bob West RCAF, bombing locomotive sheds south of Boulogne. Clear skies, well placed markers and negligible opposition, all helped to make this a memorable attack. A searing orange coloured explosion lit the sky for about six seconds, this eruption being reported by several crews. Before long volumes of black smoke with the angry lick of fire faintly visible curled across the sheds, thus making it difficult for the late arrivals to bomb with any confidence. Altogether the mainforce unleashed over 113 tons of bombs on this target, before the smoke completely hid the markers from view.

Two nights later, on the 22nd, Wing Commander 'Hank' Iveson took his squadron to the marshalling yards at Orleans, well to the south of Paris. The target defences were alert and the *flak* was accurate. At least two bombers were hit and sent down out of control in the vicinity of the Aiming Point, but Iveson's men came through unscathed. Aachen on the 24th tells a different story. Patchy cloud was encountered en route, but the mainforce started well, such was the excellence of the PFF markers lying in and around the confines of the yards. The initial bombing accuracy was good, but the defenders were responding with equal venom. Flying Officer Clifford Waite, the sole Canadian in Flight Sergeant Bill Palmer's crew, had already witnessed the destruction of three bombers as their own aircraft approached Aachen. He had tried counting the parachutes:

'... but there were precious few. Our turn was next. The rear-gunner shouted "fighter, corkscrew port, go" and in the next second our starboard outer engine was knocked out and the wing set on fire. We went into a steep dive which blew the fire out, but in the process we built up a tremendous speed and it took the combined efforts of three of us to flatten the aircraft out.'

Bill Palmer would fly home low across the channel, his hydraulics shot away, to crash-land at Tangmere.

Flight Lieutenant Humphrey's crew had an adventuresome sortie fighting off three separate night-fighter attacks, and for the first time in several weeks the course of the raid was marked by fierce aerial battles. Flying north of Antwerp the withdrawing bomber force was further inconvenienced by flares going down over the docks here.

From all directions it seemed the enemy were in hot pursuit. By this time the Halifaxes of Flight Sergeant Wade, an Australian pilot with just three operational sorties behind him, and Warrant Officer Bishop had been destroyed, both claimed, it is thought, in quick succession by Hauptmann Heinz Strüning. From Bishop's crew everyone lived, his bomb-aimer Flight Sergeant Rae successfully evading the countless ground searches that followed this costly operation. The Australian Wade and his crew were nowhere near as lucky. Brought down south of Tilburg at Goirle, only Sergeant Head survived and he was captured in a wounded state.

in the wake of Aachen, it was perhaps with some feelings of trepidation that twenty-three crews emerged from briefing on the 27th. They had been told their target was the Wehrmacht camp at Bourg Leopold lying roughly midway between Antwerp and the border with Germany. Allied intelligence believed the camp to contain a full Panzer division and in view of the fluid state of enemy military movements, it was imperative to mount an attack without undue delay. At Holme the weather was far from promising and when the first Halifax took-off, shortly before midnight, a lingering mist hung over the airfield and surrounding fields. A damp smell of wet grass invaded the nostrils and there was a distinct chill in the air.

Airborne, the bombers flew into clearing skies, but over the Belgian mainland pockets of haze gave rise to momentary doubts. These doubts were soon dispelled when the leading aircraft saw Bourg Leopold clearly illuminated by the PFF flares. Within the quarter-of-an-hour that followed, over 300 bombers laid to waste most of the camp area. Explosion followed explosion amongst the lines of parked armour, throwing debris high into the air. Fires broke out as petrol tanks and fuel stores were hit and Pilot Officer Huckerby reported that the entire target area was ablaze when he made his approach. Some night-fighter activity was reported, Pilot Officer Neil Conway RAAF, on return, placing a claim for an enemy aircraft destroyed by his gunners, Sergeants Roy Bleach and Ron Minion.

For the German High Command wrestling with the problem of pinpointing where the Allied armies would come ashore, the spread and intensity of the bombing campaign these two months passed was causing its generals much concern. Evidence still led them to believe that Eisenhower would commit his forces to beachheads in the Pas de Calais area. On one factor most of the generals were in private agreement - once the Allied troops were ashore the war for Germany was as good as lost.

The final pieces in the complex pattern of deception woven by the Allies were steadily falling into place. Unknown to all but a chosen few, Eisenhower had long since made his choice and as May gave way to June preparations for dispatching the largest seaborne invasion force the world had ever witnessed was fast coming to a head.

Continuing in the present mode of operations twenty-three crews went to Trappes on 2 June. Altogether 128 bombers were employed, including Pathfinders. The outward leg passed without problem, Paris and the spread of marshalling yards in the western suburb of Trappes came into view. Target indicators cascaded on time and the familiar pattern of attack commenced. For several minutes those sheltering on the ground listened to the swish and roar given off by the high explosive bombs, followed by the slap of disturbed air as the blast effects ripped across the open yards. Rail lines were twisted and broken, sidings cratered and freight sheds were reduced to heaps of smouldering rubble. Then all was still, though the throbbing sound of departing bombers lingered awhile yet. Perhaps to those blessed with a discerning ear the alien note of fast flying fighters could be detected, high above the city streets. But even if heads still buzzed from the storm of bombs, eyes would undoubtedly see the first unmistakable signs of combat.

Within minutes of leaving Paris the mainforce were picked up by a strong force of night-fighters. The killing quickly commenced. From northwest of Paris, where the first encounter took place, to the point on the channel coast planned as their exit point was less than a hundred miles. In flying time all should have cleared this distance easily within thirty minutes. In the turmoil of battle this proved just time enough to die for many of the sixteen crews sent down. it is not possible to say who was first of the three squadron crews to fall in that desperate flight towards the sea. The plot suggests their order could have been Flight

Sergeant Smith shot down at Bretigny, Sergeant Woods near Faverolles and Pilot Officer Innes close to Treon, but one may have been ahead of the other - who can say for certain? What can be ascertained is that only one airman lived, the navigator from Smith's bomber, Flight Sergeant Hood.

This had been a sorry night for the 4 Group squadrons. Just a few miles up the road, north of Holme, at Lissett 158 Squadron would wait in vain for news of five crews. The Leconfield and Melbourne based squadrons had also suffered. Yet the squadrons employed on six other primary targets bombed that night returned virtually unscathed, such were the fortunes of war.

A brief respite of just over seventy-two hours ended with orders to bomb a coastal defence battery located at Mont Fieury on the Normandy coast. Unknown to the twenty-three crews gathered in the Holme briefing rooms, similar orders were being conveyed to equally attentive faces listening to instructions at bomber bases throughout the command. To illustrate the magnitude of that task expected from Bomber Command in the next few hours, a close study of the target list is essential.

Target	Group	Type and Number of Aircraft required		
Crisbecq	8	Mosquito	5	
	1	Lancaster	96	
St Martin	8	Mosquito	5	
de Varreville	1	Lancaster	95	
Ouistreham	8	Mosquito	5	
	8	Lancaster	5	
	3	Lancaster	106	
Maisy	8	Mosquito	5	
	8	Lancaster	5	
	4	Halifax	106	
Mont Ficury	8	Mosquito	5	
	4	Halifax	114	(23 from 76 Sqd)
La Pernelle	8	Mosquito	5	
	5	Mosquito	4	
	5	Lancaster	122	
St Pierre	8	Mosquito	5	
du Mont	5	Mosquito	5	
	5	Lancaster	115	
Houlgate	8	Mosquito	5	
	8	Lancaster	5	
	6	Halifax	106	
Merville	8	Mosquito	5	
Franceville	8	Lancaster	5	
	6	Halifax	86	
	6	Lancaster	13	
Longues-sur-	8	Mosquito	5	
Mer	8	Lancaster	69	
	6	Lancaster	25	

149

In addition to the ten coastal defence Aiming Points, thirty-one Mosquito crews from 8 Group were ordered to raid Osnabruck. But perhaps the most exacting role in this complex plan fell to the crews of 1,3 and 5 Groups. Flying a mixture of Stirlings and Lancaster's these crews were tasked to fly low over the channel on predetermined courses, dispatching Window to a precise timetable. Gradually, before the dawn was up, the radar sets on the enemy coast would glow with all the unmistakable signs of an invasion fleet steadily approaching the beaches in the Pas de Calais. The final links to deceive the enemy mind had been forged.

With the background to this historic operation now sketched in, the events of the hours remaining before the first waves of troops waded ashore in Normandy can be told by a few of the airmen involved. First, from Sergeant Ernest Turtle, flight engineer to Pilot Officer Neil Conway, flying over Hotham a few miles to the east of Holme in a brand new Halifax. The time, nearly an hour after midday:

'One by one the engines stopped with the propellers feathered. I was mad with the skipper when the first engine stopped, because I thought he had either decided to practice three-engined flying, which was stupid at our present height, or he had accidentally knocked a feathering button. Before I could vent my feelings the other motors cut and we had to get down to the serious business of a forced-landing. This came in a field close to a farm and after sliding through several hedges we came to a stop just before a farmhouse. The rear-gunner gave his head a nasty whack, but the only fatality was a rabbit which had died from shock as we passed through the hedgerow in which he was sitting.'

Conway and crew would not be going to Mont Fleury, they would go to St Lo twenty-four hours hence. One pilot who was destined to fly to the beachheads was Flight Sergeant 'George' Rowley. It would be his third operational sortie:

'At briefing it was obvious that something big was afoot. The CO said "well chaps this looks like it, but your guess is as good as mine".'

Airborne and flying south Rowley's feeling that something big was afoot was fully realised:

'Wherever we looked the sky was full of aircraft and the further south that we flew, so more aircraft kept emerging from the clouds to join the throng. Mixed with the bombers were troop transports, gliders wallowing behind tugs, fighters as well, all sporting what was then unfamiliar white invasion stripes. I suppose we were looking at the greatest assembly of aircraft ever airborne at the same time. either before or since.'

Even the groundcrews at Holme were not denied part of this airborne scene:

'We had been working around the clock and that evening was a tremendous thrill to watch. Hundreds of Halifax's were meeting overhead as squadron after squadron joined up. I went back to the hut and placed a five bob bet with an armourer that the next day would be D-Day.' *Corporal Bertram Marsb - Armourer.*

Out over the storm tossed channel the air armada flew. Conditions for the men packed in the troop transports churning through the grey waters was awful, but for those in the air it was a much smoother passage. Through the occasional breaks in the cloud cover the wake left by the invasion fleet could be clearly seen. Carl Larsen's mid-upper gunner Maurice Ransome was one of several who caught a fleeting glimpse of events below:

'I looked over my left shoulder and there below were hundreds of ships. Then we flew back into cloud. In general I thought the night was fairly tame, but the sight of all those ships is something I will never forget.'

The squadron CO recalls:

'By the time we recrossed the French coast, homeward bound, there was sufficient light to see the invasion fleet. It was a magnificent sight.'

Wing Commander 'Hank' Iveson had carried out his attack from just beneath the cloud base. The vast majority of crews had followed his example for the cloud cover was quite thick and unyielding. 'George' Rowley tells of his run and subsequent return:

'In RAF parlance it was 'a piece of cake' and we hoped that the guns we had been briefed to put out of action had indeed been silenced. As we flew home to Base there was still plenty of aerial activity going on around us. For once we were able to give the groundcrews some good accounts of the morning's work.'

One crew did not return to tell of the morning's work. Pilot Officer Walker died with his crew just as the first pale shafts of light prepared to break above Graye-sur-Mer.

While the aircrews snatched a few hours sleep the groundcrews hurriedly refuelled, serviced and rearmed the Halifaxes in readiness for the next operation. in the late afternoon many of the crews who had been in action in the small hours of the morning were called to briefing. Road and rail junctions at St Lo on the Vire south of Utah beach required their attention. Bertram Marsh, five shillings better off, was feeling particularly chirpy.

Thus the die was cast for the pattern of attacks in the weeks ahead. The inclement weather that had nearly caused Eisenhower to postpone the Normandy landings continued to be most unseasonable. Juvisy, south of Paris, received a visit in conditions of low cloud from a small force of Halifaxes, sixty-three in all, on the 7th. Exactly one third of the raiding force was supplied by the squadron, 'Hank' Iveson again at their helm. Bomb-aimers aimed their loads at the skymarkers drifting like pale ghosts above the yards. over and away from Juvisy the sharp flash of tracer marked the bombers course. Sergeant Hunt RCAF and crew would not be returning to Holme, though it was later learnt that five, including Hunt, were prisoners.

Possibly in an attempt to nullify the effectiveness of the German night-fighter units based in occupied France, the command struck at four airfields, Flers, Laval, Le Mans and Rennes. All lay to the south and east of the Normandy beaches; Laval between Rennes and Le Mans being assigned to eighteen squadron crews.

The attack was not an outstanding success. Nearly a quarter of the mainforce failed to hear the Master Bomber broadcasting instructions to descend below the cloud-base and those that did ran into extremely heavy *flak*. Flying Officers Ron Cramer and Steward bombed from 1,500 feet, as did 'George' Rowley. One crew took a very big chance and went in lower still, 600 feet to be exact. A blurred vision of hangars and hutments raced into view, bombs were released and the Halifax bucked and kicked, caught in the blast effect of its own bombs. A rather chastened Pilot Officer Huckerby flew his bomb-scarred aircraft home. His crew had had their fill of low-level attack, in the future Huckerby would bomb from the prescribed height and survive his tour.

Further drama came on the Amiens raid, the seventh in this busy month. Under clearing skies 199 Halifaxes delivered a two-pronged attack on the rail junctions at St Roch and Longeau, through which the enemy were still moving up supplies to their forces fighting a slogging battle amongst the hedgerows of Normandy. Nightfighters flew back and forth. Neil Conway's Halifax was fired upon, his gunners Ron Minion and Roy Bleach replied. Conway's Halifax escaped, Minion and Bleach claim their fire damaged their assailant. It was worth putting in a claim for one damaged. Pilot Officer Robertson RCAF emerged from two attacks relatively unscathed and secured a good Aiming Point photo. But it was not the attention of a nightfighter that came so close to sending down fellow Canadian, Flight Sergeant Galbraith.

Positioned just about centre of the stream of aircraft jockeying for a place in the bombing-run, bomb-doors open in readiness, Galbraith unwittingly flew beneath another aircraft in his wave. A sound quite unlike anything heard before pierced his ear drums. For a split second he froze in his seat and then the inhuman shriek was gone. Gingerly he nudged the controls, the Halifax responded gently to his touch, but that something awful had happened there could be no doubt. He had not long to wait. A pale faced flight engineer reported that a bomb had passed clean through their aircraft. No one was hurt, but at Woodbridge where Galbraith eventually landed, an onlooker remarked that he had never known such a badly damaged aircraft to survive.

On the 15th the woods near Fouillard were heavily bombed. A wild, tumbling confusion of flame and smoke, dust and debris, filled the air. Explosions uprooted trees, limbs in the full flush of summer greenery were tossed carelessly aside. Soldier and woodland beast died in agonising company as the compact bombing set off the neat stacks of ammunition.

With the Allied invasion now in its second week - history still records this period in the abstract style of D-plus one, D-plus two, and on - Harris was ready to take up the cudgel of round-the-clock bombing. In the dark days of late May 1940, as men of the British Expeditionary Force crouched in the sand dunes around Dunkirk calmly waiting their turn to wade out to the ships sent to pluck them from the shell torn beach, the sky above seemed filled with alien shapes, Dorniers, Junkers, 109s and Stukas by the score. For had not Reichmarshal Goering boasted to his Fuhrer that his *Luftwaffe* would crush the remnants of the armies gathered there? That he was wrong then, that the whole concept of Hitler's military strategy would prove a failure, had now four long years later resulted in near complete Allied domination of the skies.

The Americans had sent their Eighth Air Force crews out in daylight right from the start of their involvement in Europe. Now the added impetus of Bomber Command's not inconsiderable might would further help the soldiers gradually fighting their way out of Normandy. Close support of the land-battles being fought was nigh, but the first daylight objectives were the pilotless-bomb sites in the Pas de Calais.

Preparation of these sites by thousands of men and women brought from the slave labour camps in the east had occupied Hitler's engineers for months past. Within six days of the first Allied troops coming ashore, the first sites were declared ready for operations. Late in the evening of the 12th the first missiles were launched against the Home Counties. Swanscombe in Kent would absorb the first shock of this new weapon. The sound from these strange looking devices was not unlike that of a bandsaw and soon the phrase 'Buzz-bomb' would be on peoples lips. The southeast in particular suffered badly and no doubt the country as a whole would have paid a high price had it not been for the success scored against Peenemunde the previous August.

Retaliatory measures were quickly taken, first under cover of darkness, but on the 24th for the first time, in daylight. Noyelle-en-Chaussde was chosen as the squadron's prime objective and twenty-one crews briefed, immediately after the messes had served an early lunch. At 1 5.18 hours, before a larger than usual crowd gathered expectantly to watch their squadron leave, Wing Commander 'Hank' Iveson advanced the throttles of his Halifax with a well practiced hand and was soon climbing quickly away towards the south. Last to leave, just over twenty minutes later, was young Emond, a Canadian. In close formation the Halifaxes passed southwards over the patchwork pattern of fields in crop, woods and meadow land. Nearing London the soft country colours gave way to urban grey mixed with rows of slate and red-tiled roofs. Smoke from industrial chimneys smudged the afternoon air. Through the haze the channel came into view. Above the roaring horde of bombers a reassuring fighter escort flew.

Penetration into France was not deep. The markers laid by a small force of Pathfinders, seven in all, came easily into view. Ross Forsyth, Humphrey, Bill Palmer and Galbraith, both now commissioned and Pilot Officer Len Slade were in the van of the attack. From their bomb-bays sticks of high explosive bombs arced towards the land below. A minute later came a second deluge, this time from Jimmy Watt flying his favourite Halifax 'The Black Prince' named in honour of his Nigerian wireless operator 'Banjo', Flying Officer Jannings, blissfully unaware that along with his crew he would be dead within a week, Pilot Officer Ted Fuery RAAF, Iveson, Squadron Leader John Harwood, Pilot Officer Catlow, the Canadian Robertson, Peter Chipping - hit by *flak* coming up from Abbeville - Carl Larsen, Flight Lieutenant Sinclair another Australian and like Jannings fated to die this broiling summer, Emond - also hit by flak and Pilot Officer Cole. Smoke wreathed the markers, ground fire at the target was causing scant concern. Four crews remained. Flying Officer O'Brian, Flight Lieutenant Neat and Pilot Officer Ian Weir RNZAF coped, but to his unsuppressed anger Flying Officer Steward was thwarted by bomb-doors jammed tightly shut. No provision was made for a second attempt and Steward would be obliged to wait until the morrow for his first successful crack at a daylight target.

The month ended with a night attack on a railway junction at Blainville near Nancy. For the second time in less than a month the squadron was savagely mauled by a mixture of *flak* and fighters. This time the night-fighters got amongst the bombers before the target was reached. A Pathfinder Lancaster from 582 Squadron and eleven Halifax crews - five from 102 Squadron out from Pocklington - provide the grim statistics. The three squadron crews lost fell inside the space of ten minutes. The New Zealander Ian Weir was first to go, followed by Flying Officer Jannings. Jannings was down at Lesges ten kilometres southeast of Soissons and there were no survivors to tell what happened. Last to fall was Warrant Officer Gramson RCAF. Gramson died whilst the remainder of his crew not only jumped from the burning Halifax, but also found shelter in the hamlets surrounding the tiny village of Ferme Long Voisin. Ian Weir, however, had not gone at the hands of a fighter, but from a well aimed salvo of *flak*. His account now takes us through those last minutes spent between a routine operation and near oblivion:

'I had seen three go before us, slightly on our port to quarter beam, and immediately afterwards two large yellow bursts of light lit the sky behind us. There was no comment from the gunners and I kept on, dead ahead. We were letting down from 11,000 to 6,000 feet gently at this time, dropping Window at the rate of one bundle every twelve seconds, a task we started thirty miles out from the enemy coast - we seemed to have a fuselage full of the stuff. After the two great balls of yellow light we got one on the starboard wing and in a matter of seconds we were on fire inside the fuselage. I knew it was curtains and gave the order to bale out boys, bale out. As he went past me the flight engineer 'Jock' Howie gave me my 'chute', which saved my neck because I'm sure I couldn't have got back to get it. As it happened, I put it on upside down.'

Within seconds of being given his parachute, the Halifax blew itself apart:

'When I came to after the explosion I remember reaching for the rip-cord handle and couldn't find it. I started to claw at the folding part of the 'chute, where the wire should have been and then felt the handle on the left side. it opened immediately, I would estimate at about 400 feet. I thought for a moment I was going to fall into the burning wreck and I reefed on the back of the cords and spilled backwards. I landed at quite a hell of a bat and I couldn't walk for about three or four weeks. A couple of Frenchmen found me and they charged about like only Frenchmen can, yelling like banshees to one another. Along with 'Jock' Howie, Ron Lidbury and Wilson, I was carted into a sort of shed with a dirt floor, and with all the noise going on the Germans were there in no time.'

Ian Weir, battered, burnt and bruised was taken away for treatment, but not before he managed to pass his escape money over to a nun, secreting the not inconsiderable sum under the folds of her dress as she bent over him, praying and fingering the beads on her rosary 'she didn't bat an eye -just gave me a knowing smile'.

Barely without pause the squadron plunged into July. Bill 'Farmer' Brown, a New Zealand Squadron Leader recently arrived from 158 Squadron as replacement for poor Bob West killed in late June, headed eighteen crews bombing a supply site at St Martin L'Hortier during the early evening of the 1st. On the 4th he led the squadron for a second strike on this target. A third assault on St Martin was sent in the early hours of the 6th, the force of just over one-hundred Halifaxes being a seventh of the command's resources committed to action that busy night.

Croix D'Alle, Chateau Benapre east of Dieppe, the caves at Thiverny and Nucort north of the Seine above Vernon followed in a whirl of activity. A year ago the target names had a much more familiar ring, Cologne, Gelsenkirchen, Aachen, Essen - Hamburg to come. At Nucort the cutting leading to the caves was cratered, the road and rail routes also suffered some damage. Flying Officer Steward did not return from this operation, the wreckage of his Halifax and four bodies lay scattered around the area of Courcelles-ies-Gisors.

It was now mid-July. Raiding by day was an established feature in the pattern of almost non-stop bombing on tactical and strategic targets. The rare incursions over the battlefront by the *Luftwaffe* were easily dealt with. Time was now ripe to demonstrate the effectiveness of Bomber Command to the armies on the ground. On the 15th over 1,000 crews were briefed to bomb five Aiming Points cast and southeast of the ruined city of Caen, in Allied hands since the 9th, Montgomery's men were pushing towards Falaise on a steadily widening front. With the sun already high the first marker bombs were accurately placed. At Colombelles, Mondeville, Sannerville and Manneville where 'Hank' Iveson, with flight commanders 'Farmer' Brown and John Harwood, took his squadron in a maximum effort, and little Cagney, the ground shook and folded beneath the weight of over 5,000 tons of high explosives. Only Flying Officer Inglis missed seeing the clouds of dust and smoke drift towards the nearby sea - he was on the ground at Oakley, his starboard inner engine having lost power on the flight south.

In due course a congratulatory telegram on the morning's work would be sent from General Montgomery to Air Chief Marshal Harris. The squadron's copy arrived on the 21st, Sinclair's crew would never read it for they were dead, hammered down by the guns of Oberleutnant Werner Hopf while flying to Acquet during the night of the 18th. Despite these successes the continued destruction of the Ruhr targets still occupied the minds of Harris and his staff. Bomber Command's chief was never really happy operating under the rigid constraints and directives flowing from Eisenhower's headquarters. But, despite his misgivings, he had put the full weight of his command behind the spring offensive and his men had served him well. With few exceptions marshalling yards and rail centres throughout the occupied countries lay in ruins, whilst since the D-Day landings he had ably demonstrated his tactical prowess in close support of the military commanders on the ground.

On the 20th, however, he turned his attention to a synthetic oil producing plant at Bottrop, located midway between Cladbeck in the north and Gelsenkirchen to the south. For a good percentage of the 4 Group crews supplying the bulk of the force, this would be their Ruhr baptism. If any had lingering doubts as to the ferocity of the defences here the next few hours would quickly dispel such thoughts. The *flak* was strong and accurate, fighter flares shone brightly turning black night into naked white day. Bottrop burned below. Pilot Officer Mottram noted a large area of fire to the east, Emond experienced a heart stopping moment when his Halifax brushed against a similar machine; the veterans no doubt thought little had changed in this the cockpit of Germany.

The Baltic Sea port of Kiel was raided by over 600 bombers on the 23rd. Pilot Officer Len Slade had with him a Canadian second pilot:

'I told this chap my crew did not indulge in idle chatter. Anything said on the aircraft was in the interest of the prime objective to get to the target, bomb and return in one piece. The Kiel plan was to stay below 2,000 feet over the North Sea in order to avoid radar detection for as long as possible, climb to our bombing-level, find the target, drop our bombs and then descend to below 2,000 feet again for the return, the idea being to get it over with before too many fighters got airborne. This was fine in theory, but it did not work too well in practice for the defences were well and truly alerted when we arrived. Our Canadian friend had heeded my warning and had not spoken more than a few words on the way over, but the Brocks display over Kiel was too much. "Jesus Christ we are not going through that sodding lot are we" he shouted. He was promptly told to shut up and we carried on. Over the meal after debriefing he confided in me that he wished he could train his crew the way mine were trained. I told him it was essential if he wanted to survive. Sadly they did not.'

The attack left substantial damage on the east side of the docks, while to the south of the Aiming Point half-a-dozen gas holders burned with an eerie blue-tinged flame, this sight being witnessed by Sergeant Fieldson. Carl Larsen, the last of the Norwegian pilots left flying with the squadron, may well have set off these fires for his night-photo plot picture shows a vivid circular flash, so intensely bright that no surrounding ground detail can be seen. judicious route planning foxed the night-fighters and only four crews, none from the squadron. were lost. At Holme Larsen's crew celebrated well for they were screened from further operations.

Stuttgart suffered badly in three bruising attacks delivered between the 24th and the 28th. Fires burned the heart out of the town, leaving seven million square feet of visual damage. But the end of the month was spent blasting supply dumps secreted deep inside the woods at Foret du Crocq and southeast of Calais at Forêt de Nieppe, while on the ground the advance towards the Orne gathered momentum.

On the 30th 'Hank' iveson, his Distinguished Service Order having been gazetted three days earlier, led his squadron into action for the final time. To everyone's bitter disappointment the attack was abandoned just two minutes before Zero Hour. Villers Bocage lay hidden beneath a band of cloud and the proximity of the Allied battlelines deemed it imprudent to continue.

An evening attack on newly located supply dumps reported in the Forêt de Nieppe opened the squadron's August account. The groundfire was fierce. A salvo exploded in the path of Bill Palmer's aircraft. Lying prone in the nose, concentrating his mind on the bombing-run, Flying Officer Clifford Waite:

'Flak came through the Perspex nose and I was hit in the right side of the face blinding me in my right eye and partly in the left as well. I was able to clear my left eye vision sufficiently to bomb the target, but then blood came down on to my flying-suit and because of the cold, it froze. The navigator winced visibly at my condition, but the boys soon rallied around and bandaged me up. The chocolate rations were brought out and these helped to make the return flight bearable.'

Clifford Waite was on his 36th sortie when wounded. on return to Holme he was taken to hospital where surgeons saved the sight of his badly damaged right eye. At the time it was not possible to remove every splinter of Perspex and for many years he was inconvenienced by minute slivers working their way to the surface.

Just short of midnight on the 7th, frustration for a dozen crews attacking enemy strong points held by the German 89th Infantry Division at May sur Orne, south of Caen. Dust and smoke thrown up by the first waves all but obliterated the Target Indicators. However, George Rowley spotted a distinctive red glow through the haze and bombed. His was the only squadron crew to attack the enemy that night. In daylight on the 9th oil dumps southeast of Cambrai in the Forêt de Mormal were set on fire, smoke from this assault rising to 10,000 feet as the bombers cleared the target area unopposed.

The marshalling yards at Dijon in eastern France and a flying bomb site concealed in woods near Wemaers-Cappel occupied the squadron for their next two attacks. Then came a heavy raid by nearly 300 bombers on the Opel vehicle works at Russelsheim southwest of Frankfurt. It proved a disappointment. A thick ground haze persisted and for most of the attack instructions being broadcast by the Master Bomber were indistinct. Searchlight activity was intense and the flak gunners pumped thousands of shells high into the cones of light. Flight Sergeant Neill's aircraft was hit in the rear fuselage, killing his rear-gunner Sergeant Appleby instantly. Shrapnel from this near lethal burst wounded Neill, Causton his wireless operator, and Sergeant Levy in the mid-upper turret. Displaying tremendous fortitude Neill kept control, crash-landing several pain-wracked hours later at Woodbridge. By this time two squadron crews had gone to their deaths in the running battle with night-fighters. First to fall at Quint near the border between Luxembourg and France had been Flight Lieutenant Ron Cramer, well short of the target. Almost an hour later Flying Officer Ings went down like a fiery torch to crash northeast of Hamm. Both had been experienced pilots when killed with a combined total of thirty-six sorties between them.

The sad memories of Russelsheim were quickly erased by two hugely successful daylight raids. Enemy troop positions at Fontaine le Pin were saturated for a full ten minutes in the early afternoon of the 14th, the bombing-line on this occasion being only 2,000 yards ahead of the Canadians advancing on Falaise. The next day nineteen crews headed by Squadron Leader John Harrison flew to Tirlemont, one of nine airfields in Belgium and Holland singled out for concentrated attack. The bombing was quite inspiring, even when measured against the high standards set since the invasion. The weather was clear as over a 1,000 bombers and their escorts crossed the low countries, no enemy fighters in sight. Tirlemont was reached at midday and in almost casual order the assigned force of 109 Halifaxes followed the PFF Lancasters across the field, 17,000 feet below. Flying officer MacDonald RCAF watched a stick of bombs stitch their way across the southwest corner of the aerodrome. Immediately a sheet of flame leapt upwards, suggesting a direct hit on a fuel tank. Then the scene vanished in a welter of dust, smoke rising high into the mid-August sky.

Next on the busy agenda, for there was scant time for rest, was shipping at Brest. No longer to be visited under the shield of darkness, but in the full light of day. The last time Brest had featured at a squadron briefing was over three-and-a-half years ago. Then it was the threat of the *Scharnhorst and Gneisenau* that had compelled Bomber Command to fly at great risk in daylight. On that memorable occasion the squadron had mustered six crews - now twenty-four listened to the detailed instructions; weather, courses, bomb and fuel loads, the latest Intelligence assessment. Only 4 Group would be involved, seventy-nine aircraft in all. Many of those destined to fly this day would have been but boys at school when Wing Commander David Young led his squadron through the corridor of shot and shell that bleak December afternoon.

Over the harbour the *flak* was fierce, that at least had not changed, but no fighters rose like angry dogs to harry and snap as the bombers ran their course. But whereas David Young and his men had been granted an all too perfect view, this time drifting cloud made the bombing-runs very difficult to observe. Flying Officer Carr thought his bombs burst close to a ship lying against one of the moles. George Rowley, hit by flak, was confident he obtained a straddle across his target, Flight Lieutenant Neat likewise. Flight Sergeant Gee's first bomb sent water cascading like a fountain over the bows of a freighter, then a dark cloud obscured the remainder of his stick from view. Pilot Officer Fieldson was equally unfortunate, but his crew reported several columns of grey smoke rising from the harbour and its surrounds.

A night raid on the Ruhr Benzin synthetic oil plant at Sterkrade twelve miles north of Duisburg was accomplished without loss. The squadron was in high spirits and these rose further still when it was announced that twenty-one crews, led for the first time by 'Hank' Iveson's successor, Wing Commander Ralph Cassels, would carry out a daylight attack on the synthetic oil works at Homberg in the Ruhr. The lot for this first tentative penetration of the Ruhr in daylight fell to a small force of Pathfinders headed by 635 Squadron's Commanding Officer Wing Commander 'Tubby' Brooks, backed by his deputy Squadron Leader Peter Swan, and supported by over 200 4 Group Halifaxes.

A stiff reception was expected and the hearts of everyone taking part must have beat in apprehension at what lay before. Over the North Sea, dark shaded even on this late summer's day, across the still occupied low countries and on into the Ruhr the steady, purposeful beat of aero-engines gave warning of man's intent. in the van of the squadron's box flew Jack Espie, an Australian Flight Sergeant pilot:

'We approached with the aircraft in a race course pattern all jockeying for position. Some of the leading crews seemingly impatient and firing many Verey cartridges as if to order lesser aircraft to heel. Then all the smaller gaggles started to interweave into compact groups. Slowly at first the groups built up, until as we neared the Ruhr everyone was in tight formation. To me it looked like mile upon mile of aircraft, those in the distance like motionless insects. The gentle relative movement of the nearer aircraft sometimes changing abruptly into swift crossovers which was quite stunning to see.'

Below, on the edge of the Ruhr, the smoke-blackened ruins of towns bore silent witness to the effects of raids past. Ahead the sky was stained by the first searching salvos of *flak*. Sunlight blinked from bundles of Window hastily jettisoned to foil the radar predicted guns. Holding an immaculate line through the barrage which increased as the mainforce bore down on Homberg, 'Tubby' Brooks placed the first set of Target Indicators. A gash of red fire sprang from the spot where his first marker fell, then, 200 yards beyond, a bright green fire took hold. Cloud and smoke denied his deputy, Swan, but Brooks was already broadcasting instructions 'bomb between the reds and greens'. No one needed second bidding and at two o'clock precisely that August afternoon Flight Lieutenant O'Brian led the first squadron crews over Homberg. Within a few minutes over 700 tons of high explosives cut a swathe of death and destruction through the Meerbeck district. Choking clouds of brick dust gagged at the throats of those running towards the crumbling buildings, fire hoses kicked and bucked, the spray from their jets vanishing into the billowing clouds of smoke and flame. Two minutes after the start of the assault a huge column of thick brown coloured smoke mushroomed into the air. By this time most of the squadron had bombed and were fast clearing the area. Aboard Jack Espie's aircraft Sergeant' Wally' Waddington broke off from his job of dispensing bundles of Window and came up into the cockpit. From the corner of his eye Espie watched the reactions of his awe struck wireless operator:

'A Halifax, slightly higher and in front of us filled the windscreen. Black balls of expended explosives from anti-aircraft shells sped past and fresh black puffs kept appearing from all directions. That was enough for Wally and he disappeared back to the Window chute and the timely dispatch of those thousands of silvered-paper strips. To my knowledge Wally never put his head up into my office again when we were over enemy territory.'

Some of the bombing, but not a lot, went astray. Flying Officer Kerr RCAF bombed at the end of a

Dead Reckoning run, cloud at the time masking his approach. Two minutes later he saw Brooks' red markers slightly to port and realised immediately that his load had not fallen where it was intended. Some damage had been inflicted to the oil installations, but the cloud that had thwarted Peter Swan and others had partially saved Homberg. The seed, however, had been sown. Further daylight raids on the Ruhr industry could be expected to follow.

It was during this late August period that the dominance of the Allied ground forces at last turned the battle in their favour. From the first day of the June landings the enemy had fought stubbornly, though without air-cover the Wehrmacht was continuously forced to retire to new defensive positions. This lack of air-cover manifested itself south of Caen when rocket-firing Typhoons roaming at will caused dreadful carnage amongst the German motorised divisions retreating through the Falaise gap. For several days the area was transformed into one enormous killing ground, after which the Allied armies brushed aside the weakened lines of defences to charge almost unchallenged along the coast of northern France and into Belgium. This rapid advance enabled the leading elements of The Guards Armoured Division to breach the Belgian frontier in the early hours of 3 September and by nightfall their armour was clattering over the broad paved avenues leading into the centre of Brussels. Unchallenged, the 11th Armoured Division dashed for Antwerp, entering the city the next day. On the right flank of the British. the Americans were busy rolling back the enemy from north of the Seine. This indeed was the stuff of war.

These sudden advances left several German garrisons isolated, notably those at Le Havre and Calais, whilst trapped around the Scheldt Estuary stood von Zangen's Fifteenth Army. in retrospect, the failure of the British to capitalise on the enemies weak order north of Antwerp would, in the days to come, have the most dire consequences. On 6 September, just two days after taking control of the disorganised Western Front armies, von Rundstedt signalled the commander of the Fifteenth Army to fall his men back across the Scheldt to Flushing and then by way of Bergen op Zoom on to Breda and relative safety. Had the British 11th Armoured Division, suitably supported, moved up from Antwerp to Woensdrecht the outcome at Arnhem may have been so different.

Meanwhile, the squadron was playing its role in attacks on the beleaguered enemy garrisons. Gun emplacements and strong points at Le Havre received a caning, two major raids being flown on the 10th leaving the defenders shocked and confused. just before the middle of September, two attacks on synthetic oil installations at Gelsenkirchen were launched. Well over a year had passed since the squadron last visited this prime target, then one of the many objectives in the first Battle of the Ruhr. The first raid was aimed at plant in the Buer district, commencing in the early afternoon of the 12th. A strong barrage of *flak* rose to buffet the mainforce pouring across the town between 17,000 and 18,000 feet. Nearly every squadron bomber was hit, though none broke station. Warrant officer Les Dowling RAAF, however, decided to make a second run as Sergeant George Bailey, one of his air-gunners, will now explain:

'At the last moment cloud obscured the Aiming Point and the bomb-aimer did not press the release button. Then the cloud drifted clear, so the skipper plumbed for another go. By the time we started our second run we were practically on our own and the *flak* gave us a renewed hammering. Talk about sweating cobs, I was glad to see the back of Gelsenkirchen that day.'

Flight Sergeant Elchuck RCAF, a wireless operator, was wounded quite badly in the legs by shell splinters piercing the forward compartment of Flying Officer Karr's Halifax. The next day sixteen crews, jointly headed by the New Zealand flight commanders, Bill Brown and John Harrison, braved the gauntlet of fire to deliver an evening attack on the Nordstern area. A thick ground haze made life difficult for the bomb-aimers, the smoke screen put down by the defenders added to their problems, and in consequence most of the bombs fell on, or around a steel plant close to the refineries.

Keeping abreast with this almost continuous call for operations were the groundcrew. Despite the unending grind, Al Hurst, a young Leading Aircraftsman from Wigan, recalls some of the lighter moments of the time:

'One crew returned with the side exit door jammed. The mid-uppergunner signalled for a ladder and I had just placed it in position when I heard the WAAF driver, who had arrived with the crew coach, give out quite a loud cry. The rear-gunner, it appears, had swivelled his turret round, got out and made off to show how affectionate he could be. Meanwhile, the pilot had got out of the aircraft and when I asked what was going on, he replied somewhat laconically "Oh he is a little highly strung from the trip, but she'll be OK".'

Perhaps this was after one of the forays to Gelsenkirchen. On another occasion:

'Usually it fell to me to ask the pilots if there were any snags and if his answer was &no', I would hurry down the fuselage to see if the crew had left any of their sweet ration behind. After one trip the pilot said "yes, there's a 500-Ib bomb hanging out of the bomb-doors". I locked the controls and did not concern myself about the search for sweets.'

A comment now from Wing Commander Ralph Cassels:

'I must say a word for the armourers. With the variety of targets - close support of troops one moment requiring high explosives, industrial targets with a requirement for incendiaries the next, then perhaps high explosives against railways, coupled with a swiftly changing military situation, it was a case of 'bombs on', 'bombs off' two or three times a day. They never faltered.'

A serious take-off accident heralded the start of the Kicl operation on the 15th. Sergeant Throssell's Halifax was barely airborne when the nose dipped and the fully laden bomber crashed heavily into a field and caught fire. Rescue teams were quickly at the scene and their prompt action saved the lives of all those on board. Throssell, Flying Officer Cattelier, a Canadian and the mid-upper gunner, Sergeant Ireland, were quite badly hurt, all being taken to hospital and detained. Over Kiel the *flak* was as fierce as ever. Dick Cowl, a bomb-aimer, had a piece of shrapnel smash the coffee flask lying beside him. Another piece lodged itself deep in the heel of his left flying boot - he was completely unaware of the latter until his return to Holme.

Apart from an evening visit to marshalling yards at Neuss on the 23 rd, the remaining five attacks were aimed at softening up the German strong points at Boulogne and Calais cut off in the Allied advances at the end of August. It was during this busy period that the enemy inflicted a bloody defeat on the British and Polish airborne forces parachuted on to the small Dutch town of Amhem. Any thoughts of victory by the turn of the year were quickly removed by this hard fought battle. Now with the first golden hues of autumn tinting the leaves on the hedgerows, the harvest gathered and thanksgiving done, the men of Holme, innocent bystanders to such peaceful scenes, would turn their eyes ever increasingly towards the Ruhr. The first battle had been fought between March and July 1943 when an Allied victory was still a dream, the second was destined to last throughout what would prove to be the last winter of the war. But before concerning ourselves with the final round a few impressions from aircrew starting and aircrew finishing their tours. First, from Sergeant John Mason RAAF, a wireless operator and the sole Commonwealth airman in Flying Officer Peter Collin's crew:

'Three of our first four trips were unusual in that they were low-level attacks on ground targets in the Calais area. in the parlance of the day, these were 'a piece of cake', although in looking back I think we must have been blissfully ignorant as our Halifaxes were not the best type of aircraft for this type of work. On several occasions we were holed by light *flak.'*

From Warrant Officer Peter Chipping, with the squadron since the time of Nuremburg:

'After D-Day Bomber Command became more and more involved in daylight operations. Despite the fact that the casualty rate was very low in comparison with night operations, I was never particularly keen on daylights. No doubt my dislike was due to the long training and experience devoted to night operations.' And in a similar vein:,

'Having been trained and by now accustomed to flying at night, the idea of daylight operations was distinctly unpleasant. At first, the sense of nakedness or relative defencelessness was somewhat similar, though to a lesser degree, to that of being caught at night in a searchlight beam, an unforgettable experience and certainly one of the most terrifying. At least on approaching the 'Happy Valley' in the dark one could try and wait until some unfortunate colleague had been caught in a cone and then take advantage of his misfortune to nip through. By daylight we were all exposed and the puffs of anti-aircraft fire and tracer bullets took on a totally different and decidedly more hostile appearance. Moreover, to see one of one's own aircraft shot down, break up or explode that much more clearly produced a sickening feeling in the pit of the stomach and a desire to get the job in hand over as quickly as possible.'

Chapter Nine

OCTOBER 1944 to MARCH 1945

Around twenty crews had during the last few months completed their tours of operations, many having flown on well beyond the magical number of '30'. Such a total could not have been contemplated a year ago, but since April the wearing down of *the Luftwaffe's* capability to function in the face of continuous attack had swung the odds once more in favour of the bomber crews. The sheer pace of operations was also helping and instead of the protracted affairs of 1942/43 when a tour could take up to nine months, or more, to complete, crews were now being screened after six months, or less.

In the four months since the beginning of June, the squadron had dispatched a total of 1.140 sorties on fifty-nine major attacks for the loss of fourteen aircraft. Trappes and Blainville, both in June, had between them claimed six crews, but since 12 August the squadron had operated without loss. This good fortune was destined not to last, but even so the loss rate from now on would be negligible in comparison with the dreadful winter of 1943/44 when thirty-two crews failed to return between the beginning of October and the end of March.

The opening attack in October 1944 came on the 6th when in the late afternoon the command visited the synthetic oil plant at Scholven. The *flak* was quite awful. Flying along the narrow corridor that formed the approach into the target area, seventeen aircraft from the twenty-one sent were hit by the barrage, but no one was physically hurt. Mentally, for some, the fearsome barrage of ground fire, the nightfighters and the always numbing cold was having its effect :

'On return from raids I used to shut my eyes and try to compose myself to induce sleep, but all I could see were images of aircraft on fire and breaking up in the air, and the *flak*. In fact every detail stood out very clearly in my mind. My thoughts would race from one subject to another until I began to doubt my ability to carry on.'

'Clear memories of those days, I have none. it is as if the cells of my brain have totally rejected what I went through and experienced. Some years ago in a general tidy up of my possessions, I burnt every scrap of paper that reminded me of the war photographs, the lot,'

'Some, I suppose, did adapt to the call of bombing, indeed our bomb-aimer immediately volunteered for a second tour on ending his first, but I was only too pleased to be finished. To say that I was afraid would be an understatement and at least I am beholden to my crew for seeing me through what I now remember as the most frightening period of my life.'

I have taken these three honest accounts from correspondence with squadron aircrew who completed their tours of duty during the last winter of the war; all were decorated for their devotion to duty.

The day following the Scholven raid, twenty crews, Bill Brown at their head for the last time, went to the ancient town of Kleve, now clogged with enemy troops. it was a lovely early autumn day, clear skies, and under different circumstances ideal for a leisurely flight over the wooded countryside bordering the Rhine northwest of the Ruhr. But on this day, the savagery of Arnhem fresh in mind, there was no time to take in the rolling splendour of the hills, the meandering streams and the neat clusters of dusty villages nestling between the Niers and the Rhine. Approaching from the direction of Nijmegen the bombers came down upon Kleve in all their might, bomb-doors open, bomb-aimers prone and tensely watching for the first markers. Flak, as usual, signposted the way and the leading Pathfinder Lancaster flown by Wing Commander Bingham-Hall was hit and damaged, but his deputy Wing Commander Ison was on hand to guide the mainforce in.

Quickly, so it seemed, the town below crumbled under the weight of bombing. Across the Rhine and northwards at Emmerich a similar scene of total destruction was in hand. The threat to Montgomery's Second Army, moving on beyond Antwerp, was lifted.

The coal and steel centre of Bochum was thrashed by over 400 aircraft on the 9th, twenty of these from the squadron. Nineteen returned, leaving the Halifax of young Wall, a Canadian who had been with the squadron for little over a month, broken and burning on the ground at Arpath, the crew dead, victim of a night-fighter.

Duisburg followed. Two crushing attacks delivered with all the power and precision that Bomber Command could muster left the town quite bewildered. Both raids came within a span of twenty-four hours and involved nearly 2,000 aircraft. The first raid started shortly after nine o'clock in the morning of the 14th. George Rowley took a pilot from an Elementary Flying Training School, just for the experience. He could only have been suitably impressed by what he saw. From the area of the docks explosions ripped through the wharves and storage sheds, fires swiftly broke out as buildings burst asunder. Flying Officer Stu Orser RCAF saw oil tanks blazing fiercely beneath much black smoke. Flight Sergeant White saw his bombs leap-frog across the marshalling yards. All saw and felt their adrenaline rise as the *flak* puffs split the air, but the twenty-eight crews employed came safely through[28]. Holme was reached in ample time for lunch.

Debriefed, the weary crews fell into a fitful sleep, only to be woken and ordered to attend a second briefing for Duisburg. With the midnight hour approaching twenty bombers stood lining the perimeter, each waiting for the signal that would send them winging once more towards the Ruhr. To the hurly-burly of roaring engines, the hiss of air from hydraulic brakes, the drumming of rubber upon concrete, silent waving, muffled cheers, all were soon on their way.

Climb, trim, check the throttle and boost settings, weave, call the crew, look about, course set, instruments functioning, noise, the ever constant vibrant noise, now where are you Duisburg? On the horizon a dull red glow, nearer now, like a web the uncontained rivers of fire set a certain marker. The thump and bump of bomb-bays opening, holding steady, steady, fleeting shapes skid and slide, rock and buffet. Then it's over. Below, the town is a raging inferno of fire, the defences seem quite bemused by the ferociousness of the raid. Bank away, nose down slightly and fly away from the false dawn of Duisburg lighting the sky above the Rhine in a mocking red and yellow light.

Barely rested, the call is Kiel and for four crews, George Rowley's, Flying Officer K Carr's and the Canadians Reilly and Bateman, it is their third major operation inside of thirty-six hours. Over Kiel Flying Officer Reynolds was treated to the terrible sight of a bomber running full tilt into a fighter flare. A white and gold ball of fire spiralled down.

---

28   This attack cost the command fifteen aircraft.

During the late afternoon of the 23 rd over 1000 bombers set out for Essen. The evening sky was grey and forbidding and the entire Ruhr valley lay hidden beneath the dark mass of floating clouds. Two years ago such conditions would have been a boon to Essen and a cause of bitter frustration to the bomber crews groping aimlessly in the darkness for some clue that would reveal their position. Now the weather no longer provided an effective shield, the march of science had seen to that. Flying ahead of the mainforce the Pathfinder crews laid a complex set of route and Target Markers. Essen was bombed with enthusiasm, 4,129 tons of high explosives and a further 409 tons of incendiaries rained down. A year ago the bombers flew loaded mainly with incendiaries, now with little left to burn the bomb-bays were packed with lethal charges of high explosive bombs.

Two days later Essen received a second drubbing, the two attacks had cost the squadron a single crew. Flight Sergeant White, who had watched in awe as his bombs cascaded across the marshalling yards at Duisburg on the 14th, was dead, killed in a crash near Old Buckenham southwest of Attleborough in Norfolk. Sergeant Jim Hampton, a flight engineer who had already lost two brothers on operations flying with Bomber Command and who had flown with Flight Sergeant White to within a few days of the crash writes:

'He was a most likable person, quiet with a good sense of humour. Of very slight build this made it very difficult for him to see ahead and he found taxying extremely trying. once airborne he had as good a control as any other pilot. I felt this loss quite keenly.'

A reversal to ground support broke temporarily the renewed attacks on the Ruhr. On the 28th fifteen crews bombed the sea defences at Walcheren island in the Scheldt estuary. As recounted, the Allies in their lightning advance in early September had reached Antwerp with relative ease. Now, much to the concern of the Supreme Commander and his staff, the port facilities of this Belgian port were still being denied as the enemy still commanded the northern banks of the Westerschelde. Despite his many problems, von Runstedt realised that a continued presence on Walcheren would seriously contain the ambitions of Montgomery to pivot his armies towards the borders of Holland and Germany. Allied intelligence suggested that the island contained some fifty artillery pieces, their calibres ranging between 75 and 220 mm. Furthermore, the majority were well sited in concrete bunkers and manned by experienced naval gunners. Supporting this formidable array of heavy guns were numerous mobile flak and searchlight batteries. The taking of Walcheren was going to be no picnic. But there was a flaw in the defences, a flaw realised by the Allied ground commanders very mindful of the casualties that could be expected from a conventional assault. The main defences were sited below the level of the surrounding sea and herein lay the island's Achilles heel. Smash the sea defences and Walcheren would be untenable. The task of doing this was handed to Bomber Command.

The opening attack came on 3 October when a force of 259 Lancasters and Mosquitoes, suitably protected by a strong fighter escort, smashed a one-hundred yard gap in the Westkapelle dyke which follows the coastline for about three miles around the island's western shoreline. Thousands of tons of seawater poured through the breach, isolating a number of batteries and making others unusable. The west seawall at Flushing was broken on the 7th and on the same day the sea wall bordering the Sloe channel was also holed. Four days later a small force of Lancasters broke the dyke at Veere, whilst on the 17th Westkapelle was again pounded. The predicament of those defending the island was fast becoming critical. Only the centres of Flushing and Middleburg, along with a small area of dunes to the east were free of flood-water.

The squadron joined the assault on the 28th, again Westkapelle being the focal point of attention. Few had difficulty in picking out the green Target indicators and some good bombing was achieved both by the experienced and by the two crews making their operational debut, Flight Sergeant Eyres RAAF and Sergeant Harold Bertenshaw. Of late even the well defended areas of the Ruhr had failed to seriously damage any of the squadron's aircraft, but to the dismay of those crews flying in Squadron Leader Langton's formation, their leader's Halifax was hit by the accurate ground fire. Trailing a plume of smoke it dived into the sea and was lost from sight.

The sea has a notorious record for giving up her victims and Langton's loss was no exception, only the body of his wireless operator, Flight Sergeant Care, being eventually washed onto the sandy shores of the Dutch coast. No doubt it was with a degree or two of trepidation that seventeen crews joined in an area attack on the last of the remaining gun sites, some standing on their own private islands, others waterlogged but still manned. Shortly after midday on the 29th and in wonderfully clear visibility the attack commenced. A vivid red flash, followed by a rush of black smoke was seen spewing up from below by Flight Sergeant Globe. Bert Whittaker saw something much closer. Making his run over the flooded island, Whittaker was holding parallel station with a Pathfinder Lancaster. Without warning the Lancaster turned from its position to the left of the Halifax and headed towards him. There was no time to take avoiding action, barely time to shout a warning, before the starboard wing of the Lancaster struck home with a fearsome blow, wrenching the control column from his strong hands. The collision ripped a massive gash in the rear fuselage from just aft of the port entrance door to a point directly beneath the tailplane leading edge. Protruding from the torn cladding, a twisted section of Lancaster wing, but the rear fuselage structure was holding. Exercising extreme caution Bert Whittaker kept his Halifax flying and after several anxious hours spent recrossing the North Sea he landed safely at Holme. Peter Chipping's old aircraft was a sorry sight and it would spend several months undergoing repairs. Later in the day news came through to say that the Lancaster crew had returned safely and the pilot had taken full responsibility for the unfortunate accident. With the good news that no lives had been lost, the mangled remains of the Lancaster's wing were returned to its squadron with suitable comments and compliments attached.

On the first day of November a small Allied seaborne force waded ashore at Walchcren to mop up the defenders. Thanks in no small way to Bomber Command the sea approaches to Antwerp were now clear.

After the alarms of Walcheren, the squadron welcomed the return to night operations and two attacks on Cologne. The centre of this once beautiful city had suffered badly, though the smoke-blackened walls of the Gothic style cathedral still stood relatively unscathed.

On Dusseldorf on 2 November the squadron records say that the mainforce was assailed by night-fighters. Not an unusual occurrence, even though the *Luftwaffe* was by now hard pressed to provide effective cover for the homeland. Under normal circumstances such an entry would not merit too much attention, but on this occasion the squadron combat reports enthuse over the destruction of jet propelled fighters. In the light of such startling news it is worth spending a moment or two examining the validity of these claims. Undoubtedly, if such aircraft had been encountered, then the bombers had met a derivative of the Messerschmitt Me 262. But had they? First, an account written shortly after the war by Syd Tumham, flight engineer to Flying Officer 'Slim' LeCren, a French Canadian and skipper of the victorious Halifax. The crew had been alerted to the presence of an enemy fighter over the target area by their bomb-aimer, MacAdoo. Syd Turnham had just poked his head up into the astrodome, when he saw the fighter, guns firing, bearing down on them from astern:

'The rear-gunner shouted "he's having a go". I watched absolutely terrified, but unable to move. The fighter was still coming at us, though it had ceased firing. Our rear-gunner was still giving it a good hosing and I heard him cry out "I've got it, I've got it, it's alight". And he had, I yelled "You've hit it Bev". The enemy aircraft, a mass of flames now, turned on its back and blew up leaving a shower of small blazing pieces like a child's firework.'

At this stage of the action, it is quite obvious that no one in LeCren's crew had recognised their attacker as being anything other than a conventional night-fighter. Most certainly there is no hint, or suggestion, that a jet had been destroyed. indeed, after landing and going into the interrogation room, LeCren seemed rather reluctant to put forward a claim, but an Intelligence Officer was roaming about the room excitedly saying the *Luftwaffe* had for the first time sent up jets against the bomber force. Syd Turnham continues: 'Apparently the destruction of one, or two of these machines had been seen by other crews. This encouraged Bev to describe the particular attack made upon us, the details of which were later confirmed by other crews. After considering all the evidence the Commanding Officer decided to claim the destruction of the fighter by our rear-gunner, We were very pleased about this and went off for our meal feeling on top of the world.'

Holme was not the only 4 Group bomber station bubbling with excitement that early November morning. At Lissett, just inland from the resort of Bridlington, the intelligence Officers of 158 Squadron were busy processing the claims for three such aircraft destroyed. Heady news indeed, and for 'Slim' LeCren there was more to follow. In best bib and tucker the tall gaunt Canadian, still not fully recovered from the pneumonia that had grounded him earlier in the year, accompanied by his crew similarly attired, reported to the BBC radio studios at Leeds. Not surprisingly all were more nervous here than in the full heart stopping cry of battle. Fussed and fawned over by a zealous producer, LeCren retold the events of their combat.

Two nights later whilst he was running in over Bochum, the story of their battle with a German jet fighter was being broadcast into the homes of anyone who cared to listen.

But the question remains; did LeCren's crew destroy a jet fighter that dark November night over Dusseldorf? I think not. First, a cursory look at the most likely contender, the Me 262. By November 1944 the jet was at last in quantity production for the *Luftwaffe*, but theoretically not as the fighter envisaged by Professor Messerschmitt, but as a 'bomber'. This reversal of role was by order of the Fuhrer himself, who had never warmed to the enthusiasm shown by Goering and his *Luftwaffe* generals, Galland in particular. Hitler had attended a demonstration of the Me 262 in November 1943, a few weeks before the battle over his capital city commenced. From the outset he demanded this sleek thoroughbred fighter be called a bomber, and as a result development was a protracted affair. But the precarious German position in the winter of 1944 found a variety of designs being pushed into all manner of roles and at about this time a Me 262A was undergoing trials fitted with an SN-2 'Lichtenstein' radar array fitted in the nose. However, the majority of successful combats achieved by the Me 262 and there were many - were achieved by day. Evidence of the true night-fighter version appears to be restricted to experimental prototypes and the only documented material relating to night combats rests with Oberleutnant Waiter who employed Wilde Sau' tactics in February 1945 to intercept Mosquitoes over Berlin.

It is, of course, possible that a decision to employ the Me 262 as a 'night-fighter' in November 1944 was made at a local level and that Wilde Sau sorties were flown with disastrous results. Nonetheless, the more likely explanation is that Allied intelligence, suspecting that the *Luftwaffe* might use their jets by night, briefed the squadron intelligence Officers accordingly. Thus, suitably primed, possibilities quickly turned to facts in the minds of the debriefing teams, the end result being a spate of claims made in all sincerity, but in truth concerning conventional piston-engined night-fighters.

A welcome stand-down for ten days ended with a heavy daylight attack on Julich, a peaceful town sitting astride the Roer river. Once more the course of war had singled out a target that normally would have been left aside. But in mid-November 1944 the Allied lines were extending eastwards through the forests of the Ardennes, whilst in the centre and on the southern flanks of this early winter advance, American troops were moving up through Luxembourg towards the Saar Palatinate. The Roer and the Moselle were within striking distance, Cologne was a tantalising prize beckoning in the distance.

A general mauling of the enemy lines of communications west of the Rhine was called for and Julich was one of several targets earmarked for punishment. To the great delight and pride of all at Holme, 76 Squadron was chosen to spearhead the Julich attack. In tight order, Wing Commander Ralph Cassels leading, the squadron executed a compact bombing pattern. Within two minutes all twenty-three crews had passed over the Aiming Point and only Flight Sergeant Largary's aircraft had been damaged by the *flak* barrage.

The raid on Munster, north of the Ruhr Valley, delivered on the 18th was very disappointing. Large amounts of cloud hid the target area and the few skymarkers seen, as the mainforce approached, were soon swallowed up in the mass of cloud. Bombs were released more in hope than in expectation and little material damage was done. Sterkrade was, however, a much different story. Here the synthetic oil plant of Holten, which had already been at a standstill for three days, though this fact was unknown at the time of the attack, took a tremendous pounding. Flying Officer Roope reported bright red fires mushrooming amongst the profusion of exploding bombs. There can be no doubt these blistering attacks on the Ruhr industries were now having a very disruptive effect on production. The manufacturing: centres of Essen and Duisburg, now little more than bomb-blasted ruins, were further punished towards the end of the month, but not on the Titanic scale of the October raids.

The impetus of attack was carried on into December. Liagen was visited on the 2nd, Soest three nights later. In the early stages of the Soest raid the bombing was weak and scattered, but sharp instructions from the Master Bomber quickly rectified the situation and the town was left gutted and torn apart, fire licking from the heaps of rubble, dead and dying everywhere.

Continuing strikes on Essen brought a sharpish response and six crews from a mainforce of slightly less than 530 aircraft did not return.

The weather, meanwhile, was dreadful. On the Continent snow fell in mid-December so adding to the discomfort of the Allied armies, weary from the strength sapping autumn battles. Christmas was fast approaching and in general the main battle areas were fairly quiet. Amongst the chill pine forests of the Ardennes the Allied lines were thin and lightly defended, but, so it was thought, a similar situation prevailed with the Germans opposite. No one was expecting any major developments along this section of the front.

This feeling of calm was rudely shattered in the early hours of 16 December, when in a lightning attack von Runstedt sent his Panzers roaring through the snow covered woods. On a broad front of some fifty miles, stretching from Monschau in the north to Echternach in the south, the German armour sliced into the American lines. The Wehrmacht's initial advance was rapid. Forward lines were overrun and within hours headquarters staffs in several areas were fighting for their lives as the Tiger tanks blasted a path for the close following infantry. The aim was to drive through to Antwerp and isolate the two major Allied army groups. The success of von Runstedt's plan hinged on the weather remaining bad, coupled with the speed of his forward echelons.

While the weather remained in his favour he stood an outside chance of success, but he was committing his forces with little, or no air support and very meagre supplies of fuel. it was a huge gamble which so nearly succeeded.

For several days the clouds almost hugged the tops of the trees. The Typhoons and Tempests, Mustangs and Thunderbolts sat on the ground, completely ineffective. The advance continued, though Allied resistance was stiffening.

Forty-eight hours after the first Panzers brushed aside the forward defenders, Squadron Leader John Crampton took off from Holme with eighteen crews to bomb enemy supplies passing through Duisburg. A mainforce of 523 bombers were employed; in the event few saw anything of the markers being put down on two Aiming Points. The attack failed.

On the 22nd fifteen crews were briefed for a strike at rail communications at Bingen well down the Rhine beyond Koblenz. The weather forecast was not inspiring. Only Bert Whittaker, Carr and Leakey, the Australian Eyres, MacDonald, Ball and Thompson, Canadians all, took-off. Some measure of success was accomplished.

Then, on the 24th the British 29th Armoured Brigade halted the panzers at Foy Notre Dame near Dinant. At Holme plans for the festive season were in the balance.

'Christmas Eve came along and we were detailed for another raid. The weather was still awful, hard frost and fog. As a result of these conditions the trip was postponed for twenty-four hours. This meant we would be flying on Christmas Day.'

So wrote Syd Turnham in his diary. Huw Morgan, Bert Whittaker's bomb-aimer, gives his impressions of events on the 25th[29]:

'We were briefed several times during the day, but couldn't take-off because of the fog. Stand-down did not come until early evening, after which we ate a belated Christmas dinner. A hastily arranged all-ranks dance in the Sergeants Mess followed, but it was a rather gloomy affair with most of us drinking hard, yet seemingly remaining sober.' Another fellow-mess member, however, thought it was a much brighter occasion:

'Needless to say as the booze flowed, so the fun increased and the high spot of the evening came when some bright type challenged the Wingco to climb up the tables and chairs, stacked like a pyramid to the ceiling, with one hand and drink a pint of beer at the same time. He was all set to drink his pint when the lot collapsed, leaving the Wingco on the floor flat on his back. A Sergeant walked over to where he lay and proceeded to empty his drink all over him saying, "that was a bloody poor effort". For a second or two the situation could have gone either way, but the Wingco said "it's alright, it's only my drinking suit". His popularity simply soared from that moment on.'

In Al Hurst's billet everyone was getting merry on beer from a bucket resting on the stove, when their privacy was invaded by a young Canadian pilot, Flying Officer Woolfe. 'Woolfy' was by this time in quite a state and after a rousing chorus or two, made off for his own quarters. Huw Morgan again:

'Woolfy charged into our billet in the small hours, demanding we return his hat. We didn't know what he was talking about, and with much good natured jostling, hustled him out into the night. Around dawn we were woken and ordered straight to briefing where we were told St. Vith was our target.'

Again there was a frustrating delay, but at midday the order to go was given. The weather was still far from encouraging when Jack Espie took-off:

'It was an instrument take-off and the airfield was closed after about two thirds of us were airborne.

---

29   Although 76 Squadron did not fly on Christmas Day, raids to the St. Vith area were carried out.

With so few aircraft the sky was lonely. The fog spread across the sea and into Northern France. Nearing the target there was a break in the clag, this was confirmed with the arrival of accurate shelling from some 88 mm guns.'

Espie was one of the fifteen pilots who had managed to get away from Holme before the weather closed in. Woolfe, also, was amongst the fifteen now closing in company with a sizeable mainforce on the small Belgian town of St. Vith. 'Slim' LeCren was on operations for the twenty-first time since mid-September. Syd Turnham was with him:

'The Met. man was right on form, the weather being almost clear as we reached the target. We were flying in the second of three waves and bombed after one false run. Below I could see a convoy of tanks and armoured vehicles. The defensive fire was very hot and we were holed in one or two places, but it did not do any vital damage. Some were not so lucky and at least two of our number went down out of control.'

From another crew, the pilot remembers:

'The Halifax to the right of us must have received a direct hit. The nose, forward of the wing, disintegrated. The nose-less aircraft then climbed, paused, a wing dropped, and then dived earthwards. I think we all held our breath during that dive. My reargunner, 'Lefty' Wright counted just one parachute opening before the crash.'

Jack Espie had witnessed the end of poor Woolf. The direct hit had killed the boisterous Canadian who had celebrated so well the previous evening. The parachute seen by Jack Espie's rear-gunner belonged to Woolf's mid-upper gunner, Flight Sergeant Mason RCAF. The rest were dead, their corpses scattered over a wide area of the Ardennes near Nassogne.

St. Vith and its surrounds were quickly shaken to the core, smoke and flames engulfed the tiny community luckless enough to be caught up in the web of retreating enemy armour.

'It had been snowing and one could clearly see the hundreds of tank tracks winding in all directions. The flak was heavy, but there was a complete absence of fighters. Our bombing was quite devastating.' *Flying Officer Doug Bennett - Bomb Aimer.*

Indeed Doug Bennett is quite correct in his assessment. Frau Margret DoepgenBeretz had survived the raid sent on Christmas Day. Now, with the return of the bombers, she had taken shelter in a cellar, along with others from the town.

'All at once there was a tremendous explosion of a heavy bomb. Everyone was gasping for breath, a stove exploded and the chimney was crushed. Smoke and soot shot out making us as black as a negro and we all thought we would suffocate. But just then a second bomb exploded, making a hole in the vault and we all got out into the open. How long the bombing had gone on, no one could say - maybe half-an-hour. Burning phosphorus[30] was everywhere and the German soldiers were helping the civilians. The town seemed to be an ocean of fire.'

About three miles to the south of St. Vith, lies the village of Lommersweiler. An eye witness here writes:

'It was a calm day. About 3.30 in the afternoon there was a heavy air raid on St. Vith, continuing for about twenty minutes. As the defending ack-ack guns are destroyed, the bombers were able to discharge their loads without interference. During the evening the first refugees from St. Vith arrived in the village.

---

30   This reference to burning phosphorus has been questioned. It is very likely that fuel stocks were on fire and in the confusion, with flames and smoke everywhere, the term 'Phosphorus' was used to describe the scene

A German soldier who was amongst them said "It was just hell. I fought in Russia and survived Normandy, but I can assure you that was nothing in comparison to St. Vith".'

No one is able to say for certain how many people died during the attacks on this community. Kurt Fagnoul, author and local historian, writes:

'Three hundred bodies were recovered from the crypt under the church, but it is estimated that the number killed was between 1,000 and 1,500 which is quite a lot for a town having nowadays 3,000 inhabitants.'

The Met. man who had forecast clearing skies over Belgium had also warned of fog over England on return. For the second time he was proved correct. Jack Espie tried to get onto a FIDO equipped aerodrome. He was on his final approach to land when the airfield controller ordered him to divert, there was no space remaining on his field. Jack flew off to Leuchars in Scotland. 'Slim' LeCren was down, along with Peter Collins and others, at another Scottish aerodrome, East Fortune. Their arrival here at what was normally a Coastal Command Operational Training Unit threw the station into a turmoil. The aircrews, thickly clad in fur-lined boots, sweaters and all manner of garments necessary for winter operations in the Halifaxes, soon began to feel most uncomfortable. in the crowded mess ante-room the temperature was unpleasant to say the least. Syd Turnham, in company with other NC0s, decided to explore his temporary home:

'We walked down to the guardroom, as I wanted to find a telephone and ring my wife. "Are you the members of the Halifax crews that have just arrived"? asked one of the Service Policemen. On being told we were, he took us into a billet adjoining the guardroom, loaned us towels, soap, razor, brush and comb. He also supplied us with collars and ties and for me a pair of gym shoes. Later, when we were washed and shaved, he directed us to a local hostelry where we spent the evening revelling in true Scottish hospitality.'

Peter Collins crew were also out and about. Peter, rather unfairly, though he took it cheerfully enough, had earned himself the title of 'land away Collins'. This was his fifth away from Base landing and by now he and his crew always operated well prepared for such eventualities.

At Holme Huw Morgan celebrated his twenty-third birthday, unaware that his pal 'Woolfy' would not be coming back anymore.

For the last attack of 1944, by which time the Ardennes offensive had swung in favour of the Allies, the squadron went to Cologne. in the early evening gloom Flight Lieutenant Harrison's aircraft took a direct hit from *flak* and exploded. Harrison, by a miracle, was blown clear. The rest of his crew were not so fortunate and Holme lost a very popular Bombing Leader in Flight Lieutenant May DFM. He had been filling in for Harrison's regular bomb-aimer, such are the fortunes of war. The raid itself barely warranted mention in the press:

'After many years' writes John Mason 'the exploits of Bomber Command had become so common that the fact that the boys were out in force last night had little news value. It was the days of the Battle of the Bulge, buzz bombs and V2 rockets. The army was the news. The end was in sight and to the people at home the news was that the army was pushing on to a final victory. Nonetheless, Bomber Command continued to press on untiringly as it had done from the beginning. Feats of bravery and fortitude had become the norm, rather than the exception. The standard had been set and you were expected to press on regardless.'

During the early evening of New Year's Day 1945, Squadron Leader 'Maxie' Freeman headed the squadron contingent of eighteen crews heading for the Ruhr, their primary objective a coking plant at Dortmund. It was altogether an eerie night, nightfighters were seen, but no combats are reported; the bombing seemed confused and scattered. No tangible results were achieved and all were thankful to feel the frost covered runways of Holme beneath them on return. Not so the following night, when Bomber Command turned night into day over the I C Farbein chemical works at Ludwigshafen. This pulverising attack got under way just before seven o'clock in the evening. The Pathfinders had done their work well. Target indicators burned brightly near the works, believed to be the largest in Germany and the mainforce saturated the town with a mixture of high explosives and incendiaries. The hackneyed phrase 'fires visible for over fifty miles on the return leg' was duly entered in the squadron records, as indeed they were.

With all the familiar hallmarks of air battles marking the bombers course, raids on Hannover, communications at Hanau, and the marshalling yards at Saarbrucken followed. The latter target was bombed on a bright frosty afternoon and the entire sweep of the yards vanished beneath an erupting cloud of dust, smoke and flying debris.

Two nights after Saarbrucken, eighteen crews were ordered to go in ahead of the Pathfinders over Magdeburg. The records state to divert attention by the enemy nightfighters from the PFF'. The thoughts of those so employed are not recorded, but a number of enemy fighters were seen, though no claims were lodged.

in the first seventeen days of January the squadron flew 109 sorties, a superb effort as the weather was far from easy. Then for twelve days a blissful rest. No operations, just the routine of training, plus a change of command. On the 25th the very popular Ralph Cassels handed over the running of the squadron to Wing Commander 'Chic' Whyte, but we will meet Ralph Cassels again later in the story.

For the 28th a night raid on Stuttgart was planned, and executed in rather indifferent weather. Radar aids were used to assist the bombing, but in the words of Flight Lieutenant Perry afterwards, it was all rather a chancey business and lacking in concentration. on return the weather took a turn for the worse and crews were forced to scramble in under lowering clouds, or seek refuge at bases in southern England. The brave got in, the wise diverted; Kennard, a Canadian to Manston, Maxie Freeman, Orser, Gracie, Williams, Hannan and Gerald Lawson all to Benson, Thompson and 'Mac' McBrinn to the coastal delights offered by Ford. All were safely back at Holme in time to go to Mainz on the opening day of February.

Coming home in the late evening in 'Vera the Virgin', a veteran of nearly eighty missions, 'Mac' McBrinn crashed near Tibbenham in Suffolk. Flying Officer Wheatley his bomb-aimer, Farley the navigator and Flight Sergeant Rogers his wireless operator baled out. Flying Officer Ken Oddy who had been posted in for a second tour of duty the previous November[31] was last seen trying to get back to his mid-under position and, along with the others he died.

Oil targets at Wanne Eickel came in for attention on the 2nd and 9th, Flight Lieutenant Ted Fuery RAAF, now well into his second tour of duty with the squadron, reported seeing vivid yellow explosions west of the main patch of Target indicators on the second attack. Further destructive raids on the synthetic oil works at Bohlen near Leipzig and at Wesel followed. Over Bohlen crews complained that the Master Bomber was indistinct, the flak heavy and nightfighters were nosing around too close for comfort. it was also bitterly cold.

---

31   At the same time as Flying Officer Ken Oddy's arrival on the squadron, Flying Officers Bill James and Erie Furness arrived for second tours as air-gunners. It is believed that when Ken Oddy was killed, the squadron was employing the mid-under gunner for the last time as Eric Furness writes 'it was the coldest, most unenviable position in Bomber Command.'

The first of two attacks on Wesel was a complete failure. Thick cloud shielded the upper Rhine and the raid was called off by the Master Bomber. Pilot Officer Oleynik RCAF failed to hear the broadcast cancelling the attack and he completed his bombing run using radio aids. Returning to Holme in the half-light of a typical, grey, misty February afternoon, Squadron Leader Whitty had the misfortune to crash near Brough.

His bomb-aimer Flying Officer Bobby was killed, but the rest escaped with only minor cuts and bruises to show for their frightening experience.

The second attempt at Wesel went off without a hitch and a jubilant Pilot Officer Barrell returned to say that his gunners, Flight Sergeants Tennant and Terry had destroyed a Bf 109. Flying Officer Roope did not return, he was down at Epinoy in France, but he was home in time to go to Mainz on the 27th, by which time his promotion to Flight Lieutenant had come through. Squadron Leader Whitty, recovered from his crash on the 17th, was also operating, but in common with his squadron companions he was not too enthusiastic about the results. A strong easterly wind was blowing, sending the PFF flares cavorting wildly about the sky. Bombs were scattered over a wide area as bomb-aimers gamely tried to allow for the drift, their efforts, in the main, failing. But no more would Sir Arthur Harris ask his crews to go to the old Roman settlement of Mainz. This was the fourth and last mainforce attack on this target. After the war it was assessed that sixty-one per cent of this industrial complex and centre before and since, of the Rheinischen wine trade, had been destroyed. For Pilot Officer Barrell this was purely academic for he, along with his rear-gunner Flight Sergeant Terry, was a prisoner. The remainder of his crew were found dead in the wreckage of their Halifax strewn over a snow covered field close to the town. Theirs was the last squadron aircraft to fall on German soil.

Prior to Mainz, the long haul to Chemnitz had been accomplished on the 14th. Crews flew on this raid with leaflets printed in Russian, just in case any were forced down near the advancing Soviet armies.

And so the might of Bomber Command steam rollered without pause over the bruised and broken towns of Germany. On the ground the net was being drawn tight, the news from Italy told of further advances towards the Po River, from the cast the Russians were closing with a vengeance towards Germany's eastern borders, whilst in the west the reverses of the Ardennes were just a bitter memory.

March 1945, the last full month of the bombing campaign, commenced with Wing Commander 'Chic' Whyte leading his men for the second time since taking over from Ralph Cassels. Their objective, as part of a mainforce of over 850 bombers, was Cologne. By now the forward American troops were within five miles of the city suburbs, though aiming to cross the Rhine at Remagen, down stream south of Bonn. 'Chic' Whyte and his men were not concerned with smashing factories, or destroying plant. This time their task was to help destroy the highways leading into Cologne. Cut them, block them, deny the enemy the opportunity to move his troops and armour in defence of the Rhineland. History now remembers this attack as the 22nd major assault on this target since March 1942. In those three intervening years the style of operations had changed completely and it is true to say that the crews flying to Cologne that early March day in 1945 belonged to another world when compared with their brave forerunners who carried the war to the enemy camp in 1942.

One common factor remained, binding those who had survived those perilous years to the aircrew now flying in the full flush of certain victory - their commander, Air Chief Marshal Sir Arthur Harris. in charge by March 1942, he was still at the helm three years later. No story involving the men and women of Bomber Command can be told without some reference to his leadership. He had made his mistakes. His unbending attitude at times frustrated even his closest colleagues on the planning staff at High Wycombe and within the Air Council. Furthermore, it must be admitted that he had not achieved his ultimate aim of bringing Germany to her knees by bombing alone. That dream faded on a stormy June morning in 1944 when the first Allied soldiers ran onto a cold, barren beach in Normandy, and stayed there. But despite these remarks, despite the criticism of recent years, no one can deny that Arthur Harris conducted the bombing campaign with a single mindedness and a tenacity that was at times frightening to behold. He had bowed to authority, notably to Eisenhower in the run-up to 'Overlord', but he was never broken in his own unshakeable confidence in the ability of his aircrews and he had most ably demonstrated to the world what his men could do. Testament to their achievement lay stark in the ruins of Hamburg, the Ruhrland towns and cities and at countless other places that had felt the weight of a Bomber Command attack. Equally, it is indisputable that Allied casualties on D-Day and beyond were effectively reduced by the effort and sacrifice of Bomber Command. In the critical middle war period, the persistent chipping away at the cornerstone of German industry had compelled the German High Command to deploy men and materials on an ever increasing scale to the unproductive task of home defence. On several fronts, notably in Russia, the Wehrmacht suffered as a direct result of Bomber Command's continual presence over the Ruhr and other manufacturing towns of Germany. But perhaps most important of all, his aircrews believed implicitly in him and practically without exception all served him to the very best of their ability. Now one last Herculean effort was being asked of them, freely and not without further sacrifice it was going to be given.

Chapter Ten

THE DAWN BREAKS

Everyone had returned safely from Cologne. Warrant Officer Collins and Pilot Officer Rowland had excitedly given their first post-raid reports, and now twenty-four hours later, the squadron was busy preparing for a heavy strike on a synthetic oil producing plant northeast of Dortmund at Kamen. None of the twenty crews employed had great difficulty in locating Kamen and the return flight passed without hint of trouble until the bombers were streaming in over the Wash, navigation lights on, all making their calls in readiness for landing, Not long to go. Holme was primed, ready to recover her charges. The tea urns were hot and steaming, the Intelligence Officers and their little bands of helpers were waiting. The babbling ritual of debriefing would soon begin, afterwards 'bacon and eggs', swop a yarn or two before drifting off to bed. And then the intruders struck:

'I was occupying the second pilot's seat when I noticed air to air firing and soon afterwards the red marker beacons went out. This was the signal that enemy aircraft were in the vicinity. I advised my pilot to switch off his navigation lights and reduce height by 2,000 feet in order to bring us out of the main stream.' writes Flying Officer Eric Furness, flying with Pilot Officer Globe. Globe did as he was bid, but as he landed so a Ju 88 made one firing pass - and missed. Pilot Officer Paul Oleynik was not so lucky:

'We were raked from rear to front, the attack coming from the rear port quarter. There were bullet holes from the port side window going through the cockpit and out the right side. Normally I would lean forward over the control column in preparation for landing, but this time I was leaning backward, with my arms fully extended. Had I been in my normal flying position I would have had a couple of bullets go through the back of my head.'

His mid-upper gunner, Flight Sergeant Maltby RCAF from Kamloops, British Colombia, was not so fortunate. He was struck in the forehead and died instantly. Oleynik diverted to Carnaby, the emergency aerodrome north of Holme near Bridlington. En route he was attacked again, but with his wireless operator flashing SOS on the bottom signal light and the flight engineer firing off red Very cartridges, this attack was successfully evaded, and Paul Oleynik set his badly damaged bomber down on the Carnaby strip:

'The port tyre collapsed and we started to ground-loop to the left, which was taking us directly into the control tower. I could not straighten out, so I increased the radius of the ground-loop in order to avoid colliding with the tower and crashed head on into another Halifax.'

The attack on Oleynik's aircraft and the ensuing general melee was seen by the crew of Pilot Officer Harold Bertenshaw's aircraft. His bomb-aimer, George French takes up the story:

'We were turning to port when the fighter struck from below on the starboard side, hitting us in the starboard outer engine and in the petrol tanks, which quickly burst into flames sending rivulets of burning fuel streaming across the damaged wing. The force of the attack sent us into a dive and I distinctly remember seeing trees flashing past as I helped the pilot to pull out. At about 600 feet we levelled off and the order to abandon the aircraft was given. Bunny Austin, Dave Skilton and Timber Wood went without trouble, but Holly Sporne in the rear turret got his flying-boots entangled as he tried to roll out backwards and he had to pull himself back into the aircraft to free himself. By the time he left, we were below 400 feet. Whilst Holly was sorting himself out, I collected Harold's 'chute and clipped it in position, forgetting his safety harness was still in place. Moments later the fire burnt through the control wires and I went out through the forward escape hatch, followed by the skipper who had had the good fortune to realise my error. Unknown to us at the time the mid-upper gunner, Morgan Shearman, must still have been in the aircraft for he was found alive lying by one of the engines, eight loops of his parachute cords still in the pack. He must have jumped very late.'

Morgan Shearman lived, though he subsequently underwent more than twenty operations in the process of his recovery.

The rest of the crew were badly shaken from this very low-level escape. Harold Bertenshaw sprained an ankle, but by blowing on his whistle he was soon found by three of the crew and together they made their way to a farm at Cadney, just south of the Humber. From here they were able to telephone Holme, and later transport arrived from Kirton Lindsey where they were to spend the night.

This had been a sharp reminder that the *Luftwaffe* could still present a threat, when it was least expected. Why the *Luftwaffe* did not concentrate more on this type of attack is one of the major mistakes of the German air war and like so many more is directly attributable to Hitler himself.

An oil processing plant at Hemmingstedt was left burning on the 7th, the U-boat construction yards at Hamburg were savaged on the 8th. Slim LeCren was home way ahead of all others. Hamburg had been his 36th sortie and after bombing the yards it had been 'home James and don't spare the horses'. His crew had come through their tour relatively untroubled, though LeCren himself had flown the last half dozen operations wracked with pain. For weeks his right thigh had been troubling him and the Medical Officer had diagnosed muscular rheumatism. Over Hemmingstedt their Halifax had been hit by *flak* and the hydraulics damaged, resulting in a very anxious landing on return to Holme. The next night as his crew left the briefing room, LeCren turned to his rear-gunner and said:

'Boy if you see any fighters tonight, you will have to hit them first because I won't be able to do any evasive action with this leg, so be on your toes.' Near him was his flight engineer, Syd Tumham:

'We could see that he was in pain. His face, which was normally thin, was now drawn and white and his whole attitude was that of a man who was driving himself on to do his job. For the first time since our flight together, I found myself looking at him in a different light. He may not have been a social success, but he had a lot of guts.'

On the 11th, for the last time, the command went to Essen. Twenty-two crews, including Maxie Freeman, now in charge of A Flight after serving as deputy to John Crampton, who was this day heading the B Flight contingent and Paul Oleynik flying on operations for the first time since the intruder incident[32], took part in this historic operation. By tea time the ruined city of Essen had soaked up a further 4,662 tons of bombs, a far different story from when this target was first visited in strength on 8 March 1942. No other German town had attracted the target selectors at High Wycombe like Essen. it had occupied the command on twenty-eight major occasions since March 1942 and only Berlin had taken a greater weight of bombs. The squadron will remember it for the *flak* and searchlights, the haze and perhaps the feeling of apprehension felt when the covers were pulled back at briefing to reveal the ugly smudge of Essen waiting.

32   Erie Furness was in the mid-upper turret.

But Arthur Harris was not yet finished with the Ruhr. Dortmund, the marshalling yards at Wuppertal/Barmen, Homberg - scene of the commands first daylight intrusion over seven months ago - a colliery at Bottrop, all were bombed on four violent days between the 12th and 15th and for good measure Hagen was blasted in a mid-evening raid on the last day of this mini offensive. Flight Lieutenant 'Mac* MacFarlane took part in four of the five raids, Ted Fuery RAAF, Largary, Paul Oleynik, Inglis, Boswell, Reilly, Thompson, Chiddenton, Stu Orser and Gerald Lawson, all Canadians, Flight Lieutenant Campbell, Warrant Officer Collins, Flight Lieutenants Reynolds and Roope and Flying Officer Howe all chalked up three apiece. The pincer movement to encircle the Ruhr was gaining momentum. A bridgehead south of Bonn, established by the Americans, was firm and troops with armour in support were ready to swing northwards. Wesel, meanwhile, had been chosen for the northern crossing point and here Eisenhower planned to use his airborne forces. To avoid any repercussions of Arnhem, Bomber Command was handed the job of disrupting enemy troop movements through the few remaining Ruhr railheads.

Witten, south of Bochum, was bombed at four am on the 19th and left burning. Failure, however, on the 20th when high winds over a cloudy Ruhr valley blew the skymarkers well away from the intended Aiming Point at Bochum, but against Dulmen on the northern edge of the Ruhr, the command triumphed. Raided on the 22nd, just two days ahead of the planned parachute drop, Dulmen was left ablaze from end to end. The few remaining stocks of fuel left to the *Luftwaffe* were engulfed by the flames and destroyed. Only Flight Lieutenant Inshaw missed seeing the massive orange eruptions; he was forced to turn back to Holme with failing engines.

On the day of the Allied airborne landings, a strong force of bombers, twenty-two from the squadron, flew over the ruins of what once had been the oil town of Sterkrade. This time their target was the railway station. Four crews, Ted Fuery, Flight Lieutenant Carter RCAF, Flying Officer Morris and Flight Sergeant Arnston RCAF were piloting brand new Halifax B VIs; the days of the faithful B III were numbered.

No one could fail to be awed by the destruction now being handed out. By and large the PFF were marking targets with unerring accuracy and for the unfortunate German civilians, caught up in the turmoil of the last few weeks of the war, life must have seemed like Armegedon itself. What remained of the principal Ruhr communities was little more than heaps of fire blackened rubble. In many places where the outer shells of buildings remained, the interiors were gutted from incendiary fires of raids past. What life remained existed in cold, dank cellars, or in makeshift shelters fashioned out of the ruins of what had once been cosy homes, cherished and cared for. All pattern of normal life had long since vanished, the fight to survive in the face of such abject misery was won by some, lost by many.

Shut away in his Berlin bunker, divorced both mentally and physically from the reality of what was happening to his people, Adolf Hitler, his brain fogged from the massive daily intake of drugs, continued to berate his Generals, issue orders to formations that had ceased to function and bestow decorations on the few hirelings even now deluding themselves that victory could still be theirs.

With the Ruhr encircled, the Wehrmacht fell back deeper into what remained of Germany. The Allies were now in hot pursuit. In Holland men of the First Canadian Army were moving northwards, aiming for the German ports of Emden and Wilheimshaven. From the centre of the Allied lines the American Ninth Army pushed on towards Hannover, their left flank covered by the British Second Army advancing on the Weser river. In the south American armour was driving hard in two directions, one towards the Harz mountains, the other making for Lippstadt to join up with the Ninth.

Such activity on the battle fronts left the command with little to do, but during

the first ten days of April the squadron joined in mainforce attacks directed against Harburg and

Hamburg. At Harburg, a town standing on the south bank of the Elbe and little more than an extension of the sprawl of Hamburg, oil storage tanks were left burning fiercely on the 4th. Of the twenty-one squadron crews operating, five were making their operational debut. Flying Officers Amundrud RCAF and MacPhee RCAF made their marks in the new B VIs, while Flight Sergeants Eases, Hems RCAF and Joe Penner RCAF were flying the few remaining B IIIs. It was the last time the squadron used this version, and four nights later when twenty-one crews took-off for the submarine building yards at Hamburg, the transition to the much improved Halifax B VI was complete.

in its death throes the Hamburg defences sent up a stiff barrage of *flak*, while Flying Officer Amundrud was set upon by a night-fighter. Considerable damage was inflicted before he threw off his assailant, but sensibly Amundrud held his course, bombed, and returned under the protective mantle of the mainstream.

During the mid-afternoon of the 11th the Bayreuth marshalling yards north of Nuremburg were plundered in no uncertain fashion, the squadron diarist remarking 'no opposition whatsoever, and on departure smoke was rising to 12,000 feet.' For seven days the squadron rested, but on the 18th a maximum effort was called for against Heligoland, a small island guarding the sea approaches to the Elbe. From the concrete dispersals surrounding Holme-on-Spalding Moor, twenty-six Halifaxes began the familiar journey out to the duty runway. Under a clear April sky the first Halifax moved off down the runway, black streaked, hallmark of thousands of landings. A second bomber moved into position, engines throbbing. Nothing disturbed the orderly flow until the eleventh aircraft started its roll, the clock in the control tower showing 11.33 am. Piloted by Warrant Officer Holmes, things went wrong:

'The aircraft started to swerve from side to side as it went down the runway. The pilot tried to correct, but the swerve increased and finally the Halifax turned completely round, the undercarriage legs gave way and the aircraft crashed on the airfield with the bomb-load spilling out. I was in the rest position at the time and managed to get the escape hatch above me off. However, I had some difficulty in climbing out until somebody put their hands under my backside and I came out like a cork from a bottle. Fortunately for us our erratic take-off had been seen from the tower and crash and ambulance vehicles had been running practically alongside us. As I came out of the wreck I ran along the wing, straight into the ambulance.'

The crew had had a most fortuitous escape and for the navigator, Squadron Leader Haskett [33], it had been a very eventful start to his second tour of operations. Now came the task of marshalling the remaining Halifaxes back to their dispersals, a pall of smoke marking the area where Holmes had so nearly met his end. For those that had taken off, Heligoland is best remembered by one crew for the clear spring skies. Flight Sergeant Tim Cooke navigating for Flying Officer Bonnie Morris found himself looking up from his charts:

'It was such a beautiful day as we flew out over the North Sea. The sky was a deep blue and it was difficult to realise there was still a war on.'

'Another seven days drifted away. The Allied armies continued their advance towards the Elbe. On the 25th operations were ordered against an island lying at the eastern end of the Frisian islands chain, Wangerooge. Crammed with heavy calibre guns the island was deemed to present a threat and Bomber Command was ordered to nullify its fortifications.

Lunch was taken early at Holme where twenty-five aircraft were made ready. At 2.25 pm in the afternoon

33 Recently arrived from 578 Squadron Burn, to takeover duties as Squadron Navigation Leader.

Flying Officer Eyres RAAF commenced the familiar ritual, unaware that for the last time the squadron was being called upon to operate in anger. Flight Lieutenant Chiddenton RCAF was next to go, followed smartly by Flight Sergeant judge. Then came Flying Officer MacPhee RCAF and Pilot Officer Simons RCAF, before Wing Commander Chic Whyte opened the throttles, watched his revs climb and with practised calm, took to the air.

By now the roar of engines could be heard all over the field and its surrounds. People waved, cheered and shouted all manner of good wishes. Pilot Officer Turner was in position, then he too was gone. Watchful eyes saw Warrant Officer Holmes go, this time successfully, though John Crampton gave him a two-minute start, just in case. Flight Lieutenant Kennedy slotted in behind John Crampton, Gerald Lawson, Bell, Calcutt, Eames and Joe Penner quick to follow.

From Leconfield and Lissett, Breighton and Melbourne and a host of other dromes, Halifaxes and Lancasters were rising into a clear late April sky. At Holme Flight Lieutenant Reynolds was airborne at just after a quarter to three, Inshaw next and then Flight Sergeant Arnston RCAF, all were safely away. Scrappy Outerson, another Canadian, gunned his motors and was gone, Flight Lieutenant Perry beating down the long concrete strip in close pursuit. Still the crowd lingered on; five to go. Flight Lieutenant Carter RCAF was first with Flying Officer Amundrud following. A special cheer for Flight Sergeant Cuscaden making his first operational sortie and eager to get going. On the stroke of three Ted Fuery RAAF departed and lastly Warrant Officer Kerrigan RCAF climbed away to join the gathering throng. The process of take-off had taken thirty-six minutes.

Less than an hour later Kerrigan was back at Holme, his mission terminated by an unserviceable starboard inner engine. The remainder carried on over the North Sea untroubled.

As the hour of five approached, the mainforce, stepped up between 8 and 10,000 feet, swung in towards Wangerooge. Shell bursts stained the afternoon air and as the leading waves crossed over the island the barrage increased in intensity. Flying Officer MacPhee RCAF and Pilot Officer Turner bombed in unison, the sweep of their watches showing five o'clock precisely. A minute later bomb4oads tumbled from the Halifaxes flown by Pilot Officer Simons RCAF and Flight Lieutenant Kennedy, the sharp outline of Wangerooge already dissolving beneath volumes of smoke and dust thrown high by the close knit pattern of bombing.

With Simons and Kennedy fast leaving the area, seven more squadron aircraft converged on the Aiming Point, the flak by this time being both concentrated and accurate. Flight Sergeant Ray Tiffin RCAF, the mid-upper gunner in Joe Penner's crew, was watching a gaggle of bombers some 2 to 300 yards away on his starboard side:

'I saw two come together, and I immediately notified the skipper. There were some fighters covering us and these were very much on the alert following this unfortunate accident. One, it was either a Mustang or a Typhoon, came down and circled the two aircraft as they fell.'

Ray Tiffin had been spectator to the end of Scrappy Outerson and Gerald Lawson, and it is Gerald Lawson who now continues:

'Someone shouted "look out skipper". I looked ahead and up, and on both sides, but could see nothing to indicate a possible collision, or other danger. All of a sudden I felt a jolt and the whole aircraft seemed to lift up. Geoff Artus, my wireless operator, was standing beside me and he immediately went back to his compartment. The aircraft then went completely out of control. I shouted over the intercom for everyone to get out, at the same time pushing the emergency warning button on the instrument panel. For the next few seconds I am not sure of what happened. I seemed to be held against the side of the aircraft. Vaguely

I remember hunching myself down and then I probably went out through the cockpit roof for when I regained my senses I was outside, under the port wing behind the engine. The prop was still turning over, so I kicked like mad and fell away, pulling the D-ring of my parachute pack after a short count.

No one else left Gerald Lawson's Halifax, and not a soul got away from Scrappy Outerson's bomber spinning towards the sea 8,000 feet below. As the truncated remains of Lawson's aircraft fell, Flight Lieutenant Perry's camera clicked, securing a quite dramatic photograph showing the tail section well ahead of the rest of the airframe.

Four minutes after this horrific mid-air collision that had claimed the lives of seven Canadians and six Englishmen, Wing Commander Whyte and Ted Fuery sent their loads arching into the confusion below. They were the last from the squadron to bomb.

For some the flight home took less than two hours. Squadron Leader John Crampton was first back, while the Australian Eyres who had been first to go, rounded off his day by being last to land. The time was 7.32 pm. It was all over.

Crews were collected and whisked away for debriefing. An ordered calm settled over the once busy scenic of taxying bombers, scurrying crew buses and the like. The groundcrews accepted back their charges, engines giving off curious pinging sounds as hot metal cooled in the still chill evening air. Soon the dark mantle of night would brush away the last shades of light from the sun settling low to the west. Someone remembered to tell the crews waiting at A Apple's and T Tommy's pads that Outerson and Lawson would not be returning. In the brightly lit debriefing room crews were busy describing the pounding given to Wangerooge. Ray Tiffin again:

'At debriefing I never heard much mentioned about the loss of the two crews. Scrappy Outerson was a good friend of our skipper, and we sorely mourned his death. Many a night our crews had got together, either in the Mess or at the local village pub, which we called Dogpatch.'

But what happened to Gerald Lawson?

'I floated out to sea and came down about a hundred yards off shore. After the bombing stopped, I came up on to the beach to be greeted by an officer holding a hand-gun. He took me up the beach and through the town to a guard house. On our way, a German civilian, who I presume had just lost his home, came running towards me with a brick in his hand, but my officer guard drew his gun and told him to lay off, which, I am relieved to say, he did.'

For nearly a week Lawson was held on the bomb-pitted island, after which he was ferried to the mainland and taken to a camp a few miles east of Wilhelmshaven. From here he was liberated on 6 May by Royal Marine Commandos, though already the camp had been surrendered to the prisoners by the German commander. No one in authority, it seems, wanted to be taken by the Polish Army for fear of reprisals. The next few days passed in a heady whirl. A breakfast of bacon and eggs washed down with champagne was taken with a nearby French squadron, then on to Nijmegen where his shirt was stolen, Brussels and home to England in a Lancaster.

Already much had changed at Holme. All Canadian aircrew had been posted out to the RCAF Depot at Warrington near Manchester on 8 May in readiness for their return home to Canada. But of even greater importance, the squadron's role had changed from bombing to transport. The days of the Halifaxes were numbered, twin engined Dakotas were being made ready for issue. Overnight, as the squadron took its leave of Bomber Command to come under the aegis of Transport Command, the airgunners became redundant and were posted away. Throughout the month of June the squadron busied itself flying Cook's tours over the silent, broken towns of Germany, showing as many of the groundcrews as possible the achievements of the five years past. it was their victory as well. The Ruhr valley was the top attraction.

On the 14th Wing Commander Ralph Cassels resumed command from Chic Whyte, by which time the first of the Dakotas[34] had arrived. Now the squadron programme included ground lectures, map reading and astro navigation training exercises. Gradually the Halifaxes were withdrawn to Maintenance Units where the majority were quickly reduced to scrap, so rapid was the run-down of Bomber Command's reserves. On the 20th two Halifaxes spent a total of ten hours thirty-five minutes touring over Germany, the flight times suggest the Ruhr. One further Halifax entry is recorded on the 25th, after which the flying entries are concerned only with Dakota conversion training. Life was now taking on a quite different meaning. New crews were arriving, many without experience of the long drawn out bombing campaign. Their skills lay in dropping supplies, ferrying mail and freight. A new dawn was about to break for the squadron.

---

34   The squadron records show familiarisation flying in Dakotas taking place on 4 June, two hours thirty-five minutes in all.

Chapter Eleven

INDIA

In the early hours of 1 November 1945 [35], three squadron Dakotas were loaded with a mixture of passengers and freight, engines were started and as the hands on the watch office clock at Poona, southeast of Bombay, pointed to four o'clock, all three took off and headed for Mauripur. Later that same morning four more Dakotas left Poona, this time heading for Arkonam, while before the day was out, single flights had departed f or Santa Cruz and Palam. Life as a transport squadron in India had begun. Behind the squadron lay three busy months. Ralph Cassels had been posted to Staff College in mid-July, Wing Commander Nicholson DFC arriving to take his place. Training and a certain amount of upheaval had taken a toll amongst the carefully laid plans:

'We flew down to Portreath (in Cornwall) in readiness to go to India, but at this point my pilot Bill Walsh decided to return home to New Zealand under the scheme to return farmers. I was sent to Dishforth for retraining and so missed the opportunity of going with the squadron.'

So writes Flight Sergeant Leonard Eckhoff, Bill Walsh's wireless operator, who eventually reached this exotic land as a member of 232 Squadron. Prior to the Portreath staging post, the squadron had spent most of August in Oxfordshire, based at Broadwell:

'... where we practised dropping paratroops and supply containers. Here we heard the news of VJ Day, actually as our aircraft was taxiing out to do yet another supply practice drop. Everyone just 'switched off' and left the planes where they stood. We had a good party that night, my crew having a wonderful time at the local hospital as guests of the matron and her nurses.' *Flight Sergeant Stan Pearson - Second Pilot.*

Unlike Len Eckhoff, Stan Pearson flew out to India with his regular pilot, Flight Lieutenant Dickie Bird, still somewhat bemused at his present role for Stan had been recalled from leave to join the squadron having previously flown as a bomb-aimer with 51 Squadron from early February 1945, until the end of the war in Europe. There was, he recalls, a shortage of second pilots and:

'I don't think my crew, who had served in Transport Command for some considerable time, took too kindly to having a bomb-aimer as a fourth member of 'their' crew, and who would sit in the second pilot's seat. However, we soon got on extremely well together and I was very sorry when the day came for my release and I had to leave them in India.'

Similarly employed was George French, who only a few months previously had had the escape of his life on return from Kamen. Now he was sitting alongside Flight Lieutenant Birley and enjoying every moment of his new 'trade'. Although many of the Halifax pilots had been posted away, a few still

---

35   This is the date entered in the squadron records as the start of operations in India. However, at least one crew - and
        probably there are others - started operating in late September.

remained, Wally MacFarlane and Throssell to name just two, and it is the latter's navigator, Squadron Leader Haskett, who describes his crew's early days spent in India:

'The move to India was a very prolonged affair, but eventually most crews arrived at Tilda, a base in the central province which had been originally earmarked as our home for the airborne invasion of Singapore. We, however, went to Drigh Road, staying here for three days before flying on to Mauripur on 29 September. The next day we were detailed to fly the British Services football team to Ceylon. This trip was very enjoyable as the team included a lot of footballers that were household names at the time - Tommy Lawton for one. We watched them play a combined services team before they went on, I believe, to the Far East, while we flew back to Mauripur on 2 October.'

Flight Lieutenant John Howard, who had joined the squadron in July, also spent a memorable first few weeks that started for him at Karachi where some of the squadron were living under canvas:

'On the 7th (October) my crew had the pleasant task of taking the Chinese Foreign Minister and two of his staff from Karachi to Calcutta, via Delhi. Wang Shih-Chich was on his way back to China from attending the Big Five Conference. We were met in Calcutta by the Chinese Consul, who was instructed to look after us and we had a wonderful ten-course Chinese meal in Calcutta with the Consul the next day. On the 9th we did the return journey to Karachi, this time taking ex-prisoners of war on their way back to England.'

Between November 1945 and April 1946, the squadron was mainly engaged in flying British servicemen due for demobilisation on the first stages of their journey home. Two principal routes were used: Poona to Arkonam in Madras and Poona to Mauripur. Squadron Leader Haskett, despite the office work which his position as Squadron Navigation Leader demanded from him, managed to fly these routes on forty-eight occasions. From April 1946 the squadron found itself reverting gradually to the close support role in which it had been trained, though there were diversions. in late May the squadron commenced moving from Poona to Palam. Flight Lieutenant Wright took charge of the advance party, and the entire move was completed by early June. Squadron Leader Renolds handed over responsibility of the Training Flight to Flight Lieutenant Jepps and the care of the Operations Flight passed from Squadron Leader Lyall to Flight Lieutenant Roberts. Some leaflet dropping sorties were flown on three days soon after arrival at Palam, the Bamrauli, Agra and Ganges valley areas being the principal dropping areas. On the 17th the squadron was tasked to move number 1 RIAF Spitfire Squadron from Samungli to Yelahanka, and this job occupied life until 4 July. Exhibition supply drops were flown by two crews at Dum Dum on the 2nd of the month, while on the 21st, during the movement of stores for number 23010 AMES, a Dakota became bogged down at Charachapli and was declared a write-off'.

But the active days of the squadron were numbered. On the last day of July 1946, four aircraft were employed on passenger and freight runs, the first leaving at 07.30 hours for Samungli and Mauripur. Thirty minutes later three crews took-off, one making for Santa Cruz with twelve passengers and 730-lbs of freight, a second laden with 1,110-lbs of freight and three passengers to Chaklala and Peshawar, while the third crew flew seventeen passengers west to Shaibah.

August may have passed in similar fashion, but the records for this month have not been kept and on 1 September 1946 the squadron was re-numbered 62 Squadron. Crews had already started to split up, some going to other squadrons and units, but many were taking their discharge. John Howard, anxious to make the start of the Cambridge autumn term, and frustrated by delays at Bombay, got together a scratch crew and flew a Royal Navy Expeditor light-twin communications aircraft from Jodhpur home to Sealand in Cheshire. He made the start of term with time to spare. For another pilot, Flight

181

Lieutenant Wally MacFarlane, it was his immediate post-war flying that helped to make up his mind for the future:

'It was the switch to Dakotas that finally propelled me into civil aviation. I had only considered the war as an interference with my education of going on to university, acquiring a degree in engineering and going out to Africa to a vision of building yet another bridge across the Zambezi.'

Without doubt there must be similar stories as this period in the squadron's history came to a close. Thousands of aircrew were making the adjustment from war to peace, some being more successful than others in this respect. For those leaving the service it was the opportunity to start new ventures, or to pick up the threads of a pre-war occupation, but whatever path followed, 76 Squadron would soon be just a memory.

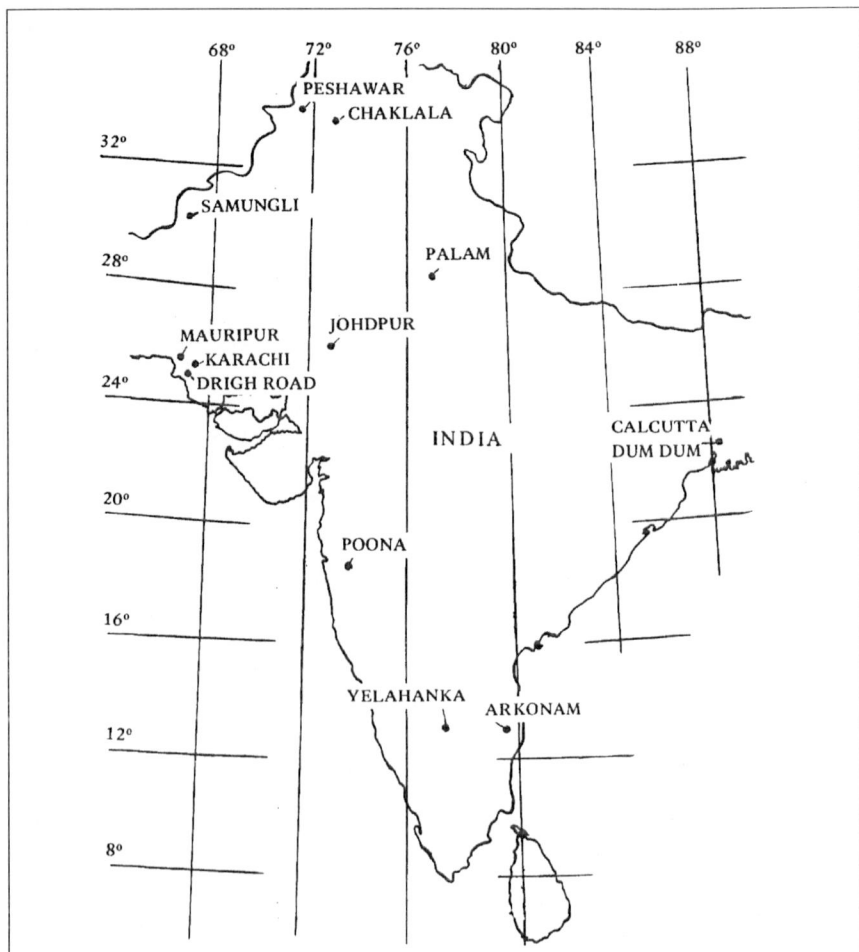

Chapter Twelve

CANBERRAS

Seven years after re-numbering to 62 Squadron at Palam, the squadron was reformed, this time in the light bomber role equipped with twin-jet Canberras and based at Wittering in Northamptonshire. The reformation came on a cold, dank, December day in 1953, through the gloom of which Squadron Leader Wynne DFC paraded his 'new' squadron before the Air Officer Commanding 3 Group, Air Vice Marshal Hudleston CB CBE. During the course of his short address to the chilled assembly of officers and men, the AOC handed over the aircraft log-books for the squadron's first Canberra, a B.2, serial number WJ991.

Equipment, however, was slow in arriving and it was into mid-January 1954 before the CO was able to collect the squadron's eighth aircraft from Lindholme. For the remainder of the winter months and well into the spring, training exercises involving the squadron high level CEE-H bombing practice were carried out, the training sorties being flown over the United Kingdom and Germany.

By the summer of 1954 the squadron was functioning well and between 16 and 25 July it was caught up in Exercise Dividend, a major air exercise designed to test both the defensive and offensive elements of the Royal Air Force. During this period of increased activity, the squadron shared its Canberras with crews from 40 Squadron, but on the 22nd it was four squadron crews that carried out successful high level visual attacks on the docks at Tilbury. Earlier in the month, on the 7th, the squadron took delivery of its ninth aircraft, the ferry flight from Lindholme being undertaken by Flight Lieutenant Taylor and his navigator Flight Lieutenant Marsden. Tragically, both were killed six weeks later when their aircraft crashed during a night approach into Wittering. This dreadful accident, which also claimed the life of the aircraft's radar plotter, Sergeant Addy, was followed by a spate of minor spills. Flight Lieutenant Slessor suffered an undercarriage failure on 9 September, and he landed with the wheels still retracted. On the 24th Flying Officer Jackson lost his nosewheel on takeoff, and six days later one of the Canberras was damaged at Marham when the nose wheel was accidentally retracted with the aircraft parked.

The winter of 1954/55 passed without further incident, and early in the New Year Squadron Leader Wynne led the first of two detachments to Habbaniya in Iraq, where a series of radio trials were conducted.

On 10 November of that same year came a change in command, and a change in role. Squadron Leader Boyd took over from Squadron Leader Wynne and on the same day the squadron, reduced now to seven aircraft, flew down to Weston Zoyland in Somerset, here to prepare for a move to Australia and major participation in what would be known as Operation Grapple, the British nuclear tests in the Pacific. Before proceeding on this far flung journey, the Canberra B.2s were exchanged for B.6s, conversion training taking up most of December, while the first two months of 1956 were spent in tying up all the loose ends prior to setting out on Sunday 18 March on the first stage of the journey which would take the squadron to RAAF Pearce in Western Australia. Pearce was reached on the 25th, the last stages being flown from Changi to Darwin, and Darwin to Pearce and their new home. Here the squadron remained until early August, after which a move was made to Edinburgh Field, a base near Adelaide in South Australia.

At the present time little can be said about the squadron's work in Australia; suffice to say it was fully involved in the nuclear weapons tests carried out at Maralinga and at Christmas island, the specially modified Canberras being used to take cloud samples in the wake of the test explosions. This exacting work necessitated the frequent rotation of aircraft and crews back to the United Kingdom and it was during one of these rotations in April 1958 that Flight Lieutenant De Salis and Flying Officer Lowe were involved in the spectacular loss of one of the specially modified Canberra bombers. Flying at 56,000 feet on an acceptance trial from Hemswell, the aircraft, which had been recently fitted with Napier Double Scorpion rocket motors, began to break up over Derbyshire. Both aircrew used their ejector seats and in doing so gained the doubtful distinction of making the highest-ever emergency escape from an aircraft. Surprisingly, bearing in mind the altitude and an air temperature of 97 degrees of frost, neither man suffered too badly, though De Salis considers he spun beneath his parachute for around nine of the eleven mile descent. Lowe, after separating from his seat, found himself facing face downwards and he timed his free-fall for four minutes, though he later remarked it seemed like a day and a half. It was, indeed, a most fortunate escape and bears comparison with Pilot Officer Bertenshaw's very low level escape from a Halifax in March 1945.

Between late July and the end of September 1958, the squadron, now commanded by Squadron Leader Gledhill AFC, concentrated at the Christmas island base for the last time. However, it was destined to remain at Edinburgh Field for over another year, Squadron Leader Stonham DFC arriving on 1 February 1959 to take command. Life during this time was pleasant. The Australian climate agreeable and training flights to New Zealand were the occasion for much enjoyment. But all good things must end. Farewells were said on 21 November 1959, and the delights of this hospitable country were exchanged for the gloom of an English winter. Thorney island, haven on more than one occasion for squadron aircraft during the grim years of 1941/45, was reached on the 27th and three days later the squadron was settling in at Upwood, a well appointed pre-war station in Huntingdon.

An escape to Luqa in Malta for three weeks was engineered the following February, but after this brief sojourn life was rather humdrum and the end was signalled in the December. A disbanding party was thrown on the 16th and on the 19th the task of ferrying the squadron's remaining Canberra bombers to Wroughton in Wiltshire was put in hand. Fittingly it fell to Squadron Leader Stonham, accompanied by his navigator Flight Lieutenant Osborne, to make the squadron's last Canberra sortie. Upwood was left at 2.15 pm on 22 December 1960 and Wroughton was reached forty-five minutes later. With this flight the longest chapter in 76 Squadron's fine history was brought to a close. Perhaps one day the '76' number plate will be resurrected once more to serve in the nation's defence. If so, its members will have the benefit of the proud tradition of one of the Royal Air Force's finest squadrons.

'Over the years since I left the service, I wonder at times if the Halifax was only a dream. It's been all 'Lancs' the better kite, but the Halifax was a good aircraft and it did play an important part in 'Butch 'Harris's bombing offensive. *'Leading Aircraftsman George Wadsworth - FME.*

'One night in the mess the boys wanted some excitement. There was always a bottle of lighter fuel on the bar, which with some twisted up papers was used to start a bonfire on the floor in front of the bar. Then they grabbed anyone who happened to be around and took his tie to add as fuel for the fire. I was playing snooker and had removed my tie - with a cry of "you son of a bitch" they threw me to the floor chanting "if we don't get your tie, we'll tear off your collar", so with that I quickly gave them my tie. Then they called the fire marshal and as he come through the doorway, off came his tie too. Finally, they got tired of it all and stood around the fire, unzipped and proceeded to put the fire out with a gusto. Mops, brooms and pails were found and everyone got stuck in to clean up the mess. Even the padre, who was a jolly sort, took part. *'Flight Lieutenant Fred Armstrong RCAF - Pilot.*

'In my minds eye I can see again 'Knocker' (Flight Sergeant White, killed on operations to Essen 23 October 1944) and the rest of them, and I do believe that it would only need the characteristic smell of the Halifax to make me think I was back there again. One can only speculate about what might have become of 'Knocker' and crew, my brothers and all the other Bomber Command types if fate had been different, but we will never know. One thing I do know, I miss them and I will never forget them.' *Sergeant Jim Hampton -Flight Engineer.*

'Part of the joy of operations was to watch the sunrise. it didn't just indicate the start of a new day, it meant so much more. Our flight engineer, George Jones and myself always enjoyed a cigarette and the drill was, once we crossed our own coast and were below oxygen level, George would bring a flask of coffee down to the rear-turret and I would have a couple of cigarettes ready. George, I believe, never lived to see the end of the war, but on those occasions as we relaxed together oh how he loved his cigarette and coffee watching the dawn breaking. *'Sergeant Al Atkinson —Air Gunner.*

185

BIBLIOGRAPHY

Bowyer, Chas.   *Hampden Special* (Ian Allan, 1976)
Cheshire, Leonard   *Bomber Pilot* (Hutchinson, 1943)
Fagnoul, Kurt   *Kriegsschicksale 1944-1945* (Society St Vith, 1971)
Fagnoul, Kurt   *St Vith im Schatten des Endsiegs* (Society St Vith, 1980)
Hastings, Max   *Bomber Command* (Michael Joseph, 1979)
Hornsey, Denis   *The Pilot Walked Home* (Collins Blue Circle, 1946)
Jones, Geoffrey   *Raider: The Halifax and its Flyers* (Kirnbers, 1978)
Middlebrook, Martin   *The First Day on the Somme* (Alien Lane, 1971)
Middlebrook, Martin   *The Nuremberg Raid* (Alien Lane, 1973)
Middlebrook, Martin   *The Battle of Hamburg* (Alien Lane, 1980)
Moyes, Philip   *Bomber Squadrons of the RAF* (Macdonald, 1964)
Musgrove, Gordon   *Pathfinder Force* (Macdonald and Janes, 1976)
Price, Alfred   *Battle over the Reich* (Ian Allan, 1973)
Rapier, Brian   *White Rose Base* (Aero Litho Co, 1972)
Rawlings, John   *Fighter Squadrons of the RAF* (Macdonald, 1969)
Robertson, Bruce   *Beaufort Special* (Ian Allan, 1976)
Shores, Christopher   *Mediterranean Air War* (Ian Allan, 1972)

Aeroplane   various issues
Flight   various issues
The Times   various issues

Postscript

MEMORIES

For various reasons I have not found it possible to include every recollection and anecdote sent to me during the preparation of this book. in no way has this been the fault of the contributor and in presenting the following small selection of accounts, I hope to rekindle some of the memories shared by those who served with 76 Squadron. So, without further ado, let us just turn back the clock:

'What a life it was, sharing the end of tour booze-ups down in the village with the aircrews; the more sobering sight of a bomber with only one undercarriage leg down heading for Carnaby.' *Leading Aircraftsman Al Hurst - FME.*

'The luxury used to he a night at the Station Hotel in Hull, bed and breakfast for 14/6d, with a hot bath thrown in. No one ever needed to go without a drink for lack of money, and socially there was plenty of activity to choose from every free evening from Betty's Bar in York, the Londesborough Arms at both Market Weighton and Selby, to the New Inn at Holme. In reality, there were too few evenings in the week.' *Flying Officer Dick Cowl - Bomb-Aimer.*

'I recall that the Station Dance Band used to play from time to time in the mess during lunch on Sundays. The most popular tune (1944) was 'Sand in my Shoes', a particularly appropriate melody for one of our prettier WAAF Officers when she was posted to North Africa. *'Squadron Leader John Crampton Pilot,*

'Time mellows one s impressions and time did not mean very much then. it was an existence of literally hour to hour. if your crew, or your name was not on the 'Battle Order', usually issued about ten o'clock in the morning for an operation that evening, it meant that you should be alive to face the following morning.' *Pilot Officer Eric Wright — Pilot.*

'They were pretty free and easy days at Holme with little of the 'bull' which was all too prevalent in our pre-squadron days, though there was good discipline amongst the air and groundcrews. I can only recall one incident of what was fondly known as an officer's inspection of the hut. This happened one fine summer day when this hod poked his head through an open window of our Nissen hut, cosy with some carpet on the floor and a jam jar full of flowers on the table: "everything alright you chaps", to which we replied "yes thanks", and with that off he went.' *Flight Sergeant Bernard* Gurr — *Flight Engineer.*

From Pilot Officer Bob Perry, a pilot who was dreadfully injured when his Halifax crashed in the Vale of York, ten miles south of Catterick on 16 June 1942:
'It was a happy squadron with a high morale, always, and I was very sad to leave it.'

'The day we arrived (6 October 1943) a briefed operation had been cancelled and the hilarity that followed had to be seen to be believed. A few days later we saw the squadron CO and he told us we could have a week's leave before starting operations. As we were packing, ready to leave for this unexpected bonus, our flight engineer was called on the Tannoy and was detailed to replace a sick engineer for that night's operation. Through a series of odd circumstances he had not flown before, though he had done all his ground training. Subsequently he made his first flight on a trip to Hannover, which must have been an experience for him.' *Sergeant Bryan Williams - Wireless Operator.*

'Our raid ended quite near the target when a night-fighter set fire to the starboard wing. The mid-upper gunner died at his post from burns before the bomb-aimer said to the skipper "Is'nt it time we got out". Being the navigator I was first to leave, but before I could do so the aircraft went into a dive, completely enveloped in flames. Eventually four of us managed to get clear before it hit the ground, but I'm afraid our bomb-aimer was not amongst us.' *Flying Officer John Pakeman,* shot down on operations to Frankfurt in December 1943.

'On arrival at Dulag-Luft I was put in a solitary cell as I had been rude to a German officer. I spent the usual five, or six days in the interrogation camp, but thanks to the superb lectures that we hid had in the squadron, I was able to cope with every trick from the bogus Red Cross forms, to the friendly German interrogator who followed the bullying type. It was exactly as the lecturer had described it.' *Flight Sergeant Guy Edwards — Air Gunner.*

'One crew had a mid-upper gunner, Bill Brewer, who had a very unusual lucky charm. On every trip he carried in his battle-dress pocket a heavy horse-shoe. He said it was his intention when he finished his tour to have all the target names painted on the shoe - I wonder if he ever did.' *Flight Sergeant Roy Clarke - Wireless Operator.*

'For me Augsburg was the worst target in that period (early 1944). We were attacked by a Ju 88, just seconds after we had dropped our bomb-load, coming in from the port quarter. I shouted to the skipper to corkscrew to port and as he did so the nightfighter came in through our combined fire. We reported this at debriefing and put in a claim for a probable. 'Flight *Sergeant 'Tich'Day -Air Gunner.*

'We had been briefed to carry out an air-test and on this particular day a number of bombs had been stacked very close to our dispersal, which happened to be quite small. In turning to get out of the pan, my tailwheel collided with the stack of bombs and sent them tumbling in all directions. Most of the groundcrew, who were in the immediate area, made a run for it, but one chap just stood still with his hands over his ears with the hardware rolling past him. It was a most frightening few moments for all the bombs were fully serviceable and had had their fins fitted. What good fortune they had not been fused. *'Flying Officer Bill Palmer - Pilot,*

'The next morning after our final trip, I was awakened by the Adjutant and requested, along with the rest of my crew, to accompany the bodies of four Mosquito aircrew who had been killed in accidents nearby to the undertakers at York, and then to the railway station. Not a pleasant duty on completion of a tour of operations. We were due to have an end of tour party at the Parkway in Leeds that evening, but my flight engineer (Ferris Newton) had to give it a miss as he was Duty Flight Engineer. For me it was all something of an anti-climax. 'Pilot *Officer George Dunn - Pilot.*

Appendix One

SQUADRON BASE,COMMANDERS AND EQUIPMENT

SECTION ONE - SQUADRON BASES
Formed as 76 Home Defence Squadron RFC at:

Ripon, Yorkshire	15 Sep 16 - Mar 19	with detachments at:
Copmanthorpe,Yorkshire		A Flight
Helperby, Yorkshire		B Flight
Catterick, Yorkshire		C Flight
Tadcaster, Yorkshire	Mar 19 - 13 Jun 19	Squadron disbanded.

Re-formed as 76 (Bomber) Squadron from B Flight, 7 Squadron at:

Finningley, Yorkshire	12 Apr 37 - 23 Sep 39	
Upper Heyford, Oxfordshire	23 Sep 39 - 22 Apr 40	Disbanded, following merger with 7 Squadron and SHQ Upper Heyford, to become 16 OTU.

Re-formed as 76 Squadron from C Flight, 35 Squadron at:

Linton-on-Ouse, Yorkshire	12 Apr 41 - 4 Jun 41	
Middleton St. George, Co. Durham	4 Jun 41 - 17 Sep 42	with detachments to:
Lossiemouth, Moray	27 Jan 42 - 6 Feb 42	'Tirpitz' operations.
Tain, Ross and Cromarty	27 Mar 42 - 8 Apr 42	'Tirpitz' operations.
Tain, Ross and Cromarty	21 Apr 42 - 30 Apr 42	'Tirpitz' operations.
Aqir, Palestine	12 Jul 42 - 12 Aug 42	Using Advance Base at Shallufa and LG 224,Egypt for operations.
Fayid, Egypt	12 Aug 42 - 7 Sep 42	Middle East detachment merged with 10 Squadron detachment to form 462 (RAAF) Squadron.
Linton-on-Ouse, Yorkshire	17 Sep 42 - 16 Jun 43	
Holme-on-Spalding Moor, Yorkshire	16 Jun 43 - 7 Aug 45	Transferred from Bomber Command to Transport Command on 7 May 45.
Broadwell, Oxfordshire	4 Aug 45 - 27 Aug 45	
Portreath, Cornwall	27 Aug 45	In preparation for move to India.
Poona, India	1 Nov 45 - 25 May 46	
Palam, India	25 May 46 - 1 Sep 46	Re-numbered 62 Squadron.

Re-formed as 76 Squadron in the Light Bomber role at:

Wittering, Northants	9 Dec 53 - 10 Nov 55	with detachments to:
Habbaniya, Iraq	22 Feb 55 - 19 Mar 55	
Habbaniya, Iraq	16 May 55 - 6 Jun 55	

Wildenrath/Wahn, West Germany	30 Sep 55 - 1 Oct 55	
Weston Zoyland, Somerset	10 Nov 55 - 18 Mar 56	Squadron commenced moving to Australia.
RAAF Pearce, Western Australia	25 Mar 56 - 9 Aug 56	with a detached flight at
Weston Zoyland, Somerset	Mar 56 - Jul 56	
RAAF Edinburgh Field, South Australia	9 Aug 56 - 21 Nov 59	During this period the Squadron led a complicated existence, explained as follows:
Maralinga, Australia	6 Sep 56 - 30 Nov 56	Detachment.
Weston Zoyland, Somerset	30 Nov 56 - Feb 57	To change equipment and personnel.
Christmas Island, Pacific	4 Mar 57 - 11 Mar 57	Detachment.
Christmas Island Pacific	18 Apr 57 - 10 Jul 57	During this period, Christmas Island became the squadron's main base and the Edinburgh Field element reverted to a detached flight status until 10 Jul 57.
Maralinga, Australia	2 Sep 57 - 18 Oct 57	Detachment.
Christmas Island, Pacific	23 Oct 57 - 25 Nov 57	Detachment.
Christmas Island, Pacific	7 Mar 58 - 27 May 58	Detachment.
Christmas Island, Pacific	21 Jul 58 - 1 Oct 58	Main base, then returned to RAAF Edinburgh Field.
Upwood, Huntingdon	30 Nov 59 - 30 Dec 60	with detachment to:
Luqa, Malta	6 Feb 60 - 29 Feb 60	

Note. Throughout the squadron's service in Australia, training flights to New Zealand were carried out, and throughout most of 1957 - '59, aircraft were rotated between the UK and Australia for the purpose of servicing, modification and change of aircrews.

SECTION TWO - 76 SQUADRON CONVERSION FLIGHT
Formed at:

Middleton St. George, Co. Durham	5 Feb 42 - 9 Jun 42	
Dalton, Yorkshire	9 Jun 42 - 31 Aug 42	
Middleton St. George, Co. Durham	31 Aug 42 - 16 Sep 42	
Riccall, Yorkshire	16 Sep 42 - 7 Oct 42	Merged with 10, 78 and 102 Squadron Conversion Flights to become 1658 Heavy Conversion Unit.

SECTION THREE - SQUADRON COMMANDING OFFICERS

Major E M Murray DSO MC	15 Sep 16 - 6 Feb 18
Major A C Wilson	6 Feb 18 - 13 Jun 19
W/Cdr S Graham	12 Apr 37 - 25 Apr 37
S/Ldr E J George.	25 Apr 37 - 16 Jul 38

S/Ldr N A Pearce	16 Jul S8 -	1 Jan 39	Died at Marlborough.
F/Lt L R Stewart	1 Jan 39 -	10 Jan 39	Temporary CO.
S/Ldr J B T Whitehead	10 Jan 39 -	13 Apr 39	
W/Cdr D S Allan	13 Apr 39 -	26 Jun 39	
S/Ldr J H R Oldfield	26 Jun 39 -		
W/Cdr D S Allan by	3 Sep 39 -	22 Apr 40	
W/Cdr S O Bufton DFC	12 Apr 41 -	28 May 41	Promoted to G/Capt.
W/Cdr G T Jarman DSO DFC	28 May 41 -	4 Sep 41	Posted to HQ 4 group.
W/Cdr J J A Sutton DFC	4 Sep 41 -	9 Nov 41	Posted to HQ Bomber Command.
S/Ldr J T Bouwens DFC	10 Nov 41 -	15 Dec 41	Posted to HQ6 Group.
W/Cdr D O Young DFC AFC	15 Dec 41 -	7 Sep 42	Assumed command of 462 (RAAF) Squadron.
S/Ldr C C Calder DFC	14 Jul 42 -	5 Aug 42	CO of Home Echelon
W/Cdr G L Cheshire DSO DFC	5 Aug 42 -	7 Apr 43	Posted to Marston Moor.
W/Cdr D C Smith DFC	7 Apr 43 -	22 Dec 43	Posted to 42 Base.
W/Cdr D Iveson DSO DFC	22 Dec 43 -	14 Aug 44	Posted to 1669 HGU.
W/Cdr R K Cassels DFC	14 Aug 44 -	24 Jan 45	Posted to 42 Base.
W/Cdr L G A Whyte	24 Jan 45 -	14 Jun 45	Posted to 44 Base.
W/Cdr R K Cassels DFC	14 Jun 45 -	13 Jul 45	Posted to Staff College.
W/Cdr P A Nicholson DFC	15 Jul 45 -	1 Sep 46	
S/Ldr J G Wynne DFC	9 Dec 53 -	10 Nov 55	
S/Ldr J N B Boyd	10 Nov 55 -	17 Dec 56	
S/Ldr G Bates DFC	17 Dec 56 -	20 Dec 57	
S/Ldr T C Gledhill AFC	20 Dec 57 -	1 Feb 59	
S/Ldr J F G Stonham DFC	1 Feb 59 -	30 Dec 60	

Note. Wing Commander G L Cheshire arrived on the squadron in the rank of Squadron Leader and was promoted to the rank of Wing Commander shortly after taking up his appointment as Commanding Officer.

SECTION FOUR - SQUADRON EQUIPMENT

BE.2c	Sep 16 -	18	
BE.2e	Sep 16 -	18	
BE.12	Sep 16 -	18	
BE.12a	Sep 16 -	18	
BE.12b	18 -	18	
Bristol 14 F2B	18 -	19	
Avro 504K	-	19	
Vickers Wellesley	Apr 37 -	Apr 39	
Avro Anson	Mar 39 -	Apr 40	
Handley Page Hampden I	Mar 39 -	Apr 40	
Handley Page Halifax B.I	Apr 41 -	Dec 42	
Handley Page Halifax B.II	Oct 41 -	Sep 43	
Handley Page Halifax B.V	Feb 43 -	Jul 44	
Handley Page Halifax B.III	Jan 44 -	May 45	
Handley Page Halifax B.VI	Feb 45 -	Oct 45	
Douglas Dakota C.4	Jun 45 -	Aug 46	
English Electric Canberra B.2	Dec 53 -	Dec 55	
English Electric Canberra B.6	Dec 55 -	Dec 60	Some fitted with Scorpion rocket motor.

Appendix Two

OPERATIONAL SORTIES
SECTION ONE

Operational sorties flown by 76 Squadron in the role of a Home Defence Squadron.

Date 1917	Flight/Base Type	Aircraft Desp	No	Remarks
21/22Aug	A Copmanthorpe	BE 2e	2	One crashed on landing.
	B Helperby	BE 2e	2	One crashed on landing.
		BE 12	1	Zeppelin L41 tracked over northern Yorkshire. In addition to L41 , Zeppelins L42, 44, 45, 46 and 47 claim to have been in the general area of north Yorkshire.
24/25 Sep	A Copmanthorpe	RE 2e	2	One crashed on landing.
		BE 12	2	One crashed on landing at Shipton,
	B Helperby	BE 2e	1	2nd Lt W W Cook engaged
	C Catterick	BE 2e	1	Zeppelin L42 over the North Sea.
		BE 12	1	Other Zeppelins tracked over northern England included L35, 41, 46,53 and 55.
19/20 Oct	A Copmanthorpe	BE 2e	3	Night of the famous 'silent raid'
		BE 12	1	when 11 Zeppelins were reported
	B Helperby	BE 2e	1	over England. From this total,
		BE 12	1	five were lost over Europe during the return flights after being driven off course by gale force
1918				winds.
12/13 Mar	B Helperby	BE 12	1	Zeppelins L61, 62 and 63 tracked
		BE 12b	1	over Yorkshire.
	C Catterick	BE 12	1	
13/14 Mar	A Copmanthorpe	BE 2e	1	Zeppelin L42 over Hartlepool.
		BE 12b	1	Engaged by an AA battery at
	B Helperby	BE 12	1	Howden.
		BE 12b	1	
	C Catterick	BE 2e	1	
		BE 12	2	
5/6 Aug	A Copmanthorpe	BE 12b	1	False alarm. No Zeppelin reached
	B Helperby	BE 12b	2	the area, but there was airship activity over East Anglia and L70
Total sorties			**31**	wss shot down off the Norfolk coast by a DH 4 operating from RAF Yarmouth.

		BE 2e	BE 12	BE 12b
Sortie table by Flights and aircraft:	A Flight	8	3	2
	B Flight	4	4	4
	C Flight	2	4	-
	Totals	**14**	**11**	**6**

SECTION TWO

A table listing the attacks carried out, or attempted by 76 Squadron in the role of a
Bomber Squadron between 12 June 1941 and 25 April 1945, as recorded in the F 540
and F 541 sections of AIR 27/650, 651, 652 and 653. An attempt has been made to
identify the purpose for these attacks, and to identify by areas some of the lesser
known French targets raided in the summer of 1944.

Date 1941	Target	No Desp	No Attack	Alt	DNCO	FTR	Remarks
12 Jun	Huls	3		1	2		Chemical works.
16 Jun	Cologne	3	2		1		Main railway station.
20 Jun	Kiel	5	5				Shipyards.
23 Jun	Kiel	4	3			1	Shipyards
26 Jun	Kiel	1	1				Shipyards.
29 Jun	Hamburg	2	1	1			
2 Jul	Bremen	4	4				
5 Jul	Magdeburg	3	2	1			
7 Jul	Frankfurt	4	3		1		
8 Jul	Merseburg	6	6				Leuna oil plant.
14 Jul	Hannover	7	7				Railway station.
19 Jul	Hannover	4	4				Railway station.
21 Jul	Mannheim	3	3				
24 Jul	La Pallice	6	2		1	3	Daylight raid on the Scharnhorst.
30 Jul	Cologne	4	4				
2 Aug	Berlin	4	4				Friedrichstrasse station.
5 Aug	Karlsruhe	5	4			1	Railway workshops.
7 Aug	Essen	4	4				Krupps works.
12 Aug	Berlin	7	2	1	1	2	Friedrichstrasse station. Sgt McHale crashed.
14 Aug	Magdeburg	2	2				
16 Aug	Cologne	2	2				
19 Aug	Kiel	2	2				Shipyards.
24 Aug	Düsseldorf	2	2				
28 Aug	Duisburg	3	3				
29 Aug	Frankfurt	2	1	1			S/Ldr Bickford crashed.
31 Aug	Cologne	2	1	1			
2 Sep	Berlin	2	2				
7 Sep	Berlin	1	1				
11 Sep	Turin	4	4				Royal Arsenal.
13 Sep	Brest	4	3				Battle cruisers. P/O Hutchin crashed.

Date 1941	Target	No Desp	No Attack	Alt	DNCO	FTR	Remarks
15 Sep	Hamburg	2	2				
19 Sep	Stettin	1	1				Main railway station.
29 Sep	Stettin	3	2	1			Shown in the squadron records as Stenner Haxen.
2 Oct	Brest	3	2		1		Battle cruisers.
12 Oct	Nuremburg	4	4				Siemens Schuckert works.
	Bremen	1				1	
20 Oct	Wilhelmshaven	1	1				
	Emden	1	1				
22 Oct	Mannheim	3	3				
26 Oct	Cherbourg	3	1		2		Invasion port.
	Hamburg	2	2				
31 Oct	Hamburg	3	3				
	Dunkirk	1				1	Invasion port.
7 Nov	Berlin	5	2	1	2		
9 Nov	Hamburg	3	2	1			Blomm and Vos shipyard.
25 Nov	Brest	4	4				Battle cruisers. Squadron used the Halifax B II for the first time.
30 Nov	Hamburg	5	5				
18 Dec	Brest	6	5		1		Daylight raid on the Scharnhorst and Gneisenau.
30 Dec	Brest	6	5			1	Daylight raid on the Scharnhorst and Gneisenau.

1941 Totals:

	Target	No Desp	No Attack	Alt	DNCO	FTR	Remarks
	Halifax B.I	**149**	**115**	**11**	**11**	**10**	**Two sorties undetermined.**
	Halifax B.II	**13**	**12**		**1**		

Date 1942	Target	No Desp	No Attack	Alt	DNCO	FTR	Remarks
7 Jan	St.Nazaire	3	3				Invasion port.
8 Jan	Brest	1	1				Dockyard power station.
30 Jan	Tirpitz	5	1		4		Sgt Harwood ditched.
11 Feb	Mannheim	6	5	1			
12 Feb	German battle cruisers at sea	2			2		Daylight.
13 Feb	Cologne	4	4				
22 Feb	Lista	3	2		1		Aerodrome in Norway.
3 Mar	Billancourt	3	3				Renault works in the western suburbs of Paris.
30 Mar	Tirpitz	12		11	1		
8 Apr	Hamburg	6	6				
10 Apr	LeHavre	3	3				Invasion port.
	Essen	5	2		2	1	8,000-1b bomb usea on operations for the first time.

Date 1942	Target	No Desp	No Attack	Alt	DNCO	FTR	Remarks
26 Apr	Dunkirk	1	1				Invasion port.
27 Apr	Dunkirk	2	1			1	Invasion port.
	Tirpitz	11	10		1		Two aircraft borrowed
28 Apr	Tirpitz	9	9				from 78 Squadron.
3 May	Hamburg	7	6			1	
5 May	Stuttgart	5	4		1		Docks area.
	Nantes	1			1		Invasion port.
6 May	Stuagart	1		1			Docks area.
8 May	Warnemünde	8	3	3	1	1	Heinkel aircraft works.
19 May	Mannheim	7	3	1	2	1	
22 May	St. Nazaire	5	4		1		Invasion port.
29 May	Gnomeet Rhône	7	6			1	Aero engine works at Gennevilliers (north of Paris).
30 May	Cologne	21	19		2		1,000 plan raid.
1 Jun	Essen	21	20			1	1,000 plan raid.
3 Jun	Bremen	10	7		1	2	
5 Jun	Essen	4	3		1		Krupps works.
8 Jun	Essen	6	6				Krupps works.
19 Jun	Emden	6	6				
20 Jun	Emden	5	4			1	
25 Jun	Bremen	14	10		3	1	Millennium Two.

The Middle East table of attacks will follow the December 1942 targets.

Date 1942	Target	No Desp	No Attack	Alt	DNCO	FTR	Remarks
19 Jul	Vegesack	1					Submarine and ship-building yards. F/Sgt Belous crashed.
26 Jul	Hamburg	3	1		1	1	
29 Jul	Saarbrucken	2	2				
30 Jul	Düsseldorf	2	2				
11 Aug	Mainz	1	1				
20 Aug	Dijon	1	1				'Nickel' sortie.
28 Aug	Saarbrucken	4	3		1		
1 Sep	Saarbrucken	3	2			1	
2 Sep	Karlsruhe	3	2	1			
4 Sep	Bremen	4	3		1		
6 Sep	Duisburg	3	3				
8 5ep	Frankfurt	6	5				Sgt Nicholson crashed.
10 Sep	Düsseldorf	5	5				
23 Sep	Bremen	3	3				
14 Sep	Wilhelmshaven	3	3				
16 Sep	Essen	3	2			1	
19 Sep	Saarbrucken	1	1				
23 Sep	Flensburg	4	3			1	Submarine base.
26 Sep	Flensburg	3			3		Submarine base. Group sent a recall signal.
10ct	Flensburg	3	2			1	Submarine base.

Date 1942	Target Desp Attack	No	No	Alt	DNCO	FTR	Remarks
2 Oct	Krefeld	4	4				
5 Oct	Aachen	5	2		2	1	
6 Oct	Osnabrück	2	2				
8 Oct	Minelaying	5	5				
11 Oct	Minelaying	1	1				Nectarines.
13 Oct	Kiel	6	6				Shipyards.
15 Oct	Cologne	5	3	1	1		
23 OCt	Genoa	7	7				
6 Nov	Minelaying	4	3		1		Nectarines.
7 Nov	Genoa	7	6			1	
8 Nov	Minelaying	2	1			1	Nectarines.
9 Nov	Hamburg	6		6			
15 Nov	Genoa	7	7				
16 Nov	Toulon	1	1				'Nickel' sortie.
17 Nov	Lyonsand St. Étienne	2	2				'Nickel sorties.
18 Nov	Turin	5	4		1		
20 Nov	Turin	9	7		1	1	
22 Nov	Stuttgart	6	5		1		
23 Nov	Minelaying	3	3				Nectarines.
25 Nov	Minelaying	2	2				Nectarines.
26 Nov	Minelaying	5	5				Nectarines.
28 Nov	Turin	10	8		2		
2 Dec	Frankfurt	9	7		2		
6 Dec	Mannheim	13	10	1	1	1	
8 Dec	Minelaying	5	5				North east of Langeog Is.
9 Dec	Turin	10	9	1			
11 Dec	Turin	10	1	1	8		
14 Dec	Minelaying	7	5		2		Nectarines.
17 Dec	Minelaying	8	1		7		Baltic sea.
20 Dec	Duisburg	12	10			2	

MIDDLE EAST OPERATIONS:

Date	Target	No	No	Alt	DNCO	FTR	Remarks
10 Jul		8	8				Operational transit.
14 Jul		8	8				Operational transit.
15 Jul	Tobruk	5	5				Harbour installations.
17 Jul	Tobruk	2	1		1		
19 Jul	Tobruk	4	2		2		
	Tdbruk	1	1				F/Sgt Granger with a 10 Squadron crew.
21 Jul	Tobruk	6	4	1	1		
23 Jul	Tobruk	4	4				
24 Jul	Tobruk	1	1				
25 Jul	Tobruk	8	7		1		
27 Jul	Tobruk	4	4				
29 Jul	Tobruk	9	7		2		

Date 1942	Target Desp Attack	No Desp	No Attack	Alt	DNCO	FTR	Remarks
31 Jul	Tobruk	7	5		2		F/O Wickham crashed.
1 Aug	Tobruk	2	2				One aircraft borrowed from 10 Squadron.
2 Aug	Tobruk	6	5		1		
4 Aug	Tobruk	7	5		2		
5 Aug	Tobruk	2	2				
6 Aug	Tobruk	3	3				
8 Aug	Tobnuk	4	3		1		
9 Aug	Tobnuk	1	1				
10 Aug	Tobruk	5	5				
12 Aug	Tobruk	4	4				
13 Aug	Tobruk	3	3				
15 Aug	Tobruk	6	5	1			
17 Aug	Tobruk	6	5		1		
19 Aug	Tobruk	9	9				
21 Aug	Tobruk	8	8				
23 Aug	Tobruk	8	8				
25 Aug	Tobruk	10	10				
28 Aug	Tobruk	7	7				
30 Aug	Tobruk	5	4		1		P/O Raymond crashed.
1 Sep	Tobruk	8	7		1		
3 Sep	Tobruk	7	6		1		
5 Sep	Heraklion	5	3		1	1	Aerodrome on the Island of Crete.

1942	Totals:						
	Halifax B.I	12	9		3		
	Halifax B.II Eur.	434	323	28	56	25	**Two sorties undetermined.**
	Halifax B.II ME	183	162	2	18	1	
	Combined	**629**	**494**	**30**	**77**	**26**	**Two sorties undetermined.**
	1941/42	**791**	**621**	**41**	**89**	**36**	**Four sorties undetermined.**

1943							
9 Jan	Minelaying	11	10		1		Silverthorn.
14 Jan	Lorient	12	11		1		Docks and submarine pens.
15 Jan	Lorient	1	1				Docks and submarine pens.
16 Jan	Berlin	2	2				
17 Jan	Berlin	7	5			2	
21 Jan	Minelaying	4	2		1	1	Nectarines.
23 Jan	Lorient	6	5		1		Docks and submarine pens.
27 Jan	Düsseldorf	8	7		1		
29 Jan	Lorient	5	4		1		Docks and submarine pens.
2 Feb	Cologne	5	5				
3 Feb	Hamburg	6	5		1		
4 Feb	Turin	2	2				
7 Feb	Lorient	6	6				Docks and submarine pens.
11 Feb	Wilhelmshaven	7	6		1		

Date 1943	Target	No Desp	No Attack	Alt	DNCO	FTR	Remarks
13 Feb	Lorient	11	11				Docks and submarine pens.
14 Feb	Cologne	9	9				
16 Feb	Lorient	14	13		1		Docks and submarine pens.
18 Feb	Wilhelmshaven	8	8				
	Minelaying	4	4				Nectarines III.
19 Feb	Wilhelmshaven	13	13				
25 Feb	Nuremburg	17	15		1		Sgt Sanderson crashed.
26 Feb	Cologne	14	14				
28 Feb	St.Nazaire	14	14				Docks and submarine pens.
1 Mar	Berlin	14	12			2	
2 Mar	Minelaying	2	2				Nectarines I.
3 Mar	Hamburg	12	11			1	
5 Mar	Essen	12	9		2	1	Krupps works. Battle of the Ruhr commenced.
8 Mar	Nuremburg	12	9	1	2		
9 Mar	Munich	8	8				
11 Mar	Stuttgart	11	9		2		
12 Mar	Essen	11	8		2	1	
22 Mar	St.Nazaire	9	9				Docks and submarine pens.
26 Mar	Duisburg	13	11		2		
27 Mar	Berlin	11	9	1	1		
28 Mar	St.Nazaire	3	3				Docks and submarine pens.
29 Mar	Berlin	11	3		6	2	
2 Apr	St.Nazaire	1	1				Docks and submarine pens.
3 Apr	Essen	12	10		1	1	
4 Apr	Kiel	12	11		1		
8 Apr	Duisburg	8	5		2	1	
10 Apr	Frankfurt	10	9			1	
14 Apr	Stuttgart	10	10				
16 Apr	Pilsen	10	6		1	3	Skoda armament works.
	Mannheim	1	1				
20 Apr	Stettin	14	13		1		Docks and industry.
26 Apr	Duisburg	10	9			1	
27 Apr	Minelaying	6	4		2		Silverthorn,
28 Apr	Minelaying	6	6				Nectarines I.
30 Apr	Essen	8	6		1	1	
4 May	Dortmund	15	14			1	
12 May	Duisburg	12	10		2		
13 May	Bochum	17	15		2		
23 May	Dortmund	15	13			2	
25 May	Düsseldorf	14	13		1		
27 May	Essen	14	13			1	
29 May	Wuppertal	12	12				
11 Jun	Düsseldorf	18	13		3	2	
12 Jun	Bochum	15	13		1	1	
19 Jun	Le Creusot:	9	9				Schneider armament factory in Central France
21 Jun	Krefeld	20	17		3		

Date 1943	Target	No Desp	No Attack	Alt	DNCO	FTR	Remarks
22 Jun	Mülheim	19	18			1	
24 Jun	Wuppertal	20	16	1	2	1	
25 Jun	Gelsenkirchen	16	11		5		
28 Jun	Cologne	19	14		3	2	
3 Jul	Cologne	19	17		2		Raid on the east side.
9 Jul	Gelsenkirchen	20	19		1		
13 Jul	Aachen	14	13				2Lt Hulthin RNAF crashed.
15 Jul	Montbéliard	23	21		2		Peugeot works in Eastern France near the border with Switzerland.
24 Jul	Hamburg	24	19		4	1	Battle of Hamburg.
25 Jul	Essen	22	19		3		
27 Jul	Hamburg	24	24				
29 Jul	Hamburg	23	20		2	1	
30 Jul	Remscheid	20	18		1	1	
2 Aug	Hamburg	20	7	3	9	1	
9 Aug	Mannheim	16	14		1	1	
10 Aug	Nuremburg	20	18		2		
12 Aug	Milan	22	21			1	Lt Hulthin RNAF landed at Protville.
17 Aug	Peenemünde	20	20				Rocket testing station.
22 Aug	Leverkusen	22	20		2		
23 Aug	Berlin	23	20		3		
27 Aug	Nuremburg	24	18		5	1	
30 Aug	Munchen-Gladbach	15	12		1	1	F/Lt Lemmon crashed.
31 Aug	Berlin	16	7	1	8		
3 Sep	Minelaying	3	1		2		Silverthorn.
5 Sep	Mannheim	21	18		2	1	
6 Sep	Munich	18	13		4	1	
15 Sep	Montlucon	19	19				Dunlop tyre factory in Central France.
16 Sep	Modane	16	9		7		Marshalling yards in the French Alps.
22 Sep	Hanover	21	18		1	2	
23 Sep	Mannheim	18	13	2	3		
27 Sep	Hannover	20	15	1	2	2	
29 Sep	Bochum	11	10	1			
3 Oct	Kassel	20	16			4	
4 Oct	Frankfurt	13	7	1	5		
8 Oct	Hannover	21	16		5		
22 Oct	Kassel	22	14		7	1	
3 Nov	Düsseldorf	20	17		1	2	
11 Nov	Cannes	10	9	1			Marshalling yards.
18 Nov	Mannheim	23	17	1	4	1	Battle of Berlin commenced
19 Nov	Leverkusen	19	19				
22 Nov	Berlin	19	17		2		
25 Ndv	Frankfurt	21	15	2	2	2	

Date 1943	Target Desp Attack	No	No	Alt	DNCO	FTR	Remarks
26 Nov	Stuttgart	11	8		1	2	
3 Dec	Leipzig	19	14		4	1	
20 Dec	Frankfurt	21	15	2	1	3	
29 Dec	Berlin	22	19	1	2		
1943	**Totals:**						
	Halifax B.II	**374**	**325**	**2**	**31**	**15**	**1 sortie undetermined**
	Halifax B.V	**1079**	**888**	**17**	**128**	**44**	**2 sorties undetermined**
	Combined	**1453**	**1213**	**19**	**159**	**59**	**3 sorties undetermined**
	1941/42/43	**2244**	**1834**	**60**	**248**	**95**	**7 sorties undetermined**
1944							
20 Jan	Berlin	23	16	2	2	3	
21 Jan	Magdeburg	19	14			4	F/Sgt Firth crashed.
28 Jan	Berlin	17	10	1	5		F/Sgt Ward cPashed.
15 Feb	Berlin	9	7		1	1	
24 Feb	Schweinfurt	3	3				Squadron used the Halifax B.III for the first time.
25 Feb	Augsburg	4	4				
1 Mar	Stuttgart	11	8		1	1	F/Sgt Richards crashed.
6 Mar	Trappes	14	14				Marshalling yards southwest of Paris.
7 Mar	LeMans	11	6		5		Marshalling yards.
13 Mar	LeMans	16	16				Marshalling yards.
15 Mar	Stuttgart	18	17			1	
18 Mar	Frankfurt	18	13		3	2	
22 Mar	Frankfurt	17	16		1		
24 Mar	Berlin	16	9	4	2	1	
26 Mar	Essen	16	15		1		
30 Mar	Nuremburg	14	10		1	3	
9 Apr	Lille	14	14				Marshalling yards.
10 Apr	Tergnier	10	10				Marshalling yards in Northern France, in the Aisne.
20 Apr	Ottignies	23	21		2		Marshalling yards in the south of Belgium, near Charleroi.
22 Apr	Dusseldorf	22	19		1	2	
24 Apr	Karlsruhe	20	20				
26 Apr	Villeneuve-St. Georges	22	22				Marshalling yards south of Paris.
27 Apr	Montzen	21	21				Marshalling yards in East Belgium.
30 Apr	Achères	20	19		1		Marshalling yards northwest of Paris.
1 May	Malines	17	13		4		Marshalling yards north of Brussels.

Date 1944	Target	No Desp	No Attack	Alt	DNCO	FTR	Remarks
6 May	Mantes-Gassicourt	11	10		1		Marshalling yards west of Paris.
9 May	Berneval	13	13				Heavy gun battery on the Normandy coast, near Dieppe.
10 May	Lens	17	16		1		Marshalling yards.
11 May	Trouville	16	13		2		Coastal defence battery on the Normandy coast, in the Calvados. F/Sgt Strattford crashed.
12 May	Hasselt	18	16		1	1	Marshalling yards in East Belgium.
19 May	Boulogne	24	22		2		Marshalling yards.
22 May	Orleans	23	23				Railway centre.
24 May	Beaumont	3	3				Gun emplacement on the Normandy coast, west of Cherbourg.
	Aachen	18	16			2	The Rothe Erde marshalling yards.
27 May	Bourg-Leopold	23	22		1		Panzer camp east of Antwerp.
1 Jun	Ferme D'Urville	22	21		1		A radar and w/t station west of Cherbourg.
2 Jun	Trappes	23	20			3	Marshalling yards.
5 Jun	Mont Fleury	23	19		3	1	Coastal defence battery on the Normandy coast northeast of Bayeux.
6 Jun	St.Lo	19	18		1		Choke point south of the Normandy beach-head.
7 Jun	Juvisy	21	18		2	1	Marshalling yards south of Paris.
9 Jun	Laval	18	10		8		Aerodrome.
12 Jun	Amiens	22	21			1	Rail junction at Longueau.
14 Jun	Douai	21	21				Locomotive depot in Northern France.
15 Jun	Fouillard	21	21				Fuel and ammunition dumps near Rennes.
16 Jun	Domleger	12	12				V1 launching site northeast of Abbeville.
22 Jun	Laon	21	18		1	1	Marshalling yards. S/Ldr West RCAF crashed
24 Jun	Noyelle-en-Chaussée	21	20		1		V1 launching site northeast of Abbeville.
25 Jun	Montorgueil	19	17		2		V1 launching site, southeast of Hesdin.
27 Jun	Mont Candon	16	16				V1 launching site south-southwest of Dieppe.

Date 1944	Target	No Desp	No Attack	Alt	DNCO	FTR	Remarks
28 Jun	Blainville sur L'Eau	19	15		1	3	Railway junction between Nancy and Luneville.
1 Jul	St. Martin l'Hortier	18	18				Supply dumps northwest of Neufchâtel
4 Jul	St. Marrin l'Hortier	19	19				Supply dumps.
5 Jul	St. Martin l'Hortier	19	19				Supply dumps.
6 Jul	Croixdalle	19	19				Constructional works southeast of Dieppe.
9 Jul	Chateau Benapre*	27	26		1		Vl launching site.
12 Jul	Thiverny	20	20				Supply depot near Senlis in the Oise.
15 Jul	Nucort	25	24			1	Modified Vl launching site northwest of Pontoise in the Val d'Oise.
18 Jul	Manneville	28	27		1		Troop concentration east of Caen.
18 Jul	Acquet	24	23			1	Vl launching site northeast of Abbeville.
20 Jul	Bottrop/ Welheim	27	25		2		Synthetic oil plant.
23 Jul	Kiel	21	21				
24 Jul	Stuttgart	5	4		1		
25 Jul	Forêt du Crocq	22	21		1		Launching site Le Crocq, north of Beauvais in the
28 Jul	Forêt de Nieppe	16	16				Oil Supply depot near
29 Jul	Forêt de Nieppe	11	11				Dunkirk
30 Jul	Villers-Bocage	28			28		German armour Southwest of Caen. Cancelled.
3 Aug	Forêt de Nieppe	10	10				Supply depot.
	Bois de Cassan	20	19		1		Constructional works.
5 Aug	Forêt de Nieppe	25	25				Supply depot.
7 Aug	May sur Orme	13	1		12**		Battle area.
9 Aug	Forêt de Mormal	27	26		1		Oil stores.
10 Aug	Dijon	16	16				Marshalling yards.
11 Aug	Wemaers-Cappel	10	10				Vl launching site south of Dunkirk.
12 Aug	Russelsheim	23	21			2	Opel works.
14 Aug	Fontaine-le-Pin	19	19				Troop concentration south of Caen.
15 Aug	Tirlemont	18	18				Aerodrome.
17 Aug	Brest	24	21		3		Shipping.
18 Aug	Sterkrade	22	21		1		Synthetic oil plant.

* Possibly 'Bernatre' northeast of Abbeville.
** Sorties cancelled on the instructions of the Master Bomber.

Date 1944	Target	No Desp	No Attack	Alt	DNCO	FTR	Remarks
25 Aug	Watten	6	6				Constructional works southeast of Calais.
25 Aug	Pontscorff	16	7		9		Gun battery near Lorient.
27 Aug	Honberg	21	20		1		Synthetic oil plant.
1 Sep	La Pourchinte	25	25				Supply dumps, southwest of St. Omer in the Pas de Calais.
3 Sep	Soesterberg	16	16				Aerodrome.
10 Sep	Le Havre	17	17				German garrison.
	Le Havre	8	7		1		German garrison.
12 Sep	Gelsenkirchen-Buer	26	24	1	1		Synthetic oil plant.
13 Sep	Gelsenkirchen-Nordstern	16	15		1		Synthetic oil plant.
15 Sep	Kiel	16	15				Sgt Throssell crashed.
17 Sep	Boulogne	21	21				Gun emplacements.
20 Sep	Calais	23	23				German garrison.
23 Sep	Neuss	23	21		2		
25 Sep	Calais	22			22*		German garrison.
26 Sep	Calais	15	15				German garrison.
27 Sep	Calais	15	15				German garrison.
6 Oct	Scholven	21	21				Synthetic oil plant.
7 Oct	Kleve	20	20				Communications.
9 Oct	Bochum	20	17		2	1	
14 Oct	Duisburg	28	27		1		
15 Oct	Duisburg	20	19		1		
15 Oct	Wilhelmshaven	16	16				
23 Oct	Essen	25	19		5		F/Sgt White crashed.
25 Oct	Essen	22	22				
28 Oct	Westkapelle	15	14			1	Gun emplacements.
28 Oct	Cologne	4	4				
29 Oct	Walcheren	17	17				
30 Oct	Cologne	21	21				
31 Oct	Cologne	19	15				
2 Nov	Düsseldorf	15	15				
4 Nov	Bochum	18	13		3	2	
6 Nov	Gelsenkirchen	13	12		1		Synthetic oil plant.
16 Nov	Julich	23	19		4		Communicatiohs.
18 Nov	Münster	15	15				
21 Nov	Sterkrade	21	19		2		Synthetic oil plant.
28 Nov	Essen	26	26				
30 Nov	Duisburg	19	19				
2 Dec	Hagen	22	21		1		
5 Dec	Soest	22	20		2		Marshalling yards.
6 Dec	Osnabrück	18	16		2		
12 Dec	Essen	20	20				

* Sorties cancelled on the insrructions of the Master Bomber.

Date 1944	Target	No Desp	No Attack	Alt	DNCO	FTR	Remarks
18 Dec	Duisburg	18	18				
22 Dec	Bingen	7	7				Marshalling yards.
26 Dec	St.Vith	15	13		1	1	Communications.
28 Dec	Opladen	12	11		1		Railway workshops.
29 Dec	Koblenz	22	20		2		Communications.
30 Dec	Cologne	20	19			1	Kalk/Nord marshalling yards
1944	**Totals:**						
	Halifax B V	**68**	**47**	**3**	**8**	**8**	**2 sorties undetermined**
	Halifatr B.III	**2224**	**2014**	**5**	**167**	**33**	**5 sorties undetermined**
	Combined	**2292**	**2061**	**8**	**175**	**41**	**7 sorties undetermined**
	1941/42/43/44	**4536**	**3895**	**68**	**423**	**136**	**14 sorties undetermined**
1945							
1 Jan	Dortmund-Hoesch	18	16		2		Coking plant.
2 Jan	Ludwigshaven	15	15				Chemical plant.
5 Jan	Hannover	20	19		1		
6 Jan	Hanau	16	16				Communications.
14 Jan	Saarbrucken	18	18				Marshalling yards.
14 Jan	Dulmen	4	4				Fuel depot.
16 Jan	Magdeburg	18	17		1		Marshalling yards.
28 Jan	Stuttgart-Kornwestheim	22	21		1		
1 Feb	Mainz	19	17		1		F/Sgt McBrinn RCAFcrashed.
2 Feb	Wanne Eickel	16	16				Synthetic oil plant.
4 Feb	Bonn	21	19		2		Communications.
7 Feb	Goch	19	8		11*		Communications.
9 Feb	Wanne Eickel	17	16		1		Synthetic oil plant.
13 Feb	Bohlen	23	22		1		Synthetic oil plant.
14 Feb	Chemnitz	13	13				Support to eastern front.
17 Feb	Wesel	19	1		18*		
20 Feb	Wesel	16	I5		1		4 Group records show Reisholz as the target.
21 Feb	Worms	18	17			1	Communications.
23 Feb	Essen	22	22				
24 Feb	Kamen	17	17				Synthetic oil plant.
27 Feb	Mainz	22	19		2	1	
2 Mar	Cologne	21	20		1		Communications.
3 Mar	Kamen	20	20				SyntheEic oil plant.
5 Mar	Chemnitz	20	19		1		Support for eastern front.
7 Mar	Hemmingstedt	17	16		1		Oil refinery.
8 Mar	Hamburg	18	18				Submarine building yards.
11 Mar	Essen	22	22				Communications.

* Sorties cancelled on the insructions of the Master Bomber.

Date 1945	Target	No Desp	No Attack	Alt	DNCO	FTR	Remarks
12 Mar	Dortmund	20	19		1		Communications.
13 Mar	Wuppertal-Barman	20	20				Marshalling yards.
14 Mar	Homberg	7	7				
15 Mar	Bottrop	13	13				
	Hagen	9	9				
19 Mar	Witten	20	20				
20 Mar	Bochum	15	IS				
22 Mar	Dulmen	17	16		1		Troop concentrations.
24 Mar	Sterkrade	22	22				Communications.
25 Mar	Osnabrück	22	22				Marshalling yards.
4 Apr	Harburg	21	21				Oil storage depot.
8 Apr	Hamburg	21	21				Submarine building yards.
11 Apr	Bayreuth	26	24		2		Marshalling yards.
18 Apr	Heligoland	11	10				W/O Holmes crashed.
25 Apr	Wangerooge	25	22		1	2	Gun emplacements.

1945	Totals:						
	Halifax B.III	652	602		47	2	1 sortie undetermined
	Halifax B.VI	108	102		3	2	1 sortie undetermined
	Combined	760	704		50	4	2 sorties undetermined
1941/42/43/44/45		5296	4599	68	473	140	16 sorties undetermined
Operational sorties by type:							
	Halifax B.I	161	124	11	14	10	2 sorties undetermined
	Halifax B.II	1004	822	32	106	41	3 sorties undetermined
	Halifax B.V	1147	935	20	136	52	4 sorties undetermined
	Halifax B.III	2876	2616	5	214	35	6 sorties undetermined
	Halifax B.VI	108	102		3	2	1 sortie undetermined
	Totals	5296	4599	68	473	140	16 sorties undetermined

SECTION THREE

A breakdown of 76 Squadron's operational flying in India.

Nov 45	120 operational flights to Mauripur	961.15 hours
	41 operational flights to Arkonam	288.05 hours
	36 special lifts	424.20 hours
	Continuation training	187.20 hours
	Passengers carried	6326
	Freight lifted	183056-bs

Dec 45	91 operational flights to Mauripur	689.40 hours
	32 operational flights to Arkonam	206.35 hours
	25 speciallifts	225.10 hours
	Continuation training	247.30 hours
	Passengers carried.	4918
	Freight lifted	71040-1bs

Jan 46	91 operational flights to Mauripur	606.10 hours
	32 operational flights to Arkonam	206.35 hours
	40 special lifts	349.10 hours
	Passengers carried	5574
	Freightlifted	149111-1bs

Feb 46	84 operational flights to Mauripur	494.10 hours
	30 operational flights to Arkonam	369.45 hours
	23 special lifts	220.30 hours
	Passengers carried	4644
	Freight lifted	75383-1bs

Mar 46	106 operational flights to Mauripur	784.00 hours
	21 operational flights to St. Thomas Mt	190.05 hours
	9 operational flights to Dum-Dum	124.30 hours
	29 special lifts	632.30 hours
	Passengers carried	4550
	Freight lifted	106219$_{1/2}$ lbs

Apr 46	85 operational flights to Mauripur	663.00 hours
	29 special lifts	567.25 hours
	Passengers carried	2721
	Freight lifted	113553-1bs

May 46	35 operational flights to Mauripur	260.15 hours
	73 special lifts	637.00 hours
	Passengers carried	1388
	Freight lifted	249452-1bs

Jun 46	77 special lifts	849.00 hours
	Passengers carried	598
	Freight lifted	192045-1bs
	Total weight of mail carried	227-1bs

Jul 46	81 special lifts	865.00 hours
	Passengers carried	937
	Freight lifted	1363684-1bs[36]
	Supply drops at Chittagong	171

Aug 46	No entries recorded	

---

[36] Compared with previous months this figure is extraordinarily high, and I suggest an error has.occurred in the squadron records. It is regretted that the records for October 1945 and August.1946 have not been entered in the Operational Record Book, for without these statistics a complete assessment of the squadron's achievements in India cannot be made.

Appendix Three

76 SQUADRON 'ROLL OF HONOUR'

SECTION ONE
Aircrew failing to return from operational sorties over Germany, Italy and the Middle East, the occupied countries and mining operations.

23 Jun 41 (L9492) Kiel/Wilhelmshaven		5 Aug 41 (L9516) Karlsruhe	
P/O W K Stobbs	+	Sgt T A Byrne	pow
Sgt J L Cullum	+	Sgt C B Flockhart	pow
Sgt G H Barnard	+	Sgt L A Thompson	pow
Sgt J S Lipton	pow	Sgt G W S Taylor	pow
Sgt R S Adair	+	Sgt R Brown	+
Sgt A Turner	+	Sgt J H Pitt	pow
		F/Lt T B Leigh	pow[37]

24 Jul 41 (L9529) Scharnhorst		13 Aug 41 (L9530 MP:L) Berlin	
F/Lt A E Lewin	+	F/Lt C C Cheshire	pow
Sgt W H J Gourley RAAF	+	Sgt P H T Horrox	pow
FISgt C H Horner	+	Sgt G J Smalley	pow
Sgt B Phillips	pow	Sgt E C Gurmin	pow
Sgt P J Vickery	+	Sgt A T Niven	+
Sgt W A Finlayson	pow	Sgt R C Wash	pow
F/Lt N W McLeod	pow	F/Sgt W Woods	+

24 Jul 41 (L95 17) Scharnhorst		13 Aug 41 (L9531) Berlin	
P/O J F P J McKenna	+	Sgt C E Whitfield	+
Sgt R F Ford-Hutchinson	+	Sgt J J Berry	+
Sgt G Summers	+	P/O V D Durham	+
Sgt V A Davis	+	Sgt A Critchlow	+
Sgt J M Pilbeam	+	SGT N F Brotherton	+
Sgt L T Rice	+	Sgt K Kenworthy	pow
F/S9t R W J Hill	+	F/Sgt W A Bone	pow[38]

24 Jul 41 (L9494) Scharnhorst		12 Oct 41 (L9561MP:H) Bremen	
S/Ldr W R Williams	pow	Sgt E B Muttart RCAF	+
P/O J G Ireton	pow	P/O N F Trayler	pow
Sgt L J Butler	pow	Sgt R W P Alexander	pow
Sgt N Kershaw	pow	Sgt W H Hunt	pow
Sgt S Jones	pow	Sgt G H Patterson	pow
Sgt A H J Turner	pow	Sgt L A Roberts	pow
Sgt G R Wedderburn	pow	Sgt J W Duffield	pow
		Sgt D Cotsell	pow

---

37   Died in captivity 25 Mar 44

38   Died in captivity 19 Apr 45

31 Oct 41 (L9602 MP:N) Dunkirk
Sgt C S O'Brien RCAF   +
P/O N F McLean RNZAF   +
Sgt J R Johnson RCAF   +
F/Sgt J Flannigan   +
P/O F C Brooks RCAF   +
Sgt C E Wood   +
Sgt J Mycock   +

30 Dec 41 (L9615 MP:X) Brest
P/O D S King RCAF   +
Sgt W R Gales RCAF   +
Sgt S M Wilson RAAF   +
Sgt L Blair   +
Sgt H J Toski   +
Sgt P D Randall   +
Sgt F J Eaton   +

3IMar 42 (R945 3 MP:K) Tirpitz
S/Ldr A P Burdett   +
P/O N F Bowsher RCAF   +
F/Sgt W J Cadger RCAF   +
F/Sgt L W Fletcher RCAF   +
Sgt S Davis   +
Sgt D C Martin   +
Sgt L W Hanson RAAF   +

10 Apr 42 (R9484 MP:G) Essen
F/Sgt J H Lambeth   +
Sgt R Kitchen   +
P/O J R Connolly   +
Sgt M C F Swain   +
Sgt S F Parker   +
Sgt W D R George   +
Sgt C H Reynolds RAAF   +

12 Apr 42 (R9487 MP:X) Essen
Sgt K F Lloyd-Jones RAAF   +
P/O W Culmsee   +
P/O R Fairclough   pow
F/Sgt R W A Hawksworth   +
Sgt H E Hothersall   +
Sgt P E Wheeldon   +
Sgt W A R Moule RCAF   +

27 Apr 42 (W1017 MP:T) Dunkirk
Sgt P C Morris   +
Sgt G A Simpson   +
P/O W A Trickett RAAF   pow
Sgt J Potts   +
P/O W A Shiels   pow
Sgt J W Brown   pow
F/Sgt G Sanderson   +

3 May 42 (R9451 MP:H) Hamburg
Sgt J B Willaims   +
Sgt H Ellis-Owens   +
Sgt N H Leaman   pow
Sgt B B Jackson   +
Sgt C R Fox   pow
Sgt A W Jones   +

8 May 42 (R9456 MP:F) Warnemünde
P/O H B Moorhouse   +
F/O W L Long   +
Sgt J J O'Reilly   +
Sgt T P Smith   +
Sgt D R Neve   +
Sgt R Davison   +

l9 May 42 (W7660 MP:L) Mannheim
F/Sgt F W Anderson   pow
Sgt R H Baird RCAF   pow
Sgt C Ilian   pow
Sgt G B Gowers   pow
Sgt A E Redding   pow
Sgt E K Southward   pow
F/Sgt R A LaFranchise RCAF   pow

29 May 42 (W1065 MP:G) Gnome et
                              Rhone
P/O J D Anderson   +
Sgt T R Marshall   +
P/O N H Bowack   +
F/Sgt D A Miner   +
Sgt W Brown   +
Sgt J Nicol   +
Sgt M S D Corker   +

1 Jun 42 (W1064 MP:J) Essen
Sgt T R A West   +
Sgt P Wright   esc
Sgt J A Oldfield   pow
Sgt J R Thompson   +
Sgt W J Norfolk   esc
P/O W B Mulligan RNZAF   pow

3 Jun 42 (R9457 MP:A) Bremen
F/Sgt J W Stell   +
Sgt R C Cockburn   pow
Sgt W Archer   +
Sgt D P Brooks   +
Sgt C R Metcalfe   +
Sgt D H Nelson   pow
Sgt R Greenwood   +

3 Jun 42 (Wl104 MP:F) Bremen

P/O J A Philip	+
Sgt F E Ormerod	+
P/O R S Mulhauser RCAF	+
Sgt J H Harte	+
Sgt J Battersby	+
Sgt W Watson	+

20 Jun 42 (W1114 MP:F) Emden

P/O H Norfolk	+
Sgt R W F Painter	pow
P/O E A White RACF	pow
Sgt W Charlesworthy	+
Sgt D S Smith	pow
Sgt H D Jones	pow
F/Sgt E Salway	+

25 Jun 42 (W7747 MP:G) Bremen

Sgt J E Meyer RCAF	+
F/Sgt W C Francouer RCAF	+
Sgt J M Cameron	+
Sgt A M C Gasson	+
Sgt W J Mills	+
Sgt J Almond	+
Sgt A Wearmouth	+

26 Jul 42 (R9485 MP:H) Hamburg

Sgt E J Butt	pow
Sgt R J Woollard	pow
P/O A S Hawkins	+
Sgt C M Muir	pow
Sgt D L Osborne	+
Sgt P Barr	+
Sgt E C Sudbury	pow

1 Sep 42 (W1244 MP:D) Saarbrucken

P/O H G Sherwood	+
Sgt D W Coverly	pow
Sgt C H M Smith	pow
Sgt E J Kingston	pow
Sgt H Fowler	pow
Sgt L Park	pow
Sgt H E Turvey	pow

5 Sep 42 (Wl 144 MP:Q) Heraklion**

F/Lt J Bryan	+
Sgt S H Robinson	pow
Sgt A Potts	+
Sgt C R Jones	pow
Sgt W R Young	pow
Sgt T P E Blatch	pow

16 Sep 42 (R9365 MP:C) Essen

P/O A G Campbell RAAF	+
F/Sgt M J Standley RAAF	+
Sgt S A Witchell	+
F/Sgt W N Geddie	+
Sgt J R Runnicles	+
Sgt S G White	+
Sgt A Moffatt	+

23 Sep 42 (DT508 MP:K) Flensburg

S/Ldr J O Barnard	pow
P/O G T Lester	pow
P/O S E Groves	+
Sgt D M Elliott	pow
Sgt R Gadd	pow
Sgt R Douglass	pow
Sgt N J Hill	+

1 Oct 42 (W7812 MP:B) Flensburg

P/O M W Atkinson RCAF	+
Sgt T W Peacock RNZAF	+
Sgt E Topping	+
Sgt P D Skerman	+
Sgt P van Lelyveld RRAF	+
Sgt H S Greenwood	+
Sgt L H Lavis	+

5 Oct 42 (DT496) Aachen

	+
Sgt K A Peters RCAF	+
P/O B G Robinson	+
Sgt A Waring	+
F/Sgt T I R Owen	+
Sgt V J Coombs	+
Sgt J F Killilea	+
Sgt A E Holding	+

7 Nov 42 (DT515 MP:T) Genoa

F/Sgt G Thom RCAF	pow
Sgt H J R White RCAF	pow
Sgt H Gorfunkle	pow*
Sgt D J McBride RNZAF	pow
Sgt L W Horne	esc
Sgt H W Owen	pow
Sgt D L Reed	pow

*   Died shortly after admission to a Rheims Hospital
** The Areodrone

8 Nov 42 (DT5 50 MP:B) Minelaying
Sgt G G Sawatzky RCAF +
Sgt J McGauchie +
P/O W G Barrett +
Sgt G B Finley RCAF +
Sgt R H Bowkett +
Sgt E H Seares +
Sgt T A Keech +

20 Nov 42 (DT571 MP:M)) Turin
Sgt B A Wisely RNZAF +
Sgt J Warren +
P/O P J Morice +
Sgt W McAsh +
Sgt T Casbolt +
Sgt G E Rawson +
Sgt J Murchison +

6 Dec 42 (BB242 MP:P) Mannheim
P/O W C Hillier +
Sgt R L McDonald RCAF pow
Sgt H J B Canter esc
Sgt H L Robertson esc
Sgt J E Theckston pow
Sgt J A Parkin pow
Sgt A F Smith +

20 Dec 42 (DT511 MP:D) Duisburg
F/O D Anderson +
F/Sgt W Henschel +
Sgt W A Brimble +
Sgt F Tredinnick +
Sgt J Davey +
Sgt W E Adams +
Sgt T H Walpole +
Sgt R W Forman +

20 Dec 42 (DT570 MP:R) Duisburg
S/Ldr R N Pearce +
Sgt E Jones +
Sgt C R Ray +
Sgt J E N Warner +
Sgt L E Herbert +
Sgt A R O'Dell +
Sgt D Brierley +
Sgt C F Gilder +

17 Jan 43 (DT647 MP:P) Berlin
Capt B Naess RNAF +
Sgt L Lamb +
Lt R Indseth RNAF +

Sgt A V D Stinton +
Sgt A R Saunders +
Sgt M C Moody +
Sgt P H B P Green +

17 Jan 43 (DT569 MP:C) Berlin
Sgt D A Gold +
Sgt A W Stevenson +
Sgt D R Dewar +
Sgt C A Gruchy +
Sgt A D Tidmarsh +
Sgt J Ward +
P/O A H Piggs +

21 Jan 43 (DT621 MP:D) Minelaying
Sgt D Holmes +
Sgt J F McFarlane +
Sgt P Ferguson +
Sgt D C H Hunt +
Sgt T W E Robson +
Sgt F E Williams +
Sgt F A Hughes +

1 Mar 43 (DT5 56 MP:U) Berlin
S/Ldr J L Fletcher +
F/Lt A T Wheatley +
P/O B B Blackman pow
F/O L Souter-Smith esc
F/Sgt G G Stanley RCAF +
Sgt L A Trinder +
Sgt E J Crutch pow
Sgt K V Moore RCAF +

1 Mar 43 (DT767 MP:V) Berlin
F/O N S Black RNZAF +
P/O E A Taylor +
Sgt L H Gregson +
Sgt G Prigent +
Sgt J R Barrett +
Sgt H J Gruntman +
Sgt J Ryder +

3 Mar 43 (W7678 MP:L) Hamburg
F/O W R Golding +
Sgt R L Culverson +
P/O L A Allan +
Sgt G C D Sayer +
Sgt K Hitchen +
Sgt R R Webber +
Sgt J J Thompson +

5 Mar 43 (BB282 MP:R) Essen
F/Sgt C A Milan RCAF	+
P/O E J Fry RCAF	+
F/O C G Hitt	+
Sgt H W Edwards	+
Sgt H C Cope	+
Sgt D J Trainor	+
Sgt R B van Buren RCAF	+

12 Mar 43 (DT751 MP:C) Essen
Sgt P Nevines	pow
Sgt R G Poland	pow*
P/O J B Locke	pow
Sgt W S Wright	pow
Sgt R C Ratcliffe	pow
Sgt A C Sharpe	+
Sgf F J G Stapleton	pow

29 Mar 43 (DT744 MP:K) Berlin
F/Lt J H Wetherly	+
Sgt A H J Whittle	+
F/Lt H J Beck	+
P/O A H G Paxton	+
F/Sgt J R Orr	+
Sgt L Havenhand	+
Sgt C H Mitton	+

29 Mar 43 (DT563 MP:O) Berlin
Sgt L J Cursley	+
Sgt J Taylor RCAF	+
Sgt T Edwards	+
Sgt A B Boyd	+
Sgt R G Wright	+
Sgt F J Platt	+
F/Sgt R W MacNeill RCAF	+

3 Apr 43 (W7805 MP:M) Essen
Sgt J K Howarth	+
Sgt J W S Blakey	pow
Sgt G H Egan	pow
P/O F W Digby	+
Sgt F G Williams	+
Sgt W C Pitt	+
Sgt H N Richards RCAF	pow

8 Apr 43 (W1236 MP:G) Duisburg
F/O M A S Elliott	+
F/O H H Rogers DFM	+
P/O R R Johnston	+
P/O A M Houston	+
F/Sgt J Appleton	+

Sgt R J Maffhews	+
Sgt T K Wagstaff	+
Sgt J.D. Armstrong	+

10 Apr 43 (JB871 MP:V) Frankfurt
F/Lt A H Hull	+
Gr Capt J R Whitley	esc
Sgt M A I Davies	esc
Sgt W J Painter	+
Sgt G A Bozier	+
Sgt P E Matthews	+
Sgt B Strange	esc
P/O J A A M David	esc

16 Apr 43 (JB800 MP:U) Pilsen
Sgt G C Wright	+
F/O A N Cooper	+
P/O H E Smith	+
F/O J F Webb	+
Sgt D B Wombwell	pow
Sgt A G C Read	+
Sgt F A Robb RCAF	+

16 Apr 43 (DT575 MP:Y) Pilsen
Sgt B W E Wedderburn	+
Sgt F O Ross RCAF	+
Sgt B J Clinging	+
Sgt F C Fidgeon	+
Sgt L N Jonasson RCAF	+
Sgt J Strachan	+
Sgt S C H Brown	+

16 Apr 43 (DK165 MP:E) Pilsen
Sgt E K Webb	+
Sgt J Kay	+
Sgt K R G Williams	+
Sgt A R Ross RCAF	+
Sgt L B Mitchell	pow
Sgt S Braybrook	+
F/Sgt G Brown	+

26 Apr 43 (DG423 MP:H) Duisburg
Sgt D C McNab RNZAF	+
P/O N D Fleming	+
Sgt F N Slingsby	+
Sgt B F Keable	+
Sgt C C Strain RCAF	+
Sgt J Wood	+
Sgt J Clegg	+

* Died in captivity 19 Jan 44.

30 Apr 43 (DK171 MP:J) Essen
Sgt B W Thomas RAAF	+
Sgt F Norris	pow
Sgt E H Wood	+
Sgt F J Chandler	+
Sgt G E Testal	pow
Sgt A Hawley	+
Sgt R E Hemsworth	pow

4 May 43 (DK134 MP:Y) Dortmund
P/O J I M Bell	*pow
Sgt A E Bumstead	*pow
Sgt H J Hamlyn	*pow
Sgt H Farrington	*pow
Sgt D J Marshall	*pow
F/Sgt D B Brown RCAF	*pow
Sgt A Forster	*pow
Sgt B Thompson	*pow

23 May 43 (DK172 MP:L) Dortmund
F/Sgt E S Bawden	+
Lt P Waaler RNAF	pow
Sgt T Musgrove	+
Sgt L W S Thick	pow
Sgt J W Smith	pow
Sgt C Greenhalgh	+
Sgt T Knowles	pow
Sgt T L V Hitchcock	+

23 May 43 (DK169 MP:M) Dortmund
Sgt C H Cousins	pow
Sgt J F Hughes	pow
P/O A W L Pruce	pow
Sgt A G Dale	pow
P/O J W Coleman	+
Sgt J Parr	pow
Sgt H A Crouse RCAF	+

27 May 43 (DK147 MP:A) Essen
P/O D S Ross RCAF	pow
Sgt G J Beckford	pow
Sgt H Anderson	+
Sgt W G Styles	pow
P/O H Langlois RCAF	pow
Sgt R Jones	pow
F/O E F Campbell	+

11 Jun 43 (DK200 MP:L) Düsseldorf
Sgt D S Phillips	+
Sgt G A Burdett	pow
Sgt J Hills	pow
Sgt N W S Clack	+
Sgt E Cadmore	+
Sgt C G Bird	pow
Sgt E W A Brise	pow

11 Jun 43 (DK170 MP:C) Düsseldorf
Sgt A J N Wilson	+
Sgt J Domnitz	+
Sgt J A Lobban	pow
Sgt J J Pawsey	+
Sgt D Tibble	+
Sgt C K Burton	+
Sgt K W Lawson RCAF	+

12 Jun 43 (DK177 MP:H) Bochum
F/Sgt A A H Pullan RNZAF	+
Sgt J G Brown .	+
P/O J Kay	+
Sgt L C Gearing	+
Sgt H Baker	+
Sgt I B Nicol	+
F/Sgt J E Buxton	+

22 Jun 43 (DK224 MP:Q) Mülheim
P/O J Carrie	pow
Gr Capt D E L Wilson RAAF	pow
Sgt R W Hibbs	pow
Sgt G B Thomason	pow
Sgt E L McVittie	pow
Sgt R H Hammett RCAF	pow
Sgt R Huke	+
Sgt S M Davies	pow

24 Jun 43 (DK166 MP:D) Wuppertal
F/Lt G H Cheetham RCAF	+
Sgt G I Simkin	+
P/O J D Danks	pow
Sgt K R Newton	pow
Sgt J Sweeney	pow
Sgt R H Evans	pow
Sgt E Harper	+

*   From this crew. four are reported to have evaded capture in the days immediately following their loss. Later, three were picked up and became prisoners. while the fate of the fourth man is undetermined.

28 Jun 43 (DK137 MP:R) Cologne
Sgt G C Parritt   +
Sgt B Howard   +
Sgt L Harris   +
Sgt R E Archer   +
Sgt C G Vallance   +
Sgt J L Burnside   +
Sgt R J Coggins   +

28 Jun 43 (DKl50 MP:E) Cologne
Sgt D Coles   +
P/O H W Chester   +
P/O K E Moon   +
Sgt T C R James RCAF   +
Sgt L Glover-Price   +
Sgt R J McAuley   +
Sgt R B Twitchen   +

24 Jul 43 (DK187 MP:M) Hamburg
F/O G Such   +
Sgt F J Jackson   +
Sgt F E McMakin   +
F/O R C Ross   +
Sgt H Nelson   +
Sgt R Cowell   +
Sgt H A Morris   +
Sgt D R Bell   +

29 Jul 43 (EB244 MP:X) Hamburg
Sgt A R Bjercke RNAF   +
Sgt H Roberts   pow
F/O C Daniel   +
Sgt O C Olsen RNAF   pow
Sgt V C Daniels   pow
Sgt D M Morrison   pow
Sgt S H Bates   pow

30 Jul 43 (DK202 MP:Q) Remscheid
Sgt R A Cole   +
Sgt A B Harper   +
Sgt R F Russell   +
Sgt J W Pothecary   +
Sgt J R Williams   +
Sgt J Lewis   +
Sgt D T Shaw RCAF   +

2 Aug 43 (EB249 MP:E) Hamburg
F/O S I Dillon RNZAF   +
F/O J Pattison RNZAF   +
F/Sgt A K Baxter RNZAF   +

F/Sgt E O'Shaughnessy RNZAF   +
Sgt R S Fry   +
Sgt H V Mullane   +
Sgt A T Lees   +

9 Aug 43 (LK892 MP:C) Mannheim
F/Lt C M Shannon RAAF   +
Sgt T Buchan   +
F/O G A Turner   +
F/O W C Ellis   +
Sgt J Smith   +
Sgt F Walton   +
Sgt J Dodson   +

12 Aug 43 (DK240 MP:G) Milan
P/O B S McCann   +
F/O J W Brace   pow
Sgt A C Samuel   +
Sgt J R Luxton   +
F/Sgt H S Martin RCAF   +
Sgt W H Jones   pow
Sgt L F Jackson   +

27 Aug 43 (DK269 MP:J) Nuremburg
F/Sgt W P Ward   +
F/O P Carling   +
F/Sgt G Pearson   +
Sgt G R Elks   +
F/O E Hyett   +
Sgt J E P Morton   +
Sgt J E Camerson RCAF   +

30 Aug 43 (DK207 MP:S) München-
                                    Gladbach
S/Ldr A L C A Stuart   +
F/O W G Williams   pow
P/O K Holme   +
 Sgt D J Doe   pow
Sgt V T Bradley   +
Sgt D G Powell   +
Sgt S McLennan RCAF   +

5 Sep 43 (DK223 MP:N) Mannheim
P/O S T Schmidt RNZAF   +
P/O A F Smith   pow
F/O W W Goldberg   +
Sgt E V Dean   +
Sgt F Watling   +
Sgt W H Saunders   +
Sgt A F Todd RCAF   +

6 sep 43 (EB250 MP:R) Munich

F/Sgt E G Little RNZAF	+
F/Sgt L H E Gittins	+
Sgt B A Phillis	+
P/O E M Farrington	pow
Sgt J H Naylor	+
Sgt R E Lewis	+
Sgt J P Amold	+
Sgt G W Broadbent	pow

22 Sep 43 (EB253 MP:C) Hannover

SGT D Fjaervoll RNAF	+
Sgt L L Kerr RCAF	+
Sgt F G Old	pow
Sgt E Stotthard	+
Sgt J K Dennis [40]	pow
Sgt K Meredith	+
Sgt A Osnes RNAF	+

22 Sep 43 (LK645 MP:S) Hannover

S/Ldr F W S Turner	+
Sgt G F Bryant	pow
Sgt R Wray	+
F/O J A Beggs	pow
Sgt B C Bailey	pow
Sgt J Cole	pow
P/O D O Cull RAAF	pow

27 Sep 43 (DK266 MP:O) Hannover

P/O S W Hickman	+
Sgt A S Pring	+
F/O G W Keene	+
Sgt L C A Walters	+
Sgt J M Emerson	+
Sgt F Brierley	+
Sgt G Scott	+

27 Sep 43 (LK891 MP:X) Hannover

P/O D G Griffiths	+
F/Sgt B A Shortland	+
P/O K A Barber	+
Sgt A E H Holmes	+
Sgt R C H Freeman	+
Sgt L Glentworth	+
Sgt C R Walker	+
Sgt D M R B Entwisle	+

3 Oct 43 (DK201 MP:P) Kassel

P/O A Thorp	+
Sgt K D Butters	pow
Sgt G P Barrell	pow
P/O J P Suzor	pow
Sgt J F Perry	pow
Sgt J Zuidmulder	+
Sgt E Luder	pow
P/O W W Wanless RCAF	pow

3 Oct 43 (DK247 MP:W) Kassel

F/O W S Wilson RAAF [39]	pow
F/Sgt J C Boyd RNZAF	pow
Sgt K Herring	+
Sgt W E Price	+
P/O J R Hillhouse RCAF	+
Sgt A J Murtagh	+
Sgt R M Watson RCAF	+

3 Oct 43 (LK904 MP:T) Kassel

F/Sgt W T Waitt	+
Sgt R A Blackburn	+
Sgt A M McKinlay	+
Sgt L Turner	+
Sgt J E A Beecher	+
Sgt S E Waldron	pow
Sgt D Pickersgill	+

3 Oct 43 (DK203 MP:A) Kassel

2Lt N Eckhoff RNAF	+
Sgt R Coupe	pow
Sgt S Meieran RNAF	pow
Sgt J Skjelanger RNAF	pow
Sgt C H E Coster	pow
Sgt A Hayes [41]	pow
F/O M G Sheerman	+

22 Oct 43 (LK664 MP:U) Kassel

Lt L E Hulthin RNAF	+
W/O I H Blackburn	+
P/O A V C Barden	+
P/O C M Murfitt	+
Sgt F Southern	+
Sgt L T Brawn	+
Sgt R J K Machan	+
P/O L J Pringle RAAF	+

---

39   Died in captivity 17 Nov 43.

40   Repatriated Sep1944.

41   Died of wounds 6 Oct 43.

3 Nov 43 (LK948 MP:T) Düsseldorf

F/Lt D E Hicks RCAF	+
Sgt G Morrison	+
Sgt S W Lucyk RCAF	+
Sgt A E Bristow	pow
Sgt R W Elder	+
Sgt R Clough	pow
Sgt T W Davis	+

3 Nov 43 (LK932 MP:X) Düsseldorf

F/Lt D G Hornsey	esc
Sgt D C Clark-Carter	pow
Sgt R W Glover	pow
Sgt J S Carnill	pow
Sgt K J Davis	pow
Sgt F A Fewson	pow
Sgt R E Stokes	pow

18 Nov 43 (LK957 MP:H) Mannheim

F/Sgt J Wade-Seymour	+
Sgt S Iving	+
F/Sgt C T Talkington	pow
Sgt W C Hughes	+
Sgt F Hemingway	+
Sgt D C S Davie	+
Sgt E C Goodwin	+

25 Nov 43 (LK903 MP:G) Frankfurt

2Lt K Lindaas RNAF	+
Sgt E L Guertin RCAF	pow
F/Sgt D L Melhuish	pow
Sgt R E Beer	pow
Sgt H S Seatter	pow
Sgt D H Short	pow
Sgt F V Beadle	pow

25 Nov 43 (DK231 MP:B) Frankfurt

P/O S J Troake	+
F/O T G Paton	pow
P/O R J Fayers	pow
Sgt P L Weeks	+
S/Sgt P W Flewell USAAF	pow
Sgt L H Barnes	+
F/Sgt R S Orr RCAF	+

26 Nov 43 (LK946 MP:F) Stuttgart

F/O N W Mann RCAF	pow
F/Sgt E L Capreol RCAF	pow
Sgt F Winterbottom	pow
Sgt J Hodgson	pow
Sgt P Drummond	pow

Sgt A C Fuller	pow
Sgt E J Berndt RCAF	+

26 Nov 43 (LK687 MP:P) Stuttgart

P/O H R W Whittle	+
F/Sgt A Roy RCAF	pow
P/O J R Rogers	pow
F/O R C Saunders	pow
Sgt W Coates	pow
P/O W J Morgan	pow
Sgt F F MacPhearson	+

3 Dec 43 (LK902 MP:H) Leipzig

F/Sgt I M Lowe RCAF	+
F/O J Stott	+
F/Sgt W R K Boles RCAF	+
Sgt L S Newey	+
Sgt J R W Kerner	+
Sgt S Jones	+
Sgt J N E Nadeau RCAF	+

20 Dec 43 (LK911 MP:Y) Frankfurt

F/Sgt J T Boddington	+
Sgt J Barrington	+
Sgt T Wilson	pow
Sgt E Andrews	pow
Sgt F J McMillan	pow
Sgt A J Cope	pow
Sgt F Tessick	+

20 Dec 43 (LK7 32 MP:F) Frankfurt

F/Sgt W D V Cable	+
F/O J Blair	+
F/O J O Pakeman	pow
F/Lt I G Evans	pow
Sgt N W E Blatch	+
Sgt C J Castleton	pow
Sgt L H Rollingson	pow

20 Dec 43 (LK926 MP:C) Frankfurt

F/Sgt C W Matthews	+
F/Sgt L F Gillingham	+
F/Sgt J A Lamb RNZAF	+
Sgt H C Cohen	+
Sgt D S McClelland RCAF	+
Sgt R F Taylor	+
F/Sgt L J Sheean RAAF	+

20 Jan 44 (LK958 MP:Q) Berlin
F/Sgt G C Ive RAAF	+
Sgt K C Buchan RAAF	pow
Sgt K F Hutson	+
F/Sgt M F Curry RAAF	pow
Sgt J C Stones	+
Sgt R V Turner	+
Sgt A J E Raven	+

20 Jan 44 (LK921 MP:R) Berlin
F/Sgt V Parrott RCAF	+
F/Sgt A L P Gibson RCAF	+
F/Sgt J L Miriams	+
F/Sgt F W Hickman	+
Sgt J T Hadland	+
Sgt J Vicary	+
F/Sgt L J McCrachy RAAF	+

20 Jan 44 (LL116 MP:X) Berlin
P/O G G A Whitehead	esc
Sgt R J Prior	pow
F/O H D G Morris	+
W/O J McTrach RCAF	esc
Sgt L Stokes	pow
Sgt J M Fisher	pow
Sgt H Fisher	pow
Sgt B Compton	esc

21 Jan 44 (LK912 MP:N) Magdeburg
Sgt H W Bloomfield	+
Sgt K A Hicks	+
Sgt V W Piedot	+
Sgt E G Bird	+
Sgt D Pinkard	+
Sgt A C Pope	+
Sgt A W McGrath RCAF	+

21 Jan 44 (LK922 MP:L) Magdeburg
F/Sgt H Boyes	+
F/O D H McVie RAAF	pow
Sgt T Fraser	pow
Sgt C M Bennett	pow
Sgt J McCurry	+
Sgt R S Western	+
Sgt R Forte	+

21 Jan 44 (LK733 MP:B) Magdeburg
Lt T Anundskaas RNAF	+
F/O B R James RAAF	+
Sgt S R Jessamy	+
Sgt L G Driver	+

P/O H Wyatt	+
Sgt J Gorrie	+
Sgt J Rose	+

21 Jan 44 (LL185 MP:G) Magdeburg
Sgt C Walker	+
Sgt A Abrahams	+
F/Sgt J Sutherland RCAF	+
Sgt P Gizzi	+
Sgt K C Southward	+
Sgt F Hughes	+
Sgt G A Shield	+

15 Feb 44 (LL140 MP:A) Berlin
F/Sgt D A Eaton	pow
F/Sgt R Neal	pow
F/Sgt G K Wilson	pow
Sgt J C Harding	pow
Sgt E B Upton	+
Sgt R S Becker	pow
Sgt J A Watson	pow

1 Mar 44 (LW629 MP:M) Stuttgart
F/Sgt H T Davies	+
Sgt R B Basford	+
F/Sgt C W Jackson	pow
Sgt A Drake	+
Sgt C D Greenhill	+
Sgt A Fenwick	+
F/Sgt K G Wilson	+

15 Mar 44 (LW657 MP:G) Stuttgart
P/O A Jones RCAF	+
Sgt L G Scott RCAF	+
Sgt R Golding	+
Sgt J R Quicke	+
Sgt W Robson	+
Sgt W N Hedges	+
Sgt D A Bean	+

18 Mar 44 (LK791 MP:H) Frankfurt
F/Sgt P R Noyes	+
W/O C L Reed RCAF	+
F/O C G S Heaton	pow
Sgt A C Buckel	pow
Sgt L A Basting	pow
Sgt R A Ray	pow
F/Sgt J A van Marle	+

18 Mar 44 (LW655 MP:V) Frankfurt
F/Sgt D Joseph	pow
F/Sgt E Wirth RCAF	pow
F/O K G Ramsey RCAF	+
Sgt G F J Haskett	pow
Sgt J K Kirton	pow
Sgt E T H Giles	pow
Sgt W Sinclair	pow
Sgt L Makens	pow

24 Mar 44 (LK790 MP:F) Berlin
F/Sgt L Marshall RCAF	+
F/Sgt T Wilkinson RCAF	+
F/Sgt F W Kinch	pow
Sgt P Cramp	pow
Sgt W Longhorn	pow
Sgt W Lawton	*pow
Sgt E J Albon	pow

30 Mar 44 (LK795 MP:P) Nuremburg
F/Lt H D Coverley	pow
F/Sgt W A Blake	pow
F/Sgt K A H Trott	pow
Sgt P G Wilmshurst	pow
Sgt G M Smitham	pow
Sgt G E Motts	+
Sgt D M Bauldie	*pow

30 Mar 44 (LW696 MP:X) Nuremburg
S/Ldr K A Clack DFM	+
F/Sgt R E Mogalki RCAF	+
F/Sgt K J Shropshall	+
F/O R K Thomson RCAF	+
Sgt L W A Peall	+
Sgt G L Edwards	pow
P/O D C Nowell DFM	+
P/O D H Edwards	+

30 Mar 44 (LW647 MP:W) Nuremburg
F/O G C G Greenacre	+
F/Sgt A S Arneil	+
F/O A Thorpe	+
Sgt J A Henthorn	pow
P/O A D Maw RCAF	+
P/O A Monk	pow
P/O A H Death RCAF	+

22 Apr 44 (MZ578 MP:I) Düsseldorf
S/Ldr S A Somerscales	+
F/O S T Wingham	esc
F/O J H Lewis	esc

F/O J H Reavill	pow
F/Sgt H R Poole	+
F/O S W Stephen	pow
F/Sgt F J Rowe	pow

22 Apr 44 (MZ530 MP:U) Düsseldorf
F/Lt R A M Lemmon	+
F/O J G Gunnell	pow
P/O W Booth	pow
W/O E Butcher	pow
F/Sgt J W Chapman	+
P/O G Griffiths	pow
F/Sgt D Yuille	+

12 May 44 (MZ575 MP:W) Hasselt
F/O J Newcombe	+
F/O C H Stewart DFC	+
S/Ldr N L Shove DFC	+
F/O H D Reeder	esc
F/Sgt R Reading	pow
F/O A J Crouch DFM	+
F/O C Saunderson	+

24 May 44 (MZ623 MP:P) Aachen
W/8 F Bishop	pow
F/Sgt A H Rae	esc
F/O I H Greer	pow
F/Sgt W Cliff	pow
Sgt J Danes	pow
Sgt W T Mays	pow
Sgt C Cassidy	pow

24 May 44 (MZ622 MP:L) Aachen
F/Sgt P S Wade RAAF	+
Sgt S Patterson	+
Sgt K H Allaker	+
F/Sgt M H Graydon RAAF	+
Sgt J Horrocks	+
Sgt R E D Robinson	+
Sgt R J Head	pow

2 Jun 44 (LK783 MP:C) Trappes
P/O A J Innes	+
W/O J Paige RCAF	+
F/Sgt E Bryan	+
Sgt E Tonge	+
Sgt G N Clithero	+
Sgt J W Golder	+
Sgt G R Whittle	+

* Died in captivity 19 April 45.

2 Jun 44 (LK784 MP:D) Trappes
Sgt F G Woods   +
Sgt R Stewart   +
Sgt H C Johnson RCAF   +
F/Sgt L S Bryan   +
Sgt I W Davis   +
Sgt R Lee Mee Power   +
Sgt W E Woodbine   +

2 Jun 44 (MZ604 MP:W) Trappes
F/Sgt L J R Smith   +
F/Sgt H C Caswell RAAF   +
F/Sgt R T Hood   pow
Sgt J Thompson   +
Sgt C A Teasdale   +
Sgt A Ferguson   +
Sgt C Lowrie   +

6 Jun 44 (LW638 MP:W) Mont Fluery
P/O S A D Walker   +
F/O I R Draper   +
Sgt M C Murray RCAF   +
Sgt D W H Edsall   +
Sgt P Craig   +
Sgt N J Neal   +
Sgt T A McRobbie   +

7 Jun 44 (MZ531 MP:D) Juvisy
Sgt P R Hunt RCAF   pow
Sgt G C Heddle RCAF   pow
Sgt F McGarvey RCAF   pow
W/O D Clark RCAF   pow
Sgt T C Guy RCAF   pow
Sgt W H Eggleston   esc
Sgt R Dodds RCAF   esc

12 Jun 44 (LW644 MP:O) Amiens
P/O A L Johnston RCAF   +
F/Sgt G F Griffiths   +
F/Sgt H Earl   +
Sgt C J Trott   +
F/Sgt D Burton   +
Sgt E F Lewis   +
Sgt A Moult   +

22 Jun 44 (LW656 MP:B) Laon
W/O H L Cribb   +
F/Sgt M W Cosgrove RNZAF   +
Sgt D A Danbury   +
F/Sgt P S May RAAF   +
Sgt I H Ross   +

Sgt R E Royal   +
Sgt J S Webster   +

28 Jun 44 (MZ736 MP:B) Blainville
P/O I R M Weir RNZAF   pow
F/Sgt R L Lidbury   pow
F/O K J Bunn   +
Sgt A W Offer   esc
Sgt J P Gregory   +
Sgt G T Howie   pow
W/O S Wilson   pow

28 Jun 44 (MZ679 MP:C) Blainville
F/O J G Jannings   +
F/O T W Thompson RCAF   +
F/Sgt R L Givens   +
Sgt C F Poole   +
Sgt R P Lucas   +
Sgt J E Beeson   +
Sgt B C Acourt   +

28 Jun 44 (MZ539 MP:X) Blainville
W/O WT Gramson RCAF   +
Sgt G E Salisbury   esc
Sgt A Jones   esc
Sgt F McKechnie   esc
Sgt W J Bennett   esc
Sgt F Palmer   esc
Sgt S E Munslow   esc

6 Jul 44 (MZ524 MP:P) Nucort
F/O H M Steward   +
Sgt C S Menzies   +
Sgt R R Hughes   pow
Sgt F Pierson   pow
Sgt P Bryden   pow
Sgt E W McSaunders   +
Sgt P V Boyter   +

18 Jul 44 (LK873 MP:S) Acquet
F/Lt P E Sinclair RAAF   +
F/Sgt A G Rodgers RAAF   +
F/O G Watkins   +
Sgt W Ray   +
Sgt F Phillips   +
Sgt R Nevill   +
P/O D E Blockley   +

12 Aug 44 (LW695 MP:M) Russelsheim
F/Lt O R Cramer   +
F/Sgt O Thomas   +

Sgt J Duncan +
F/Sgt L W Powis +
Sgt C Astall +
Sgt W B Collins +
Sgt K S Bolton +

12 Aug 44 (LL578 MP:H) Russelsheim
F/O R V Ings
F/Sgt K P Sampson RAAF +
F/Sgt R Etherton RAAF +
Sgt W E Twigg +
Sgt F Williams +
Sgt R M McLaren +
F/Sgt I Brownlee RCAF +

9 Oct 44 (NA567 MP:W) Bochum
F/Sgt A L Wall RCAF +
Sgt T G Morin RCAF +
Sgt L R Kay RCAF +
Sgt P E Bennett +
F/Sgt M Gnida RCAF +
Sgt L T Webster +
F/Sgt K J Edmison RCAF +

28 Oct 44 (MZ599 MP:U) Westkapple
S/Ldr R T Langton +
F/O J S Corry +
F/O J C Cossins +
Sgt E Care +
Sgt R W McGraine +
Sgt F G Whittaker +
Sgt W L Sandiland +

4 Nov 44 (LW648 MP:Q) Bochum
P/O J L Thompson +
Sgt D Holcroft pow
F/Sgt F Chaplain pow
Sgt J McKee +
Sgt A G Frost pow
Sgt S Wilson pow
Sgt J Young +

4 Nov 44 (LL577 MP:M) Bochum
F/Sgt D N Cole +
Sgt D Plumley +
Sgt E Goudie +
Sgt D Dodgson +
Sgt W Day +
Sgt F Craddock +
Sgt E Fitton +

26 Dec 44 (MZ740 MP:R) St Vith
F/O D Woolf RCAF +

F/O G Floyd RCAF +
F/O R H Emerson RCAF +
P/O A B Clark RCAF +
F/Sgt K M Mason RCAF pow
Sgt J S Gray +
F/Sgt O F Newton RCAF +
W/O T Smith +

30 Dec 44 (NA171 MP:E) Cologne
F/Lt S B Harrison pow
F/Lt P T F May DFM +
Sgt D W Holmes +
Sgt J M Johnstone +
Sgt A Waterhouse +
Sgt J Wright +
Sgt R F Bloy +

21 Feb 45 (NR121 MP:E) Worms
P/O H L Ball RCAF +
P/O W J Phillips RCAF +
F/O W B Mallen RCAF +
W/O E Boydell +
F/Sgt J N Pennington RCAF +
F/Sgt J Faulkner +
F/Sgt J J McNeill RCAF +

27 Feb 45 (LL5 79 MP:L) Mainz
P/O R J P Barrell pow
F/O R J L Boucher RCAF +
F/Sgt L E Cannock +
F/Sgt F W Heron +
F/Sgt H Tennant +
P/O H Osbourn +
F/Sgt G F Terry pow

25 Apr 45 (RG591 MP:A) Wangerooge
W/O J R Outerson RCAF +
F/Sgt C Livemore RCAF +
F/O J Ramsey RCAF +
Sgt J Nicholson +
F/Sgt E T Sutton +
Sgt E J Burdall +
F/Sgt G Gibson +

25 Apr 45 (RG553 MP:T) Wangerooge
P/O G W Lawson RCAF pow
F/O M Slaughter RCAF +
F/O C R Morrison RCAF +
F/Sgt A G Artus +
P/O R I Sweet RCAF +
Sgt D B N Stanes +
P/O L L Slauenwhite RCAF +

SECTION TWO

Aircrew killed, wounded, or prisoners as result of enemy action, not covered by Sec. One

24 Jul 41 (L95 3 1 MP:R) Scharnhorst
F/Sgt Begbie	w

13 Aug 41 (L9562) Berlin
Sgt J McHale	+
Sgt R J McInnes RCAF	+
Sgt S C Mayes	+
Sgt E P Hogan	+
Sgt L E Brown RCAF	+
Sgt C Austin	+
Sgt J G S West DFM	+

29 Aug 41 (L95 18) Frankfurt
S/Ldr R R Bickford DFC '	+
Sgt G W Duckmanton	+

14 Sep 41 (L9567 MP:N) Brest
P/O R E Hutchin	+

19 Jul 42 (W7670 B) Vegesack
F/Sgt N L Belous	+
Sgt F Hebron	+

31 Jul 42 (BB195 MP:B) Düsseldorf
Sgt J A McAuley	+

8 Sep 42 (W1228 MP:A) Frankfurt
Sgt J E Nicholson	+
F/Sgt A N Thompson	+
P/O A Robson	+
Sgt L G Harvey	+
Sgt R L Stevens	+
Sgt J T Murray	+
Sgt C R Rundle	+

9 Nov 42 (DT511 MP:B) Hamburg
Sgt V F R Killner	pow
Sgt K A Peacock	pow

14 Apr 43 (DT698 MP:B) Stuttgart
Sgt M F Weir	*w

28 Jun 43 (DKISl MP:K) Cologne
Sgt J C McDougall	w

3Jul 43 (DK174 MP:W) Cologne
Sgt L T Brawn	w

_____

* Died of wounds 15 Apr 43.

25 Jul 43 (DK148 MP:G) Essen
Sgt E W Waterman	pow

27 Jul 43 DK188 MP:J) Hamburg
Sgt A Smith	+
Sgt W Berry	w
F/Sgt J Heggarty	w

10 Aug 43 (DK245 MP:H) Nuremburg
Sgt H T Whittlesea	+

12 Aug 43 (LK890 MP:T) Milan
Sgt W T Waitt	w
Sgt C Ramsden	w

17 Aug 43 (DK194 MP:U) Peenemunde
Sgt K Parry	w

30 Aug 43 (DK195 MP:P) München-
Gladbach
F/Sgt C Kirkham	w
Sgt H G Foster	w
Sgt C Wicks	w

5 Sep 43 (EB240 MP:P) Mannheim
Sgt E P L Marvin	w

3 Nov 43 (LK949 MPtV) Düsseldorf
Sgt D H Stocker	pow
Sgt S J W Cancea	pow
Sgt G C Harris	w

21 Jan 44 (LK630 MP:D) Magdeburg
F/Sgt E Firth	+
Sgt G L Young	w

28 Jan 44 (DK245 MP:G) Berlin
Sgt D Munson	+
Sgt G Channon	+

1 Mar 44 (LW6 36 MP:X) Stuttgart
F/Sgt J L Richards RCAF	+
F/Sgt R Sirluck RCAF	+
P/O F C Flitcroft	+
Sgt P C Bates	+
Sgt R Tipaldi	+
Sgt G H Hawkins	+
F/Sgt C A Rye RAAF	+

25 April 44 (LK789 MP:L) Karlsruhe
P/O D R Dibbins	+
F/Sgt J R Bathe	+
Sgt K C Oswald	+
Sgt J G Davenport	+
Sgt N M Harrison	+
Sgt G J Head	+
F/Sgt J Anderson	w

22 Jun 44 (LW620 MP:G) Laon
S/Ldr R G West RCAF	+
F/Sgt J Johnston	+
F/Lt P S Milliken RCAF	+
P/O W J Lowe	+
F/Sgt L J Barnard	+
P/O A T Clarke	+
F/Sgt T Glen	+

12 Aug 44 (LW637 MP:B) Russelsheim
F/Sgt T G Neil	w
Sgt R H Causton	w
Sgt B J Levy	w
Sgt J Appleby	+

12 Sep 44 (LL577 MP:M) Gelsenkirchen-Buer
F/Sgt G Elchuck RCAF	w

15 Sep 44 (MZ526 MP:N) Kiel
Sgt D Throssell	w
F/O L Cattelier RCAF	w
Sgt P E Bates	w
F/Sgt A Hamy	w
Sgt N L Ireland	w
F/Sgt E Pickles	w
Sgt P Crisswell	w

23 Oct 44 (MZ691 MP:Q) Essen
F/Sgt L W White	+
F/Sgt R Dawson	+
F/Sgt H Winder	+
Sgt T Lawson	+
Sgt A Thornhill	+
F/Sgt G J Brown	+
Sgt C Waltham	+

1 Feb 45 (MZ516 MP:V) Mainz
F/Sgt P J McBrinn RCAF	+
P/O R J Cowie RCAF	+
F/O H R Mock	+
Sgt J Ellingson RCAF	+
F/O K W Oddy	+

17 Feb 45 (RG444 MP:U) Wesel
F/O C W Bobby	+

3 Mar 45 (NA 584 MP:E) Kamen
F/Sgt W T Maltby RCAF	+

SECTION THREE
Aircrew casualties not covered in Sections One and Two

11 Dec 39 (P1267)
P/O C D Stevens	+

4 Mar 40 (P1270)
P/O W G C Edmonds	si

22 Jul 41 (L9533)
P/O L R Blackwell	
Sgt T N Hudgell	+
Sgt J W R Boggis	+
Sgt A J Howes	+
Sgt A J Grenyer	+

16 Jun 42 (BB199 MP:A)
P/O R L Perry	si
Sgt B F Hoskins	+

24 Jun 42 (W7661 MP:D)
Sgt J H G Bingham	+
F/Sgt M H Roberts RCAF	+
Sgt J B Fanning	+
Sgt R G Warkcup	+
Sgt M C Glover	+
Sgt R N Birder	+

25 Jun 42 (R9482 MP:D)
Sgt A Ashton	+
P/O W J Cole	+
Sgt C D Barnett	+
Sgt L D Richardson	+
Sgt H R Smith	+
P/O Higgins DFM	+

28 Jun 42 (W7665 MP:N)
F/Sgt S Tackley   *si
Sgt Wilson   si
Sgt Morgan   si
AC Robertson   si

18 Aug 42 (V9992 MP:M)
F/Sgt J Gillies   +
Sgt C C Lee   +
F/Sgt J H F Sydes   +
Sgt A Collins   +
Sgt J A Triscott   +
Sgt W C Bacon   +
Sgt S Dowling   +

3 Nov 43 (LK681 MP:A)
F/Lt J Steele   *si
F/O W Laskie   +
Sgt D Kneale   +
Sgt J G Kirby   +
F/Sgt R A Brawn RAAF   +
F/Sgt H M Welch RCAF   *si
Miss D Robson B.Sc   *si

16 Aug 54 (WH873) Canberra B2
F/Lt K W Taylor   +
F/Lt J K G Marsden   +
Sgt A R Addy   +

CASUALTY TOTALS, BY SECTIONS:

	+	pow	esc	w	si
Section One	683	281	27		
Section Two	60	5		27	
Section Three	32				6
Totals	**775**	**286**	**27**	**27**	**6**

Note 1. Of the 286 airmen taken prisoner, eight died in captivity and one was
        repatriated.
Note 2. Of the 27 wounded, one died from his wounds.
Note 3. Of the 6 seriously injured (including Miss Robson), four died from their
        injuries.

* Died as a result of injuries received.

Appendix Four

SQUADRON AIRCRAFT

These lists have been compiled from information obtained from a variety of sources and are intended to indicate, briefly, their Operational life with 76 Squadron.

The columns after the aircraft serial show:
- i) Previous Unit or source of manufacture.
- ii) Date of allocation to the Squadron.
- iii) Code letters either applied or assumed in chronological order.
- iv) The total number of Operations commenced. The symbol + indicates that the aircraft was borrowed from another Unit at the time it operated.
- v) Subsequent fate or disposal.

Aircraft were frequently 'borrowed 'within the Squadron to replace those not immediately available for a particular sortie; in such cases, the Operation has been credited to the assumed aircraft letter.

The reasons for an aircraft being Struck off Charge are shown where such information is available. Where no subsequent details are given, it can be assumed that they were consequently Struck off Charge or were not repaired and returned to Squadron strength before the War in Europe ended.

The crash site of aircraft missing on Operations has been given in nearly all instances; many of the towns or villages named are quite small and are not easily found on the average map; others have been renamed and can only be located after consulting maps of the period involved.

ABBREVIATIONS AND EXPLANATORY NOTES

A&AEE	Aircraft and Armament Experimental Establishment'
ACSEA	Air Command South East Asia
BAT	Beam Approach Training
CF	Conversion Flight
CU	Conversion Unit
D/F	Direction Finding
EE	English Electric
ElFA	Write-off, non operational
FIU	Fighter interception Unit
Flt	Flight
Flt Ref	Flight Refuelling
FTR	Failed to Return
Gardening	Minelaying
Hal CF	Halifax Conversion Flight
HP	Handley Page
km	Kilometres

LAP	London Aircraft Production		
LRDU	Long Range Development Unit		
ME	Middle East		
mu	Maintenance Unit		
N S E W etc	Points of the compass		
n/f	Night-fighter		
Ops	Operations		
OTU	Operational Training Unit		
RAE	Royal Aeronautical Establishment		
recaptured	Returned to United States control		
SoC	Struck off Charge		
Sqn	Squadron		
u/c	Undercarriage		
3/FB	Write-off (in North Africa), operational causes		
+	Operations flown when aircraft not on 76 Sqn charge		

WELLESLEY I   (April 1937 to April 1939)

K7715	7 Sqn B Flt	12.04.37	to ME and 148 Sqn 20.8.37
K7716	7 Sqn B Flt	12.04.37	to ME and 148 Sqn 18.8.37
K7717	7 Sqn B Flt	12.04.37	to ME and 148 Sqn 20.8.37
K7718	7 Sqn	19.04.37	to ME and 148 Sqn 26.8.37
K7719	7 Sqn	19.04.37	sunk in Bay of Biscay enroute to ME 6.9.39
K7720	7 Sqn	30.04.37	to ME and 148 Sqn 1.8.37
K7722	Factory	30.04.37	to ME and 47 Sqn
K7725	Factory	29.05.37	to ME and 47 Sqn
K7726	Factory	27.05.37	to ME and 47 Sqn
K7730	Factory	25.06.37	to ME and 148 Sqn
K7731	Factory	25.06.37	to ME and 223 Sqn
K7735	LRDU	28.06.37	to ME and transferred to Egyptian Air Force 14.2.39
K7740	Factory	21.07.37	to A&AEE 18.11.38
K7741	Factory	21.07.37	SoC 11.11.40
K7742	Factory	26.07.37	to ME and 45 Sqn
K7743	Factory	26.07.37	to ME and 14 Sqn
K7744	Factory	27.07.37	to RAE
K7746	Factory	30.07.37	became 1041M circa March 38
K7748	LRDU	16.09.38 NM:H	sunk in Bay of Biscay enroute to ME 6.9.39
K7752	35 Sqn	30.09.38	to ME and SoC 17.4.40
K7767	Factory	14.09.37	to ME and 47 Sqn
K7790	77 Sqn	18.11.38	sunk in Bay of Biscay enroute to ME 6.9.39
K8522	77 Sqn	18.11.38	sunk in Bay of Biscay enroute to ME 6.9.39
K8527	Factory	04.11.37	to ME and 47 Sqn
K8528	Factory	04.11.37	to ME and 223 Sqn
K8530	35 Sqn	15.06.38	to ME and 223 Sqn
K8531	207 Sqn	18.07.38	to ME and 14 Sqn
K8532	207 Sqn	18.07.38	sunk in Bay of Biscay enroute to ME 6.9.39
L2641	77 Sqn	10.11.38	to ME and 47 Sqn
L2642	148 Sqn	31.01.39	to ME and SoC 25.1.41
L2648	77 Sqn	23.11.38	to ME and 223 Sqn

L2689 Factory   22.02.38   to ME and FTR 1.9.40
L2690 Factory   22.02.38   to ME and 223 Sqn

ANSON I (March 1939 to April 1940)

N4988	44 Sqn	02.06.39	to 16 OTU 18.4.40
N4989	44 Sqn	12.06.39	to 16 OTU 18.4.40
N4995	44 Sqn	02.06.39	to 16 OTU 18.4.40
N4998	44 Sqn	02.06.39	to 16 OTU 18.4.40
N4999	44 Sqn	17.06.39	to 16 OTU 18.4.40
N5000	44 Sqn	09.06.39	to 16 OTU 18.4.40
N5001	44 Sqn	02.06.39	to 16 OTU 18.4.40
N5014	7 Sqn	10.03.39	
N5025	7 Sqn	10.03.39	
N5026	7 Sqn	10.09.39	
N5032	52 Sqn	10.10.39	to 16 OTU 18.4.40

HAMPDEN I   (March 1939 to April 1940)

L4044	49 Sqn	16.01.40	to 16 OTU 18.4.40
L4137	Factory	30.03.39	to 144 Sqn 1.10.39
L4138	Factory	30.03.39	to 7 Sqn 30.11.39
L4139	Factory	31.03.39	to 106 Sqn 22.12.39
L4140	Factory	01.04.39	to 7 Sqn 30.11.39
L4141	Factory	03.04.39	to 144 Sqn 7.11.39
L4142	Factory	06.04.39	to 16 OTU 18.4.40
L4143	Factory	12.04.39	to 144 Sqn 1.10.39
L4144	Factory	06.04.39	to 16 OTU 18.4.40
L4145	Factory	12.04.39	to 16 OTU 18.4.40
L4146	Factory	14.04.39	to 61 Sqn 30.11.39
L4147	Factory	14.04.39	crashed in forced-landing Bicester 25.11.39
L4148	Factory	17.04.39	to 16 OTU 18.4.40
L4149	Factory	17.04.39	to 106 Sqn 17.10.39
L4150	Factory	18.04.39	to 106 Sqn 17.10.39
L4151	Factory	18.04.39	to 16 OTU 18.4.40
L4152	Factory	19.04.39	to 83 Sqn 3.11.39
P1179	Factory	17.08.39	to 16 OTU 18.4.40
Pl 180	Factory	18.08.39	to 16 OTU 18.4.40
P1181	Factory	21.08.39	to 16 OTU 18.4.40
Pl182	Factory	26.08.39	to 16 OTU 18.4.40
P1250	9 MU	23.01.40	to 16 OTU 18.4.40
P1251	9 MU	23.01.40	to 16 OTU 18.4.40
P1267	10 MU	28.09.39	crashed near Princes Risborough 11.12.39
P1268	10 MU	28.11.39	to 16 OTU 18.4.40
P1269	10 MU	28.11.39	to 16 OTU 18.4.40
P1270	10 MU	28.11.39	crashed taking off from Upper Heyford 4.3.40
P1271	10 MU	28.11.39	to 16 OTU 18.4.40

HALIFAX I   (May 1941 to December 1942)

L9488 35 Sqn		10.06.41	2 Ops	swung on take-off at Middleton-St-George and u/c collapsed 2.8.41, to HP 13.8.41
L9492	35 Sqn	19.06.41	2 Ops	FTR KIEL 23124.6.41 shot down near Buxtehude, Germany
L9494	35 Sqn	20.06.41	2 Ops	FTR La PALLICE *(Scharnhorst)* 24.7.41 ditched near La Rochelle, France
L9496	35 Sqn	19.06.41	5 Ops	to 28 Hal CF 28.10.41
L9510	*35* Sqn	12.05.41	4 Ops	to 102 Sqn CF 2.7.42
L9513	35 Sqn	05.05.41	4 Ops	to 28 Hal CF 28.10.41
L9514	35 Sqn	25.05.41	1 Ops	u/c collapsed on landing at Middleton-St-George 15.6.41.to 3506M
L9516	3 5 Sqn	03.05.41	11 Ops	FTR KARLSRUHE 5/6.8.41 crashed at Louvain, Belgium
L9517	35 Sqn	12.05.41	10 Ops	FTR La PALLICE *(Scharnhorst)* 24.7.41 shot down by harbour defences and crashed off La Rochelle, France
L9518	35 Sqn	05.05.41	5 Ops	Aircraft abandoned near Pocklington due to fuel shortage, on return from FRANKFURT 29/30.8.41
L9519	35 Sqn	08.05.41		u/c collapsed on landing at Marston Moor 6.1.42, whilst on loan to 1652 CU,to HP 28.1.42
L9523	35 Sqn	12.05.41 MP:Y	15 Ops	to 78 Sqn CF 13.7.42
L9528	35 Sqn	06.06.41 MP:P	3 Ops	to 1658 CU 31.12.42
L9529	35 Sqn	06.06.41	7 Ops	FTR La PALLICE *(Scharnhorst)* 24.7.41 shot down near Aigudlon, France
L9530	35 Sqn	06.06.41 MP:L	5 Ops	FTR BERLIN 12/13.8.41 crashed at Parnewinkel, 40 km NE of Bremen, Germany
L9531	HP	07.06.41 MP:R	2 Ops	FTR BERLIN 12/13.8.41 shot down and crashed between Weser-munde and Geestemuende, Germany
L9532	HP	12.06.41	1 Op	to 1652 CU 16.1.42
L9533	HP	14.06.41		stalled in the circuit at Middleton-St-George and crashed 21.7.41
L9534	HP	15.06.41 MP:T MP:N MP:T	9 Ops	to 28 Hal CF 2.11.41
L9561	HP	30.06.41 MP:H	12 Ops	FTR BREMEN 12/13.10.41 shot down near Wons, Holland
L9562	HP	07.07.41	3 Ops	stalled in the circuit at Middleton-St-George on return from BERLIN 12/13.8.41
L9563	HP	28.06.41 MP:U	4 Ops	to 78 Sqn CF 17.6.42
L9564	12 MU	02.08.41 MP:A	5 Ops	to 28 Hal CF 18.11.41

L9565	8 MU	02.08.41 MP:B	6 Ops	to 28 Hal CF 28.10.41
L9567	45 MU	27.08.41 MP:N	1 Ops	Crashed three miles E of Bedford on return from BREST 13/14.9.41
L9570	8 MU	10.10.41 MP:E	2 Ops	Swung on landing at Tain and u/c collapsed 6.2.42.SoC 19.2.42
L9573	HP	12.08.41 MP:D	1 Op	to 1658 CU 31.12.42
L9574	HP	16.08.41 MP:R	5 Ops	to 76 Sqn CF 30.6.42
		MP:C		Cat E/FA 9.10.42 and SoC
L9577	HP	26.06.42		76 Sqn CFto 1658 CU
L9578	12 MU	29.08.41 MP:C	2 Ops	u/c collapsed on landing at Middleton-St-Georee 15.1.42
L9581	37 MU	08,11.41 MP:Q	1 Op	Ditched four miles off Aberdeen, due to fuel shortage, on return from TRONDHEIM (Tirpitz) 30.1.42
L9583	45 MU	17.10.41 MP:M	8 Ops	to 78 Sqn 20.2.42
L9601	8 MU	27.09.41 MP:F	6 Ops	to 78 Sqn 20.2.42
L9602	45 MU	15.10.41 MP:N	1 Op	FTR DUNKIRK 31.10.41 believed ditched off Dunkirk, France
L9604	12 MU	20.10.41 MP:W	3 Ops	overshot on landing at Linton-on-Ouse on return from BREST 30.11.41,to HP 23.12.41,to 3161M
L9608	24 MU	17.10.41 MP:H	3 Ops	to 1652 CU 14.2.42
L9609	37 MU	08.11.41 MP:V	2 Ops	to 1652 CU 14.2.42
L9611	45 MU	24.10.41 MP:J	3 Ops	u/c collapsed on take-off at Middleton-St-George 17.1.42

HALIFAX II   (October 1941 to September 1943)

L9615	24 MU	25.10.41 MP:X	2 Ops	FTR BREST 30/31.12.41 crashed in the sea twenty miles off the French coast
L9617	37 MU	15.11.41 MP:A	4 Ops	to 78 Sqn 27.2.42
			+2 Ops	borrowed from 78 Sqn as EY:Y
L9620	HP	28.10.41 MP:O	6 Ops	to 76 Sqn CF 12.5.42,to 1658 CU
R9364	35 Sqn	25.01.42		to 78 Sqn 27.2.42
R9365	10 Sqn	19.03.42		issued to 76 Sqn CF
		MP:W	6 Ops	to 76 Sqn
		MP:C		FTR ESSEN 16/17.9.42 crashed at Rabrouck, Dept du Nord, France
R9366	10 Sqn	29.03.42 MP:U	2 Ops	issued to 76 Sqn CF to 1658CU
R9373	10 Sqn	.42 MP:W	3 Ops	to 78 Sqn 27.2.42
R9375	HP	27.11.41 MP:T	1 Op	to 78 Sqn 27.2.42
R9378	78 Sqn	18.04.42		issued to 76 Sqn CF
		MP:K	2 Ops	to 76 Sqn caught fire whilst bombing-up for Ops BREMEN 25.6.42
R9379	12 MU	06.12.41 MP:L	1 Op	overshot on landing 17.1.42 to 12 MU 30.5.42
R9382	10 Sqn	17.03.42		issued to 76 Sqn CF, to 408 Sqn CF 22.10.42
R9384	12 MU	29.08.42		to 10 Sqn 3.9.42

R9385	Flt Ref	42	1 Op	to R A E 8.10.42
R9386	35 Sqn	25.01.42 MP:J	3 Ops	to 78 Sqn 27.2.42
R9387	10 Sqn	17.03.42 MP:Z	2 Ops	issued to 76 Sqn CF
				to 1658 CU 31.12.42
R9391	102 Sqn	15.01.42 MP:K	2 Ops	to 78 Sqn 22.2.42
R9420	HP	25.01.42 MP:G	1 Op	to 78 Sqn 27.2.42
R9427	HP	25.01.42		to 78 Sqn 27.2.42
R9430	10 Sqn CF	18.03.42		issued to 76 Sqn CF
				to 78 Sqn CF 17.5.42
R9434	HP	30.01.42		to 78 Sqn 27.2.42
R9447	HP	24.02.42 MP:R	14 Ops	to 78 Sqn 22.6.42
R9451	HP	14.02.42 MP:H	6 Ops	FTR HAMBURG 3/4.5.42 crashed at Ottensen, near Buxtehude, Germany
R9452	HP	14.02.42 MP:L	3 Ops	aircraft abandoned on return from ESSEN 12/13.4.42 crashed near Hunmanby 12 miles S of Wold Newton
R9453	HP	16.02.42 MP:L	1 Op	FTR AAS FJORD (*Tirpitz*) 30/31.3.42 ditched 16 miles S of Sumburgh due to fuel shortage
R9454	HP	27.02.42 MP:S	11 Ops	to 78 Sqn 24.6.42
R9455	HP	16.02.42 MP:C MP:O	10 Ops	to 78 Sqn 24.6.42
R9456	HP	16.02.42 MP:F	6 Ops	FTR WARNEMUNDE 819.5.42 shot down near Rostock, Germany
R9457	HP	16.02.42 MP:A	6 Ops	FTR BREMEN 3/4.6.42 shot down near St Maartenvlotbrug, Holland
R9482	HP	24.02.42 MP:D	8 Ops	crashed on take-off 25.6.42
R9484	HP	24.02.42 MP:G	3 Ops	FTR ESSEN 10/11.4.42 shot down at Oer-Erckenschwick, 4 miles N of Recklinghausen, Germany
R9485	HP	26.02.42 MP:P MP:H	5 Ops	to 76 Sqn CF 29.6.42 FTR HAMBURG 26/27.7.42 crashed at Buxtehude, Germany
R9486	HP	27.02.42 MP:Q	6 Ops	to 1652 CU in March 42, returned to 76 Sqn, to 78 Sqn CF 25.8.42
R9487	HP	27.02.42 MP:X MP:M MP:X	6 Ops	FTR ESSEN 12/13.4.42 shot down near Buer, Germany
V9980	8 MU	07.11.41 MP:B	6 Ops	to 10 Sqn 27.2.42
V9992	1427 Flt	23.07.42		crashed on three engines at Thirsk 18.8.42
W1006			+2 Ops	borrowed from 78 Sqn as EY:K
W1013			+1 Op	borrowed from 78 Sqn as EY:E
W1014	EE	11.02.42		to 78 Sqn 27.2.42
			+1 Op	borrowed from 78 Sqn as EY:V
W1016	EE	16.02.42 MP:B	8 Ops	FTR OSNABRUCK 9/10.8.42 whilst on loan
W1017	EE	16.02.42 MP:T	4 Ops	FTR DUNKIRK 27/28.4.42 believed crashed in the sea off Dunkirk, France
W1018	12 MU	26.02.42 MP:M	9 Ops	to 78 Sqn 22.6.42

Serial	Unit	Date MP	Ops	Remarks
			+1 Op	borrowed from 78 Sqn as EY:D
W1035	EE	26.02.42 MP:U	3 Ops	u/c collapsed on landing on return from BREMEN 3/4.6.42
W1036	EE	26.02.42 MP:Y	12 Ops to	78 Sqn 24.6.42
			+2 Ops	borrowed from 78 Sqn as EY:K
W1063			+1 Op	borrowed from 78 Sqn as EY:T
W1064	EE	17.04.42 MP:J	3 Ops	FTR ESSEN 1/2.6.42 shot down near Grez Doiceau, Belgium
W1065	EE	17.04.42 MP:G	4 Ops	FTR PARIS 29/30.5.42 crashed at Gennevilliers (NW Paris), France
W1093			+1 Op	borrowed from 78 Sqn as EY.S
W1104	EE	09.05.42 MP:F	3 Ops	FTR BREMEN 3/4.6.42 crashed in the Waddenzee between Vlieland and Harlingen, Holland
W1114	8 MU	09.06.42 MP:F	1 Op	FTR EMDEN 20.6.42 crashed at Vierhuizen, Holland
W1115	8 MU	10.06.42		to 78 Sqn 23.6.42
W1144	EE	25.05.42		to 78 Sqn 27.5.42 returned to
		MP: Q	12 Ops	76 Sqn 24.6.42, to the Middle East 10.7.42 FTR HERAKLION 5.9.42
Wl 148	8 MU	09.06.42 MP:P	12 Ops	to the Middle East 16.7.42;SoC 1.3.44
Wl 149	78 Sqn	22.06.42 MP:R	14 Ops	to the Middle East 16.7.42. SoC 1.3.44
W1150	78 Sqn	22.06.42 MP:M	1 Op	to 78 Sqn 1.8.42
W1156	78 Sqn	24.06.42 MP:Y	11 Ops	to the Middle East 10.7.42. SoC 1.3.44
Wl 161	78 Sqn	24.06.42 MP:O	15 Ops	to the Middle East 17.7.42. FTR 20.7.43
Wl 168	102 Sqn	29.10.42 MP:O	1 Op	to 1658 CU 8.2.43
Wl 169	45 MU	28.06.42 MP: S	3 Ops	to the middle East 10.7.42.SoC 1.3.44
W1177	EE	27.06.42 MP:G	10 Ops	to the Middle East 17.7.42. SoC 27.4.44
Wl 180	77 Sqn	29.06.42		to 78 Sqn 29.6.42
W1183	77 Sqn	29.06.42 MP:M	15 Ops	to the Middle East 17.7.42 SoC 6.10.42
W1184	EE	02.07.42		to 78 Sqn 2.7.42
W1228	78 Sqn	24.07.42 MP:A	6 Ops	crashed at Haltby, 4 miles E of York, 8/9.9.42
W1236	460 Sqn	25.10.42 MP:G	31 Ops	FTR DUISBURG 8/9.4.43 lost without trace
W1244	EE	03.08.42 MP:D	3 Ops	FTR SAARBRUCKEN 1/2.9.42 crashed at Chateau Blankaart, Woumen, Belgium
W7655	HP	08.04.42 MP:C MP:L MP:C	19 Ops	to the Middle East 10.7.42.SoC 1.1.47
W7660	HP	14.04.42 MP:L	3 Ops	FTR MANNHEIM 19/20.5.42 shot down near Marche, Belgium
W7661	78 Sqn	.42		collided with Oxford V4140 of 1516 BAT Flight near Middleton-St-George 24.6.42 and crashed

W7664	R A E	28.04.42 MP:T	11 Ops	to the Middle East 17.7.42 SoC 1.2.44
W7665	HP	24.04.42 MP:N	8 Ops	stalled on a three-engined approach at Middleton-St-George 28.6.42
W7670	78 Sqn	20.06.42 MP:B	1 Op	crashed at Yarm on return from VEGESACK 19/20.7.42
W7671	78 Sqn	29.06.42 MP:H	9 Ops	to the Middle East 17.7.42, SoC 1.9.43
W7672	RAE	02.05.42 MP:E	16 Ops	to the Middle East 10.7.42. SoC 6.10.42
W7678	10 Sqn	09.02.43 MP:L	4 Ops	FTR HAMBURG 3/4.3.43 lost without trace
W7702	45 MU	30.05.42 MP:L	13 Ops	to the Middle East 16.7.42 Cat 3/FB 16.1.44
W7747	HP	11.06.42		to 78 Sqn 13.6.42
		22.06.42 MP:G	1 Op	Returned to 76 Sqn FTR BREMEN 25/26.6.42 lost without trace
W7754	12 MU	23.06.42 MP:F	12 Ops	to the Middle East 10.7.42 crashed two miles W of Bilbeis, Egypt, 31.8.42
W7755	12 MU	22.06.42 MP:A	12 Ops	to the Middle East 16.7.42 SoC 1.3.44
W7762	HP	27.06.42 MP:D	5 Ops	to the Middle East 6.10.42 SoC 30.9.43
W7781	460 Sqn	07.11.42 MP:U	7 Ops	to 1658 CU 2.2.43
W7805	HP	11.08.42 MP:L MP.M	20 Ops	issued to 76 Sqn CF but immediately re-allocated to 76 Sqn FTR ESSEN 314.4.43, crashed at Hervest, E of Dorsten, Germany
W7812	78 Sqn	20.08.42 MP:B	9 Ops	FTR FLENSBURG 112.10.42 crashed at Flensburg, Germany
W7813	78 Sqn	20.08.42 MP:E	32 Ops	to 77 Sqn 21.4.43
W7820	460 Sqn	27.08.42 MP:G MP:B	23 Ops	to 102 Sqn 14.4.43
W7856	78 Sqn	17.09.42		to 77 Sqn 21.12.43
W7868	HP	30.09.42 MP:R	3 Ops	to 1658 CU 2.2.43
W7879	HP	14.10.42		to 102 Sqn 31.10.42
W7882	HP	18.10.42		to 102 Sqn 31.10.42
W7937	HP	08.12.42		to 78 Sqn 10.2.43
BB189	8 MU	27.08.42 MP:H	3 Ops	to 158 Sqn 15.10.42
BB195	12 MU	21.07.42 MP:B	2 Ops	crashed at Stock, Essex, on return from DUSSELDORF 30/31.7.42
BB196	12 MU	28.07.42 MP:O	1 Op	u/c collapsed on take-off from Catfoss 31.8.42 - SoC
BB199	78 Sqn	07.06.42 MP:A		engine caught fire in the air, over Yorkshire 16.6.42. SoC 19.6.42
BB221	103 Sqn	28.01.43		to 103 Sqn 2.2.43
BB222	LAP	04.09.42		issued to 76 Sqn CF SoC 16.3.43
BB237	LAP	16.09.42 MP:C	7 Ops	crashed on landing at Benson on return from GENOA 23/24.10.42. SoC 29.10.42
BB238	L A P	22.09.42 MP:J MP:P	27 Ops	to 77 Sqn 18.5.43

BB239	LAP	25.09.42		to 78 Sqn 25.9.42
BB242	LAP	05.10.42 MP:P	9 Ops	FTR MANNHEIM 6/7.12.42 crashed at Bar le Duc, France
BB245	158 Sqn	31.10.42 MP:V 16.03.43	10 Ops	to 1658 CU 3.2.43 returned to 76 Sqn, to 1658 CU
BB246	LAP	18.10.42		to 1658 CU 2.2.43
BB282	1658 CU	02.02.43 MP:R	10 Ops	FTR ESSEN 5/6.3.43 lost without trace
BB284	1658 CU	02.02.43 MP:D	20 Ops	to 77 Sqn 14.4.43
BB300	1658 CU	03.02.43 MP:A	15 Ops	to 10 Sqn 14.4.43
BB324	LAP	28.02.43 MP:Q	3 Ops	to 10 Sqn 18.4.43
BB365	LAP	30.03.43 MP:T	3 Ops	to 102 Sqn 1.5.43
DC220	78 Sqn	22.08.42 MP:F		to 76 Sqn CF 19.9.42 to 1658 CU 23.1.43
DT490	EE	30.08.42 MP:F 19.09.42	26 Ops	issued to 76 Sqn CF to 76 Sqn, to 1658 CU 18.4.43
DT492	158 CF	14.10.42 MP:H	25 Ops	damaged on Ops STUTTGART 11/12.3.43 crew baled out over the English coast on return
DT496	EE	12.09.42 MP:A	3 Ops	FTR AACHEN 516.10.42 crashed between Heusy and Verviers Belgium
DT508	EE	13.09.42 MP:K	1 Op	FTR FLENSBURG 23/24.9.42 crashed in the sea off Rømø Denmark
DT509	78 Sqn	13.09.42		to 78 Sqn 31.10.42
DT511	EE	13.09.42 MP:D MP:B MP:D	9 Ops	FTR DUISBURG 20/21.12.42 crashed between Liedern and Bocholt, Germany
DT515	405 Sqn	27.09.42 MP:T	5 Ops	FTR GENOA 7/8.11.42 crashed between Chaumont and St Aignan, France
DT522			+1 Op	borrowed from 78 Sqn as EY:R
DT526			+1 Op	borrowed from 78 Sqn as EY.L
DT541	EE	01.10.42 MP:S	31 Ops	to 10 Sqn 21.4.43
DT545	EE	01.10.42 MP:Q	14 Ops	crashed on take-off for NUREMBURG 25/26.2.43
DT550	EE	10.10.42 MP:B	2 Ops	FTR 'Gardening'8/9.11.42 crashed in the sea W of Rottumeroog, Holland
DT554	78 Sqn	05.12.42 MP:T	7 Ops	to 1652 CU 20.7.43
DT556	78 Sqn	10.10.42 MP:A MP:U	17 Ops	FTR BERLIN 1/2.3.43 crashed 4 km N of Kasterlee, Belgium
DT563	77 Sqn	25.10.42 MP:L MP:O	30 Ops	FTR BERLIN 29/30.3.43 crashed off Vlieland, Holand
DT569	158 Sqn	25.10.42 MP:C	13 Ops	FTR BERLIN 17/18.1.43 crashed 1 km SE of Glashütte, Germany
DT570	158 Sqn	25.10.42 MP:R	8 Ops	FTR DUISBURG 20/21.12.42 shot down by a n/f between Weeze and Geldern, near Goch, Germany
DT5 71	EE	24.10.42 MP:M	2 Ops	FTR TURIN 20/21.11.42 crashed at Bardonecchia, Italy
DT574	EE	27.10.42		damaged on landing on return from Ops 8.12.42 whilst on loan. SoC 29.12.42

DT575	EE	27.10.42 MP:Y	18 Ops	FTR PILSEN 16/17.4.43 crashed near Liesse, France
DT621	12 MU	23.12.42 MP:D	2 Ops	FTR 'Gardening' 21.1.43 lost without trace, believed crashed off the Ems estuary
DT647	12 MU	29.12.42 MP:P	3 Ops	FTR BERLIN 17/18.1.43 lost without trace, believed in the North Sea, NW of juist, Germany
DT698	EE	20.12.42 MP:W	21 Ops	damaged by a n/f on Ops STUTTGART 14/15.4.43.SoC 22.5.43
DT744	EE	21.01.43 MP:K	18 Ops	FTR BERLIN 29/30.3.43 shot down at Welmbuttel, Germany
DT751		24.01.43 MP:C	20 Ops	FTR ESSEN 12/13.3.43 crashed 3 km SW of America, Holland
DT767	EE	21.01.43 MP:J	12 Ops	FTR BERLIN 1.3.43 lost without trace
DT782	EE	05.02.43 MP:J	7 Ops	force landed at base on return from ESSEN 12/13.2.43
HR727	HP	22.04.43		to 102 Sqn 18.5.43
HR748	HP	22.03.43 MP:R	4 Ops	to 78 Sqn 26.4.43
HR874	HP	26.06.43		FTR MANNHEIM 6/7.9.43 whilst on loan to 78 Sqn
JB800	48 MU	23.03.43 MP:U	4 Ops	FTR PILSEN 16/17.4.43 crashed at Mundelsheim, Germany
JB870	EE	20.03.43 MP:H	6 Ops	FTR PILSEN 16/17.4.43 whilst on loan to 78 Sqn
JB871	EE	20.03.43 MP:V	4 Ops	FTR FRANKFURT 10/1 1.4.43 crashed at Hirson, France
JB872	EE	30.03.43 MP:C	9 Ops	to 78 Sqn 26.4.43
JB873	EE	23.03.43 MP:J	7 Ops	to 78 Sqn 26.4.43
JB874	EE	23.03.43 MP:L	5 Ops	to 78 Sqn 3.6.43
JD145	EE	11.05.43		to 78 Sqn 18.5.43

HALIFAX V   (February 1943 to July 1944)

DG234	1663 CU	01.09.43		to 1663 CU
DG353	8 MU	28.07.43		to 1663 CU 6.8.43
DG394	1663 CU	18.04.43		to 1663 CU 27.4.43
DC420	1663 CU	16.04.43 MP:Q	4 Ops	to 1663 CU 3.5.43
DC421	1663 CU	18.04.43		to 1663 CU 27.4.43
DG422	1663 CU	16.04.43 MP:S	4 Ops	to 1663 CU 3.5.43
DG423	1663 CU	16.04.43 MP:H	2 Ops	FTR DUISBURG 26/27.4.43 crashed in Amsterdam, Holland
DK128	Fairey	20.02.43		to 1652 CU 8.3.43
DK132	1663 CU	16.04.43 MP:V	7 Ops	to 1663 CU 25.5.43
DK134	45 MU	21.04.43 MP:Y	3 Ops	FTR DORTMUND 4/5.5.43 crashed near Kilder, Holland
DK136	8 MU	05.08.43 MP:U	1 Op	u/c collapsed on landing, return from NUREMBURG 10/11.8.43
DK137	8 MU	23.04.43 MP:R	8 Ops	FTR COLOGNE 28.6.43 shot down

					over Vottem, N of Liege, Belgium
DK138	8 MU	23.04.43	MP:T	11 Ops	to 1663 CU 13.1.43
			MP:V		
			MP:X		
DK147	8 MU	07.04.43	MP:A	4 Ops	FTR ESSEN 27/28.5.43 crashed
					near Laer, NW of Munster, Germany
DK148	8 MU	06.05.43	MP:J	16 Ops	crash landed on retrn from ESSEN
			MP:G		25/26.7.43
DK149	Fairey	07.04.43	MP:A	23 Ops	to 1663 CU 26.9.43
			MP:B		
			MP:D		
			MP:G		
DK150	Fairey	20.04.43	MP:E	11 Ops	FTR COLOGNE 28.6.43
					crashed at Angermund, Germany
DK151	8 MU	30.05.43	MP:T	16 Ops	to 1663 CU 10.11.43
			MP:K		
			MP:T		
			MP:M		
			MP:Q		
			MP:Q		
DK165	Fairey	10.04.43	MP:E	1 Op	FTR PILSEN 16/17.4.43 crashed
					between Lachen and Speyerdorf,
					Germany
DK166	Fairey	07.04.43	MP:D	15 Ops	FTR WUPPERTAL 24.6.43 shot
					down at Lovenich (NW Cologne),
					Germany
DK167	Fairey	12.04.43	MP:F	35 Ops	hit a DIF hut on approach, and
			MP:A		belly landed on return from
			MP:F		STUTTGART 26/27.11.43
			MP:A		
DK168	Fairey	12.04.43	MP:G	24 Ops	to 1663 CU 10.11.43
			MP:H		
			MP:H		
DK169	Fairey	12.04.43	MP:B	7 Ops	FTR DORTMUND 23/24.5.43
			MP:M		shot down by a nif and crashed at
			MP:B		Broekland, Holland
			MP:M		
DK170	Fairey	20.04.43	MP:C	7 Ops	FTR DUSSELDORF 11/12.6.43
					crashed near Bladel, Holland
DK171	Fairey	20.04.43	MP:J	2 Ops	FTR ESSEN 30.4 - 1.5.43
					crashed at Estern, Germany
DK172	Fairey	20.04.43	MP:L	7 Ops	FTR DORTMUND 23/24.5.43 crashed
					3 km NW of Greven, Germany
DK173	Fairey	20.04.43	MP:P	20 Ops	to 1663 CU 8.9.43
			MP:C		
			MP:P		
DK174	Fairey	20.04.43	MP:W	14 Ops	crash landed at Hartford Bridge on
			MP:A		return from COLOGNE 3/4.7.43
			MP:W		
DK175	Fairey	23.04.43	MP:O	13 Ops	u/c collapsed on take-off for Ops
			MP:T		AACHEN 13/14.7.43

DK176	Fairey	23.04.43 MP:U	12 Ops	crash landed on return from GELSENKIRCHEN 9/10.7.43
DK177	Fairey	28.04.43 MP:H	8 Ops	FTR BOCHUM 12/13.6.43 crashed 6 km N of Neinborg, Germany
DK178	Fairey	28.04.43 MP:Q MP:R MP:Y MP:U	16 Ops	to 166 3 CU 2 3.6.44
DK179	Fairey	28.04.43 MP:S	5 Ops	to 1663 CU 31.12.43
DK187	Fairey	08.05.43 MP:Y MP:M	16 Ops	FTR HAMBURG 24/25.7.43 lost without trace, believed crashed off the Elbe estuary
DK188	Fairey	08.05.43 MP:V MP:J	12 Ops	crash landed at Shipdham on return from HAMBURG 27/28.7.43
DK193	48 MU	29.05.43 MP:Y	18 Ops	swung on take-off for MUNCHEN-GLADBACH 30/31.8.43 and caught fire
DK194	48 MU	30.05.43 MP:H MP:U MP:T	26 Ops	to 1663 CU 15.2.44
DK195	8 MU	02.06.43 MP:O MP:J MP:D MP:O MP:P	20 Ops	damaged by a nif of Ops MUNCHEN-GLADBACH 30/31.8.43
DK200	Fairey	27.05.43 MP:L	1 Op	FTR DUSSELDORF 11/12.6.43 crashed at Scherlebeck, Germany
DK201	Fairey	27.05.43 MP:P MP:Q MP:P	33 Ops	FTR KASSEL 3/4.10.43 crashed at Leistrup, near Detmold, Germany
DK202	Fairey	28.05.43 MP:Q	12 Ops	FTR REMSCHIED 30/31.7.43 crashed between Leverkusen and Wiesdorf, Germany
DK203	Fairey	27.05.43 MP:A	33 Ops	FTR KASSEL 3/4.10.43 crashed in the Waddensee, E of Terschelling, Holland
DK204	Fairey	31.05.43 MP:L	20 Ops	to 1663 CU 20.9.43
DK205	Fairey	31.05.43 MP:C MP:P	12 Ops	non-operational damage 20.11.43. SoC March 45
DK207	Fairey	04.06.43 MP:X MP: S	16 Ops	FTR MUNCHEN-GLADBACH 30/31.8.43 crashed at Grathem, Holland
DK223	Fairey	06.06.43 MP:W MP:N MP:N	17 Ops	FTR MANNHEIM 5/6.9.43 crashed at Jägersburg, Germany
DK224	Fairey	07.06.43 MP:Q	3 Ops	FTR MULHEIM 22/23.6.43 crashed near Zuilen, Holland
DK231	Fairey	28.06.43 MP:B	29 Ops	FTR FRANKFURT 25/26.11.43 crashed between Wiesloch and Malschenberg, Germany
DK236	Fairey	23.06.43 MP:V	15 Ops	to 431 Sqn 6.3.44

DK240	Fairey	29.06.43 MP:G	13 Ops	FTR MILAN 12/13.8.43
				crashed near Bernay, N France
DK241	Fairey	28.06.43 MP: Q	14 Ops	crashed on overshoot on return
		MP: Q		from BERLIN 23/24.8.43
		MP: Q		
DK245	Fairey	04.07.43 MP:H	20 Ops	hit a tree on take-off for Ops
		MP:G		BERLIN 28/29.1.44 and crashed
		MP:G		
		MP:G		
DK247	Fairey	06.07.43 MP:W	21 Ops	FTR KASSEL 314.10.43
				crashed at Vehne Moor, 18 km SW
				of Oldenburg, Germany
DK266	Fairey	05.08.43 MP:O	11 Ops	FTR HANNOVER 27/28.9.43
				crashed at Grapperhause,Germany
DK269	Fairey	06.08.43 MP:J	4 Ops	FTR NUREMBURG 27/28.8.43
				crashed near Mailach, Germany
EB138	Rootes	03.05.43		to 1663 CU 18.5.43
EB204	Rootes	08.06.43 MP:H	32 Ops	to 77 Sqn 10.3.44
		MP:H		
		MP:H		
		MP:E		
EB240	Rootes	28.06.43 MP:P	16 Ops	damaged by a n/f on Ops MANNHEIM
		MP:P		5/6.9.43, on return diverted to
				Ford and collided with a Mosquito,
				DZ299 of FIU, on landing
EB244	Rootes	30.06.43 MP:X̄	6 Ops	FTR HAMBURG 29/30.7.43
		MP:X		crashed between Oberndorf and
		MP:X		Bentwisch, Germany
EB245	192 Sqn	04.07.43 MP:K	26 Ops	to 1663 CU 5.2.44
EB249	Rootes	04.07.43 MP:E	7 Ops	FTR HAMBURG 2/3.8.43
				crashed into Hesedorf Wood,
				22 miles ENE of Bremen, Germany
EB250	Rootes	03.07.43 MP:R	17 Ops	FTR MUNICH 6/7.9.43 crashed
				20 miles SW of Munich, Germany
EB253	Rootes	08.07.43 MP:Ȳ	17 Ops	FTR HANNOVER 22/23.9.43
		MP:C		crashed near Ströhen, Germany
LK630	Fairey	17.08.43 MP:D	22 Ops	after take-off for MAGDEBURG
				21/22.1.4-4, crew abandoned air-
				craft which crashed at Hotham village
LK631	Fairey	23.08.43 MP:X̄	3 Ops	to 1663 CU 14.5.44
		MP:P		
LK645	Fairey	07.09.43 MP:N	3 Ops	FTR HANNOVER 22/23.9.43
		MP:S		crashed near Verden, Germany
LK646	Fairey	08.09.43 MP:Q	18 Ops	to 1663 CU 15.2.44
LK660	Fairey	28.09.43 MP:S	8 Ops	to 77 Sqn 23.2.44
LK664	Fairey	30.09.43 MP:U	4 Ops	FTR KASSEL 22/23.10.43
				crashed near Bilhne, 20 miles NW
				of Kassel, Germany
LK667	Fairey	03.10.43 MP:O	14 Ops	to 77 Sqn 18.2.44
LK681	Fairey	08.10.43		crashed at Enthorpe, 3 miles NE
				of Market Weighton, on an Air Test
				3.11.43

LK687	Fairey	11.10.43 MP:P	6 Ops	FTR STUTTGART 26/27.11.43 crashed at Retzbach, Germany
LK732	Fairey	12.12.43 MP:F	1 Op	FTR FRANKFURT 20/21.12.43 crashed at Dachsenhausen, Germany
LK733	Fairey	19.12.43 MP:B	2 Ops	FTR MAGDEBURG 21/22.1.44 lost without trace
LK737	Fairey	22.12.43 MP:H	2 Ops	to 77 Sqn 19.3.44
LK744	Fairey	04.01.44 MP:Y	3 Ops	to 77 Sqn 17.2.44
LK890	Rootes	18.07.43 MP:T MP:J	21 Ops	to 1663 CU 15.2.44
LK891	Rootes	18.07.43 MP:X̲ MP:X MP:X	19 Ops	FTR HANNOVER 27/28.9.43 lost without trace
LK892	Rootes	25.07.43 MP:C	3 Ops	FTR MANNHEIM 9/10.8.43 crashed at Aubeques, Pont du Garennes, 5 miles N of Boulogne, France
LK902	Rootes	11.08.43 MP:N MP:H	22 Ops	FTR LEIPZIG 3/4.12.43 crashed at Achteberg, Germany
LK903	Rootes	13.08.43 MP:G	21 Ops	FTR FRANKFURT 25/26.11.43 crashed at Schorbach, Germany
LK904	Rootes	14.08.43 MP:T	8 Ops	FTR KASSEL 3/4.10.43 crashed at Moorhausen, Germany
LK910	Rootes	29.08.43 MP:P MP:J̲ MP:H	12 Ops	to 1663 CU 15.2.44
LK911	Rootes	02.09.43 MP:Y	10 Ops	FTR FRANKFURT 20/21.12.43 Giessen, Germany
LK912	Rootes	02.09.43 MP:N	18 Ops	FTR MAGDEBURG 21/22.1.44 crashed at Hordorf, Germany
LK921	Rootes	15.09.43 MP:R	13 Ops	FTR BERLIN 20/21.1.44 crashed 15 km NW of Burgkemnitz, SE of Dessau, Germany
LK922	Rootes	15.09.43 MP:L	13 Ops	FTR MAGDEBURG 21/22.1.44 crashed at Helmstedt, Germany
LK926	Rootes	23.09.43 MP:C	12 Ops	FTR FRANKFURT 20/21.12.43 crashed in the North Sea, W of Goeree island, Holland
LK929	Rootes	27.09.43 MP:M	16 Ops	to 1663 CU 15.2.44
LK932	Rootes	30.09.43 MP:X	4 Ops	FTR DUSSELDORF 3/4.11.43 crashed near Lanaken, Belgium
LK946	Rootes	30.09.43 MP:F	8 Ops	FTR STUTTGART 26/27.11.43 crashed near Malborn, Germany
LK948	Rootes	01.10.43 MP:T	3 Ops	FTR DUSSELDORF 3/4.11.43 crashed near Miinchen Gladbach, Germany
LK949	Rootes	05.10.43 MP:V	1 Op	damaged by a n/f on Ops DUSSEL-DORF 3/4.11.43, SoC 16.11.43
LK951	Rootes	05.10.43 MP:Y̅ MP:Y	8 Ops	to 1663 CU 15.2.44

LK95 5	Rootes	11.10.43 MP:<u>W</u>	14 Ops	to 77 Sqn 18.2.44
LK957	Rootes	13.10.43 MP:H	2 Ops	FTR MANNHEIM 18/19.11.43 crashed in the Zotzenbach area of Germany
LK958	Rootes	14.10.43 MP:<u>Q</u> MP:Q	6 Ops	FTR BERLIN 20/21.1.44 crashed at Liickstedt, Germany
LK999	Rootes	07.11.43 MP:V	9 Ops	to 77 Sqn 17.2.44
LL116	Rootes	09.11.43 MP:X	8 Ops	FTR BERLIN 20/21.1.44 crashed at Lievin, 5 km W of Lens, France
LL130	Rootes	24.11.43 MP:<u>P</u>	5 Ops	to 77 Sqn 17.2.44
LL140	Rootes	29.11.43 MP:A	6 Ops	FTR BERLIN 15/16.2.44 crashed near Schwerin, Germany
LL184	Rootes	23.12.43 MP:F	4 Ops	to 77 Sqn 17.2.44
LL185	Rootes	23.12.43 MP:G	3 Ops	FTR MAGDEBURG 21/22.1.44 lost without trace, off the coast of Holland
LL189	Rootes	30.12.43 MP:C	3 Ops	engine failure on take-off for an Air Test - crashed - 11.2.44
LL215	Rootes	31.12.43 MP:S	2 Ops	to 1663 CU 15.2.44
LL234	Rootes	21.01.44 MP:E	2 Ops	to 77 Sqn 17.2.44
LL235	Rootes	20.01.44		to 77 Sqn 5.2.44
LL237	Rootes	20.01.44 MP:R MP:G	2 Ops	to 77 Sqn 17.2.44
LL242	Rootes	23.01.44 MP:L	1 Op	to 77 Sqn 18.2.44
LL244	Rootes	23.01.44		to 77 Sqn 5.2.44
LL246	Rootes	23.01.44 MP:X	1 Op	to 77 Sqn 19.2.44

HALIFAX III   (January 1944 to May 1945)

LK747	Fairey	12.03.44 MP:B MP:J MP:Z MP:L	69 Ops	to 1663 CU 6.12.44
LK754	432 Sqn	02.03.44 MP:W MP:M MP:I MP:S MP:Q MP:F MP:N	44 Ops	to 45 MU 25.4.45
LK783	Fairey	20.02.44 MP:C	16 Ops	FTR TRAPPES 2/3.6.44 crashed at Treon, France
LK784	Fairey	20.02.44 MP:D	26 Ops	FTR TRAPPES 2/3.6.44 crashed 2.5 km from Faverolles, France
LK785	Fairey	20.02.44 MP:T	56 Ops	to 1658 CU 23.11.44
LK788	Fairey	20.02.44 MP:Q MP:B MP:O MP:Z MP:O	78 Ops	to 29 MU 29.4.45

			MP: B		
			MP:O		
			MP:E		
			MP: J		
			MP:N		
LK789	Fairey	20.02.44	MP:L	12 Ops	shot down by an'Intruder'on return from KARLSRUHE 24/25.4.44 and crashed near Welney
LK790	Fairey	20.02.44	MP:K	5 Ops	FTR BERLIN 25.3.44 crashed near Gatow, Germany
LK791	Fairey	21.02.44	MP:H	1 Op	FTR FRANKFURT 18/19.3.44 crashed in the Ulmenstrasse, Frankfurt, Germany
LK795	Fairey	02.03.44	MP:P	5 Ops	FTR NUREMBURG 30/31,3.44 crashed 1 km NE of Hamm an der Sieg, Germany
LK831	Fairey	22.03.44	MP:<u>N</u>	83 Ops	to 45 MU 16.4.45
			MP:H		
			MP:A		
			MP:B		
			MP:C		
			MP:E		
LK832	Fairey	26.03.44	MP:H	82 Ops	to 48 MU 10.5.45
			MP:V		
LK867	Fairey	12.04.44	MP:P	9 Ops	aircraft ground looped and u/c collapsed on take-off for TROUVILLE 11/12.5.44
LK873	Fairey	20.04.44	MP:S	28 Ops	FTR ACQUET 18/19.7.44 crashed between Sailly and Flibeaucourt, France
LL554	Rootes	29.06.44	MP:<u>X</u>	54 Ops	to 29 MU 29.4.45
			MP:H		
			MP:Q		
			MP:D		
			MP:U		
			MP: L		
			MP: <u>L</u>		
			MP:G		
			MP: I		
			MP:Q		
			MP: S		
			MP:G		
			MP:D		
			MP:A		
			MP:B		
			MP:Y		
LL577	Rootes	14.07.44	MP:W	35 Ops	FTR BOCHUM 4.11.44 crashed near Jalhay, Belgium
			MP: U		
			MP:V		
			MP:L		
			MP:M		

LL578 Rootes		14.07.44 MP:<u>Y</u> MP: C MP: I MP:<u>A</u> MP:Q MP:M MP:<u>L</u> MP:H	9 Ops	FTR RUSSELSHEIM 12/13.8.44 crashed 2 kms NE of Hamm, Germany
LL579 Rootes		15.07.44 MP:G MP:W MP:Y MP:E MP:L	46 Ops	FTR MAINZ 27/28.2.45 crashed near Mainz, Germany
LL598 Rootes		18.08.44		to 462 Sqn 19.8.44
LL599 Rootes		22.08.44		to 462 Sqn 22.8.44
LL606 Rootes		22.01.44 MP:<u>H</u> MP:H MP:<u>B</u> MP:H MP:B MP:Z MP:N MP:E MP:D MP:H MP:<u>U</u>	52 Ops	to 10 Sqn 9.4.45
LL607 Rootes		22.08.44 MP:Y MP:X MP:J MP:O	44 Ops	to 78 Sqn 26.3.45
LL608 Rootes		24.08.44 MP:<u>A</u> MP:G MP:F MP:O MP:H MP:G MP:J MP:E MP:L	44 Ops	to 45 MU 20.4.45
LV868	HP	19.02.44 <u> </u>		to 78 Sqn 26.2.44
LV869	HP	15.02.44 MP:<u>P</u>	2 Ops	to 78 Sqn 22.3.44
LV872	HP	19.02.44 MP:H	1 Op	to 78 Sqn 24.2.44
LV873	HP	15.02.44 MP:U	8 Ops	to 78 Sqn 28.3.44
LV874	HP	15.02.44		to 78 Sqn 28.3.44
LV876	HP	19.02.44		to 78 Sqn 24.2.44
LV877	HP	19.02.44		to 78 Sqn 26.2.44
LV901	HP	28.02.44		to 78 Sqn 29.2.44
LV91 5	HP	05.03.44		to 78 Sqn 22.3.44
LV916	HP	07.03.44		to 78 Sqn 11.3.44
LV947	433 Sqn	13.01.45 MP:Z	21 Ops	to 45 MU 13.4.45
LV957	HP	26.03.44		to 78 Sqn 31.3..44

LV958	HP	26.03.44		to 78 Sqn 31.3.44
LW178	HP	21.05.44		to 78 Sqn 24.5.44
LW346	578 Sqn	12.01.45 MP:G	15 Ops	to 5226M 28.4.45. for Airborne
		MP:A		Forces
		MP:O		
		MP:K		
		MP:Y		
		MP:K		
LW363	12 MU	03.11.43 MP:F	40 Ops	to 1658 CU 22.9.44
		MP:Z		
		MP:B		
LW573	HP	28.01.44 MP:S	1 Op	to 425 Sqn 1944
LW620	EE	11.02.44 MP:G	22 Ops	crashed at Hotham on return
		MP:G		from LAON 22/23.6.44
		MP:G		
		MP:G		
LW627	EE	16.02.44 MP:Q	84 Ops	to 45 MU 13.4.45
		MP:Q		
		MP:Q		
		MP:J		
		MP:Q		
		MP:Y		
		MP:K		
		MP:M		
		MP:H		
		MP:Q		
		MP:H		
		MP:H		
		MP:W		
LW628	EE	16.02.44 MP:J	8 Ops	damaged on Ops NUREMBURG
				30/31.3.44
LW629	EE	16.02.44 MP:M	3 Ops	FTR STUTTGART 1/2.3.44
				crashed at Celles-sur-Plain, near
				Nancy, France
LW630	EE	16.02.44 MP: S	6 Ops	to 347 Sqn 10.8.44
LW631	EE	21.02.44 MP:X	76 Ops	to 45 MU 13.4.45
		MP:X		
		MP:X		
		MP:Z		
		MP:C		
		MP:R		
		MP:M		
		MP:W		
		MP:Q		
		MP:O		
		MP:W		
		MP:E		
		MP:P		
		MP:J		
		MP:Y		
		MP:Y		

Serial	Unit	Date & Codes	Ops	Notes
LW636	EE	08.12.43 MP:X	1 Op	crashed 1 mile NW of Base after take-off for STUTTGART 1/2.3.44
LW637	EE	19.02.44 MP:R / MP:C / MP: B / MP: S	45 Ops	to 1658 21.11.44
LW638	EE	18.02.44 MP:Y / MP:W	11 Ops	FTR MONT FLEURY 6.6.44 crashed at Graye-sur-Mer, France
LW639	EE	19.02.44 MP:G / MP:O / MP:X / MP:B / MP:C	32 Ops	to 1658 CU 25.11.44
LW644	EE	19.02.44 MP:O	26 Ops	FTR AMIENS 12/13.6.44 crashed between Authieux and Ratieville, France
LW646	78 Sqn	26.02.44 MP:E	77 Ops	to 1663 CU 5.12.44
LW647	EE	21.02.44 MP:W	3 Ops	FTR NUREMBURG 30/31.3.44 crashed at Nieder-Moos, Germany
LW648	EE	21.02.44 MP:A / MP:Q	66 Ops	FTR BOCHUM 4.11.44 crashed between Vohwinkel and Rutenbach, Germany
LW649	EE	20.02.44 MP:B	1 Op	aircraft crashed after take-off, out of control, at Scunthorpe 3.3.44
LW655	78 Sqn	26.02.44 MP:V	4 Ops	FTR FRANKFURT 18/19.3.44 crashed at Preist, Germany
LW656	78 Sqn	24.02.44 MP:H̄ / MP:B	33 Ops	FTR LAON 22/23.6.44 crashed near Montchalons, France
LW657	78 Sqn	24.02.44 MP:G	4 Ops	FTR STUTTGART 15/16.3.44 crashed at Haslach, Germany
LW681	EE	29.02.44 MP:Ȳ / MP:Y	20 Ops	damaged by a 500-Ib bomb over the target - AMIENS, 12/13.6.44 port wheel collapsed on landing and aircraft caught fire
LW683	48 MU	24.08.44 MP:D̠ / MP:Q / MP:N	28 Ops	SoC 5.7.45
LW695	EE	03.03.44 MP:M / MP: I / MP:M	35 Ops	FTR RUSSELSHEIM 12.8.44 crashed near Quint, Germany
LW696	EE	03.03.44 MP:X	2 Ops	FTR NUREMBURG 30/31.3.44 crashed near Daubhausen, Germany
MZ309	LAP	07.06.44		to 10 Sqn 8.6.44
MZ310	LAP	07.06.44		to 78 Sqn 10.6.44
MZ340	LAP	25.06.44		to 78 Sqn 27.6.44
MZ346			+4 Ops	borrowed from 640 Sqn as C8:Y
MZ353	77 Sqn	06.03.45 MP:D / MP:Z / MP:D	8 Ops	to 78 Sqn 10.4.45
MZ354	77 Sqn	10.03.45 MP:B / MP:V	4 Ops	to 10 Sqn 27.3.45

MZ405	158 Sqn	19.01.45 MP:Y MP:N	4 Ops	to 45 MU 20.4.45
MZ421	425 Sqn	26.02.45 MP:K MP:M MP: B MP:Q	5 Ops	to 10 Sqn 26.3.45
MZ460	48 MU	05.11.44 MP:Q	33 Ops	to 78 Sqn
MZ516	78 Sqn	23.03.44 MP:V	77 Ops	abandoned in the air over Tibbenham, near Diss on return from MAINZ 1.2.45
MZ524	78 Sqn	22.03.44 MP:G MP:P	35 Ops	FTR NUCORT 15/16.7.44 crashed at Courcelles-les-Gisors, France
MZ526	45 MU	25.08.44 MP:N	1 Op	crashed at Eastrington after take-off for Ops KIEL 15/16.9.44
MZ528	78 Sqn	28.03.44 MP:K MP:J	83 Ops	to 45 MU 13.4.45
MZ530	78 Sqn	30.03.44 MP:U	2 Ops	FTR DUSSELDORF 22/23.4.44 crashed at Schweinheim, Germany
MZ531	78 Sqn	28.03.44 MP:P̄ MP:D	7 Ops	FTR JUVISY 7/8.6.44 crashed near Etampes, France
MZ539	78 Sqn	30.03.44 MP:X	26 Ops	FTR BLAINVILLE 28/29.6.44 crashed near Ferme Long Voisin, France
MZ575	EE	15.04.44 MP:W	5 Ops	FTR HASSELT 12/13.5.44 crashed 3 km N of Hadschot, Belgium
MZ578	EE	16.04.44 MP: I	1 Op	FTR DUSSELDORF 22/23.4.44 crashed at Gulpen, Holland
MZ599	EE	24.04.44 MP:U̲ MP:U MP:U	51 Ops	FTR WESTKAPELLE 28.10.44 crashed into the sea off Walcheren Is, Holland
MZ604	EE	25.04.44 MP:W	6 Ops	FTR TRAPPES 2/3.6.44 crashed near Bretigny, France
MZ622	EE	27.04.44 MP:L	5 Ops	FTR AACHEN 24/25.5.44 crashed near Goirle, Holland
MZ623	EE	27.04.44 MP:P̄ MP:P	7 Ops	FTR AACHEN 24/25.5.44 crashed near Arendonk, Belgium
MZ679	EE	14.05.44 MP:T MP:A MP:C	15 Ops	FTR BLAINVILLE 28/29.6.44 crashed at Lesges, France
MZ680	EE	17.05.44 MP:Y MP:R	64 Ops	attacked by an 'intruder' over base on return from Ops KANIEN 3/4.3.45
MZ691	EE	20.05.44 MP:Q	53 Ops	crashed at Old Buckenham, Norfolk, on return from Ops ESSEN 2 3.10.44
MZ693	78 Sqn	23.05.44 MP:F MP:E MP:F MP:T	77 Ops	to 45 MU 4.5.45
MZ732	10 Sqn	08.06.44 MP:D	12 Ops	crashed at Carnaby on return from Ops CROIXDALLE 6.7.44
MZ736	78 Sqn	10.06.44 MP:B	4 Ops	FTR BLAINVILLE 28/29.6.44 crashed at Sacy-le-Grand, France

MZ740	EE	08.06.44 MP:Y MP:R	55 Ops	FTR St. VITH 26.12.44 crashed at Nassogne, Belgium
MZ902	102 Sqn	05.03.45 MP:H MP:W	8 Ops	SoC 9.4.45
MZ905	433 Sqn	17.01.45 MP:H	7 Ops	collided with NA219 whilst taxying out for Ops CHEMNITZ 5/6.3.45
MZ937	102 Sqn	05.03.45 MP:R	11 Ops	to 78 Sqn 9.4.45
NA114	Rootes	07.10.44		to 10 Sqn 17.10.44
NA149	10 Sqn	05.11.44 MP:C	32 Ops	to 45 MU 20.4.45
NA163	78 Sqn	MP:K MP:X MP:K	23 Ops	landed at Chedburgh on return from Ops BOHLEN 13/14.2.45 and wing tip hit a tree
NA164	78 Sqn	05.11.44 MP:U	23 Ops	damaged on landing on return from Ops WESEL 21.2.45
NA170	Rootes	10.11.44 MP:S	10 Ops	belly landed at Carnaby on return from Ops HANNOVER 5.1.45
NA171	Rootes	13.11.44 MP:S MP:E	12 Ops	FTR COLOGNE 30.12.44 crashed at Cologne, Germany
NA172	Rootes	10.11.44		to 78 Sqn 20.11.44
NA198	78 Sqn	29.11.44 MP:X	33 Ops	to 10 Sqn 1.4.45
NA205	Rootes	02.12.44 MP:J MP:C	15 Ops	to 192 Sqn 24.3.45
NA218	Rootes	01.12.44 MP:B	6 Ops	damaged on Ops HANNOVER 5.1.45
NA219	Rootes	02.12.44 MP:D	21 Ops	collided with MZ905 whilst taxying out for Ops CHEMNITZ 5/6.3.45
NA220	Rootes	02.12.44 MP:T	26 Ops	to 78 Sqn 23.3.45
NA522	Fairey	31.05.44		crashed at Hotham 5.6.44 during an Air Test
NA530	Fairey	13.06.44 MP:G MP:J MP:U MP:J MP:P MP:P MP:J	39 Ops	to 1652 CU 25.11.4.4
NA543	Fairey	09.06.44 MP:J MP:X MP:Z MP:S	65 Ops	to 45 MU 4.5.45
NA548	Fairey	14.06.44 MP:G	76 Ops	damaged on Ops OSNABRUCK 25.3.45
NA553	Fairey	16.06.44 MP:H MP:B MP:C MP:J MP:P	38 Ops	to 1658 CU 5.12.44
NA567	78 Sqn	28.06.44 MP:W MP:A MP:Z MP:S MP:A	31 Ops	FTR BOCHUM 9.10.44 crashed at Arpath, Germany

		MP:S		
		MP:T		
		MP:W		
NA570	Fairey	30.06.44 MP:M	67 Ops	to 45 MU 4.5.45
		MP:P		
NA571	Fairey	30.06.44 MP:D	69 Ops	to 29 MU 26.4.45
		MP:A		
		MP:V		
NA575	Fairey	06.07.44 MP:W	7 Ops	to 45 MU 21.12.44
		MP: I		
		MP:S		
		MP:P		
		MP:O		
		MP:Y		
NA584	Fairey	14.07.44 MP:Z	59 Ops	attacked by an 'intruder' over base
		MP:X		on return from Ops KAMEN 3/4.3.45.
		MP:T		written off following forced
		MP:B		landing at Carnaby.
		MP:Q		
		MP:P		
		MP:F		
		MP:E		
NA623	Fairey	25.08.44 MP:A	19 Ops	belly landed at Wold Dike Farm,
		MP:H		Middleton-on-the-Wolds on return
				from Ops ESSEN 28/29.11.44
NR121	434 Sqn	16.01.45 MP:E	9 Ops	FTR WORMS 21/22.2.45 crashed
				near Hohen Sülzen, Germany
NR200	48 MU	04.11.44 MP:M	38 Ops	damaged on Ops OSNABRUCK
				25.3.45
		MP:T		
		MP:M		
RG444	10 Sqn	MP:U	1 Op	Crashed 1 mile N of Elloughton, on
				return from Ops WESEL 17.2.45

HALIFAX VI   (February 1945 to October 1945)

PP172	44 MU	02.04.45 MP:Z	2 Ops	to 29 MU 19.7.45
RG493	48 MU	29.03.45 MP:-R	4 Ops	to 158 Sqn 1.5.45
RG496	48 MU	31.03.45 MP:W	1 Op	to 29 MU 13.7.45
RG497	29 MU	30.03.45 MP:S	3 Ops	to 44 MU 21.7.45
RG506	45 MU	16.03.45 MP:C	7 Ops	to 29 MU 17.7.45
RG546	45 MU	19.03.45 MP:J	5 Ops	to 29 MU 13.7.45
RG551	45 MU	17.03.45 MP:F	6 Ops	to 158 Sqn 1.5.45
RG553	45 MU	17.03.45 MP:T	2 Ops	FTR WANGEROOGE 25.4.45
				crashed into the sea off Wangerooge,
				Germany
RG554	45 MU	17.03.45 MP:E	3 Ops	shot up by a n/f on Ops HAMBURG
				8/9.4.45
RG555	45 MU	17.03.45 MP:H	7 Ops	to 102 Sqn 10.8.45
RG556	45 MU	17.03.45 MP:D	5 Ops	to 102 Sqn 10.8.45

RG558	45 MU	17.03.45 MP:B	6 Ops	to 102 Sqn 10.8.45
RG567	EE	20.03.45 MP:K	4 Ops	to 346 Sqn 10.8.45
RG568	45 MU	30.03.45 MP:U	3 ops	to 29 MU 13.7.45
RG583	EE	18.03.45 MP:G	5 Ops	to 347 Sqn 10.8.45
RG591	EE	20.03.45 MP:A	4 Ops	FTR WANGEROOGE 25.4.45 crashed into the sea off Wangerooge, Germany
RG597	EE	22.03.45 MP:M	4 Ops	to 158 Sqn 1.5.45
RG598	EE	22.03.45 MP:N	4 Ops	to 44 MU 21.3.46
RG599	EE	23.03.45 MP:L	3 Ops	to 29 MU 13.7.45
RG602	EE	23.03.45 MP:O	4 Ops	to 29 MU 13.7.45
RG608	EE	24.03.45 MP:P	4 Ops	to 29 MU 17.7.45
RG612	EE	22.03.45 MP:X	4 Ops	to 29 MU 13.7.45
RG613	EE	29.03.45 MP:Q	4 Ops	tail-wheel collapsed on landing at West Freugh 23.5.45
RG618	EE	04.04.45 MP: I	2 Ops	to 158 Sqn 1.5.45
RG622	EE	07.04.45 MP: I	1 Op	swung on take-off for Ops HELIGOLAND 18.4.45 , u/c collapsed, bomb load exploded
RG623	EE	07.04.45 MP:D	I Op	to 158 Sqn 1.5.45
RG624	EE	07.04.45		to French Air Force 31.10.45
RG656	EE	16.04.45		to 45 MU 2.8.45
RG658	EE	20.04.45		to 44 MU 21.7.45
TW790	45 MU	06.04.45 MP:E	3 Ops	to 29 MU 17.7.45
TW793	48 MU	05.04.45 MP:F	1 Op	to 158 Sqn 1.5.45
TW794	29 MU	31.03.45 MP:V	3 Ops	to 102 Sqn 1945
TW796	48 MU	31.03.45 MP:Y	3 Ops	to 44 MU 21.7.45

DAKOTAIV   (June 1945 to September 1946)

KJ863	108 OTU	1945		to 77 Sqn 7.9.45
KJ864	108 OTU	1945		to 575 Sqn 27.11.45
KJ872	108 OTU	22.08.45		to 78 Sqn 7.9.45
KJ934	108 OTU	1945		to 77 Sqn 11.9.45
KJ969	151 RU	1945		to ACSEA 16.9.45
KK156	525 Sqn	1945		to 78 Sqn 1.9.45
KN293	ACSEA	1945		recaptured 27.11.47
KN398	Kemble	1945		to 78 Sqn 3.9.45
KN425	Kemble	1945		to 525 Sqn 1.9.45
KN432	Kemble	1945		to 525 Sqn 3.9.45
KN437	ACSEA	1945		recaptured 27.11.47
KN446	Kemble	1945		to 525 Sqn 11.9.45
KN452	Kemble	1945		to 12 MU 8.12.47
KNS26	Kemble	1945		to ACSEA 20.9.45 SoC 28.3.46
KN549	Kemble	1945		to ACSEA 21.9.45 recaptured 27.11.47
KNSSO	Kemble	1945		to 12 MU 28.7.47
KN559	Kemble	1945	:S	to ACSEA 14.9.45
KN664	Kemble	1945	:D	to 12 MU 10.10.47
KN667	Kemble	10.08.45		to 12 MU 9.7.47

KP237	Kemble	14.08.45	to ACSEA 20.9.45 SoC 25.7.46
KP243	Kemble	10.08.45 :N	to ACSEA 20.9.45
			recaptured 27.11.47
KP246	Kemble	18.08.45	to 12 MU 8.8.47
KP256	Kemble	19.08.45 :W	to 12 MU 2.10.47
KP257	Kemble	18.08.45 :Y	to ACSEA 21.9.45
			recaptured 27.11.47
KP259	Kemble	10.08.45	to ACSEA 15.9.45
			recaptured 27.11.47
KP260	Kemble	19.08.45 :K	to ACSEA 17.9.45 SoC 24.4.47
KP261	Kemble	1945	to ACSEA 17.9.45 Cat E 7.6.46
KP262	Kemble	19.08.45 :M	to ACSEA 17.9.45
			recaptured 27.11.47
KP263	Kemble	18.08.45 :X	to 204 Sqn 29.1.48
KP266	Kemble	18.08.45	to 12 MU 11.9.47
KP267	Kemble	18.08.45 :J	to 12 MU 21.7.47
KP268	Kemble	18.08.45 :F	to ACSEA 15.9.45
			recaptured 27.11.47
KP269	Kemble	14.08.45 :B	to 12 MU 29.7.47
KP271	Kemble	18.08.45 :G	to ACSEA 14.9.45 SoC 11.7.46

Note: Although the squadron was re-numbered 62 Squadron in September 1946, the aircraft cards have not been amended, hence dates extending in some cases to as late as November 1947.

Appendix Five

THE MIDDLE EAST DETACHMENT

On 10 July 1942, eight Halifax bombers left Middleton-St-George on the first stage of their journey which would take them to the Middle East. The second flight of eight aircraft departed Middleton-St-George on the 14th, and with remarkably few problems, all reached their destination, Aqir in Palestine, by the 20th. The details of those who participated in this detachment now follow, in take-off order:

FIRST FLIGHT:

Halifax B II W7672 MP:E
Airborne 04.00 hours
PilotS/LdrDIvesonDFC
Obs F/Sgt A W Batchelor
W/Op P/O F Bell DFM
Engr Sgt E A Morrell
W/Op Sgt A H Denton
RG Sgt J Holmes
Med F/Lt Francis
FAE Sgt Hill
Fitt Cpl Chubb

Halifax B II W7762 MP:D
Airborne 04.09. hours
PilotP/OHWickham
Obs W/O D Boyd
W/Op Sgt R E Chambler
MUG Sgt E E Maltwood
Engr Sgt D Fitzerald
RG F/Sgt W A Gillies
Arm Sgt Gold
Fitt Sgt Rushton
Fitt LAC Messer

HalifaxBIIW1156MP:Y
Airborne 03.52 hours
Pilot F/O W R Kofoed
Obs Sgt G Miles
W/Op Sgt I F F Batchelor
MUG Sgt H V Morton
Engr Sgt T Latham
RG Sgt F J Gerrish
FME Cpl Walker
Arm Cpl McLeod
FMA LAC Watson

HalifaxBIIW1161MP:O
Airborne 04.04 hours
Pilot F/Sgt J S Thomas
Obs F/O A D Dobson
W/Op Sgt J M Reilly
W/Op Sgt H O Hollis
Engr Sgt D W ilson
RG F/O M A Street
Fitt Sgt Staley
Elect Cpl Twiss
FME LAC McGann

HalifaxBIIW7655MP:C
Airborne 04.10 hours
Pilot P/O G W Raymond
Obs F/O F G T P Earle
W/Op P/O R M Craine
MUG Sgt L G Hill
Engr Sgt H Coates
RG Sgt W J Paine
Tech F/Lt Patterson
Fitt Cpl Burge
Fitt Cpl Holloway

Halifax B II W1169 MP:S
Airborne 03.59 hours
Pilot F/Sgt H C Granger
Obs Sgt C P Harrold
W/Op Sgt W H Mennell
MUG Sgt G P Carrell
Engr Sgt H W Gorton
RG F/Sgt L F T Noakes
Fitt Cpl Culkin
Fitt Cpl Heavens
Instr Cpl Fox

Halifax B II W7754 MP:F
Airborne 04.06.hours
Pilot F/O H F Bickerdike
Obs P/O J E Earnshaw
W/Op Sgt F W Rouse
MUG Sgt J M Morrison
Engr Sgt N Temperley
RG Sgt R Vere
WEM F/Sgt Co!burn
Fitt Cpl Black
FMA L A C Robson

Halifax B II W1144 MP:Q
Airborne 04.13 hours
Pilot F/Lt J Bryan
Obs F/Sgt R SCOtt
W/Op Sgt A Potts
W/Op Sgt A E Lythgoe
Engr Sgt W R Young
RG Sgt T P E Blatch
Elect Cpl Dixon
Fitt Cpl Wiggins
FMA ACl Littlewood

Halifax B tl W7671 MP:H
Airborne 04.00 hours
Pilot F/O V D Knox
Obs FIO J C Davidson
W/Op F/Sgt J D Rogers
MUG Sgt E D Thorn
Engr Sgt G H Nicholson
RG Sgt L G Burden
FAE Sgt Davies
Fitt Cpl Crutchfield
Instr Cpl Marshall

Halifax B II Wl148 MP:P
Airborne 0.400 hours
Pilot P/O K Clack DFM
Obs F/Sgt Thomson RCAF
W/Op Sgt R C Williams
MUG Sgt F F Wigby
Engr Sgt H W Lawes
RG F/Lt J D Croft
Fitt Sgt Morrison
Elect F/Sgt Lendy
FME LAC Lancaster

Halifax B II W7702 MP:L
Airborne 04.01 hours
Pilot F/Lt W M Renaut
Obs P/O F G T Collins
W/Op Sgt J Carrad
MUG Sgt R S Mortham
Engr Sgt R H Duncanson
RG Sgt Wiltshire
Fitt F/Sgt Smith
Instr F/Sgt Sharp
Fitt Cpl Russell

Halifax B II W7664 MP:T
Airborne 04.05 hours
Pilot F/Sgt H D Alcock
Obs Sgt A J Hawkin
W/Op Sgt A E Oram
MUG Sgt J H Hart
Engr Sgt A R McKay
RG Sgt K G Mitchell
Fitt Sgt Heuser
FME LAC Rolland
Arm Cpl Shearer

SECOND FLIGHT:

Halifax B II W7755 MP:A
Airborne 03.50 hours
Pilot W Cdr D C Young
　　　　　DFC AFC
Obs Sgt N S R McMinn
W/Op Sgt J H Dickson
MUG Sgt A E Patchett
Engr Sgt J A Sprigge
RG Sgt D Moore
A&SD F/O Clulow
Met R Sgt Norris
Fitt Cpl Lee

HalifaxBIIW1183MP:M
Airborne 03.55 hours
Pilot S/Ldr P G V Warner
Obs F/Lt F T Collins
W/Op Sgt A Watson
MUG Sgt C R Jones
Engr Sgt G Waddington
RG P/O E J Greenway
Fitt Sgt Camp
Fitt Cpl Hill
Clerk LAC Tarling

HalifaxBIIW1177MP:G
Airborne 04.00 hours
Pilot F/Sgt H A Brown
Obs W/O G M Armstrong
W/Op Sgt R W Long
MUG Sgt E G Westall
Engr Sgt J Inward
RG Sgt G L Shaw
Fitt Cpl Phillips
Fitt Cpl Cordery
Obs Sgt S H Robinson

HalifaxBIIW1149MP:R
Airborne 04.06 hours
Pilot P/O J D McIntosh
Obs Sgt D H Acworth
W/Op Sgt R Fulton
W/Op Sgt D Brown
Engr Sgt H van Schaick
RG Sgt K A J Scammell
Met R Sgt Russel
Arm Cpl Atkinson
FME LAC Renton

Appendix Six

EXTENDED PHOTOGRAPH CAPTIONS AND CREDITS

Page 97   (Upper) B.E.12 C3114, possibly not a 76 Squadron machine, but representative of the type used by the squadron between September 1916 and 1918. This particular aircraft was built by The Daimler Company Ltd., Coventry. *(J M Bruce / G S Leslie collection)*

                 (Lower) Squadron Leader E J George, the tall officer centre with a moustache, with officers and NCO aircrew of 76 Squadron, Finningley 1937. *(Flight International 15374s)*

Page 98   76 Squadron Wellesleys, stepped up in echelon with K7744 in the centre. *(Flight Iternational 15384s)*

Page 99   (Upper) Wireless Operators undergoing training at Finningley in 1939 pose beneath the nose of a Hampden. Left to right: unknown, LAC Burke, LAC Cecil Smith, LAC Mollineauy, AC Hutchinson, LAC Bennet, unknown. *(C Smith)*

                 (Lower) Halifax B.1 (MP:D) piloted by Pilot officer Len Smith, August 1941. *(L Smith)*

Page 100 A particularly good side view of Halifax B.1 L9530 (MP:L) being flown by Flight Lieutenant Christopher Cheshire just a few days before he was shot down and made prisoner on operations to Berlin August 1941. Note the 'Cheshire' crest beneath the cockpit. *(via L Smith)*

Page 101 (Upper) Middle East, summer 1942. Left to right: Sergeant Payne, Sergeant Coates, Flying Officer Earle, Flying Officer Geoff Raymond and Sergeant Gill stand beneath the nose of a Halifax B.II with nineteen bomb symbols. *(G Raymond)*

(Lower)   An example of the formidable ju 88 night-fighter. This particular example, a Ju88C6, belongs to the E/NJG2 based at Gilze Rijen in Holland, and was often flown by Leutnant Bruno Heilig, Heinrich Scholl and Karl Chuss. *(H Scholl)*

Page 102 A mixture of 10 and 76 Squadron aircrews in the Middle East, summer 1942. Squadron Leader 'Hank' Iveson is sitting third from left with Wing Commander Seymour Price, the CO of 10 Squadron, on his left. Douglas Knox is standing on the far right of the third row, while third from the left in the back row is young Pilot Officer Kenny Clack DFM. *(D Iveson)*

Page 103   (Upper) Captain Gunnar Halle RNAF standing to the right of the rear entry door of Halifax B.11 JB872 (MP:C) in April 1943. The officer with his head in the hatch is Squadron Leader Nigel Bennett, behind is Lieutenant Vikholt RNAF and the crew's wireless operator, Flight Sergeant Evans. The three Sergeants are believed to be Boanas, Jacobs and Walters. *(N G Bennett)*

(Lower) Halifax B.V DK148 (MP:G) *Johnnie the Wolf* on it's belly after crash-landing on return from Essen 25-26 July 1943. On this occasion it was piloted by Flight Lieutenant Shannon RAAF, but normally it was flown by Sergeant George Dunn.

Page 104   (Upper) Squadron aircrew aboard one of the many lorries used to take crews out to their aircraft. This particular vehicle is marked 'OP' which may signify it was used to transport the crews for 'MP:O' and 'MP:P' respectively. It is believed this photograph was taken on 27 July 1943 when the target was Hamburg. Sergeant Maurice Manser seated front gives a cheerful smile and a victory sign, on his left is Alf Kirkham, his skipper, and next along is Flight Lieutenant Turner, pilot of Halifax B.V DK195 (MP:O). *(R Roll / C Tuckwell)*

(Lower) A carefully posed photograph taken on 27 July 1943 showing Flight Lieutenant Hodson, third from left, discussing their pending operation to Hamburg in Halifax B.V DK204 (MP:L). The pilot in the peaked cap is Flying Officer jimmy Steele, and standing next to him in the fur-lined flying jacket is Staff Sergeant Flewell USAAF. *(pbotograpb via R N Benwell)*

Page 105   Pilot Officer Bill Elder RNZAF sits on top of a servicing ladder shortly before taking off for Hamburg on 27 July 1943. Within hours of this photograph being taken the airman standing second down from the right, Sergeant Smith, was dead, killed by a cannon shell. Above him with one hand resting on a propeller blade, is a youthful Sergeant Berry who assisted his pilot in the subsequent crash-landing of their aircraft. *(R Roll/ C Tuckwell)*

Page 106   (Upper) A happy scene, probably taken before take-off as the airmens hair is unflattened from hours of being pressed beneath a flying helmet. The pretty young WAAF in shirt sleeve order is Mary Quinn. Note the aircrew whistles. *(R Roll / C Tuckwell)*

(Lower) Drawing parachutes, possibly prior to operations to Hamburg 27 July 1943. *(R Roll / C Tuckwell)*

Page 107   (Upper) An unidentified squadron Halifax climbs away from Holme-onSpalding Moor Moor into a darkening sky. Operations to Milan for one crew are under way on 12 August 1943- *(D C Smith)*

(Lower) Taff Isaacs, Ken Parry, Ken Hewson wearing a forage cap, George Jones, George Taylor, Dave Davis and AI Atkinson standing by the rear turret of their Halifax, summer 1943. *(T Isaacs)*

Page 108   (*Upper*) Pilot Officer Erie Wright and crew standing in front of a Halifax B.V,
           probably during September 1943. The tall officer in the centre of the group is Flight
           Lieutenant Ted Strange who started his tour a year previous flying with Norman Black
           RNZAF, others are Harry Jones, John Barton, George Halbert, Arthur Everst and Gilbert
           Duthic. (*G Dutbie*)

           (Lower) Pilot Officer George Dunn and crew in late Septemberlearly October 1943. In the
           background is a Halifax B.V, probably LK903 (MP:G), with twelve bomb symbols recorded
           On 3 October 1943, George Dunn and crew completed their tour in this aircraft, leading the
           squadron to Kassel. Ferris Newton is standing on his pilot's left. (*D C Smith*)

Page 109   (*Upper*) One crew destined not to complete their tour. Left to right: Sergeant
           Hayes, Sergeant Bob Coupe, Lieutenant Ncils Eckhoff RNAF, Sergeant Sigmund Meieran
           RNAF and Sergeant Jans Skjelanger RNAF. All were aboard Halifax B.V DK203 (MP:A)
           which was shot down by a night-fighter near Terschelling whilst returning from operations
           to Kassel, 3 October 1943. (*S Meieran*)

           (Lower) Parts of Halifax B.V DK203 (MP:A) recovered from the sea in 1980 off Terschelling.
           (W Coniin)

Page 110   (*Upper*) Flight Lieutenant Jimmy Steele prepares to take-off on operations to Kassel
           on 22 October 1943. His Halifax B.V DK168 (MP:H) is being waved away by Johnny Waldo
           RNAF, Major John Stene RNAF wearing the greatcoat, Squadron Leader Nigel Bennett,
           Flight Lieutenant Turner, 'Pop' Bligh and 'The Colonel'. (*N Bennett*)

           (Lower) Wing Commander Don Smith, centre, with his crew. Left to right: Flight
           Lieutenant Ashton, squadron Gunnery Leader, Steve Palmer, Frank Hart, Pete Harris,
           Geoff Cranswick and Red Thompson. in the background a brand new 'Saint', possibly
           LK645 (MP:S). (*D C Smith*)

Page 111   Squadron aircrew wait to go out to their aircraft and the start of another operation
           in late 1943. The officer with the peaked cap in the centre foreground is Flying Officer Roy
           Bolt. (F G Hall)

Page 112   (*Upper*) Pilot Officer Jimmy Row and crew stand beneath the nose of Halifax B.V
           LK630 (MP:D), late 1943. His crew, left to right: Sergeant Freddy Wood, Sergeant Jimmy
           Crick, Jimmy Roe, Flying Officer Rex Hayhurst DFC, Sergeant John Davies DFM and
           Sergeant Victor Glaysher. (*J Davies*)

           (Lower) An immaculate Flying Officer Roy Bolt and crew pose in front of Halifax B.V LK912
           (MP:N), late November 1943. Thirteen bomb symbols are painted on the nose, the last
           being an operation to Frankfurt on 25-26 November. His crew left to right: Flying Officer
           Tony Walker, Flight Sergeant Cal Rathmell, Sergeant Jack Bates, Sergeant Josy, Sergeant
           Harry van den Bos and Flying Officer Fred Hall. (*F G Hall*)

Page 113   *(Upper)* The Le Mans marshalling yards in France under attack on 13-14 March 1944. This photograph, which clearly shows several sticks of bombs falling, was secured from Halifax B.III LW655 (MP:V) piloted by Flight Lieutenant Roger Coverley. *(H D Covericy)*

(Lower) A pensive Flight Lieutenant Roy Bolt and crew being debriefed by 'The Colonel' on return from Ottignies on 21 April 1944. it will be noted his flight engineer, Jack Bates, is now commissioned and is wearing the ribbon of the Distinguished Flying Cross. *(F G Hall)*

Page 114 Warrant Officer Mickey Jenkins, standing on an oil drum, poses with his crew shortly after returning from Villeneuve St. Georges on 27 April 194.4. His aircraft, Halifax B.Ill LW695 (MP:M) is displaying ten bomb symbols and the mark above the fifth symbol indicates a claim for a Me 109 shot down on operations to Nuremburg, 30-31 March 1944 when Flying Officer Sinclair RAAF was the pilot. LW695 (MP..M) eventually failed to return from Russelsheiin on 12-13 August 1944. (A *Hurst)*

Page 115   *(Upper)* Lieutenant Carl Larsen RNAF, far right, Sergeant Maurice Ransome, his mid-upper gunner is on his right, spring 1944. *(C Larsen)*

(Lower) Pilot Officer Valle RNAF stands with his wife, in WRENS uniform, on the occasion of his award of the Distinguished Flying Cross. Left to right: General Christie RNAF, two unknown, but possibly Air Commodore Hodson standing on the Gencral's left, with Air Vice Marshal Carr, AOC 4 Group, and Group Captain Pelly-Fry, Station Commander at Holme-on-Spalding Moor, are far right. *(C Larsen)*

Page 116   *(Upper)* A happy Flying Officer Ncil Conway RAAF lines up with an equally cheerful crew with Halifax B.III MZ599 (MP:U) in the background. Left to right: Kevin Gardner RAAF, Ernie Turtle, Nathanial Futter, Roy Bleach, Bill Foreman and Ron Minion.

(Lower) St. Martin L'Hortier under attack on 5-6 July 1944, an excellent Aiming Point photograph taken from 14,000 feet from Halifax B.III LK785 (MP:T) flown by Captain Carl Larsen RNAF. *(C Larsen)*

Page 11 7   *(Upper)* On goes symbol number 43 on *Topsy,* Halifax B.III LK785 (MP:T), 24 July 1944 having recently returned from Kiel with Captain Carl Larsen RNAF at her controls.(M *Ransome)*

(Lower) Halifax B.III LW648 (MP:A) *Acbtung, The Black Prince,* after completing fifty operational sorties. This Halifax was so named in honour of it's Nigerian wireless operator, Sergeant Akin Shenbanjo, sitting on the left. Flight Lieutenant Jimmy Watt RCAF, the skipper, is standing far right. The mark above the fifth symbol indicates when LW648 was struck by an anti-aircraft shell on operations to Lille 9-10 April 1944. The key shown on the 21st bomb was applied following a trip to Aachen on 24-25 May, while the D painted above the 24th symbol signifies the eve of D-Day raid to Mont Fleury. (A *R Andrews)*

Page 118   (Upper) Halifax B.111 MZS16 (MP:V) *Vera the Virgin*, with forty-nine bomb symbols applied. This dates the photograph to between 1 and 10 September 1944, when it was being flown regularly on operations by Warrant Officer Geoff Dowling RAAF. Vera's key was attained on 12-1 3 June 1944 when Squadron Leader Pod Harrison, C Flight's commander, went to Amiens. *(G Bailey / D Sutton)*

(Lower) A close up showing the forty-nine bomb symbols applied to *Vera the Virgin*, Halifax B.III MZS16 (MP:V). *(G Bailey / D Sutton)*

Page 119   0-de-O, believed to be Halifax B.III LK788 (MP:O), showing sixty bomb symbols. Posing beneath the nose are Flight Lieutenant'Stu'Orser RCAF and crew, with members of the groundcrew. (B Gurr / L Greenham)

Page 120   (Upper) Damage inflicted to the starboard rear fuselage of Halifax B.III MZS28 (MP:K) following a collision with a PFF Lancaster on operations to Walcheren, 29 October 1944. At the time of the accident, MZS28 was being flown by Flight Sergeant Whit Whittaker. *(H Morgan)*

(Lower) Pilot Officer George Rowley and crew stand in front of a remarkably pristine Halifax B.III NA584 (MP:Z). This photograph was taken late 1944, probably in the November. (A *J Rowley)*

Page 121   Warrant Officer Jack Espie RAAF, plus crew and cocker spaniel, pose in front of a well used Halifax B.III LW646 (MP:E), November 1944. *(D D Bennett)*

Page 122   *(Upper)* St. Vith in Belgium undergoing attack on Boxing Day 1944. Note the two Halifaxes in the top left hand quarter. This photograph was taken from a 102 Squadron Halifax piloted by Flying Officer Lightbody, but pressing the bomb-tit was Gilbert Duthic, an ex-76 Squadron bomb-aimer now on the sixth operation of his second tour. *(G Duthie)*

(Lower) Halifax B.III NA570 (MP:P) *Powerful Pete* in mid-March 1945 and showing sixty-one bomb symbols. Flight Lieutenant Jim Gracie RCAF stands in the centre and the other members of his crew are Wally Hunsaker, Bill Erskine, Raymond du Pont, Jack Runyan, Dennis Reed and C Smyth. *(A Hurst)*

Page 123   *(Upper)* *Wbits Criminal* Crew pose with an attentive groundcrew. The identity of this Halifax is not known and the inscription has been chalked on and may not have been permanently applied. The aircrew, standing, left to right: Baines, Haslam, Smith, Whittaker, Bates, Morgan and Howell. *(H Morgan)*

(Lower) A really nice shot of Halifax B.VI RG591 (MP:A) taken in April 1945. This aircraft was assigned to Flight Lieutenant Peter Collins and crew, but when it was lost in tragic circumstances on 25 April 1945, it was being flown by Warrant Outerson RCAF. *(J Mason)*

Page 124   *(Upper)* Flight Lieutenant Peter Collins and crew prepare to board Halifax B.VI RG591 (MP:A), April 1945. *(J Mason)*

(Lower) Halifaxes flying towards the Bayreuth marshalling yards, 11 April 1945. *(G Butler)*

Page 125   *(Upper)* A quite dramatic photograph showing Halifax B.VI RG553 (MP:T) (Flying Officer Gerald Lawson RCAF) failing out of control with its tailplane severed over Wangerooge on 25 April 1945. Seconds earlier this Halifax had been rammed by RG591 OMP:A) (Warrant Officer Outerson RCAF) and this photograph was taken from Flight Lieutenant Perry's aircraft RG618 (MP: I). The severed tail section is just visible centre left and appears to be dropping towards a bank of cloud.(G *Lawson)*

(Lower) The smoke-blackened cathedral of Cologne with the road/rail bridge collapsed in the River Rhine. 'Cooks Tour' June 1945. Note the burnt out shells of apartment buildings surrounding the cathedral and station.

Page 126   (Upper) Groundcrews pose in front of the first Dakota delivered to the squadron at Holmc-on-Spalding Moor in June 1945. Left to right: Front, squatting: Smudger Smith, Norman Wardlow. Sitting: Corporals Tetlow, Fisher, Sergeants Glasper, Joyce, Flight Lieutenant McDonald, Flight Sergeant Munroe, Sergeants Lamplough, Johnson, Corporal Powell and LAC Dumbo Smith. Back row: LACs Fred Massey, Ted Edwards, Frank Boardman, Bill Adams, Frank Alcok, Don Mort, Allen Cowie, Ernie AndersoA Jerry Lampier, Red Endean Al Hurst and Vic Brooks. (A *Hurst)*

(Lower) 76 Squadron aircrew staging to India, autumn 1945. This photo. graph was taken in October 1945 in Palestine. *(S Pearson)*

Page 127   (Upper) Canberra B.6 WH980 in flight during the squadron's tour of duty in Australia. Note the air sampling scoop fitted beneath the bomb-bay. *(J Stonham)*

(Lower) Canberra B.6 WH976 in New Zealand during 1959. Note the serial repeated on nose wheel door. *(R W Kerr / C J Salter)*

Page 128   (Upper) Canberra B.6 WT206 staging through Gibralter, possibly during *1960. (R C B Asbworth /J D R Rawlings)*

(Lower) Canberra B.6 WJ757 at Upwood 1960. *(J Stonham)*

PERSONAL ACKNOWLEDGEMENTS

I gratefully acknowledge the help given to me by the staff of the Public Record Office. Their infinite knowledge and willingness to help saved me hours of time-consuming searches for documents, and for this I am truly grateful. I thank Air Commodore Probert, Mr Turner and Mr Munday of the Air Historical Branch, and Mrs Elderfield who gave up so much of her time at the Royal Air Force Casualty Records section assisting me with the squadron's 'Roll of Honour'.

It is now three years since I set out to write the squadron history and during this time I have sought the advice of many organisations, as well as approaching numerous individuals. In each instance help has been readily given and it gives me great pleasure to acknowledge your generous response. I will start by thanking Chris Salter of Midland Counties Publications for coming forward at the eleventh hour with production assistance, just when I had resigned myself to preparing the book by hand.

Next, to all squadron members I say a personal 'thank you' for your contributions and patience. It is impossible for me to mention all of you by name, but I particularly wish to thank Carl Larsen for coming to see me from his home in Lysaker, Norway, and to a fellow countryman of Carl's, John Stene for his quite remarkable skill in recalling events as they affected the Royal Norwegian Air Force personnel who flew with the squadron. To Maurice Manser, visiting from Australia, for providing me with much useful information, and similar gratitude I extend to John Cowl for his supply of last minute information relating to the rather obscure French targets raided in the broiling summer of 1944. Closer to home, I have pleasure in thanking Roy Bolt, Roy Clarke, Fred Hall, Ferris Newton, Mrs G Simkin, Cecil Smith, Don Smith, Leonard Smith and David Sutton for the loan of diaries and flying log-books. Also to David Young for sending me a valued document relating to the late Mike Renaut who served with such distinction throughout 1942, and beyond.

To Martin Middlebrook, author and historian from Boston, I express my very sincere thanks for checking the Nuremburg raid section and for his suggestions regarding the 'Battle of Hamburg'. Similarly, I thank Geoff Jones for allowing me to quote from his excellent book *Raider - The Halifax and its Flyers* which is published by Kimbers.

I am also grateful to the following magazines and papers for carrying my appeal, and I acknowledge their valued help. *Aeroplane, Aircraft Illustrated, Air Mail, Air Pictorial, Aviation News, British Aviation Research Group, Canadian Forces Sentinel, Express and Echo, Flight International, London Evening News, Melbourne Herald, The Australian, The Legion (Canada), The Spectator* (Hamilton, Ontario), *Toronto Daily Star.*

In preparing the appendices I have relied upon the painstaking research of many individuals. in acknowledging their help, I thank first my good friend Captain Roy Benwell who has been instrumental in preparing the aircraft histories, a truly remarkable task that involved the comparison of the squadron records against the information recorded on the aeroplane cards. Next, Jacques de Vos of Ghent in Belgium deserves special mention for the supply of detail concerning squadron evaders, and also for his translation of passages from *'St.Vith im Schatten des Endsiegs'* by Kurt Fagnoul, whom I freely acknowledge for various passages quoted in Chapter Nine. From Holland I have received fine co-operation from Will Conijn, Hans Onderwater, Leo Zwaaf and Gerrie Zwanenberg MBE. All have checked and re-checked information concerning the loss of squadron aircraft over the Netherlands. I am also grateful to Ole Kraul of Horsens for similar work in connection with losses over his native Denmark, while I am indebted to Herr Wohl of Hannover, Gus Lerch of Frankfurt and Herbert Scholl of Schliersee for much of the information relating to the reported *Luftwaffe* claims against the squadron. In connection with this part of the book, I do not forget the valued help of Peter Sharpe of Coventry. Valerie Pearman Smith has been most kind to supply me with information concerning the various squadron losses suffered in the round of attacks against the Tirpitz in 1942, and Roy Bonser kindly prepared the map that illustrates Chapter Eleven. Lastly, in this area of rescarch, I thank Christopher Cole for making available to me information he has gathered in years of careful research into the Home Defence Squadrons, of which No. 76 was a part between 1916 and 1919.

The photographs, gathered in the main from private sources, have been prepared by Robin Walker who is an acknowledged expert in this matter, also to Robin Roll for his valued contribution to the photograph section. I am also pleased to recognise the kind help given by D W Goode, Chief Librarian at the Royal Aircraft Establishment, Len Greenham of Brighton for his ever cheerful encouragement, Alan Jasper and John Tyler for much useful background information, and to Alex Thorne DFC Editor of Air *Mail,* the Royal Air Force Association journal, for his note on 635 Squadron, mentioned in respect to the Homberg raid in 1944.

For casting their experienced eyes over German documents, I am grateful to Paul Birch and Philip Scoble, and finally to Robert Kirby for giving so much of his time to reading, correcting and suggesting amendments to the draft manuscript. His good counsel has been much appreciated during the final weeks of preparing the text and appendices.

Last of all, I thank my wife and family for their support and encouragement and for enduring many evenings of solitude over the past three years.

INDEX

Note for guidance. The rank title shown after a name indicates the rank held by that person when first mentioned in the narrative and all subsequent references to this person follow this title, regardless of promotion.

257

259

Hall, Sgt Nobby, 12
Halle RNAF, Lt Gunnar, 53, 55 -5 7,
  59-61, 78
Hamborn, 57, 69
Hamburg, 17, 24, 3 7, 40, 49, 54, 60, 80-83,
  85,129,139,154,172,174,176
Hamm, 16,62,156
Hamm an der Seig, 141
Hampden bomber, 11-13, 16
Hampton, Sgt Jim, 16 3, 186
Hanau,170
Hancock, Cpl Ray, 42
Hannover, 18, 90-91, 170, 175, 186
'Happy Valley' (see Ruhr Valley)
Harburg, 176
Hardy, F/0 Judge, 52, 55
Harris, AVM Sir Arthur, 3 3, 3 6-3 8, 40,
  51-52, 58-59, 62, 66, 68, 70-71, 76,
  80, 82, 84, 89, 139-140, 144, 152,
  154,171,175,186
Harrison, F/Lt, 169
Harrison RNZAF, S/Ldr John, 156, 158
Hart light-bomber, 12
Hartford Bridge, 78
Hartnell-Beavis, F/Lt, 66
Harwood, Sgt John, 32, 34, 36, 136, 146,
  153-154
Harz mountains, 176
Haskett, S/Ldr, 176, 180-181
Hasselt, 147
Hayes, Sgt, 92
Head, Sgt, 148
Healey, F/Sgt, 130,138
Hebron, Sgt, 49
Heggarty, Sgt, 81
Heidelburg, 130
Heilig, Lt, 73
Heligoland, 176
Heliopolis, 4.4
Helmstedt, 134
Helperby, 8-9
Hemmingstedt, 174
Hems RCAF, F/Sgt, 176
Hemswell, 184
Henderson, Sir David, 7
Hendon,10
Henschel Works, 66, 91-92
Hensler, Lt, 95
Henthorn, Sgt, 141, 143
Heraklion, 4748

Herbert, Sgt, 26, 28, 30
Hewson, Sgt Ken, 72, 74-75, 78, 82, 85
Heyderkrug, 90
Heyford bomber, 9
Hickman, Sgt, 75, 91
Hicks RCAF, F/Lt David, 94-95
Higgins DFM, P/O, 42
High Wycombe, 3 1, 3 6, 5 5, 91, 136,
  171,174
Hill, Sgt, 46
Hillary, F/Lt, 16, 18, 22
Hillier, P/O, 56
Hind light bomber, 12 Hirson, 76
Hispano-Suiza engine, 9
Hitler, Herr Adolf, 12, 84, 152, 165,
174-175
Hochfeld, 57
Hodgson, F/Lt, 91
Hodson, F/Lt, 85
Hoffman, Hptm, 135
Holden, W/O, 22
Holland, 14, 49, 53, 78, 88, 94, 131,
  140,145,156,163,175
Holme-on-Spalding Moor, 75-76, 81, 84, 88,
  91, 93-94,129, 131-135, 137-139, 142-143,
  145-150, 155, 159, 162, 164-170, 173-178, 185
Holmes, Sgt, 30
Holmes, Sgt, 60, 85, 87
Holmes, W/O, 176-177
Holmsley South, 96
Homberg, 157-158, 175
Honeybourne, 77
Hood, F/Sgt, 149
Hoover, Sgt, 62, 77
Hopf, Oblt, 154
Horne, Sgt Larry, 54
Hornsea, 8
Hornsey, F/Lt Dennis, 94-95
Hotham, 150
Houlgate, 149
Houwerzijl, 40
Hoverstad RNAF, Lt Gunnar, 82
Howard, F/Lt John, 181
Howden, 9
Howe, F/0. 175
Howie, Sgt J ock, 1 5 3
Huckerby, P/O, 1485 151
Hudleston CB CBE AVM, 183
Hughes, Sgt, 135
Huke, Sgt 76

Manston, 3 3, 5 4, 1 70
Maralinga, 184
Marham, 183
Market Weighton, 94, 185
Marks, Wg Cdr, 28
Marne River, 54
Marsden, F/Lt, 183
Marsh, Cpl Bernard, 150-151
Marshall RCAF, F/Sgt, 139, 143
Marston Moor, 60, 66, 78, 1 3 5
Marvin, Sgt, 89
Mason RAAF, Sgt John, 159, 169
Mason RCAF, F/Sgt, 168
Master Bomber, 136, 144, 151, 156,
  166, 170
Matthews, F/Sgt, 131
Matthews, Sgt, 59
Mauripur, 180-181
May DFM, F/Lt, 169
May sur Orne, 155
Mayes, Sgt Stan, 24
Maze, P/0 John, 76, 82-84, 88, 91
McAuley, Sgt, 49-50
MeBrinn RCAF, F/Sgt, 170
McCadden, F/0 Reg, 85
McCann, P/O, 84
McDougall, Sgt, 77
McHale, Sgt, 17, 24
McIntosh RAAF, P/O, 42, 49
McIntyre, P/O, 35
McKechnie, Gp Capt, 51
McKenna, F/O, 22
McLeod, Sgt, 23
McTrach RCAF, W/0 John, 132-133
Meieran RNAF, Sgt Sigmund, 92
Melbourne, 149, 177
Mersburg, 18, 23, 25
Merville Franceville, 149
Messerschmitt, Prof, 165
Me262, 164-165
Middle East Command, 43
Middleburg, 163
Middleton, S/Ldr, 30
Milan, 56, 83-84
Milan RCAF, F/Sgt, 64
Milch, General, 10, 82
Mildenhall, 10
Miller RCAF, Sgt, 50
Minion, Sgt Ron, 148, 151
Misson ranges, 12

Mitchell, Sgt, 67
Modane, 89
Moehne Dam, 71
Moffatt, Sgt. 52
Mogalki RCAF, F/Sgt, 143
Moir, Sgt AI, 5 1, 5 5, 61, 78, 86
Monchengladbach, 87, 90, 95
Mondeville, 154
Monk, P/O, 141
Monschau, 166
Mont Fleury, 149-150
Montbeliard, 79
Montgassicourt, 146
Montgomery, Lt General Bernard, 45,
47-481154, 162-163
Montlucon, 89
Montzen, 144, 146
Moorhausen, 92
Moorhouse, PIO, 38
Morgan, F/Sgt Huw, 167, 169
Morin RCAF, Sgt, 30
Morris, F/O, 132-133
Morris, F/0 Bonnie, 175-176
Morris, Sgt, 37
Morrison, Sgt, 95
Morton, F/O, 145
Moselle River, 166
Mosquito light bomber, 26, 38, 63, 85,
  136, 149-150, 163, 165, 186 with
  OBOE fitted, 69.145 Mottram, P/O, 154
Motts, Sgt. 140
Mount Cenis tunnel, 89
Mulheim, 76-77
Mundelsheim, 67
Munich, 62, 89
Munich Crisis, 1 1
Munster, 166
Murfitt, Sgt. 84
Murray, Major, 8
Murray, W/O, 138
Musberg, 136
Mussolini, 14
Mustang fighter, 167, 177

Naess RNAF, Lt Bjorn, 53,55, 60
Naestved, 68
Nancy, 138, 153
Napier Double Scorpion Rocket Motor,
  184
Nassogne, 168

266

Penner RCAF, F/Sgt Joe, 176-177
Penzance,29
Perks, Sgt, 60, 62
Perriement, Sgt, 22
Perry, F/Lt, 170, 177-178
Perry, PIO, 29, 185
Persian Gulf, 41
Peshawar, 181
Peterborough, 145
Peugeot Motot Works, 79
Phillips, Sgt, 23
Phillips, Sgt, 74
Phillips Works, 79
Philp, PIO, 39
Pierce, Sir Richard, 33
Pilsen, 67, 91
'Pink Pansy', 52
Po River, 56, 144, 171
Pocklington, 25, 153
Point de Diable, 26
Poland, 12-13
Pontarlier, 96
Poole, F/Sgt, 145
Poole RCAF, Sgt, 49-50
Pooles, F/Lt, 35
Poona, 180-181
'Portemine', 63
Portreath, 180
Potts, Sgt. 47
Price, Alfred, 73
Priest, 1 3 7
Pringle RAAF, F/Sgt, 89
Prinz Eugen, 19-20, 27, 33
Protville, 84
Pyrenees, 3 9, 54, 13 3

Quimper, 20
Quint, 156

RAAF Edinburgh Field, 184
RAAF Pearce, 183
Rade Abri, 19
Radlett, 1 5
Rae, F/Sgt, 148
Ramsden, Sgt Rammy, 82, 84
Ransome, Sgt Maurice, 135, 150
Rapp, Lt, 70
Ratzeburg, 81
Raymond, P/0 Geoff, 42-46
Readhead DFC, F/Lt Tam, 86

Reading, F/Sgt, 147
Reed, Sgt Derek, 54
Reeder, F/0 Harold, 147
Reichswald Forest, 58
Reilly RCAF, F/O, 162,175
Reims, 54
Remagen, 171
Renault Works, 36
Renaut, P/0 Mike, 36-37. 40, 42, 44,
    47-48
Rennes Airfield, 151
Renolds, S/Ldr, 181
Reynolds, FIO, 162, 175, 177
Rhine River, 38, 53, 62, 76, 78, 86-87, 140,
    143, 161-1621 167v 170-171
Rhineland, 17, 38, 70, 171
Riccall, 87-88
Richards, F/Sgt, 134
Richards, P/O, 16-17
Richardson, Sgt Bill, 5 1-55, 78
Ripon, 7-8
Ritchie, General, 41
Roach, F/Lt, 31
Roberts, F/Lt, 181
Robertson, Major, 10
Robertson RCAF, P/O, 151, 1 5 3
Robinson, Sgt, 47
Robinson, Wg Cdr, 29-30
Robson B'Sc, Miss Dorothy, 93-94
Roer River, 166
Roermond, 88
Rogers DFM, FIO, 67
Rogers, F/Sgt, 170
Rolls-Royce Merlin, 20, 40, 42
Rommel, General Erwin, 41,43,45,48
Roope, F/O, 166,171,175
Ross RCAF, PIO, 70-71
Rostock, 36-38, 135
Rotterdam, 14, 24, 62, 74
Row, Sgt, 82
Rowland, PIO, 173
Rowley, F/SgtGeorge, 150-151, 155-156,
    162
Roxwell, 50
Royal Arsenal Turin, 25
Rubrouck Nord, 52
Rufforth, 48, 72, 131
Ruhr Benzin, 157
Ruhr Valley, 16, 32, 36, 38-39, 43, 51, 57, 60,
    62-639 66, 68-69, 71-751 78, 82, 87, 96, 129,